"Mark Lawrence is the best thing to happen to fantasy in recent years."
—Peter V. Brett, international bestselling author

PRAISE FOR
King of Thorns

"The whole book is really like one action scene that doesn't end . . . *King of Thorns* is epic fantasy on a George R. R. Martin scale but on speed."   —*Fixed on Fantasy*

"By the end, I found myself blown away by the deftness of Lawrence's pacing and structure, ranking it on par with *Empire Strikes Back* for greatness in second installments of trilogies I've ever had the pleasure of consuming . . . Lawrence structures every chapter, every paragraph, and every sentence with purpose, concluding with a turn of phrase that always cuts to the quick."   —*Staffer's Book Review*

"This is a breathtaking, captivating, and violent venture into a wonderful world filled with morally ambiguous characters and compelling world-building."   —*The Ranting Dragon*

"This is a dark story that demands attention from its readers but also rewards them immensely for their attention in the end. Read *King of Thorns* to be shocked and awed by the boy who would be king."   —*Fantasy Book Critic*

"This dark and gritty fantasy adventure should please fans of military fantasy and no-frills action."   —*Library Journal*

W9-ASD-990

continued . . .

"*King of Thorns* is not the run-of-the-mill fairy tale with happy endings. It is shockingly raw and a dark type of realism . . . It is horribly amazing, like a deadly storm I just couldn't escape or want to tear my eyes away from."

—*Night Owl Reviews*

"An excellent novel . . . *King of Thorns* is very good, more complex, perhaps more ambitious than *Prince of Thorns*."

—sffworld.com

"A tour de force. 'Impressive' doesn't even begin to describe its content. Truly a phenomenal series so far."

—choicebookreviews.net

"*King of Thorns* is a novel that solidifies Mark Lawrence's place as one of fantasy's most talented authors."

—*Fantasy Faction*

"*King of Thorns* builds upon the excellence started by its predecessor."

—*Elitist Book Reviews*

PRAISE FOR
Prince of Thorns

"If you've ever wanted to read a first-person book about a hero who is also the darkest of villains, try this out. It's not like anything I've ever read before."

—Rick Riordan, *New York Times* bestselling author of *The Mark of Athena*

"*Prince of Thorns* deserves attention as the work of an iconoclast who seems determined to turn that familiar thing, Medieval-esque Fantasy Trilogy, entirely on its head."

—*Locus*

King of Thorns

BOOK TWO OF
THE BROKEN EMPIRE

MARK LAWRENCE

ACE BOOKS, NEW YORK

THE BERKLEY PUBLISHING GROUP
Published by the Penguin Group
Penguin Group (USA) Inc.
375 Hudson Street, New York, New York 10014, USA

USA | Canada | UK | Ireland | Australia | New Zealand | India | South Africa | China

Penguin Books Ltd., Registered Offices: 80 Strand, London WC2R 0RL, England
For more information about the Penguin Group, visit penguin.com.

KING OF THORNS

An Ace Book / published by arrangement with Bobalinga, Ltd.

Ace Books are published by The Berkley Publishing Group.
ACE and the "A" design are trademarks of Penguin Group (USA) Inc.

For information, address: The Berkley Publishing Group,
a division of Penguin Group (USA) Inc.,
375 Hudson Street, New York, New York 10014.

ISBN: 978-0-425-25623-7

PUBLISHING HISTORY
Ace hardcover edition / August 2012
Ace mass-market edition / August 2013

PRINTED IN THE UNITED STATES OF AMERICA

20 19 18 17 16 15 14 13 12

Cover art by Jason Chan.
Cover design by Annette Fiore.
Cover hand lettering by Iskra Johnson.
Interior text design by Laura K. Corless.
Map by Andrew Ashton.

Dedicated to my son, Rhodri

ACKNOWLEDGMENTS

I need to thank my reader, Helen Mazarakis, for reading *King of Thorns* one chunk at a time as I wrote it, and telling me what she thought.

Many thanks go to Ginjer Buchanan at Ace for taking a chance on me, and to both her and Kat Sherbo for all their labour in making The Broken Empire series a success.

My editor at HarperCollins Voyager, Jane Johnson, deserves huge thanks for all her splendid efforts to date. Thanks also to Amy McCulloch and Laura Mell, who have worked various wonders on my behalf.

And finally, my agent Ian Drury must be thanked for getting me the gig in the first place and for continuing to sell my books across the world. Gaia Banks and Virginia Ascione, working with Ian at Sheil Land Associates Ltd., also need thanking for their efforts in getting Jorg's story into so many translations.

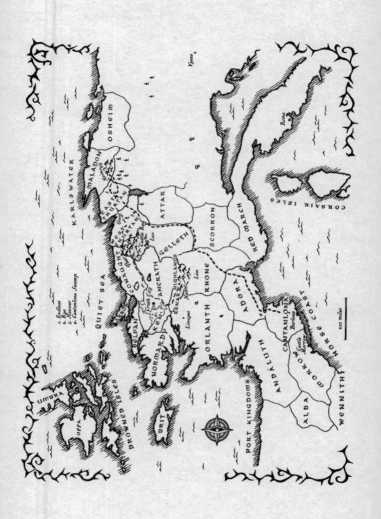

PROLOGUE

I found these pages scattered, teased across the rocks by a fitful wind. Some were too charred to show their words, others fell apart in my hands. I chased them though, as if it were my story they told and not hers.

Katherine's story, Aunt Katherine, sister to my stepmother, Katherine who I have wanted every moment of the past four years, Katherine who picks strange paths through my dreams. A few dozen ragged pages, weighing nothing in my hand, snowflakes skittering across them, too cold to stick.

I sat upon the smoke-wreathed ruins of my castle, careless of the heaped and stinking dead. The mountains, rising on all sides, made us tiny, made toys of the Haunt and the siege engines strewn about it, their purpose spent. And with eyes stinging from the fires, with the wind's chill in me deep as bones, I read through her memories.

October 3rd, Year 98 Interregnum
Ancrath. The Tall Castle. Fountain Room.

The fountain room is as ugly as every other room in this ugly castle. There's no fountain, just a font that dribbles rather than sprays. My sister's ladies-in-waiting clutter the place, sewing, always sewing, and tutting at me for writing, as if quill ink is a stain that can't ever be washed off.

My head aches and wormroot won't calm it. I found a sliver of pottery in the wound even though Friar Glen said he cleaned it. Dreadful little man. Mother gave me that vase when I came away with Sareth. My thoughts jump and my head aches and this quill keeps trembling.

The ladies sew with their quick clever stitches, line stitch, cross-line, layer-cross. Sharp little needles, dull little minds. I hate them with their tutting and their busy fingers and the lazy Ancrath slurring of their words.

I've looked back to see what I wrote yesterday. I don't remember writing it but it tells how Jorg Ancrath tried to kill me after murdering Hanna, throttling her. I suppose that if he really had wanted to kill me he could have done a better job of it having broken Mother's vase over my skull. He's good at killing, if nothing else. Sareth told me that what he said in court, about all those people in Gelleth, burned to dust . . . it's all true. Merl Gellethar's castle is gone. I met him when I was a child. Such a sly red-faced man. Looked as if he'd be happy to eat me up. I'm not sorry about him. But all those people. They can't all have been bad.

I should have stabbed Jorg when I had the chance. If my hands would do what I told them more often. If they would stop trembling the quill, learn to sew properly, stab murdering nephews when instructed . . . Friar Glen said the boy tore most of my dress off. Certainly it's a ruin now. Beyond the rescue of even these empty ladies with their needles and thread.

I'm being too mean. I blame the ache in my head. Sareth tells me be nice. Be nice. Maery Coddin isn't all sewing and gossip. Though she's sewing now and tutting with the rest of them. Maery's worth talking to on her own, I suppose. There. That's enough nice for one day. Sareth is always nice and look where that got her. Married to an old man, and not a kind one but a cold and scary one, and her belly all fat with a child that will probably run as savage as Jorg Ancrath.

I'm going to have them bury Hanna in the forest graveyard. Maery tells me she'll lie easy there. All the castle servants are buried there unless their families claim them. Maery says she'll find me a new maid-servant but that seems so cold, to just replace Hanna as if she were torn lace, or a broken vase. We'll go out by cart tomorrow. There's a man making her coffin now. My head feels as if he's hammering the nails into it instead.

I should have left Jorg to die on the throne-room floor. But it didn't feel right. Damn him.

We'll bury Hanna tomorrow. She was old and always complaining of her aches but that doesn't mean she was ready to go. I will miss her. She was a hard woman, cruel maybe, but never to me. I don't know if I'll cry when we put her in the ground. I should. But I don't know if I will.

That's for tomorrow. Today we have a visitor. The Prince of Arrow is calling, with his brother Prince Egan and his retinue. I think Sareth would like to match me there.

Or maybe it's the old man, King Olidan. Not many of Sareth's ideas are her own these days. We will see.

I think I'll try to sleep now. Maybe my headache will be gone in the morning. And the strange dreams too. Maybe Mother's vase knocked those dreams right out of me.

1

Wedding day

Open the box, Jorg.

I watched it. A copper box, thorn patterned, no lock or latch.

Open the box, Jorg.

A copper box. Not big enough to hold a head. A child's fist would fit.

A goblet, the box, a knife.

I watched the box and the dull reflections from the fire in the hearth. The warmth did not reach me. I let it burn down. The sun fell, and shadows stole the room. The embers held my gaze. Midnight filled the hall and still I didn't move, as if I were carved from stone, as if motion were a sin. Tension knotted me. It tingled along my cheekbones, clenched in my jaw. I felt the table's grain beneath my fingertips.

The moon rose and painted ghost-light across the stone-flagged floor. The moonlight found my goblet, wine untouched, and made the silver glow. Clouds swallowed the sky and in the darkness rain fell, soft with old memories. In the small hours, abandoned by fire, moon, and stars, I reached for my blade. I laid the keen edge cold against my wrist.

The child still lay in the corner, limbs at corpse angles, too broken for all the king's horses and all the king's men. Sometimes I feel I've seen more ghosts than people, but this boy, this child of four, haunts me.

Open the box.

The answer lay in the box. I knew that much. The boy wanted me to open it. More than half of me wanted it open too, wanted to let those memories flood out, however dark, however dangerous. It had a pull on it, like the cliff's edge, stronger by the moment, promising release.

"No." I turned my chair toward the window and the rain, shading to snow now.

I carried the box out of a desert that could burn you without needing the sun. Four years I've kept it. I've no recollection of first laying hands upon it, no image of its owner, few facts save only that it holds a hell which nearly broke my mind.

Campfires twinkled distant through the sleet. So many they revealed the shape of the land beneath them, the rise and fall of mountains. The Prince of Arrow's men took up three valleys. One alone wouldn't contain his army. Three valleys choked with knights and archers, foot-soldiers, pikemen, men-at-axe and men-at-sword, carts and wagons, engines for siege, ladders, rope, and pitch for burning. And out there, in a blue pavilion, Katherine Ap Scorron, with her four hundred, lost in the throng.

At least she hated me. I'd rather die at the hands of somebody who wanted to kill me, to have it mean something to them.

Within a day they would surround us, sealing the last of the valleys and mountain paths to the east. Then we would see. Four years I had held the Haunt since I took it from my uncle. Four years as King of Renar. I wouldn't let it go easy. No. This would go hard.

The child stood to my right now, bloodless and silent. There was no light in him but I could always see him through the dark. Even through eyelids. He watched me with eyes that looked like mine.

I took the blade from my wrist and tapped the point to my teeth. "Let them come," I said. "It will be a relief."

That was true.

I stood and stretched. "Stay or go, ghost. I'm going to get some sleep."

And that was a lie.

The servants came at first light and I let them dress me. It seems a silly thing but it turns out that kings have to do what kings do. Even copper-crown kings with a single ugly castle and lands that spend most of their time going either up or down at an unseemly angle, scattered with more goats than people. It turns out that men are more apt to die for a king who is dressed by pinch-fingered peasants every morning than for a king who knows how to dress himself.

I broke fast with hot bread. I have my page wait at the doors to my chamber with it of a morning. Makin fell in behind me as I strode to the throne-room, his heels clattering on the flagstones. Makin always had a talent for making a din.

"Good morning, Your Highness," he says.

"Stow that shit." Crumbs everywhere. "We've got problems."

"The same twenty thousand problems we had on our doorstep last night?" Makin asked. "Or new ones?"

I glimpsed the child in a doorway as we passed. Ghosts and daylight don't mix, but this one could show in any patch of shadow.

"New ones," I said. "I'm getting married before noon and I haven't got a thing to wear."

2

Wedding day

"Princess Miana is being attended by Father Gomst and the Sisters of Our Lady," Coddin reported. He still looked uncomfortable in chamberlain's velvets; the Watch-Commander's uniform had better suited him. "There are checks to be carried out."

"Let's just be glad nobody has to check *my* purity." I eased back into the throne. Damn comfortable: swan-down and silk. Kinging it is pain in the arse enough without one of those gothic chairs. "What does she look like?"

Coddin shrugged. "A messenger brought this yesterday." He held up a gold case about the size of a coin.

"So what does she look like?"

He shrugged again, opened the case with his thumbnail and squinted at the miniature. "Small."

"Here!" I caught hold of the locket and took a look for myself. The artists who take weeks to paint these things with a single hair are never going to spend that time making an ugly picture. Miana looked acceptable. She didn't have the hard look about her that Katherine does, the kind of look that lets you know the person is really alive, devouring every moment. But when it comes down to it, I find most women attractive. How many men are choosy at eighteen?

"And?" Makin asked from beside the throne.

"Small," I said and slipped the locket into my robe. "Am I too young for wedlock? I wonder . . ."

Makin pursed his lips. "I was married at twelve."

"You liar!" Not once in all these years had Sir Makin of Trent mentioned a wife. He'd surprised me; secrets are hard to keep on the road, among brothers, drinking ale around the campfire after a hard day's blood-letting.

"No lie," he said. "But twelve is too young. Eighteen is a good age for marriage, Jorg. You've waited long enough."

"What happened to your wife?"

"Died. There was a child too." He pressed his lips together.

It's good to know that you don't know everything about a man. Good that there might always be more to come.

"So, my queen-to-be is nearly ready," I said. "Shall I go to the altar in this rag?" I tugged at the heavy samite collar, all scratchy at my neck. I didn't care of course but a marriage is a show, for high- and low-born alike, a kind of spell, and it pays to do it right.

"Highness," Coddin said, pacing his irritation out before the dais. "This . . . distraction . . . is ill-timed. We have an army at our gates."

"And to be fair, Jorg, nobody knew she was coming until that rider pulled in," Makin said.

I spread my hands. "I didn't know she would arrive last night. I'm not magic, you know." I glimpsed the dead child slumped in a distant corner. "I had hoped she would arrive before the summer ended. In any case, that army has a good three miles to march if it wants to be at my gates."

"Perhaps a delay is in order?" Coddin hated being chamberlain with every fibre of his being. Probably that was why he was the only one I'd trust to do it. "Until the conditions are less . . . inclement."

"Twenty thousand at our door, Coddin. And a thousand inside our walls. Well, most of them outside because my castle is too damn small to fit them in." I found myself smiling. "I don't think conditions are going to improve. So we might as well give the army a queen as well as a king to die for, neh?"

"And concerning the Prince of Arrow's army?" Coddin asked.

"Is this going to be one of those times when you pretend not to have a plan until the last moment?" Makin asked. "And then turn out to really not have one?"

He looked grim despite his words. I thought perhaps he could still see his own dead child. He had faced death with me before and done it with a smile.

"You, girl!" I shouted to one of the serving girls lurking at the far end of the hall. "Go tell that woman to bring me a robe fit to get married in. Nothing with lace, mind." I stood and set a hand to the pommel of my sword. "The night patrols should be back about now. We'll go down to the east yard and see what they have to say for themselves. I sent Red Kent and Little Rikey along with one of the Watch patrols. Let's hear what they think about these men of Arrow."

Makin led the way. Coddin had grown twitchy about assassins. I knew what lurked in the shadows of my castle and it wasn't assassins that I worried about. Makin turned the corner and Coddin held my shoulder to keep me back.

"The Prince of Arrow doesn't want me knifed by some black-cloak, Coddin. He doesn't want drop-leaf mixed into my morning bread. He wants to roll over us with twenty thousand men and grind us into the dirt. He's already thinking of the empire throne. Thinks he has a toe past the Gilden Gate. He's building his legend now and it's not going to be one of knives in the dark."

"Of course, if you had more soldiers you might be worth stabbing." Makin turned his head and grinned.

We found the patrol waiting, stamping in the cold. A few castle women fussed around the wounded, planting a stitch or two. I let the commander tell his tale to Coddin while I called Red Kent to my side. Rike loomed behind him uninvited. Four castle years had softened none of Rike's edges, still close on seven foot of ugly temper with a face to match the blunt, mean, and brutal soul that looked out from it.

"Little Rikey," I said. It had been a while since I'd spoken to the man. Years. "And how's that lovely wife of yours?" In truth I'd never seen her but she must have been a formidable woman.

"She broke." He shrugged.

I turned away without comment. There's something about

Rike makes me want to go on the attack. Something elemental, red in tooth and claw. Or perhaps it's just because he's so damn big. "So, Kent," I said. "Tell me the good news."

"There's too many of them." He spat into the mud. "I'm leaving."

"Well now." I threw an arm around him. Kent don't look much but he's solid, all muscle and bone, quick as you like too. What makes him though, what sets him apart, is a killer's mind. Chaos, threat, bloody murder, none of that fazes him. Every moment of a crisis he'll be considering the angles, tracking weapons, looking for the opening, taking it.

"Well now." I pulled him close, hand clapped to the back of his neck. He flinched, but to his credit he didn't reach for a blade. "That's all well and good." I steered him away from the patrol. "But suppose that wasn't going to happen. Just for the sake of argument. Suppose it was only you here and twenty of them out there. That's not so far from the odds you'd beaten when we found you on that lakeside down in Rutton, neh?" For a moment he smiled at that. "How would you win then, Red Kent?" I called him Red to remind him of that day when he stood all atremble with his wolf's grin white in the scarlet of other men's blood.

He bit his lip, staring past me into some other place. "They're crowded in, Jorg. In those valleys. Crowded. One man against many, he's got to be fast, attacking, moving. Each man is your shield from the next." He shook his head, seeing me again. "But you can't use an army like one man."

Red Kent had a point. Coddin had trained the army well, the units of Father's Forest Watch especially so, but in battle cohesion always slips away. Orders are lost, missed, go unheard or ignored, and sooner or later it's a bloody maul, each man for himself, and the numbers start to tell.

"Highness?" It was the woman from the royal wardrobe, some kind of robe in her hands.

"Mabel!" I threw my arms wide and gave her my dangerous smile.

"Maud, sire."

I had to admit the old biddy had some stones. "Maud it is," I said. "And I'm to be wed in this, am I?"

"If it pleases you, sire." She even curtseyed a bit.

I took it from her. Heavy. "Cats?" I asked. "Looks like it took a lot of them."

"Sable." She pursed her lips. "Sable and gold thread. Count—" She bit the words off.

"Count Renar married in it, did he?" I asked. "Well, if it was good enough for that bastard it'll do for me. At least it looks warm." My uncle Renar owed me for the thorns, for a lost mother, a lost brother. I'd taken his life, his castle, and his crown, and still he owed me. A fur robe would not close our account.

"Best be quick about it, Highness," Coddin said, eyes still roaming for assassins. "We've got to double-check the defences. Plan out supply for the Kennish archers, and also consider terms." To his credit he looked straight at me for that last bit.

I gave Maud back the robe and let her dress me with the patrol watching on. I made no reply to Coddin. He looked pale. I had always liked him, from the moment he tried to arrest me, even past the moment he dared to mention surrender. Brave, sensible, capable, honest. The better man. "Let's get this done," I said and started toward the chapel.

"Is it needed, this marriage?" Coddin again, doggedly playing the role I set him. Speak to me, I had said. Never think I cannot be wrong. "As your wife, things may go hard for her." Rike sniggered at that. "As a guest she would be ransomed back to the Horse Coast."

Sensible, honest. I don't even know how to pretend those things. "It is needed."

We came to the chapel by a winding stair, past table-knights in plate armour, Count Renar's marks still visible beneath mine on the breastplates as if I'd ruled here four months rather than four years. The noble-born too poor or stupid or loyal to have run yet would be lined up within. In the courtyard outside the peasantry waited. I could smell them.

I paused before the doors, lifting a finger to stop the knight with his hands upon the bar. "Terms?"

I saw the child again, beneath crossed standards hanging on the wall. He'd grown with me. Years back he had been a baby, watching me with dead eyes. He looked about four now. I tapped my fingers against my forehead in a rapid tempo.

"Terms?" I said it again. I'd only said it twice but already the word sounded strange, losing meaning as they do when repeated over and again. I thought of the copper box in my room. It made me sweat. "There will be no terms."

"Best have Father Gomst say his words swiftly then," Coddin said. "And look to our defences."

"No," I said. "There will be no defence. We're going to attack."

I pushed the knight aside and threw the doors wide. Bodies crowded the chapel hall from one side to the other. It seemed my nobles were poorer than I'd thought. And to the left, a splash of blues and violet, ladies-in-waiting and knights in armour, decked in the colours of the House Morrow, the colours of the Horse Coast.

And there at the altar, head bowed beneath a garland of lilies, my bride.

"Oh hell," I said.

Small was right. She looked about twelve.

In peace Brother Kent reverts to type, a peasant plagued by kindness, seeking God in the stone houses where the pious lament. Battle strikes loose such chains. In war Red Kent approaches the divine.

3

Wedding day

Marriage was ever the glue that held the Hundred in some semblance of unity, the balm to induce scattered moments of peace, pauses in the crimson progress of the Hundred War. And this one had been hanging over me for close on four years.

I walked along the chapel aisle between the high and mighty of Renar, none of them so high or so mighty, truth be told. I've checked the records and half of them have goat-herders for grandparents. It surprised me that they had stayed. If I were them I would have acted on Red Kent's sentiment and been off across the Matteracks with whatever I could carry on my back.

Miana watched me, as fresh and perky as the lilies on her head. If the ruined left side of my face scared her she didn't show it. The need to trace the scarred ridges on my cheek itched in my fingertips. For an instant the heat of that fire ran in me, and the memory of pain tightened my jaw.

I joined my bride-to-be at the altar and looked back. And in a moment of clarity I understood. These people expected me to save them. They still thought that with my handful of soldiers I could hold this castle and win the day. I had half a mind to tell them, to just say what any who knew me knew. There is something brittle in me that will break before it bends.

Perhaps if the Prince of Arrow had brought a smaller army I might have had the sense to run. But he overdid it.

Four musicians in full livery raised their bladder-pipes and sounded the fanfare.

"Best use the short version, Father Gomst," I said in a low voice. "Lots to do today."

He frowned at that, grey brows rubbing up against each other. "Princess Miana, I have the pleasure of introducing His Highness Honorous Jorg Ancrath, King of the Renar Highlands, heir to the lands of Ancrath and the protectorates thereof."

"Charmed," I said, inclining my head. A child. She didn't reach much above my ribs.

"I can see why your miniature was in profile," she said, and sketched a curtsey.

That made me grin. It might be destined to be a short marriage but perhaps it wouldn't be dull. "You're not scared of me then, Miana?"

She reached to take my hand by way of answer. I pulled it back. "Best not."

"Father?" I nodded the priest on.

"Dearly beloved," Gomst said. "We are gathered together here in the sign of God . . ."

And so with old words from an old man and lacking anyone "here present" with just reason, or at least with just reason and the balls to say so; little Jorgy Ancrath became a married man.

I led my bride from the chapel with the applause and hoorahs of the nobility ringing behind us, almost but not quite drowning out those awful pipes. The bladder-pipe, a local Highlands speciality, is to music what warthogs are to mathematics. Largely unconnected.

The main doors lead onto a stairway where you can look down into the Haunt's largest courtyard, the place where I cut down the previous owner. Several hundred packed the space from the curtain wall to the stairs, more thronging out beyond the gateway, swarming beneath the portcullis, a light snow sifting down on all of them.

A cheer went up as we came into the light. I took Miana's hand then, despite the necromancy lurking in my fingers, and lifted it high to acknowledge the crowd. The loyalty of subject to lord still amazed me. I lived fat and rich off these people year after year while they squeezed a mean life out of the mountain-sides. And here they were ready to face pretty much certain death with me. I mean, even that blind faith in my ability to buck the odds had to allow a fairly big chunk of room for doubt.

I got my first proper insight into it a couple of years back. A lesson that life on the road hadn't taught me or my Brothers. The power of place.

My royal presence was requested for a bit of justice-making in what they call in the Renar Highlands a "village," though pretty much everywhere else people would call it three houses and a few sheds. The place lies way up in the peaks. They call it Gutting. I heard that there's a Little Gutting slightly higher up the valley, though it can't be much more than a particularly roomy barrel. Anyhow, the dispute was over where one scabby peasant's rocks ended and another one's started. I'd hauled myself and Makin up three thousand foot of mountain to show a bit of willing in the business of kinging it. According to reports, several men of the village had been killed already in the feud, though on closer inspection casualties were limited to a pig and the loss of a woman's left ear. Not so long ago I would just have killed everyone and come down the mountain with their heads on a spear, but perhaps I just felt tired after the climb. In any event I let the scabby peasants state their cases and they did so with enthusiasm and at great length. It started to get dark and the fleas were biting so I cut it short.

"Gebbin, is it?" I said to the plaintiff. He nodded. "Basically, Gebbin, you just hate the hell out of this fellow here and I really can't see the reason for it. The thing is that I'm bored, I've got my breath back, and unless you tell me the real reason you hate . . ."

"Borron," Makin supplied.

"Yes, Borron. Tell me the real reason and make it honest, or it's a death sentence for everyone except this good woman with the one ear, and we'll be leaving her in charge of the remaining pig."

It took him a few moments to realize that I really meant what I said, and then another couple mumbling before he finally came out with it and admitted it was because the fellow was a "furner." *Furner* turned out to mean *foreigner* and old Borron was a foreigner because he was born and lived on the east side of the valley.

The men cheering Miana and me, waving their swords, bashing their shields and hollering themselves hoarse, might have told anyone who asked how proud they were to fight for His Highness and his new queen. The truth, however, is that at the bottom of it all they simply didn't want the men of Arrow marching all over their rocks, eyeing up their goats, and maybe leering at their womenfolk.

"The Prince of Arrow has a much bigger army than you," Miana said. No "Your Highness," no "my lord."

"Yes, he does." I kept waving to the crowd, the big smile on my face.

"He's going to win, isn't he?" she said. She looked twelve but she didn't sound twelve.

"How old are you?" I asked, a quick glance down at her, still waving.

"Twelve."

Damn.

"They might win. If each of my men doesn't kill twenty of theirs then there's a good chance. Especially if he surrounds us."

"How far away are they?" she asked.

"Their front lines are camped three miles off," I said.

"You should attack now then," she said. "Before they surround us."

"I know." I was starting to like the girl. Even an experienced soldier like Coddin, a good soldier, wanted to hunker down behind the Haunt's walls and let the castle earn its keep, if you'll pardon the pun. The thing is, though, that no castle stands against odds like the ones we faced. Miana knew what Red Kent knew, Red Kent who cut down a patrol of seventeen men-at-arms on a hot August morning. Killing takes space. You need to move, to advance, to withdraw, and sometimes to just plain run for it.

One more wave and I turned my back on the crowds and strode into the chapel.

"Makin! Are the Watch ready?"

"They are." He nodded. "My king."

I drew my sword.

The sudden appearance of four foot of razored Builder-steel in the house of God resulted in a pleasing gasp.

"Let's go."

October 6th, Year 98 Interregnum
Ancrath. The Tall Castle. Chapel. Midnight.

The Ancraths' chapel is small and draughty, as if they hadn't much time for the place. The candles dance and the shadows are never still. When I leave, the friar's boy will snuff them.

Jorg Ancrath has been gone close on a week. He took Sir Makin with him from the dungeons. I was glad for that, I liked Sir Makin and I cannot truly blame him for what happened to Galen: that was Jorg again. A crossbow! He could never have bested Galen with a blade. There's no honour in the boy.

Friar Glen says Jorg near tore the dress off me after he hit me. I keep it at the back of the long closet in the bride chest Mother packed for me before we left Scorron Halt. I keep it where the maids don't look, and my hands lead me back there. I run the tatters through my fingers. Blue satin. I touch it and I try to remember. I see him standing there, arms wide, daring the knife in my hand, weaving as though he were too tired to stand, his skin dead white, and the black stain around his chest wound. He looked so young. A child almost. With those scars all across him where the thorns tore him. Sir Reilly says they found him hanging, near bloodless, after a night in the thorns with the storm around him and his mother lying dead.

And then he hit me.

I'm touching the spot now. It's still sore. Lumpy with

scab. I wonder if they can see it through my hair. And then I wonder why I care.

I'm bruised down here too. Bruised black, like that stain. I can almost see the lines of fingers on my thigh, the print of a thumb.

He hit me and then he used me, raped me. It would have been nothing to him, a mercenary from the road, it would have meant nothing to him, just something else to take. It would rank small amongst his crimes. Maybe not the largest even against me, for I miss Hanna and I did cry when we put her in the ground, and I miss Galen for the fierceness of his smile and the heat he put in me whenever he came near.

He hit me, and then he used me? That sick boy, daring the knife, barely able to stand?

October 11th, Year 98 Interregnum
Ancrath. The Tall Castle. My chambers.

I saw Friar Glen in the Blue Hall today. I've stopped going to his services but I saw him in the hall. I watched his hands, his thick fingers and his thick thumbs. I watched them and I thought of those fading bruises, yellow now, and I came to the tall closet, and here I am with the torn satin in my hands.

Skin, bones, and mischief comprise Brother Gog. Monster born and monster bred but there's little to mark him from Adam save the stippled crimson-on-black of his hide, the dark wells of his eyes, ebony talons on hand and foot, and the thorny projections starting to grow along his spine. Watch him play and run and laugh, and he seems too at ease to be a crack in the world through which all the fires of hell might pour. Watch him burn though, and you will believe it.

4

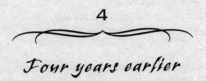

Four years earlier

I took my uncle's throne in my fourteenth year and found it to my liking. I had a castle, and staff of serving maids, to explore, a court of nobles to suppress, or at least what counted as nobles in the Highlands, and a treasury to ransack. For the first three months I confined myself to these activities.

I woke soaked with sweat. I normally wake suddenly with a clear head, but I felt as though I were drowning.

"Too hot . . ."

I rolled and fell from the bed, landing heavy.

Smoke.

Shouting in the distance.

I uncovered the bed-lamp and turned up the wick. The smoke came from the doors, not seeping under or between but lifting from every inch of the charred wood and rising like a rippled curtain.

"Shit—" Burning to death has always been a worry of mine. Call it a personal foible. Some people are scared of spiders. I'm scared of immolation. Also spiders.

"Gog!" I bellowed.

He'd been out there in the antechamber when I retired. I moved toward the doors, coming at them from the side. An awful heat came off them. I could leave by the doorway or try to fit myself through the bars on any of three windows before negotiating the ninety-foot drop.

I took an axe from the wall display and stood with my back to the stone, next to the doors. My lungs hurt and I couldn't see straight. Swinging the axe felt like swinging a full-grown man. The blade bit and the doors exploded. Orange-white fire roared into the room, furnace-hot, in a thick tongue forking time and again. And, almost as suddenly, it died away like a cough ending, leaving nothing but scorched floor and a burning bed.

The antechamber felt hotter than my bedchamber, char-black from floor to ceiling, with a huge glowing coal at its centre. I staggered back toward my bed. The heat took the water from my eyes and for a moment my vision cleared. The coal was Gog, curled like a new-born, pulsing with flame.

Something vast broke from the doorway leading to the guards' room beyond. Gorgoth! He scooped the boy up in one three-fingered hand and slapped him with the other. Gog woke with a sharp cry and the fire went out of him in an instant, leaving nothing but a limp child, skin stippled red and black, and the stink of burned meat.

Without words I stumbled past them and let my guards help me away.

They practically had to drag me to the throne-room before I found my strength. "Water," I managed. And when I'd drunk and used my knife to trim away the burned ends of my hair, I coughed out, "Bring the monsters."

Makin clattered into the hall, still pulling on a gauntlet. "Again?" he asked. "Another fire?"

"Bad this time. An inferno," I said. "At least I won't have to look at my uncle's furniture any more."

"You can't let him sleep in the castle," Makin said.

"I know that," I said. *"Now."*

"Put a quick end to it, Jorg." Makin pulled the gauntlet off. We weren't under attack after all.

"You can't let him go." Coddin arrived, dark circles under his eyes. "He's too dangerous. Someone will use him."

And there it hung. Gog had to die.

Three clashes on the main doors and they swung open. Gorgoth entered the throne-room with Gog, flanked by four of my table-knights, who looked like children beside him. Seen in amongst men the leucrota looked every bit as monstrous as the day I found them under Mount Honas. Gorgoth's cat-eyes slitted despite the gloom, blood-red hide almost black, as if infected with the night.

"What are you, Gog, eight years now? And busy trying to burn down my castle." I felt Gorgoth's eyes upon me. The great spars of his ribcage flexed back and forth with each breath.

"The big one will fight," Coddin murmured at my shoulder. "He will be hard to put down."

"Eight years," Gog repeated. He didn't know but he liked to agree with me. His voice had been high and sweet when we met beneath Mount Honas. Now it came raw and carried the crackle of flame behind it as if he might start breathing the stuff out like a damned dragon.

"I will take him away," Gorgoth said, almost too deep to hear. "Far."

Play your pieces, Jorg. A silence stretched out.

I wouldn't be sitting in this throne if Gorgoth hadn't held the gate. Or sitting here if Gog hadn't burned the Count's men. The skin on my face still clung tight, my lungs still hurt, and the stink of burnt hair still filled my nostrils.

"I'm sorry about your bed, Brother Jorg," Gog said. Gorgoth flicked his shoulder, one thick finger, enough to stagger him. "King Jorg," Gog corrected.

I wouldn't be sitting on the throne but for a lot of people, a stack of chances, some improbable, some stolen, but for the sacrifice of many men, some better, some worse. A man cannot take on new burdens of debt at every turn or he will buckle beneath the weight and be unable to move.

"You were ready to give this child to the necromancers, Gorgoth," I said. "Him and his brother both." I didn't ask if he would die to protect Gog. That much was written in him.

"Things change," Gorgoth said.

"Better they find a quick death, you said." I stood. "The changes will come too fast in these ones. Too fast to be borne. The changes will turn them inside out, you said."

"Let him take his chance," Gorgoth said.

"I nearly died in my bed tonight." I stepped down from the dais, Makin at my shoulder now. "The royal chambers are in ashes. And dying abed was never my plan. Unless t'were as emperor in my dotage beneath an over-energetic young concubine."

"It cannot be helped." Gorgoth's hands closed into massive fists. "It's in his dena."

"His dinner?" My hand rested on the hilt of my sword. I remembered how Gog had fought to save his little brother. How pure that fury had been. I missed that purity in myself. Only yesterday every choice came easy. Black or white. Stab Gemt in the neck or don't. And now? Shades of grey. A man can drown in shades of grey.

"His dena. The story of every man, written at his core, what he is, what he will be, written in a coil in the core of us all," Gorgoth said.

I'd never heard the monster say so many words in a row. "I've opened up a lot of men, Gorgoth, and if anything is written there then it's written red on red and smells bad."

"The centre of a man isn't found by your geometry, Highness." He held me with those cat's eyes. He'd never called me Highness before either. Probably the closest to begging he would ever come.

I stared at Gog, crouched now, looking from me to Gorgoth and back. I liked the boy. Plain and simple. Both of us with a dead brother that we couldn't save, both of us with something burning in us, some elemental force of destruction wanting out every moment of every day.

"Sire," Coddin said, knowing my mind for once. "These matters need not occupy the king. Take my chambers and we'll speak again in the morning."

Leave and we'll do your dirty work for you. The message was clear enough. And Coddin didn't want to do it. If he could read me I surely could read him. He didn't want to slit his horse's throat when a loose rock lamed it. But he did. And he would now. The game of kings was never a clean game.

Play your pieces.

"It can't be helped, Jorg," Makin set a hand to my shoulder, voice soft. "He's too dangerous. There's no knowing what he'll become."

Play your pieces. Win the game. Take the hardest line.

"Gog," I said. He stood slowly, eyes on mine. "They're telling me you're too dangerous. That I can't keep you. Or let you go. That you are a chance that can't be taken. A weapon that can't be wielded." I turned, taking in the throne-room, the high vaults, dark windows, and faced Coddin, Makin, the knights of my table. "I woke a Builders' Sun beneath Gelleth, and this child is too much for me?"

"Those were desperate times, Jorg," Makin said, studying the floor.

"All times are desperate," I said. "You think we're safe here, on our mountainside? This castle might look big from the inside. From a mile off you can cover it with your thumb."

I looked at Gorgoth. "Maybe I need a new geometry. Maybe we need to find this dena and see if the story can't be rewritten."

"The child's power is out of control, Jorg," Coddin said, a brave man to interject when I'm in full flow. The kind of man I needed. "It will only grow more wild."

"I'm taking him to Heimrift," I said. *Gog is a weapon and I will forge him there.*

"Heimrift?" Gorgoth relaxed his fists, knuckles cracking with loud retorts.

"A place of demons and fire," Makin muttered.

"A volcano," I said. "Four volcanoes actually. And a fire-mage. Or so my tutor told me. So let's put the benefits of a royal education to the test, shall we? At least Gog will like it there. Everything burns."

5

Four years earlier

"This is a bad idea, Jorg."

"It's a dangerous idea, Coddin, but that doesn't have to mean it's bad." I laid my knife on the map to stop it rolling up again.

"Whatever the chances of success, you'll leave your kingdom without a king." He set a fingertip to the map, resting on the Haunt as if to show me my place. "It's only been three months, Jorg. The people aren't sure of you yet, the nobles will start to plot the moment you leave, and how many men-at-arms will you take with you? With an empty throne the Renar Highlands might look like an easy prize. Your royal father might even choose to call with the Army of the Gate. If it comes to defending this place I don't know how many of your uncle's troops will rally to your cry."

"My father didn't send the Gate when my mother and brother were murdered." My fingers closed around the knife hilt of their own accord. "He's unlikely to move against the Haunt now. Especially when his armies are busy acquiring what's left of Gelleth."

"So how many soldiers will you take?" Coddin asked. "The Watch will not be enough."

"I'm not going to take any," I said. "I could take the whole

damn army and it would just get me into a war on somebody
else's lands." Coddin made to protest. I cut him off. "I'll take
my Brothers. They'll appreciate a spell on the road and we
managed to traipse to and fro happily enough not so many years
ago with nobody giving us much pause."

Makin returned with several large map scrolls under his
arm. "In disguise, is it?" he said and grinned. "Good. Truth be
told, this place has given me itchy feet."

"You're staying, Brother Makin," I told him. "I'll take Red
Kent, Row, Grumlow, Young Sim . . . and Maical, why not?
He may be a half-wit but he's hard to kill. And of course Little
Rike—"

"Not him," Coddin said, face cold. "There's no loyalty in
that one. He'll leave you dead in a hedgerow."

"I need him," I said.

Coddin frowned. "He might be handy in a fight, but there's
no subtlety in him, no discipline, he's not clever, he—"

"The way I'd put it," said Makin, "is that Rike can't make
an omelette without wading thigh deep in the blood of chickens
and wearing their entrails as a necklace."

"He's a survivor," I said. "And I need survivors."

"You need me," said Makin.

"You can't trust him." Coddin rubbed his forehead as he
always did when the worry got in him.

"I need you here, Makin," I said. "I want to have a kingdom
to come back to. And I know I can't trust Rike, but four years
on the road taught me that he's the right tool for the job."

I lifted my knife and the map sprung back into its roll. "I've
seen enough."

Makin raised his eyes and tipped his maps unopened onto
the table.

"Mark me out a decent route, will you, Coddin, and have that
scribe lad copy it down." I stood straight and stretched. I'd need
to find something to wear. One of the maids had burned my old
rags and velvet's no good for the road. It's like a magnet for dust.

Father Gomst met Makin, Kent, and me on our way to the
stables. He'd hurried from chapel, red in the face, the heaviest
bible under one arm and the altar cross in his other hand.

"Jorg—" He stopped to catch his breath. "King Jorg."

"You're going to join us, Father Gomst?" The way he paled made me smile.

"The blessing," he said, still short of wind.

"Ah, well bless away."

Kent went to his knees in an instant, as pious a killer as I ever knew. Makin followed with unseemly haste for a man who'd sacked a cathedral in his time. Since Gomst had walked out of Gelleth by the light of a Builders' Sun, without so much as a tan to show for it, the Brothers seemed to think him touched by God. The fact we had all done the same with far less time at our disposal didn't register with them.

For my own part, for all the evils of the Roma church, I could no longer bring myself to despise Gomst as I once had. His only true crime was to be a weak and impotent man, unable to deliver the promise of his lord, the love of his saviour, or even to put the yoke of Roma about the necks of his flock with any conviction.

I bowed my head and listened to the prayer. It never hurts to cover your bases.

In the west yard my motley band were assembled, checking over their gear. Rike had the biggest horse I'd ever seen.

"I could run faster than this monster, Rike." I made a show of checking behind it. "You didn't take the plough when you stole it, then?"

"It'll do," he said. "Big enough for loot."

"Maical's not bringing the head-cart?" I looked around. "Where is he anyway?"

"Gone for the grey," Kent said. "Idiot won't ride any other horse. Says he doesn't know how."

"Now that's loyalty for you." I shot Rike a look. "So where's this new wife of yours, Brother Rikey? Not coming to see you off?"

"Busy ploughing." He slapped his horse. "Got a job of it now."

Gorgoth came through the kitchen gate, looming behind Rike. It's unsettling to see something on two legs that's taller and wider than Rike. Gog popped out from behind him. He took my hand and I let him lead me. There's not many that will take my hand since the necromancy took root in me. There's a touch of death in my fingers, not just the coldness. Flowers wilt and die.

"Where we going, Brother Jorg?" Still a child's voice despite the crackle in it.

"To find us a fire-mage. Put an end to this bed-burning," I told him.

"Will it hurt?" He watched me with big eyes, pools of black. I shrugged. "Might do."

"Scared," he said, clutching my hand tighter. I could feel heat rising from his fingers. Maybe it cancelled the cold from mine. "Scared."

"Well then," I said. "We're headed the right way."

He frowned.

"You've got to hunt your fears, Gog. Beat them. They're your only true enemies."

"You're not scared of anything, Brother Jorg," he said. "King J—"

"I'm scared of burning," I said. "Especially in my bed." I looked back to the brothers, stowing weapons and supplies. "I had a cousin who liked to burn people up, did I not, Brother Row?"

"Ayuh." He nodded.

"My cousin Marclos," I said. "Tell Gog what happened to him."

Row tested the point of an arrow with his thumb. "Went up to him all on your ownself, Jorg, and killed him in the middle of a hundred of his soldiers."

I looked down at Gog. "I'm scared of spiders too. It's the way that they move. And the way that they're still. It's that scurry." I mimicked it with my hand.

I called back to Row. "How am I with spiders, Row?"

"Weird." Row spat and secured his last arrow. "You'll like this tale, Gog, what with being a godless monster and all." He spat again. Brother Row liked to spit. "Spent a week holed up in some grain barns one time. Hiding. We didn't go hungry. Grain and rats make for a good stew. Only Jorg here wasn't having any of that. Place was stuffed full of spiders see. Big hairy fellows." He spread his fingers until the knuckles cracked.

"For a whole week Jorg hunted them. Didn't eat nothing but spider for a week. And not cooked mind. Not even dead."

"And rat stew always tasted good after that week," I said.

Gog frowned, then his eyes caught the glitter on my wrist. "What's this?" He pointed.

I pulled my sleeve back and held it up for all to see. "Two things I found in my uncle's treasury that were worth more than the gold around them. Thought I'd bring them along in case of need." I made sure Rike caught sight of the silver on my wrist. "No need to be going through my saddlebags at night now, Little Rikey. The treasure's here and if you think you can take it, try now."

He sneered and tied off another strap.

"Wossit?" Gog stared entranced.

"The Builders made it," I said. "It's a thousand years old."

Row and Red Kent came over to see.

"I'm told they call it a watch," I said. "And you can see why."

In truth, I'd been watching it a lot myself. It had a face on it behind crystal, with twelve hours marked and sixty minutes, and two black arms that moved, one slow, one slower still, to point out the time. Entranced, I had opened it up at the back with the point of my knife and gazed into the guts of the thing. The hatch popped back on a minute hinge as if the Builders had known I would want to see inside. Wheels within wheels, tiny, toothed, and turning. How they made such things so small and so precise I cannot guess but to me it is a wonder past any man-made sun or glow-light.

"What else you got, Jorg?" Rike asked.

"This." I took it from the deep pocket on my hip and set it down on the flagstones. A battered metal clown with traces of paint clinging to his jerkin, hair, and nose.

Kent took a step back. "It looks evil."

I knelt and released a catch behind the clown's head. With a jerk and a whir he started to stamp his metal feet and bring his metal hands together, clashing the cymbals he held. He jittered in a loose circle, stamping and clashing, going nowhere.

Rike started to laugh. Not that "hur, hur, hur" of his that sounds like another kind of anger, but a real laugh, from the belly. "It's like . . . It's like . . ." He couldn't get the words out.

The others couldn't hold back. Sim and Maical cracked first.

Grumlow snorting through the drowned-rat moustache he'd been working on. Then Red Kent and at last even Row, laughing like children. Gog looked on, astonished. Even Gorgoth couldn't help but grin, showing back-teeth like tombstones.

The clown fell over and kept on stamping the air. Rike collapsed with it, thumping the ground with his fist, gasping for breath.

The clown slowed, then stopped. There's a blue-steel spring inside that you wind tight with a key. And when it's finished stamping and crashing, the spring is loose again.

"Burlow . . . Burlow should have seen this." Rike wiped the tears from his eyes. The first time I'd heard him mention any of the fallen.

"Yes, Brother Rike," I said. "Yes, he should." I imagined Brother Burlow laughing with us, his belly shaking.

We made our moment then, one of those waypoints by which a life is remembered, the Brotherhood remade and bound for the road. We made our moment—the last good one. "Time to go," I said.

Sometimes I wonder if we all don't have a blue-steel spring inside us, like that dena of Gorgoth's coiled tight at the core. I wonder if we don't all go stamping and crashing, crashing and stamping in our own little circles going nowhere. And I wonder who it is that laughs at us.

6

Four years earlier

Three months previously I had entered the Haunt alone, covered in blood that was not my own and swinging a stolen sword. My Brothers followed me in. Now I left the castle in the hands of another. I had wanted my uncle's blood. His crown I took because other men said I could not have it.

If the Haunt reminds you of a skull, and it does me, then the scraps of town around the gates might be considered the dried vomit of its last heave. A tannery here, abattoir there, all the necessary but stinking evils of modern life, set out beyond the walls where the wind will scour them. We were barely clear of the last hovel before Makin caught us.

"Missing me already?"

"The Forest Watch tell me we have company coming," Makin said, catching his breath.

"We really should rename the Watch," I said. The best the Highlands could offer by way of forest was the occasional clump of trees huddled miserably in a deep valley, all twisted and hunched against the wind.

"Fifty knights," Makin said. "Carrying the banner of Arrow."

"Arrow?" I frowned. "They've come a ways." The province lay on the edge of the map we had so recently rolled up.

"They look fresh enough by all accounts."

"I think I'll meet them on the road," I said. "We might get a more interesting story out of them as a band of road-brothers." The truth was I didn't want to change back into silks and ermine and go through the formalities. They would be heading for the castle. You don't send fifty men in plate armour for a stealth mission.

"I'll come with you," Makin said. He wasn't going to take "no" this time.

"You won't pass as a road-brother," I said. "You look like an actor who's raided the props chest for all the best knight-gear."

"Roll him in some shit," Rike said. "He'll pass then."

We happened to be right by Jerring's stables and a heap of manure lay close at hand. I pointed to it.

"Not so different from life in court." Makin grimaced and threw his robe into the head-cart. Maical had hitched it to the grey out of habit.

When the captain of my guard looked more like a hedge-knight at the very bottom of his luck, we moved on. Gog rode with me, clutching tight. Gorgoth jogged along, for no horse would take him, and not just because of his weight. Something in him scared them.

"Ever been to Arrow, Makin?" I asked, easing my horse upwind.

"Never have," he said. "A small enough principality. They breed them tough down there though, by all accounts. Been giving their neighbours a headache for years now."

We rode on without talk for a while, just the clatter of hooves and the creak of the head-cart to break the mountain silence. The road—or trail if I'm honest, for the Builders never worked their magic in the Highlands—wound its way down, snaking back and forth to tame the gradients. As we dropped I started to realize that in the low valleys it would be spring already. Even here a flash of green showed now and again and set the horses nosing the air.

We saw the knights' outrider an hour later and the main column a mile farther on. Row started to turn off the trail.

"I'll say when we turn aside and when we stand our ground, if it's all the same to you, Brother Row." I gave him a look. The Brothers had started to forget the old Jorg—been too long lazing around the Haunt, left too long to their own wickednesses.

"There's a lot of them, Brother Jorg," said Young Sim, older than me of course but still with little use for a razor if you discounted the cutting of throats.

"When you're making for the king's castle it's bad manners to cut down travellers on the way," I said. "Even ones as disreputable as us."

I rode on. A pause and the others followed.

The next rise showed them closer, two abreast, moving at a slow trot, a pair of narrow banners fluttering in the Renar wind. No rabble these, table-knights from a high court, a harmony to their arms and armour that put my own guard to shame.

"This is a bad idea," Makin said. He stank of horse-shit.

"If you ever stop saying that I'll know it's time to start worrying," I said.

The men of Arrow continued their advance. We could hear their hooves on the rock. I had an urge to rest in the middle of the trail and demand a toll. That would have made a tale, but perhaps too short a one. I settled for pulling to the side and watching as they drew closer. I cast an eye over our troop. An ugly lot, but the leucrotas won the prize.

"See if you can't hide behind Rike's beast, Gorgoth," I said. "I knew that plough horse would come in useful."

I took the knife from my belt and started to work the dirt from under my fingernails. Gog's claws dug in beneath my breastplate as the first men reached us.

The knights slowed their horses to a walk as they came near. A few turned their heads but most passed without a glance, faces hidden behind visors. At the middle of the column were two men who caught the eye, or at least their armour did, polished to a brilliance, fluted in the Teuton style, and scintillating with rainbow hues where the oiled metal broke the light. A hound ran between their horses, short-haired, barrel-chested, long in the snout. The leftmost of the pair raised his hand and the column stopped, even the men in front of him, though there seemed no way they could have seen him.

"Well now," he said, both words precise and tightly wrapped.

He took his helm off, which seemed a foolish thing to do when he might be the target of hidden crossbows, and shook his head. Sweat kept his blond hair plastered to his brow.

"Good day, Sir Knight," I said and nodded him a quarter of a bow.

He looked me up and down with calm blue eyes. He reminded me of Katherine's champion, Sir Galen. "How far to Renar's castle, boy?" he asked.

Something in me said that this man knew exactly how far it was, as crow flies and cripple crawls. "King Jorg's castle lies a good ten miles yonder." I waved my knife along the trail. "About a mile of it up."

"A king, is it?" He smiled. Handsome like Galen too, in that square-jawed blond manner that will turn a girl's head. "Old Renar didn't count himself a king."

I started to hate him. And not just for the pun. "Count Renar held only the Highlands. King Jorg is heir to Ancrath and the lands of Gelleth. That's enough land to make a king, at least in these parts."

I made show of peering at the fellow's breastplate. He had dragons there, etched and enamelled in red, each rampant, clutching a vertical arrow taller than itself. Nice work. "Arrow is it you're from, my lord?" I asked. Not waiting for an answer I turned to Makin. "Do you know why that land is named Arrow, Makin?"

He shook his head and studied the pommel of his saddle. The need to say "this is a bad idea" twitched on his lips.

"They say it's called Arrow because you can shoot one from the north coast to the south," I said. "From what I hear they could have called it Sneeze. I wonder what they call the man who rules there."

"You know a lot about heraldry, boy." Eyes still calm. The man beside him moved his hand to his sword, gauntlet clicking against the hilt. "They call the man who rules there the Prince of Arrow." He smiled. "But you may call me Prince Orrin."

It seemed rash to be riding into another's realm with fifty

men, even fifty such as these. The very thing I had decided against for my own travels.

"You're not worried that King Jorg will take the opportunity to thin the field in this Hundred War of ours?" I asked.

"If I were his neighbour, maybe," the Prince said. "But killing me or even ransoming me to my enemies would just make his own neighbours more secure and better able to harm him. And I hear the king has a good eye for his own chances. Besides, it would not be easy."

"I thought you came looking for a count, but now it seems you already know about King Jorg and his good eye," I said. He came prepared, this one.

The Prince shrugged. He looked young when he did it. Twenty maybe. Not much more. "That's a handsome sword," he said. "Show it to me."

I'd wrapped the hilt about with old leather and smeared that with dirt. The scabbard was older than me and shiny with the years. Whatever my uncle's sword had been, it wasn't handsome now. Not until I drew it and showed its metal. I considered throwing my dagger. Old blondie might not see so clear with it jutting out of his eye socket. He might even have a brother at home who'd be pleased to be the new Prince of Arrow and owe me a favour hereafter. I could see it in my mind's eye. The handsome Prince with my dagger in his face, and us racing away across the slopes.

I'm not given to should haves. But I should have.

Instead I stowed the knife and drew my uncle's sword, an heirloom of his line, Builder-steel, the blade taking the light of the day and giving it back with an edge.

"Well now," Prince Orrin said again. "An uncommon sword you have there, boy. From whom did you steal it?"

The mountain wind blew cold, finding every chink in my armour, and I shivered despite the heat pulsing from Gog at my back. "Why would the Prince of Arrow come all the way to the Renar Highlands with just fifty knights, I wonder?" I dismounted. The Prince's eyes widened at the sight of Gog left in the saddle, half-naked and striped like a tiger.

I stood on one of the larger rocks by the roadside, on foot to show I had no running in me.

"Perhaps such reasons are not for a bandit child by the roadside clutching a stolen sword," he said, still maddeningly calm.

I couldn't argue with the "stolen" so I took offence against the "child." "Fourteen is a man's age in these lands and I wield this sword better than any who held it before me."

The Prince chuckled, gentle and unforced. If he had studied a book devoted to the art of infuriating me he could have done no better job. Pride has ever been my weakness, and occasionally my strength.

"My apologies then, young man." I could see his champion frown at that, even behind his visor. "I travel to see the lands that I will rule as emperor, to know the people and the cities. And to speak with the nobles, the barons, counts . . . and even kings, who will serve me when I sit upon the empire throne. I would win their service with wisdom, words and favour, rather than with sword and fire."

A pompous enough speech perhaps, but he had a way with words this one. Oh, my brothers, the way he spoke them. A magic of a new kind, this. More subtle than Sageous's gentle traps—even that heathen witch with his dream-weaving would envy this kind of persuasion. I could see why the Prince had taken off his helm. The enchantment didn't lie in the words alone but in the look, in the honesty and trust of it all, as if every man who heard them was worthy of his friendship. A talent to be wary of, maybe more potent even than the power Corion used to set me scurrying across empire and to steer my uncle from behind his throne.

The hound sat and licked the slobber from its chops. It looked big enough to swallow a small lamb.

"And why would they listen to you, Prince of Arrow?" I asked. I heard a petulance in my voice and hated it.

"This Hundred War must end," he said. "It will end. But how many need drown in blood before the peace? Let the throne be claimed. The nobles can keep their castles, rule their lands, collect their gold. Nothing will be lost; nothing will end but the war."

And there it was again. The magic. I believed him. Even without him saying so I knew that he truly sought peace, that he would rule with a fair and even hand, that he cared about the people. He would let the farmers farm, the merchants trade, the scholars seek their secrets.

"If you were offered the empire throne," he said, looking only at me, "would you take it?"

"Yes." Though I would rather take it without it being offered.

"Why?" he asked. "Why do you want it?"

He shone a light into my dark corners, this storybook prince with his calm eyes. I wanted to win. The throne was just the token to demonstrate that victory. And I wanted to win because other men had said that I may not. I wanted to fight because fighting ran through me. I gave less for the people than for the dung heap we rolled Makin in.

"It's mine." All the answer I could find.

"Is it?" he asked. "Is it yours, Steward?"

And in one flourish he showed his hand. And showed my shame. You should know that the men who fight the Hundred War, and they are all men, save for the Queen of Red, fall from two sides of a great tree. The line of the Stewards, as our enemies call us, trace the clearest path to the throne, but it is to the Great Steward, Honorous, who served for fifty years when the seed of empire failed. And Honorous sat *before* the throne rather than on it. Still, a strong claim to be heir to the man who served as emperor in all but name is a better case for taking that throne than a weak claim to be heir to the last emperor. At least that's how we Stewards see it. In any case I would cut myself a path to the throne even if some bastard-born herder had fathered me on a gutter-whore—genealogy can work for me or I can cut down the family tree and make a battering ram. Either way is good.

Many of the line of Stewards are cast in my mould: lean, tall, dark of hair and eye, quick of mind. Even our foes call us cunning. The line of the emperor is muddied, lost in burning libraries, tainted by madness and excess. And many of the line, or who claim it, are built like Prince Orrin: fair, thick of arm, sometimes giants big as Rike, though pleasing on the eye.

"Steward is it now?" I rolled my wrist and my sword danced. His hound stood up, sharp, without a growl.

"Put it away, Jorg," he said. "I know you. You have the look of the Ancraths about you. As dark a branch of the Steward tree as ever grew. You're all still killing each other so I hear?"

"That's King Jorg to you," I said, knowing I sounded like a spoiled child and unable to help it. Something in Orrin's calm humour, in the light of him, cast a shadow over me.

"King? Ah, yes, because of Ancrath, and Gelleth," he said. "But I'm told your father has named young Prince Degran his heir. So perhaps . . ." He spread his hands and smiled.

The smile felt like a slap in the face. So Father had named the new son he'd made with his Scorron whore. And gifted him my birthright. "And you're thinking to give him the Highlands too?" I asked, keeping the savage grin on my face however much it wanted to slide away. "You should know that there are a hundred of my Watch hidden in the rocks ready to slot arrows through the gaps in that fancy armour, Prince." It might even be true. I knew that at least some of the Watch would be tracking the knights.

"I'd say it was closer to twenty," Prince Orrin said. "I don't think they're mountain men, are they? Did you bring them out of Ancrath, Jorg, when you ran? They're skilled enough, but proper mountain men would be harder to spot."

He knew too much, this prince. It was seriously starting to annoy. And as you know, being angry makes me angry.

"In any case," he carried on as if I weren't about to explode, as if I weren't about to ram my sword entirely through his body, "I won't kill you for the same reason you won't kill me. It would replace two weak kingdoms with a stronger one. When the road to the empire throne, to my throne, leads me here, I would rather find you and your colourful friends terrorizing the peasants and getting drunk, than find your father or Baron Kennick keeping order. And I hope that by the time I arrive you will have grown wiser as well as taller, and open your lands to me as emperor."

I jumped from my rock and the hound stood in my path quicker than quick, still no growl but way too many teeth on display, all gleaming with slobber. I fixed its eyes, which is a good way to get your face bitten off, but I meant to threaten the beast. Holding my sword by hilt and blade, flat side forward, I took another step, a snarl rising in me. I had a hound once, a good one that I loved, before such soft words were taken from me, and I had no wish to kill this one. But I would. "Back." More growl than word. My eyes on his.

And with ears flat to its head the beast whimpered and skulked back between the horses' legs. I think it sensed the death in me. A bitter meal, that necromancer's heart. Another step away from the world. It sometimes seems I stand three steps outside the lives of other men. One for the heart. One for the thorn bush. And perhaps the first for that dog I remember in dreams.

I call him mine but the hound belonged to my brother William and me. A wolf-hound of some kind, huger than the two of us, a charger fit for two young knights. He could take William on his back, Will being just four, but if I leapt on too he would shake us both off and nip my leg. We called him Justice.

"Impressive," said Prince Orrin, looking anything but impressed. "If you're finished with my dog then we'll be on our way. I plan to cross through to Orlanth via High Pass, or Blue Moon Pass if it's clear, and pay a call on Earl Samsar."

"You'll be on your way when I say so," I told him, still aching for . . . something. Fear maybe? Perhaps just a measure of respect would do it. "And by whatever route I allow." I didn't like the way he seemed to know the lie of my land better than I did.

He raised an eyebrow at that, keeping a smile at bay and irking me more than smiling would have. "And what then is your judgment in this matter, King Jorg?"

Every fibre of me ached to hurt him. In any other man his words would sound smug, arrogant, but here on this cold mountain slope they sounded honest and sincere. I hated him for being so openly the better man. I caught his eye and in that instant I knew. He pitied me.

"Cross swords with me, Brother Orrin," I said. "You're right to think of peace. Why should my goat-herders or your pig farmers suffer in a war to see which of our backsides polishes the empire throne? Cross swords with me and if I yield, then on the day you come to claim the empire I won't stand against you. Come, draw your blade. Or have your champion try his luck if you must." I nodded to the man beside him.

"Ah," Orrin said. "You wouldn't want to fight him. That's my brother Egan. God made him to stand behind a sword. Scares me sometimes! And besides, the two of you are too alike.

Egan thinks all this talk is a waste. He would set our farmers on your herders and drown the world in blood, would you not, Egan? I have a dream for the empire. For my empire. A bright dream. But I fear all Egan's dreams are red."

Egan grunted as if bored.

The Prince dismounted. "Clear the path and let no man interfere."

"This is—"

"I know, Makin." I cut across him. "It's a bad idea."

Makin climbed off his horse and stood beside me as Orrin's men pulled away. "He could be good," he said.

"Good is fine," I said. "I'm *great*."

"I won't argue that you're world class at killing, Jorg," Makin hissed. "But this is swordplay and only swordplay."

"Then I shall have to play the game," I said. The Prince hadn't asked what I would demand of him when I won. That left a bitter taste.

We stepped together then, two of the hundred, the lines of emperor and steward met for battle.

"We could do this the clever way, Jorg," Orrin said. He had enough of my measure not to say the easy way. "Support me. The new emperor will need a new steward."

I spat in the grit.

"You don't know what it is you want, or why you want it, Jorg," he said. "You've seen nothing of the empire you want to own. Have you been east, chasing the sun to the wall of Utter itself? Have you seen the shores of dark Afrique? Spoken with the jarls who sail from their northern fastness when the ice allows? If you had been spawned in the Arral wastes then all the miles you covered in those roaming years of yours would have shown you nothing but grassland. By ship, Jorg, by ship. That's the way to see the empire. Have you even seen the sea?"

The grey let out a long complacent fart, saving me from an answer. I always loved that horse.

We circled. Like much in life, a sword fight, especially a longsword fight, is about choosing your moment. A swing is a commitment, often a lifetime commitment. You wait for the best odds then bet your life on the chance offered. Against a man in plate armour you have to put muscle into it. All your strength. To put enough hurt through that metal so he won't be taking advantage as you draw back for the next attack. A lunge can be more tentative. It needs to be precise. To find and pierce that chink in the armour before he finds and pierces yours.

I swung, not to hit him but just to let our blades meet. His sword held a smoky look, something darker alloyed to the Builder-steel. The clash rang out harsh across the slopes. Somehow he rolled his blade in the instant they met and almost took mine from my hands. I didn't like that at all. I pressed him, short swings to keep him busy, to numb his hands and stop them being so tricksy. It felt like hacking at a stone pillar and left my palms aching, pain stabbing up my wrists.

"You're better than I expected," he said.

He came at me then, lunge, half-swing, lunge. Combinations too fast to think about.

We train so that our muscles learn. So that our eyes talk to our arms and hands, skipping the brain and the need to bother with decision and judgment. It's like learning the notes for a piece on the harp. First you think it through, A, C, C, D . . . and in time your fingers know it and you've forgotten the notes.

My sword arm made its moves without consulting me.

"Really not bad at all," he said.

But when you try to play the piece faster, and then faster still, and quicker again, at some point your fingers falter. What comes next? they want to know. What's next?

A heavy metal bar to the side of the head is what's next, apparently. At least that's what the flat of his blade felt like. I said something that was half-curse, half-groan, and all blood, then fell over as if he'd cut all my strings.

"Yield." It sounded as if he was calling from the far end of a long tunnel.

"Fuck that." More blood, possibly some bits of tooth.

"Last chance, Jorg," he said. The edge of his sword lay cold against my neck.

"He yields." Makin at the far end of the same tunnel. "He yields."

"Like hell I do." The difference between sky and ground had started to reassert itself. I focused on a dark blob that could well be Orrin.

"Yield," he said again. Warmth down my neck where blood trickled from his shallow cut.

I managed a laugh. "You've already said you won't kill me, Prince of Arrow. It's not in your interest. So why would I yield?" I spat again. "If you ever get to my borders with an army, I'll decide what to do then."

He turned away with a look of disgust.

"The High Pass," I said. "I'll give you free passage to the High Pass and you can bother the earl with your moralizing. You earned that much." I tried to stand and failed. Makin helped me to my feet.

We watched them ride on. The brother, Prince Egan, gave me an evil stare as he passed. Orrin didn't even turn his head.

We watched until the last horse vanished over the rise.

"We're going to need a bigger army," I said.

Sir Makin is almost the handsome knight of legend, dark locks curling, tall, a swordsman's build, darkest eyes, his armour always polished, blade keen. Only the thickness of his lips and the sharpness of his nose leave him shy of a maiden's dream. His mouth too expressive, his look too hawkish. In other matters too Sir Makin is "almost." Almost honourable, almost honest. About his friendship, though, there is no almost.

7

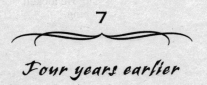

Four years earlier

We'd ridden for two hours since the Prince of Arrow left for the High Pass. Two hours in a very different kind of silence to the one that kept us company for the first part of our journey. I had the sort of headache that makes decapitation seem like a good option. Any idiot could tell that it wouldn't take much for me to make their neck the practice run.

"Ouch."

Well, not every idiot.

"Yes, Maical," I said. "Ouch." I watched him through slitted eyes, teeth tight against the throb in my skull. Sometimes you couldn't tell old Maical was broken. Whatever piece was missing from him, it didn't always show. For whole moments at a time he could look ready for anything, tough, dependable, even cunning. And then it came, that weakness about the mouth, the furrowing of the brow, and the empty eyes.

Maical had found his way back to the Brotherhood within weeks of our victory in the Highlands. Lord knows how, but I suppose even pigeons can find their way home with nothing but a drop of brain in their tiny skulls. In the months since I made the Haunt my home he'd served as stable-boy or assistant to the stable-boy, or dung-collector, or some such. I made it clear I wanted him fed and given a place to sleep. I'd killed his brother after all. Gemt hadn't cared much for him. He beat him and set him to both their tasks on the road. But he made sure Maical ate and he made sure he had a place to sleep. "He banged you up, Jorg," Maical said. He looked stupid when he spoke, lips always wet and glistening.

I saw Makin wince, Row exchange a bet with Grumlow.

"Yes, Maical, he surely did."

I didn't feel bad for knifing Gemt. Not for a heartbeat. But it hurt me to think of Maical too broken to hate me, caught in whatever hooks snagged his mind, seeing but trapped. I thought of the watch a *tick tick tick*ing on my wrist. All that cleverness, those wheels within wheels, turning, being turned, teeth biting, and yet one tiny piece of grit, one human hair in the wrong place, and it would seize, ruined, worthless. I wondered what had got into Maical way back when. What had it been that stole his wits away?

"Tell Makin to get himself up here," I said.

Maical pulled on his reins and the grey slowed. I saw Row's scowl. He'd lost his bet.

The mountains pulsed from red to green as the pain washed from front to back, from behind my eyes to the base of my skull.

"Sometimes I think you keep him around just to keep the grey happy," Makin said. I hadn't noticed him draw level.

"I want you to teach me how to use a sword," I said.

"You know how—"

"I thought I did," I said. "But now I'm going to take it seriously. What just happened . . ." I put my hand to my head and my fingers came away bloody. ". . . is not going to happen again."

"Well, at least it's a kingly way to pass the time," he said. "Help to keep your edge too. Have you even swung a sword since we took the Haunt?"

I shrugged and wished I hadn't. My teeth made a nasty squeaking as they ground over each other.

"I'm told you've been attempting to father a bastard on pretty much every serving girl in the castle." He grinned.

It's good to be the king.

Except when you get hit in the head with a sword.

"It's an effort at repopulation," I said. "Quality and quantity." I clapped a hand to my head. "Arrrgh, damn and fuck it." Some pain you can distance yourself from, but a headache sits right where you live.

Makin kept grinning. I think he quite liked seeing me knocked down.

He reached into his saddlebag, dug deep, pulled out a tight wrap of leather and tossed it over. I almost missed it. Double vision will do that for you.

"Clove-spice," he said.

"Been hoarding that one, Sir Makin." You could trade a good horse and not get enough clove-spice to fill your hand. Wonderful stuff for pain. Too much and you die of course, but it's like floating to your death, carried by a warm river. I almost opened the wrap. "Take it." I threw it back. Giving in to things becomes a habit. I made an enemy of the ache in my head and started to fight.

We rode on. I filled my mind with old venom, brought out the hate I kept for the Count of Renar. I'd had little to exercise it on since he passed out of reach. The *throb throb throb* behind my eyes made the ache from my broken tooth feel like a tingle.

Rike caught up on that monster horse of his and kept pace. He watched me for a while. Makin might have enjoyed seeing me knocked on my arse, but Rike thought all his festival days had come at once.

"You know why I keep you around, Rike?" I asked.

"Why?"

"You're like the worst part of me." That squeak of enamel on enamel again as I ground my teeth. "Damn." It slackened off. "I don't have an angel on one shoulder and a devil on the other. I got me a devil on both. But you're like the bad one. Like I'd be if I lost my charm, and my good looks." I realized I was babbling and tried to grin.

"Lose yourself, Rike." Makin again. I hadn't seen him come back.

"My father was right, Makin," I said. "Right to take his brother's money, for William and Mother. He would have lost half his army just getting to the Haunt."

Makin frowned. He held the clove-spice out again. "Take it."

"My father knew about sacrifice. Corion too. The path he set me on. The right one. I just didn't like being pushed."

I could hardly see Makin, eyes slitted against the pulse in my head.

Makin shook his head. "Some crimes demand an answer. Corion tried to take that from you. I crossed three nations to find the men who killed my girl." He sounded worried.

"Idiot." Numb lips shaped the word.

"Jorg." Makin kept his voice low. "You're crying. Take the damn spice."

"Going to need a bigger army." Everything had gone black and I felt as if I was falling. And then I hit the ground.

8

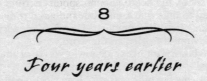

Four years earlier

I woke in a darkened room. A fly buzzed. Someone somewhere was being sick. Light filtered in where the daub cracked from the wattle. More light through the shutters, warped in their frame. A peasant hut. The retching stopped, replaced by muted sobs. A child.

I sat up. A thin blanket slipped from me. Straw prickled. The ache in my head had gone. My tooth hurt like a bastard but it was nothing compared to how my head had been. I felt around for my sword and couldn't find it.

There's something magical about a departed headache. It's a shame the joy fades and you can't appreciate not having one every moment of your life. That hadn't been a regular headache of course. Old Jorgy got himself a bruised brain. I'd seen it before. When Brother Gains fell off his horse one time and hit his head he went crazier than Maical for the best part of two days. "Did I fall off my horse?" He must have asked that a thousand times in a row. Crying one moment. Laughing the next. We're brittle things, us men.

I found my feet, still a little shaky. The door opened and the light came dazzling around the dark shape of a woman. "I brought you soup," she said.

I took it and sat again. "Smells good." It did. My stomach growled.

"Your friend, Makin, he brought a couple of rabbits for the pot," she said. "We hadn't had meat since the pigs got took."

I raised the bowl to my lips: no spoons here. She left as I started slurping, burning my mouth and not caring too much. For a long time I just sipped and watched the dust dance where fingers of light reached in through the shutters. I munched on lumps of rabbit, chewed on the gristle, swallowed the fat. It's good to eat with an empty mind.

At last I got to my feet again, steadier now. I patted myself down. My old dagger was on my hip and there was a lump in my belt pouch which turned out to be Makin's clove-spice. One more glance around for my sword and I went to the door. The day seemed a little too bright, the wind chill and sharp with the stink of old burning. I stretched and blinked. Apart from the hut I'd come from, a stall for animals by the look of it, the place lay in ruins. Two houses with tumbled walls and blackened spars, some broken fences, animal pens that looked to have been ridden through with heavy horse. I saw the woman crouched in the shell of the closer house, her back to me.

The sudden need for a piss bit hard. I went against the hut, a long hot acid flow never seeming to end. "Jesu! Have I slept for a week?"

A wise man once said, "Don't shit where you eat." Aristotle perhaps. On the road that's a rule to live by. Find your relief where you will. Move on each day and leave the shit, all manner of shit, behind you. In the castle I have a garderobe. Which, let's face it, is a hole in the wall to crap through. In a castle you shit where you eat and you have to think a bit harder about what kind of shit is worth stirring up. That's what I've learned in three months of being king.

Finished at last. Had to be a week's worth.

I felt better. Good. A yawn cracked my face. The land lay flat to the north, the Matteracks a jagged line to the south. We'd left the Highlands or near as dammit. I stretched and ambled over to the woman. "Did my men do this?" I frowned and glanced around again. "Where in hell are they anyhow?"

She turned, face worn, haunted around the eyes. "Soldiers

from Ancrath did it." A child hung in her arms, limp and grey, a girl, six years, maybe seven.

"Ancrath?" I arched a brow. My eyes kept returning to the girl. "We're close to the border?"

"Five miles," she said. "They told us we couldn't live here. The land was annexed. They started to fire the buildings."

Annexed. That rang a small bell at the back of my mind. Some dispute about the border. The oldest maps had it that Lord Nossar's estate reached out this far.

I could smell the vomit now, sour on the morning air. The girl had a blood-black smear of it in her hair.

"They killed your man?" I asked. I surprised myself. I don't care enough about such things to waste words on them. I blamed the bang on the head.

"They killed our boy," she said, staring past the black timbers, past me, past the sky. "Davie came out screaming and choking, blind with the smoke. Got too close to a soldier. Just a quick swing, like he was cutting down bindweed, and my boy was open. His guts . . ." She blinked and looked down at the girl. "He kept screaming. He wouldn't stop. Another soldier put an arrow through his neck."

"And your man?" I hadn't asked about her boy. I hadn't wanted that story. And the girl kept watching me, without interest, without hope.

"I don't know." She had a grey voice. The way it goes when emotions have burned out. "He didn't go to Davie, didn't hold him, too scared the soldiers would cut him down too." The girl coughed, a wet sound. "Now he cries all the time or stares at the ground."

"And the child?" I cursed my empty head. I had only to think a question today and it came spilling out of me.

"Sick," she said. "In her stomach. But I think it's in her blood too. I think it's the waste." She pulled the girl to her. "Does it hurt, Janey?"

"Yes." A dry whisper.

"A little or a lot?"

"A lot." Still a whisper.

Why ask such questions if there's nothing to be done? "He did right," I said. "Your man. Sometimes you need to hold back. Bide your time." The thorns had held me back when it mattered, made the decision for me. "He did right." The words that rang so true before I fell off my horse seemed empty beside the shell of their home. A blow to the skull can knock a deal of sense out of a man.

I saw horsemen across the meadow. Two men, three horses. Makin and Rike rode up, keeping an easy pace.

"Good to have you on your feet, Jorg." Makin gave me his grin. Rike just scowled. "Mistress Sara and Master Marten have been looking after you, I see." And that was Makin for you, always with the making friends, remembering names, jollying along.

"Sara, is it?" I said. I supposed these were my people after all. "And little Janey." For a moment I saw a different Jane, crushed and broken under rocks, the light dying out of her. That Jane once told me I needed better reasons. Better reasons if I wanted to win, but maybe just better reasons for everything.

"Take her inside," I said. "It's too cold here." A vague guilt crept over me, for pissing on one of the only four walls they had left.

Sara stood and carried the girl indoors.

"So you left me for dead then, Makin?" I asked. "Where are the others?"

"Camped a mile down the road." He nodded north. "Watching for any more raiding parties."

Odd to think of jolly old Nossar standing behind the raids. It put a sour edge on sweet memories. I remembered him in his feasting hall, with the faded maps stretched out across the table, how he pored over them. Nossar in his oak chair in the fort of Elm, grey beard and warm eyes. We played in that hall, Will and I, when we were no bigger than the child Sara carried past me. Nossar and his lines on the map. Gruff talk of "his boys" giving Renar's boys a hiding.

"Are you ready to ride?" Makin asked.

"Soon." I went to my horse. "Brath" the stablemaster called him and I'd not seen fit to change the name. Sturdy enough but not a patch on Gerrod who fell under that mountain I pushed over in Gelleth. I fished a few necessaries from my saddlebags and followed Sara.

The light had blinded me on the way out. The gloom left me

blind on the way in. The stall stank. I hadn't noticed it when I woke but it hit me now. Old vomit, sweat, animal dung. I believed the Prince of Arrow when he said he would protect the people, give them peace. I believed Jane when she said I needed better reasons for the things I made fate give me. I believed it all. Everything except that it meant anything to me.

I crouched by the woman. Already I had to reach for her name. "The new king didn't protect you then?"

"There's a king?" she said without interest, wanting me gone.

"Hello, Janey," I said, turning the charm onto the girl instead. "Did you see I brought the biggest, ugliest man in the world to show you?"

Half a smile twitched on her lips.

"So what do you want, little Janey?" I asked. I didn't know what I was doing here, crouched in the stink with the peasants. Maybe I just wanted to beat the Prince of Arrow at something. Or maybe it was just the echoes of that knock on the head. Perhaps Maical was knocked on the head as a baby and that knock had been echoing through his whole life.

"I want Davie." She kept unnaturally still. Only her mouth moved. And her eyes.

"What do you want to be? To do?" I thought of my childhood. I wanted to be death on wings. I wanted to break the world open until it gave me what was mine.

"A princess," Janey said. She paused. "Or a mermaid."

"I tell her stories, sir," the mother said, half-fearful even now, ruined and on the edge of despair. I wondered what she thought I might take from her. "My grandmother read," she said. "And my family keeps the tales." She stroked Janey's hair. "I speak them when she's hurting. To keep her mind from it. Fill her head with nonsense. She don't rightly know what a mermaid is even."

I bit my tongue then. Three impossible requests in as many moments. I'd followed them in thinking to be the king. Thinking of my crown and throne, my armies, gold and walls.

She wants her brother, she wants to be a princess, she wants to be a mermaid. And the waste will take her, screaming from her mother's arms, to a cold slot in the ground. And all the king's horses and all the king's men can't do a thing about it.

I touched her then, Janey, just a light touch on the forehead. She had enough death in her already and didn't need me adding to it. But I touched her, with my fingers, just to feel it pulsing under the skin, eating at the marrow of her bones. The sickness in her called out to the necromancy lying in me, making a link. I could feel her heartbeat flutter under mine.

"Ready to ride, Jorg?"

"Yes." I swung up into Brath's saddle.

We set off at slow walk.

"Any of that spice left, Brother Jorg?" Makin asked.

"I must have swallowed it all for the pain," I said, patting my belt pouch.

Makin rolled his eyes. He glanced back at the ruined farmstead. "Christ bleeding. There was enough—"

The faint sound of cymbals cut him off. The clash of cymbals, the whirr of cogs, stamping, and a child laughing.

"Leave anything else behind, Jorg?" he asked.

"Red Kent was right," I said. "It was cursed. Evil. Better the hurt fall on the peasants, neh?"

On the plains the winds can make your eyes sting.

Rike pulled on his reins and started back.

"Don't," I said.

And he didn't.

Sleep came hard that night. Perhaps soft months in the Haunt had left me wanting the comfort of a bed. Sleep came hard and the dreams came harder, dragging me under.

I lay in a dark room, a dark room sour with the stink of vomit and animals, and saw nothing but the glitter of her eyes, child's eyes. Heard only the *tick tick tick* of the watch on my wrist and the *rasp rasp rasp* of her breath, hot and dry and quick.

I lay for the longest time with the tick and the rasp and the glitter of her eyes.

We lay and a warm river carried us, thick with the scent of cloves.

Tick, breath, tick, breath, tick, breath.

And then I woke, sudden and with a gasp.

"What?" someone murmured. Perhaps Kent in his blankets.

"Nothing," I said. The dream still tangled me. "I thought my watch stopped."

But it wasn't the watch.

In the grey dawn Makin rose beside me cracking his face with a yawn, spitting, and rubbing his back. "Jesu but I'm sore." He cast a bleary glance my way. "Nothing a pinch of clove-spice wouldn't fix."

"The child died last night," I told him. "Easy rather than hard."

Makin pursed those thick lips of his and said no more about it. Perhaps thinking of his own child lost back among the years. He didn't even ask how I knew.

The years never seem to weigh on Brother Maical, as if his inability to count their passing protects him from their passage. He watches the world through calm grey eyes, broad-chested, thick-limbed. Brother Grumlow cuts Maical's hair close, with a tail at the rear, and shaves his beard leaving him clean-cheeked and sharp. And if no one told you that his thoughts rattle in an empty head, you might think Brother Maical as capable a rogue as rides among the Brothers. In battle though his hands grow clever, and you'd think him whole, until the din fades, the dying fall, and Maical wanders the field weeping.

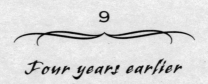

9

Four years earlier

The Highlands has lowland, though precious little of it and what there is lies stony and grows yet more stones when farmed. In my three months as king I had stuck to the mountains. Only now, when the road led me north to Heimrift, did I discover the fringes of my kingdom where it brushed against Ancrath and the Ken Marshes.

We rode from the ruined farm, from the peasants, Marten and Sara, whose names had stayed with me this once, and from their dead girl, Janey, whose breath stopped one night on the edge of spring before we'd gone twenty miles down the trail. We kept to the border lands where road-brothers are wont to travel and opportunity abounds. The farther into a kingdom a bandit-troop can venture without serious resistance is a measure of that kingdom's softness. Thurtan was always soft around the edges, the Ken Marshes softer still. Ancrath, we would say, was hard. Hard enough to break your teeth on.

"Why have we stopped?" Makin wanted to know.

The road forked. An unmarked junction, a dirt road scored through dreary hills where Ancrath met the Marshes met the

Highlands. The wind rippled through the long grass. Any place three nations touch will grow well given half a chance. Blood makes for rich soil.

"There's two choices. Take the one that's not Ancrath," he said.

I closed my eyes. "Do you hear that, Makin?"

"What?"

"Listen," I said.

"To what?" He cocked his head. "Birds?"

"Harder."

"Mosquitoes?" Makin asked, a frown on him now.

"Gog hears it," I said. "Don't you, lad?"

I felt him move behind me. "A bell?"

"The bell at Jessop where the marsh-tide brings the dead. It's got a voice so deep it just crawls over the bogs, mile after mile," I said.

That bell had called me back home once before. That bell had let me know I had a new brother lurking in a stranger's belly, being put together piece by piece beneath dresses fit for a queen. Under silk and lace. And now it reminded me of the Prince of Arrow's words. Words his sword nearly knocked clean out of my head. That my little brother had come out to play, and the cradle toys my father first gave him were the rights to my inheritance.

"We'll go this way," I said, and turned along the harder path.

"The Heimrift is *that* way," Makin said. He pointed to be clear. "I'm not arguing. I just don't want anyone saying I didn't mention it, you know, when we're all lying on the ground bleeding to death."

He *was* arguing as it happened, but he had a case and I didn't stop him.

We rode for an hour or so, leaving the sourness of the boglands behind us. Spring races through Ancrath before it starts to struggle up the slopes into the Highlands. We came to woodlands, with leaves unfurling on every branch, as if one blow of spring's green hammer had set them exploding from the bud. I took the Brothers from the road and we followed trails into the woods. If you don't want to meet anyone, take the forest path, especially in Ancrath since I stole Father's Forest Watch from him.

Spring warmth, the luminous green of new leaves, the song of thrush and lark, the richness of the forest breathed in and slowly out . . . Ancrath has charms unknown in the Renar Highlands, but I'd started to appreciate the wildness in my new kingdom, the raw rock, unobtainable peaks, even the endless wind scouring east to west.

Grumlow leaned over and snagged something from Young Sim's hair. "Woodtick." He cracked it between his nails. Even Eden had a snake problem.

The head-cart started to snag on bushes and dead-fall as the trails grew narrow. Rike's cursing came more frequent and more dire, prompted by repeated slaps in the face from branch after branch.

"Shouldn't ride so high, Little Rikey," I told him.

Makin came up, behind him Kent and Row, chuckling over some joke he'd left them with. "We'll be walking soon then?" He ducked under low-hanging greenery.

I pulled up at a stream crossed by a small clapper bridge that must have been old when Christ first learned to walk. I remembered the bridge, possibly the farthest I'd ever ventured alone before I left the Tall Castle for good. "We'll leave the horses here," I said. "You can watch them, Grumlow, you being the man with the sharp eyes today."

And that wasn't all that was sharp about Grumlow. That moustache might make him look stupid but he had a clever way with daggers, and a clever number of them stashed about his person.

I thought about leaving Gog and Gorgoth. Especially Gorgoth, for he wasn't one to be taken places unobserved. When I first brought him into the Haunt, after sitting my arse on the throne for a day or two, he caused quite a stir. Even lame, from the arrows he'd taken for me holding open that gate, he looked like a monster to reckon with. I had Coddin bring him up through the west-yard on a market day. You'd have thought someone dropped a hornets' nest for all the commotion. One old biddy screamed, clutched her chest, and fell over. That made me laugh. And when they told me she never did get back up . . . well that seemed funny too at the time. Maybe I'm getting too old, for it doesn't strike me quite so merrily any more. Let truth be told though, she did fall funny.

In the end I took them both. Gorgoth is the kind you need in a tough spot, and Gog, well he makes lighting the campfire less of a chore.

Making your way through the greenwood without people seeing you isn't too hard if you know your way and don't count charcoal burners as people. They're a lonely breed and not wont to gossip. So Rike didn't have to kill them.

And so we sliced into Ancrath easily enough, tramping along the deer paths. Even hard kingdoms have their fault lines.

"It shouldn't be this easy," Makin said. "It wasn't in my day. Damned if Coddin and his fellows would have let bandits wander so carelessly." He shook his head, though it seemed an odd thing to complain about.

"Your father's army has grown weak?" Gorgoth asked, demolishing the undergrowth as he walked.

I shrugged. "Half his forces are out in the marsh or barracked in the bog towns. Dead things keep hauling themselves out of the muck these days. There's others having similar problems. I had a merchant at court telling me the Drowned Isles have fallen to the Dead King. All of them. Given over to corpse men, marsh ghouls, necromancers, lich-kin."

Makin just crossed his chest and picked up the pace.

We travelled light, locating good shelter in the woods, and good eating. Young Sim had a way with the finding of rabbits, and I could knock the odd squirrel or wood-pigeon off its branch with a handy stone. Animals in spring are easy, too full of the new warmth, too taken with new possibilities, and not enough of watching for rocks winging their way out of the shadows.

Ancrath casts a spell on you, and nowhere more so than in the greenwood where the day trickles like honey and the sun falls golden amid pools of shade. We walked in single file with the song of the thrush and sparrow, and the scent of may and wild onions. The day set me dreaming as I walked and my nose led me back through the years to memories of William. There was a night when my brother lay sick, when my mother wept, and the table-knights would not turn their stern faces to me. I remembered the prayers I had whispered in the dark chapel when all the holy men were in their beds, the promises I made. No threats back then. I barely even bargained with the Almighty in those days. And when I crept back to our chambers I climbed in beside William and held his head. The friar had given him bitter potions and cut his leg to release the bad blood. My mother had set an ointment of honey and onion on his chest. That at least seemed to ease his breathing a little. We lay with the night sounds, William's dry wheeze, our hound Justice snoring by the doors, the click of the maid's needles in the hall, and the cry of bats, almost too high for hearing as they swung around the Tall Castle in the moonless dark.

"A penny for them," Makin said.

I snapped my head up with a start, almost tripping. "My thoughts are worth less than that today." I had been a foolish child.

Sometimes I wished I could cut away old memories and let the wind take them. If a sharp knife could pare away the weakness of those days, I would slice until nothing but the hard lessons remained.

We made our way without problem until we ran out of forest. The land around the Tall Castle is clear of trees and set to farming, to feed the king, and so that he may see his enemies advance.

I leaned against the trunk of a massive copper beech, one of the last great trees before the woods gave over to a two-acre field of ploughed earth peeping with green that might have been anything from carrots to kale for all I knew. More fields to the left and right, more beyond. A lone scarecrow watched us.

"I'll go on alone," I said. I started to unbuckle my breastplate.

"Go where?" Makin asked. "You can't get in there, Jorg. Nobody could. And what for? What are you possibly going to achieve?"

"A man's got a right to call in on his family now and again, Brother Makin," I said.

I stripped the vambraces from my forearms, my breastplate, and finally the gorget. I like to have iron around my neck, kept it from a slitting once or twice, but armour wouldn't save me where I was aimed.

I took the scabbard off my belt. "Kent, look after this for me." His eyes widened, almost as if he didn't know that's how a leader binds his men, with trust.

"A sword like this . . . Sir Makin—"

"I gave it to you." I cut him off.

"You need a sword, Jorg," Maical said, confusion in his eyes. Behind him Sim watched me without comment, unwrapping his harp. He at least knew enough to settle down for a wait.

I magicked my old knife into my hand, a trick I learned off Grumlow. "This will do for what I have in mind, Brother Maical."

"Give me two days," I said. "If I'm not back by then, send Rike to take the castle by storm."

And with a bow I left them to watch the carrots grow. Or the kale.

I made my way along the margins of the forest toward the Roma Road. They say you can put foot on that road and never leave it till you reach the pope's front door. I planned to walk the other way.

There's a cemetery near the Roma Road, mostly eaten by the forest, mostly forgotten. I hunted through it as a child, crumbled mausoleums choked with ivy, smothered with moss, cracked by trees. The cemetery covers acre upon hidden acre, a lost necropolis. Perechaise they call it in dusty books. The legends mean nothing to me, *Beloved, 1845. Dearly departed, 1710. My heart lies here, 1908.* Barely legible. So long ago even their calendar loses meaning.

The stones are set with a clear resin, harder than glass, which wards them in a skin no thicker than a hair. It took years before I noticed it. The weathering they'd suffered happened in the distant long ago. Now not even a hammer blow will mar them. The Builders held these old markers precious and kept them from the centuries.

I found my way through toppled gravestones close to the road where some of it is kept clear. Much has been robbed out. There's a peasant's cottage, a little to the west, entirely built from headstones, weathered granite markers with time-blurred legends remembering the dead for illiterate field-men. A house built of stories, to shelter a man who cannot read.

I found her by the road's edge, hair pink with fallen blossom. The cycle of seasons has worn the definition from her features.

But the beauty remains, the sharpness of her cheekbones, the grace in long limbs, the gentle swell of a child's breast, a freckling of lichen. She needs no deep-carved runes to spell out her life. Here I buried my child. A message for which reading is not required. She died in the winter of a lost year, the daughter of a wealthy man who would have given all his wealth, and more, to buy her into spring.

I saw her first in autumn, long ago, when the leaves fell so thick they hid the stone dog she chases. Whilst I watched her other travellers hurried past on the road, clenched against the sharp-fingered wind. Some paused to wonder what she chased, hugging themselves, squinting into the rain. They moved on. I stayed. Maybe they wondered what *they* were chasing.

She's after her dog. A little terrier, remembered in stone, lost that autumn in a drift of wet ochre. A centuries-old chase that has seen the death of everyone who cared, the end of every soul that knew the terrier's name. A chase that saw the stilling of each hand to touch this child, the loss of every life that shared her world.

I came again with the snows on the first day of winter, to see my statue girl. My first love maybe. I watched and the snow fell, tiny crystals, the kind so perfect they almost chime against the ground. The light failed early and a wildness infected the wind, swirling the snow into rivulets of milk across the Roma Road, ice hissing over stone. A frost came and etched silver tracery across her dress, with only me to see.

The seasons turn, and here I am again, and still she waits for spring.

They buried high lords and high ladies here. Poets and bards. Now it's a place for servant corpses. Close enough to the Tall Castle for sentimental ladies to visit their wet-nurses, far enough away to be seemly. They bury old servants, sometimes even faithful dogs, around my girl who waits for spring. Soft-hearted ladies from court come with their perfumed toys that have ceased to yap. And one time a boy of six, soaked and half-frozen, dragging something that might once have been a wolf.

"Hello, Jorg."

I turned and between the old graves walked Katherine, the sun making magic of her hair.

10

Four years earlier

Hello, Jorg. *Was that all she said to me? Katherine, there in the Rennat Forest, among the gravestones.* Hello, Jorg?

I'm trying to wake up from something. Maybe I've always been trying. I'm drowning in confusion, somewhere high above me light dances on a surface, and past that the air is waiting. Waiting for me to draw breath.

I hardly know Katherine but I want her, with unreasonable ferocity. Like a sickness, like the need for water. Like Paris for Helen, I am laid low by irresistible longing.

In memory I study the light on her face, beneath the glow-bulbs of the Tall Castle, beneath the cemetery trees. I envy those patches of sunlight, sliding over her hair, moving unopposed the length of her body, across her cheekbones. I remember everything. I recall the pattern of her breath. In the heat of Drane's kitchen I remember a single bead of sweat and the slow roll of it, down her neck, along the tendon, across her throat. I've killed men and forgotten them. Mislaid the act of taking a life. But that drop of sweat is a diamond in my mind's eye.

"Hello, Jorg." And my clever words desert me. She makes me feel my fourteen summers, more boy than man.

I want her beyond reason. I need to own, consume, worship, devour. What I've made of her in my mind cannot live in flesh. She's just a person, just a girl, but she stands at the door to an old world, and although I can't go back . . . she can come through, and maybe bring with her a scent of it, a taste of that lost warmth.

These feelings are too fierce to last. They can only burn, making us ash and char.

I see her in dreams. I see her against the mountains. High, snow-cold, snow-pure, unobtainable. I climb, and on the empty peak I speak her name to the wind, but the wind takes my words. It takes me too. Tumbling through void.

"Hello, Jorg."

My flesh prickles. I rub at my cheek and my fingers come away bloody, sliced open. Every part of me burns with pins and needles. Real pins, real needles. I scream and like buds on the branch each prickle erupts, a hundred thorns sliding from my skin, growing from the bone. There are animals impaled, stabbed through like exhibits on a gamekeeper's board. Rat, stoat, ferret, fox, dog . . . baby. Limp and watching.

I scream again and rotate into darkness. A night with only a whisper to give it form. A whispered chant, growing louder.

Topology, tautology, torsion, torture, taunt, taut, tight, taken, taking . . . taking . . . take . . . what's he trying to take?

Somebody fumbling at my arm, fingers too stupid for the clever catch on the watch. A quick move and I had his wrist, impossibly thick, strong. I dug my thumb into the necessary pressure point. Lundist showed it to me in a book.

"Arrg!" Rike's voice. "Pax!"

I sat up sharp, breaking the surface, drawing that long-awaited breath, and shaking the darkness from my mind. Topology, tautology, torsion . . . meaningless webs of words falling from me.

"Rike!" Crouched over me, blocking the too bright sun.

He sneered and sat back. "Pax."

Pax. Road-speak. *Peace, it's in my nature.* An excuse for any crime you're caught in the middle of. Sometimes I think I should wear the word on my forehead. "Where in hell are we?"

I asked. An empty feeling ran through me, welling from my stomach and behind my eyes.

"Hell's the word." Red Kent walked over.

I lifted my hand. Sand all over. Sand everywhere in fact. "A desert?"

Two of the fingernails on my right hand were torn away. Gone. It started to hurt. My other nails were torn and split. I had bruises all over.

Gog came out from behind a lone thorn bush, slow as if he thought I might bite.

"I—" I pressed my hand to the side of my head, sand gritty on the skin. "I was with Katherine . . ."

"And then what?" Makin's voice from behind.

"I . . ." Nothing. And then nothing. As if little Jorgy had been too full of the spring's warmth and possibilities, and then a stone looped out of the shadows and took him off the bough.

I remembered the thorns. The itch and sting of them stayed with me. I lifted my arms. No wounds, but the skin lay red and scabbed. In fact Kent had it too, red as his name suggests. I turned to find Makin, also scabby, leading his horse. The beast looked worse than him, ropes of mucus around its muzzle, blisters on its tongue.

"This is not a good place to be, I'm thinking." I reached for my knife and found it gone. "What are we doing here?"

"We came to see a man named Luntar," Makin said. "An alchemist from the Utter East. He lives here."

"And here is?"

"Thar."

I knew the name. On the map scroll the word had sat along the edge of the Thurtan grasslands. There had been a burn mark on the map obscuring whatever the name labelled. But perhaps the scorch mark hadn't been an accident.

"Poisoned land," Makin said. "Some call them promised."

A Builders' Sun had burned here, many centuries ago. The promise was that one day the land would be safe again. I thrust my fingers back into the sand. Not the ones missing fingernails. I could touch the death there. I could roll it between fingertip and thumb. Hot. Death and fire together.

"He lives here?" I asked. "Doesn't he burn?"

Makin shuddered. "Yes," he said. "He does." It takes a lot to make Makin shudder.

The empty feeling gnawed at me, eating away at the questions I most wanted to ask.

"And what," I said, "did we want from this east-mage?"

Makin held out what he had been holding all along. "This."

A box. A copper box, thorn-patterned, no lock or latch. A copper box. Not big enough to hold a head. A child's fist would fit.

"What's in the box?" I didn't want to know.

Makin shook his head. "There was a madness in you, Jorg. When you came back."

"What's in it?"

"Luntar put the madness in there." Makin thrust the box back into his saddlebag. "It was killing you."

"He put my memory in that box?" I asked, incredulous. "You let him take my memory!"

"You begged him to do it, Jorg." Makin wouldn't look at me. Rike on the other hand couldn't stop.

"Give it to me." I would have reached for it but my hand didn't want to.

"He told me not to," Makin said, unhappy. "He told me to make you wait for a day. If you still wanted it after that, you could take it." Makin bit his lip. He chewed on it too much. "Trust me in this, Jorg, you don't want to go back to how you were."

I shrugged. "Tomorrow, then." Because trust is how a leader binds his men. And because my hands didn't want that box. They'd rather burn. "Now, where's my fecking dagger?"

Makin would only look at the horizon. "Best forgotten."

We moved on, leading the horses, all of us reunited. We headed east, and when the wind blew, the sand stung like nettles. Only Gog and Gorgoth seemed unaffected.

Gog hung back, as if he didn't want to be near me. "Is it all like this?" I asked him, just to make him look at me. "Even where Luntar lives?"

He shook his head. "The sand turns to glass around his hut. Black glass. It cuts your feet."

We walked on. Rike marched beside me, sparing the occasional glance. Something had changed in the way he looked at me. As if we were equals now.

I kept my head down and tried to remember. I teased at the hole in my mind. "Hello, Jorg," she had said.

Memory is all we are. Moments and feelings, captured in amber, strung on filaments of reason. Take a man's memories and you take all of him. Chip away a memory at a time and you destroy him as surely as if you hammered nail after nail through his skull. I would have back what was mine. I would open the box.

"Hello, Jorg," she had said. We were by the statue of the girl and her dog, by her grave where sentimental ladies and foolish children bury their animals.

Nothing.

I learned a time ago that if you can't get what you want by going in the front door, find a back way. I know a back way to that cemetery. Not by a path I wanted to tread, but I would take it even so.

When I was very young, six maybe, a duke called on my father, a man from the north with white-blond hair and a beard down his chest. Alaric of Maladon. The Duke brought a gift for my mother, a wonder of the old world. Something bright and moving, swirling within glass, first lost in the hugeness of the Duke's hand and then in the folds of Mother's dress.

I wanted that thing, half-seen and not understood. But such gifts were not for tiny princes. My father took it and set it in the treasury to gather dust. I learned this much from quiet listening.

The treasury in the Tall Castle lies behind an iron door, triple-locked. Not a Builder-made door, but a work of the Turkmen, black iron set with a hundred studs. When you're six, most locked doors present a problem. This one presented several.

Of all memories, the first I have is of leaning from a high parapet into the teeth of a gale, with the rain lashing and me laughing. The next is of hands pulling me back.

If you're determined, if you set your mind, there are never enough hands to pull you back. By the time I reached six I knew the outside of the Tall Castle as well as I knew the inside.

The Builders left little for a climber to use, but centuries of tinkering by the Ancraths, and the House of Or before us, had provided plenty of footholds, at least plenty of ones deep enough for a child.

There is a single high window in the royal treasury, set in a plain wall a hundred feet above the ground, too narrow for a man and blocked by a forest of bars set so close as to give a snake quite a wriggle of it. On the far side of the castle, close to the throne-room, is a hole that leads to a gargoyle's head on the outer wall. If the treasury door opens, then the movement of air through the castle makes the gargoyle speak. On a still day he moans and when the wind is up he howls. He will also speak if the wind is hard in the east and a particular window in the kitchen stores is left unshuttered. When that happens there's a fuss and somebody gets whipped with rope and wire. Without the treasury's high window the gargoyle would not speak and the king would never know when the door to his treasures stood open.

I left my bed one moonless night. William lay sleeping in his little bed. No one saw me leave, only our great-hound, Justice. He gave a whine of reproach then tried to follow. I cursed him to silence and closed the door on him.

Those bars look strong but like so much we depend upon in life they are rotten to the core. Rust has eaten them. Even those with steel left at the centre will bend given sufficient leverage. One night when my nurse lay sleeping and three guards on wall-duty argued over the ownership of a silver coin found on the steps at change-over, I climbed down a knotted rope and set foot amidst my father's wealth. I brushed the rust from my tunic, shook great flakes of it from my hair, and set my lantern, now unhooded, upon the floor.

The Ancrath loot, robbed from almost every corner of empire, lay on stone shelves, belched from coffers, stood stacked in careless piles. Armour, swords, gold coin in wooden tubs, mechanisms that looked like parts of insects, gleaming in the lantern light and tainting the air with alien scents, almost citrus, almost metal. I found my prize beside a helmet full of cogs and ash.

The Duke's gift didn't disappoint. Beneath a glass dome

that wasn't glass, sealed by an ivory disk that wasn't ivory, lay a tiny scene, a church in miniature set around with tiny houses, and there a person, and another. And as I held it to the light, and turned its surprising weight this way and that to see the detail, a snowstorm grew, swirling up from the ground until whirling flakes obliterated the view, leaving nothing but a blizzard in a half-globe. I set the snow-globe back, worried for a moment that I had somehow broken it. And miracle of miracles, the snow began to settle.

There's no magic to it now. I know that the right collection of artisans could make something similar in just a few weeks. They would use glass and ivory, and I don't know what the snow would be, but as ancient wonders go, there's little wonder in such things if you're much past six. But at the time it was magic, of the best kind. Stolen magic.

I shook the snow-globe again, and once more the all-encompassing blizzard rose, chaos, followed by calm, by settling snows, and a return to the world before. I shook it again. It seemed wrong. All that storm and fury signifying nothing. The whole world upheaved, and for what? The same man trudged toward the same church, the same woman waited at the same cottage door. I held a world in my hand, and however I shook it, however the pieces fell, in whatever new patterns, nothing changed. The man would never reach the church.

Even at six I knew the Hundred War. I marched wooden soldiers across Father's maps. I saw the troops return through the Tall Gate, bloody and fewer, and the women weeping in the shadows as others threw themselves at their men. I read the tales of battle, of advance and retreat, of victory and defeat, in books I would not have been allowed to open if my father knew me. I understood all this and I knew that I held my whole world in my right hand. Not some play land, some toy church and tiny men crafted by ancients. *My whole world.* And no amount of shaking would change it. We would swirl against each other, battle, kill, and fall, and settle, and as the haze cleared, the war would still be there, unchanged, waiting, for me, for my brother, for my mother.

When a game cannot be won, change the game. I read that in the book of Kirk. Without thought I brought the snow-globe overhead and smashed it on the ground. From the wet fragments I picked out the man, barely a wheat-grain between my thumb and finger.

"You're free now," I said, then flicked him into a corner to find his own way home, because I didn't have *all* the answers, not then, and not now.

I left the treasury, taking nothing, almost defeated by the rope climb even so. I felt tired but content. What I had done seemed so right that I somehow thought others would see it too and that my crime would not follow me. With aching arms, and covered with rust and scratches, I hauled myself back over the parapet.

"What's this now?" A big hand took me by the neck and lifted me off my feet. It seemed that the wall guards had been less argumentative over my coin than I had hoped.

It didn't take long before I stood in my father's throne-room with a sleepy page lighting torches. No whale oil in silver lamps for this night's business, just pitch-torches crackling, painting more smoke on the black ceiling. Sir Reilly held my shoulder, his gauntlet too heavy and digging in. We waited in the empty room and watched the shadows dance. The page left.

"I'm sorry," I said. Though I wasn't.

Sir Reilly looked grim. "I'm sorry too, Jorg."

"I won't do it again," I said. Though I would.

"I know," Sir Reilly said, almost tender. "But now we must wait for your father, and he is not a gentle man."

It seemed that we waited half the night, and when the doors boomed open, I jumped despite the promises I made myself.

My father, in his purple robe and iron crown, with not a trace of sleep in him, strode alone to the throne. He sat and spread his hands across the arms of his chair.

"I want Justice," he said. Loud enough for a whole court though Reilly and I were his only audience.

Again. "I want Justice." Eyes on the great doors.

"I'm sorry." And this time I meant it. "I can pay—"

"Justice!" He didn't even glance at me.

The doors opened again and on a cart such as they use to bring prisoners up from the dungeon came my great-hound, mine and Will's, chained at each leg and pushed by a mild-faced servant named Inch, a broad-armed man who had once slipped me a sugar-twist on a fete day.

I started forward but Reilly's hand kept me where I was.

Justice trembled on the cart, eyes wide, shivering so bad he could barely stand, though he had four legs to my two. He looked wet and as Inch pushed him nearer I caught the stink of rock-oil, the kind they burn in servant's lamps. Inch reached into the cart and lifted an ugly lump hammer, a big one used for breaking coal into smaller pieces for the fire.

"Go," Father said.

The look in Inch's mild eyes said he would prefer to stay, but he set the hammer on the floor and left without protest.

"There are lessons to be learned today," Father said.

"Have you ever burned yourself, Jorg?" Father asked.

I had. I once picked up a poker that had been left with one end in the fire. The pain had taken my breath. I couldn't scream. Not until the blisters started to rise could I make any sound above hissing, and when I could I howled so loud my mother came running from her tower, arriving as the maids and nurse burst from the next room. My hand had burned for a week, weeping and oozing, sending bursts of horrific pain along my arm at the slightest wiggle of fingers. The skin fell away and the flesh beneath lay raw and wet, hurt by even a breath of air.

"You took from me, Jorg," Father said. "You stole what was mine."

I knew enough not to say that it was Mother's.

"I've noticed that you love this dog," Father said.

I wondered at that, even in my fear. I thought it more likely that he had been told.

"That's a weakness, Jorg," Father said. "Loving anything is a weakness. Loving a hound is stupidity."

I said nothing.

"Shall I burn the dog?" Father reached for the nearest torch.

"No!" It burst from me, a horrified scream.

He sat back. "See how weak this dog has made you?" He glanced at Sir Reilly. "How will he rule Ancrath if he cannot rule himself?"

"Don't burn him." My voice trembled, pleading, but somehow it was a threat too, even if none of us recognized it.

"Perhaps there is another way?" Father said. "A middle ground." He looked at the hammer.

I didn't understand. I didn't want to.

"Break the dog's leg," he said. "One quick blow and Justice will be served."

"No," I swallowed, almost choking, "I can't."

Father shrugged and leaned from his throne, reaching for the torch again.

I remembered the pain that poker had seared into me. Horror reached for me and I knew I could let it take me, down into hysteria, crying, raging, and I could stay there until the deed was done. I could run and hide in tears and leave Justice to burn.

I picked up the hammer before Father's hand closed on the torch. It took effort just to lift it, heavy in too many ways. Justice just trembled and watched me, whining, his tail hooked between his legs, no understanding in him, only fear.

"Swing hard," Father said. "Or you'll just have to swing again."

I looked at Justice's leg, his long quick leg, the fur plastered down with oil over bone and tendon, the iron shackle, some kind of vice from the Question Chamber, biting into his ankle, blood on the metal.

"I'm sorry, Father, I won't ever steal again." And I meant it.

"Don't try my patience, boy." I saw the coldness in his eyes and wondered if he had always hated me.

I lifted the hammer, my arms almost too weak, shaking almost as much as the dog. I raised it slowly, waiting, waiting for Father to say it, to say: "Enough, you've proved yourself."

The words never came. "Break or burn," he said. And with a scream I let the hammer swing.

Justice's leg broke with a loud snap. For a heartbeat there was no other sound. The limb looked wrong, upper and lower parts at sick-making angles, white bone in a slather of red blood and black fur. Then came the howling, the snarling fury, the straining at his bonds as he looked for something to fight, some battle to keep away the pain.

"One more, Jorg," Father said. He spoke softly but I heard him above the howls. For the longest moment his words made no sense to me.

I said, "No," but I didn't make him reach for the torch. If I made him reach again he wouldn't draw back. I knew that much.

This time Justice understood the raising of the hammer. He whimpered, whined, begged as only dogs can beg. I swung hard and missed, blinded with tears. The cart rattled and Justice jumped and howled, bleeding from all his shackles now, the broken leg stretching with tendons exposed. I hit him on my second stroke and shattered his other foreleg.

Vomit took me by surprise, hot, sour, spurting from my mouth. I crawled in it, gagging and gasping. Almost not hearing Father's: "One more."

With his third leg smashed, Justice couldn't stand. He flopped, broken in the cart, stinking in his own mess. Strangely he didn't snarl or whine now. Instead as I lay wracked with sobs, heaving in the air in gulps, he nuzzled me as he used to nuzzle William when he cried with a grazed knee or thwarted ambition. That's how stupid dogs are, my brothers. And that's how stupid I was at six, letting weakness take hold of me, giving the world a lever with which to bend whatever iron lies in my soul.

"One more," Father said. "He has a leg left to stand on, does he not, Sir Reilly?"

And for once Sir Reilly would not answer his king.

"One more, Jorg."

I looked at Justice, broken and licking the tears and snot from my hand. "No."

And with that Father took the torch and tossed it into the cart.

I rolled back from the sudden bloom of flame. Whatever my heart told me to do, my body remembered the lesson of the poker and would not let me stay. The howling from the cart made all that had gone before seem as nothing. I call it howling but it was screaming. Man, dog, horse. With enough hurt we all sound the same.

In that moment, rolling clear, even though I was six and my hands were unclever, I took the hammer that had seemed so heavy and threw it without effort, hard and straight. If my father had moved but a little more slowly I might be king of two lands now. Instead it touched his crown just enough to turn it a quarter circle, then hit the wall behind his chair and fell to the ground, leaving a shallow scar on the Builder-stone.

Father was right of course. There were lessons to be learned that night. The dog was a weakness and the Hundred War cannot be won by a man with such weaknesses. Nor can it be won by a man who yields to the lesser evil. Give an inch, give any single man any single inch, and the next thing you hear will be, "One more, Jorg, one more." And in the end what you love will burn. Father's lesson was a true one, but knowing that can't make me forgive the means by which he taught it.

For a time there on the road I followed Father's teaching: strength in all things, no quarter. On the road I had known with the utter conviction of a child that the Empire throne would be mine only if I kept true to the hard lessons of Justice and the thorns. Weakness is a contagion; one breath of it can corrupt a man whole and entire. Now though, even with all the evil in me, I don't know if I could teach such lessons to a son of mine.

William never needed such teaching. He had iron in him from the start, always the more clever, the more sure, the fiercest of us, despite my two extra years. He said I should have thrown the hammer as soon as I lifted it, and should not have missed. I would be king then, and we would still have our dog.

Two days later I stole away from both nurse and guard and found my way to the rubbish pits behind the table-knights' stable. A north wind carried the last of winter, laced with rain that was almost ice. I found my dog's remains, a reeking mess, black, dripping, limp but heavy. I had to drag him, but I had told William I would bury him, not leave him to rot on the pile. I dragged him two miles in the freezing rain, along the Roma Road, empty save for a merchant with his wagon lashed closed and his head down. I took Justice to the girl with the dog, and I buried him there beside her, in the mud, my hands numb and the rest of me wishing I were numb.

"Hello, Jorg," Katherine said. And then nothing.

Nothing? If I could remember all that. If I could remember that dark path to the cemetery of Perechaise, and live with it these many years . . . what in hell lay in that box, and how could I ever want it back?

Many men do not look their part. Wisdom may wait behind a foolish smile, bravery can gaze from eyes that cry fright. Brother Rike however is that rarest of creatures, a man whose face tells the whole story. Blunt features beneath a heavy brow, the ugly puckering of old scar tissue, small black eyes that watch the world with impersonal malice, dark hair, short and thick with dirt, bristling across the thickest of skulls. And had God given him a smaller frame in place of a giant's packed with unreasonable helpings of muscle, weakness in place of an ox team's stamina, still Rike would be the meanest dwarf in Christendom.

11

Wedding day

Mountains are a great leveller. They don't care who you are or how many.

Some have it that the Builders made the Matteracks, drinking the red blood of the earth to steal its power, and that the peaks were thrown up when the rocks themselves revolted and shrugged the Builders off. Gomst tells it that the Lord God set the mountains here, ripples in the wet clay as he formed the world with both hands. Whoever it was that did the work, they have my thanks. It's the Matteracks that put the "high" into the Renar Highlands. They march on east to west, wrinkling the map through other kingdoms, but it's in the Highlands that they do their best work. Here it's the Matteracks that say where you can and can't go.

It's been said once or twice that I have a stubborn streak. In any case I have never subscribed to the idea that a king can be told where he can't go in his own kingdom. And so in the years since arriving as a callow youth, in between learning the sword-song, mastering the art of shaving, and dispensing justice with a sharp edge, I took to mountain climbing.

Climbing, it turned out, was as new to the people of the Highlands as it was to me. They knew all about getting up to places they needed to be. High pastures for the wool-goats, the summer passes for trade, the Eiger cliff for hunting opals. But about getting to places they didn't need to go . . . well, who has time for that when their belly grumbles or there's money to be made?

"What in hell are you doing, Jorg?" Coddin asked me once when I came back bloody, with my wrist grinding bone at every move.

"You should come out with me," I told him, just to see him wince. I climb alone. In truth there's never room for two on a mountaintop.

"I'll rephrase," said Coddin. I could see the grey starting in his hair. Threads of it at his temples. "Why are you doing it?"

I pursed my lips at that, then grinned at the answer. "The mountains told me I couldn't."

"You're familiar with King Canute?" he asked. "It's not a path I advise for you—since you pay me for advising these days."

"Heh." I wondered if Katherine would climb mountains. I thought she would, given half a chance. "I've seen the sea, Coddin. The sea can eat mountains whole. I might have the occasional difference of opinion with the odd mountain or two, but if you catch me challenging the ocean you have my permission to drop an ox on me."

I told Coddin that stubbornness led me to climb, and perhaps it did, but there's more to it. Mountains have no memory, no judgments to offer. There's a purity in the struggle to reach a peak. You leave your world behind and take only what you need. For a creature like me there is nothing closer to redemption.

"Attack," Miana had said, and surely a man shouldn't refuse his wife on their wedding day. Of course it helped that I had planned to attack all along. I led the way myself, for the sally ports and the tunnels that lead to them are known to few. Or rather many know of them but, like an honest priest, few would be able to show you one.

We walked four abreast, the tallest men hunched to save scraping their heads on rough-hewn stone. Every tenth man held a pitch torch and at the back of our column they almost

choked on the smoke. My own torch showed little more than
the ten yards of tunnel ahead, twisting to take advantage of
natural voids and fissures. The *tramp tramp* of many feet, at
first hypnotic, faded to background noise, unnoticed until without warning it stopped. I turned and flames showed nothing
but my swinging shadow. Not a man of my command, not a
whisper of them.

"What is it that you think you're doing here, Jorg?" The
dream-witch's words flowed around me, a river of soft cadence,
carrying only hints of his Saracen heritage. "I watch you from
one moment to the next. Your plans are known before you so
much as unfold them."

"Then you'll know what it is I think I'm doing here,
Sageous." I cast about for a sign of him.

"You know we joke about you, Jorg?" Sageous asked. "The
pawn who thinks he's playing his own game. Even Ferrakind
laughs about it behind the fire, and Kelem, still preserved in
his salt mines. Lady Blue has you on her sapphire board; Skilfar
sees your future patterned on the ice; at the Mathema they
factor you into their equations, a small term approximated to
nothing. In the shadows behind thrones you count for little,
Jorg, they laugh at how you serve me and know it not. The
Silent Sister only smiles when your name is spoken."

"I'm pleased to be of some service then." To my left the
shadows on the wall moved with reluctance, slow to respond
to the swing of my torch. I stepped forward and thrust the
flames into the darkest spot, scraping embers over the stone.

"This is your last day, Jorg." Sageous hissed as flame ate
shadow and darkness peeled from stone like layers of skin. It
pleased me no end to hear his pain. "I'll watch you die." And
he was gone.

Makin nearly walked into me from behind. "Problem?"

I shook off the daydream's tatters and picked up my pace.
"No problems." Sageous liked to pull the strings so gently that
a man would never suspect himself steered. To make Sageous
angry, to make him hate, only eroded the subtle powers he
used. My first victory of the day. And if he felt the need to taunt
me then I must have worried him somehow. He must have
thought I had some kind of chance—which made him a hell
of a lot more optimistic than I was.

"No problems. In fact the morning is just starting to look up!"

Another fifty yards and a stair took us onto the slopes via a crawl space beneath a vast rock known as Old Bill.

When you leave the Haunt you are immediately among mountains. They dwarf you in a way that high walls and tall towers cannot. In the midst of the heave and thrust of the Matteracks, all of us, the Haunt itself, even the Prince of Arrow's twenty thousands, were as nothing. Ants fighting on the carcass of an elephant.

Out on those slopes in the coldness of the wind, with the mountains high and silent on all sides, it felt good to be alive, and if it had to be, it was a good day to die.

"Have Marten take his troops and hold the Runyard for me," I said.

"The Runyard?" Makin said, wrapping his cloak tight against the wind. "You want our best captain to secure a dead-end valley?"

"We need those men, Jorg," Coddin said, straightening from his crawl. "We can't spare ten soldiers, let alone a hundred of our best." Even as he argued he beckoned a man to carry my orders.

"You don't think he can hold it?" I asked.

And that set Makin running in a new direction. "Hold it? He'd hold the gates of heaven for you, that man; or hell. Lord knows why."

I shrugged. Marten would hold because I'd given him what he called salvation. A second chance to stand, to protect his family. For four years he had studied nothing but war, from arrow to army, the four years since he came to the castle with Sara at his side. In the end he would hold because years ago in the ruins of his farm I had given his little girl a wind-up clown and Makin's clove-spice. A Builder toy to make her smile and the clove-spice to take her pain, and her life. The drug stole her away rather than the waste, and she died smiling at sweet dreams instead of choking on her own blood.

"Why the Runyard?" Coddin wanted to know. Coddin couldn't be put off the scent so easily.

"The Prince of Arrow doesn't have assassins in my castle,

Coddin, but he has spies. I tell you what you need to know, what will make a difference to your actions. The rest, the long shots, the hunches, it's safe to keep locked away." I tapped the side of my head. For a moment though the copper box burned against my hip and its thorn pattern filled my vision.

"I'd be happier on a horse," Makin said.

"I'd be happier on a giant mountain goat," I said. "One that shat diamonds. Until we find some, we're walking."

Three hundred men walked behind us. Armies are wont to march, but marching in the Highlands is a short trip to a broken ankle. Three hundred men of the Watch in mountain grey. Exiting the sally port amid the boulder field west of the Haunt where the tunnel rose through the bedrock. No crimson tabards here, or gold braiding, no rampant lions or displayed dragons or crowned feckin' frogs, just tatter-robes in rock shades. I hadn't come out for a uniform competition. I came out to win.

Behind us rockets took flight, lacing the dull morning with trails of sparks, and leaving a loose pall of sulphurous smoke above the castle. Wedding celebrations to amuse the Highlanders, but also a convenient draw for the eyes to the north of us, the uninvited guests.

The Prince's army had started to move, units massed in their attack formations, Normardy pike-men to the fore, rank upon rank of archers on the far side, men of Belpan with longbows near tall as them, crossbow units out of Ken, beards braided, brown pennants fluttering above the drummers, each man with a shield boy hurrying before him. The archers stood ready to peel off and find their places on the ridges to our east, the useless Orlanth cavalry at the rear. Their day would come later, after wintering in the ruins of my home, after the high passes cleared and the Prince moved on to increase his tally of fallen kingdoms. The Thurtans next no doubt. And on to Germania and the dozen Teuton realms.

We came down the slopes west of the Haunt in a grey wave, swords, daggers, shortbows. I'd spent most of dear uncle's gold on those bows. The men of the Forest Watch knew the short-bow, and the Highland recruits learned it fast enough. Three hundred recurved composite shortbows, Scythian made. Ten gold apiece. I could have sat every man on a half-decent nag for that.

The Prince's scouts saw us. That had never been in doubt. A sharp-eyed observer on their front lines might have seen us across the mile or so that remained. But why would they be looking? They had scouts.

I picked up the pace. There's nothing like mountains for making you fit to run. At first when you come to the mountains everything is hard. Even the air feels too thin to breathe. Years pass and your muscles become iron. Especially if you climb.

We moved quickly. Speed on the slopes is an art. The Prince of Arrow wasn't stupid. The commanders he had picked had chosen officers who had selected scouts who knew mountains. They moved fast, but the few men that fell didn't get up again before we caught them.

It's always nice to surprise someone. The Prince of Arrow hadn't expected me to charge his tens of thousands with my three hundred. That's probably why we were able to arrive only seconds behind the first word of our advance, and long before that word could be acted on.

Three hundred is a magic number. King Leonidas held back a Persian ocean at the Hot Gates with just three hundred. I would have liked to meet the Spartans. That story has outlived empires by the score. King Leonidas held back an ocean, and Canute did not.

I could feel the burn in my legs, the cool breath hauled in and the hot breath out. Sweat inside my armour, a river of it under the breastplate. Hard leathers these, cured and boiled in oil, padded linen underneath, no plate or chain today. Today we needed to move.

When I gave the shout, we stopped on the rock field, scattered on the slope, two hundred yards from their lines, no more, close enough to smell them. On this flank, far from the archers bound for the ridge, men of Arrow formed the largest contingent, units of spearmen in light ringmail, swordsmen in heavier chain, among them the landed knights who had levied the soldiers from farm and village or emptied their castle guard in service of their prince. And all of them, at least the ones we could see before the roll of the mountains hid the vast expanse of their advance, marched without haste, confident, some joking, watching the sparks and smoke above the Haunt. The great siege engines creaked amongst them, drawn by many mules.

I didn't need to tell the Watch. They started to loose their shafts immediately. The first screams carried the message of our attack far more effectively than scouts still hunting for their breath.

Aiming at the thickest knots of men made it hard not to find flesh.

We managed a second volley before the first of the enemy started to charge. The Prince's archers, massed on the far side of the army column a quarter mile off and more, could make no reply. *Know thyself,* Pythagoras said. But he was a man of numbers and you can't count on those. Sun Tzu tells us: *Know thy enemies*. I had lost men I could ill afford patrolling these slopes, but I knew my enemy and I knew the disposition of his forces.

The Prince's archers would have found us hard targets in any case, loose amongst the rocks and the long morning shadows.

Another volley and another. Hundreds killed or wounded with each flight. Wounded is good. Sometimes wounded is better than dead. The wounded cause trouble. If you let them.

The foot-soldiers came at us in ones and twos, then handfuls, and behind that a flood, like a wave breaking and racing across sand.

"Pick your targets," I shouted.

Another volley. A single man amongst the forerunners fell, skewered through his thigh.

"Dammit! Pick your targets."

Another volley and none of the runners fell. The dying happened back in the masses still milling in confusion, caught in the press of bodies. One of mine for every twenty of theirs. Stiff odds. If we'd managed ten volleys before they reached us we might have slain three thousand men. We managed six.

12

Wedding day

"Be ready to run," I shouted.

"That's your plan, Jorg?" Makin's face could take surprise to a whole new level. Something in the eyebrows did it.

"Be ready," I repeated. In truth if I had a plan I held no more than a thread of it, teasing it out inch by inch. And the thread I held told me, *Be ready to run*. Sun Tzu instructs: *If in all respects your foe exceeds you, be ready to elude him.*

"If that were the fucking plan," said Makin, shouldering his bow, "we should have started two weeks ago."

The first of Arrow's soldiers reached me, purple-faced from the race up the mountain.

Katherine Ap Scorron fills my nights. More than is healthy. And all of those dreams are dark. Chella walks in some of them, stepping direct from the necromancers' halls beneath Mount Honas, wicked and delicious. Her smile says she knows me to my rotten core, and Katherine's face will writhe across hers as firm flesh turns to corrupt undulation.

The dead child will wander in and out of many dreams, holding the thorn-patterned box in crimson hands. He takes different names. William most often, though he is not the brother I knew. But he follows Katherine whenever I call her to my bed; fresh killed in some, the blood still running, and in others grey with rot.

The telling of dreams is a dull business, but experiencing a stranger's dreams at first hand may be another matter. Crafting nightmares as weapons or shackles and setting them loose to hunt your victims could very well be entertaining. It seems to keep a certain dream-witch busy.

My father thought Sageous to be his creature. Perhaps he thinks he sent the witch away after I broke his power in the Tall Castle, and maybe the Prince of Arrow now thinks he owns Sageous's services. Like Corion, though, and the Silent Sister and others scattered across the empire, Sageous sees himself as a player behind the thrones, pushing kings and counts, earls and princes across the board. I have never liked to be pushed. The Prince of Arrow also struck me as a man who would prove hard for the dream-witch to move, but we will see.

Sageous learned twice over not to send his creatures out to snare me in my sleep. I think each failure takes something vital from him. Certainly he did not persist. The child is not his creation. I would know if it were.

The heathen watches though. He stands on the edge of my dreaming, silent, hoping not to be seen. I have chased him to the edge of waking and fallen from my bed choking the pillow. Once my sleeping hand found a dagger. Feathers everywhere. He seeks to steer me with the most gentle of prods. Even a soft touch, if it is made sufficiently far ahead of the crucial event, can have a great impact. Sageous seeks to steer me, to steer us all, his fingers swift and light as spiders, pulling delicate threads, until the power he wants is delivered into his lap as if by accident.

Tutor Lundist said Sun Tzu should be my guide in war. My father may have executed Lundist a week after I fled the Tall Castle but what the tutor taught will stay with me longer than any lesson Olidan Ancrath inflicted on his son.

All war is deception, Sun Tzu tells me on pages yellow as jaundice, dry as sand. All war is deception but where are my chances to deceive? I have spies in my halls, watchers in my dreams. The grave's a fine and private place they say, but I suspect even there secrets can be hard to hold in these broken days.

And so I use what I have. A copper box that holds memories. One that stores a memory so terrible I couldn't keep it in me. I have the box and I use it. Long ago I learned that pressed to the forehead, hard enough to leave its thorn print marked upon the skin, it will steal a memory, a thought, a plan, whatever is foremost in your thinking. The plan is lost but safe from Sageous's kind, and all that remains is the recollection that you had a good idea, and the memory of where to find it again when needed.

Hold the box tight in your hand and you can feel the dark edges of horror inside, cutting, burning. The pain leaks out, robbed of its context, raw and cold, and with it, if you're clever, if the fingers of your mind are deft, you can draw the thread of a previously stored stratagem from a place beyond all spies. And if you can surprise your enemy, then surprising yourself is small price to pay.

13

Wedding day

The first man I killed in my eighteenth year had done most of the job for me. Running two hundred yards up a steep and rocky slope in chain armour is hard work. The soldier looked about ready to keel over, like the old woman in the market who never got up after seeing Gorgoth for the first and last time. I let him run onto my sword and that was the end of it.

The next man went pretty much the same way, only I had to be a little faster and thrust at him rather than just let him impale himself. In battle the thrust is a much cleaner death than the cut. Unless of course it's the guts where you get it and then you're going to have a long hard time of it before the rot sets in and carries you off screaming days later.

The third man, tall and bearded, took the two bodies at my feet as a hint and slowed down to face me. He should have waited for his friends behind him on the slope, but instead he came in swinging his broadsword, still huffing and puffing from his run. I stepped back to avoid the sweep of his blade then swung my own and took his throat. He turned, spraying arterial blood over the friends he should have waited for, then tripped and fell amongst the rocks. Until you've seen it you won't believe how far blood will spurt from the right cut. It's a wonder we don't feel that pressure inside us all the time, a wonder that we don't just explode sometimes.

I should have turned and run at that point. It was the plan after all. My plan. And the men of the Watch were already in full retreat behind me. Instead I advanced, moving quickly between the two blood-spattered soldiers who leapt out of Beardy's way as he fell. I made a figure-eight cut, lashing out from one side to the other, and both of them fell, their mail torn, a shattered collarbone on the right, sliced chest muscle on the left. It shouldn't have taken them both down, but it did, and I felt that four years' hard practice with the blade hadn't been entirely wasted.

Both men were flopping on the ground, calling out about their wounds, as I cut the sixth down, another staggerer, exhausted from his charge. That done, I turned and fled, outpacing the pursuit and working hard to catch the Watch.

The men of Arrow were never going to outrun us, but they could hardly stop the chase and let us come back to practise our archery again, so they kept at it. The captains driving them were making the right choices given what they had to work with. What they should have done, however, was to withdraw to the main force and rely on their commander's battle sense to deploy his archers as a defence against us. Though perhaps the Prince of Arrow was happy enough sending a few thousand soldiers up the mountain to contain the threat and to keep his army focused on the Haunt.

I caught Makin up a few minutes later, threading my path past Watch men with less go in their legs than I had that day. Watch-master Hobbs ran with him, his captains beside him, Harold, Stodd, and old Keppen who'd made the wise choice and refused to jump for a previous watch-master back at Rulow Falls years ago. I say the Watch-master ran but by that point "brisk walk" would cover it.

"Set four squads on those ridges," I said. "Let's shoot a few more Arrows."

"And when the enemy reaches them?" Hobbs asked.

"Time to run again," I said.

"At least they'll get a rest," Keppen said, and spat a wad of phlegm on the rock.

"You'll get one too, old man." I grinned. "It's your squads I'm thinking should stay."

"I should have jumped," he muttered. He shook his head and raised his shortbow high, its red marker ribbon snapping in the wind. His men started to converge behind him as he jogged off toward the ridges.

"Running's all very well," Hobbs said, striding on, "but we'll run out of mountain in the end, or be chased out of the Highlands entirely."

"Which sounds like"—Makin heaved in a breath—"the best option when all's said and done." Of all of them he looked the worst off. Too many years letting a horse do the running. He clambered up a large boulder and stood on top looking back down the valley. "Must be three thousand of the bastards after us. Maybe four."

"Likes to keep the odds in his favour does the Prince," Hobbs said. He scratched his head where the grey grew thickest and the hair thinned. "I hope you've got a hell of a plan, King Jorg."

I hoped so too. If not for Norwood and Gelleth these Watch men would have fled an age ago. How quickly fact turns into fiction, and strangely when fact becomes legend, folk seem more ready to believe it. And maybe they were right to have faith, for I did reduce the Lord of Gelleth, his mighty castle, and his armies all to dust. Maybe they were right and I was wrong, but I found it hard to believe in whatever tricks I might have stowed in a small copper box.

Believer or not, the box was all I had. So I pressed it to my forehead, hard, as if I could push the memory I needed through the bone. The feeling is like that misremembered name appearing without preamble on your tongue, ready to be spoken, after so long dancing beyond reach on its tip. Except that instead of one word, there are many, images with them, and touches and tastes. A piece of your life returned to you.

The memory flooded me, taking me from the cold slopes, back across years. Gone the crowded Watch men, gone the shouting and the screams.

I lunged for the next hold, throwing my body after my arm and hand, loosing the last hold before my fingers had found a grip on the next, before I lost momentum. Climbing is a form of faith; there's no holding back, no reserve. My fingers jammed into the crack, the sharp edge biting, toes scrabbling on rough rock, the soft leather finding traction as I started to slip.

There's a spire of stone in the Matteracks that points at the sky as though it were God's own index finger. How it came to be, who carved it from the fastness of the mountains, I can't say. One book I own speaks of wind and rivers and ice sculpting the world in the misty long ago, but that sounds like a story for children, and a dull one at that. Better to talk of wind demons, river gods, and ice giants out of Jotenheim. It's a more interesting tale and just as likely.

Arm aching, leg straining, curved in an awkward pose across the fractured stone, I gasped for air, stealing a cold lungful from the wind. They say don't look down, but I like to. I like to see the loose pieces fall away and become lost in the distance. My muscles burned, the heat stolen by the wind. It felt as though I were trapped between ice and fire.

The spire stands clear of a vast spur where one of the mountains' roots divides two deep valleys. From the scree slopes at the spire's base to the flat top of it where a small cottage might squeeze, there are four hundred feet of shattered rock, vertical in the main, in places leaning out.

A hundred feet below I could see the ledge where I had met the goat. The heights a mountain goat will scale for the possibility of a green mouthful never cease to amaze me. They must use their own kind of magic to climb without the cleverness of fingers or toes. I'd pulled myself up and come eyeball to eyeball with the beast, its long face framed by two curling horns. There's something alien in a goat's eye, something not seen in dog or horse or bird. It's the rectangular pupil. As if they've climbed out of hell or fallen from the moon. We sat together in mutual distrust while I caught my breath and waited for life to find its way back into limbs and extremities.

I found the rock pillar in my first year as King of Renar and in all my time on the throne it was perhaps that spare needle of mountain that came closest to killing me. I failed to climb it seven times, and I am not a man who gives up any attempt easily.

Coddin once asked me why I climb and I spun him some pretty lies. The truth—at least for today—is that back when I hadn't many years on me, my mother would play for William and me on an instrument from the vaults of the tall castle. A piano. A thing of magic and many keys in black and white. We were trouble, Will and I, it has to be said. Fighting, scheming, digging out mischief of any kind that might be had—but when she played we fell silent and just listened. I remember every moment, her long fingers moving on the keys so fast they blurred together, the sway of her body, her hair hanging in a single long plait between her shoulders, the light falling across the wooden body of the instrument. But I can't hear it. She plays behind glass, walled behind too many years, lost when I walked away from it all, from her, from that damn carriage and the thorns.

I see, but I can't hear.

When I climb, and only then, on the very edge of everything, I catch stray notes. Like words robbed of meaning on the cusp of hearing . . . the music almost reaches me. And for that I would dare any height.

I made an eighth assault on the Spire at the start of the summer in which the Prince of Arrow crossed my borders with his armies new laden with loot from conquests in Normardy and Orlanth. Loot and, it must be said, recruits, for the lords of those lands were not well loved and the Prince won the people's hearts almost before their dead were boxed and buried.

Climbing is about commitment. On the Spire there are places so sheer that one hold must be wholly relinquished before the next can be obtained, and sometimes then only by hurling yourself up an open expanse of rock that offers no purchase. In such moments you are falling, albeit upwards, and if the next hold escapes you then that fall will carry you to the ground. There are no half measures in such ascents: you place everything you are or will be on each decision. Lives can be lived in this manner, but I do not recommend it. In the end though, everybody dies, but not everybody lives—the climber, though he may die young, will have lived.

There comes a point on a long climb when you know you have to surrender or die. There's no quarter given. I hung to cold stone fifty feet beneath the summit, weak as a child, aching with hunger, blistered hands and feet, arms screaming. The art of survival in the mountains is knowing when to give up. The art of reaching the top is knowing when not to.

"If I die here," I whispered to the stone. "If I fall and die, I will count it a life lived, maybe not well, but fully. No book will know my end, but I will have died in battle nonetheless." And summoning my strength I started to climb again.

Like the Scots king and his famous spider, my eighth attempt proved the charm.

Retching, slobbering on the rock, I crawled over the final corner, horizontal at long last. I lay trembling, gasping, half sobbing, as close to the end of my endurance as I had ever come.

When you're climbing you take nothing with you that you do not absolutely need. That's a good discipline to acquire, and the mountains teach it to you for free. They say that time is a great teacher but unfortunately it kills all its pupils. The mountains are also great teachers, and better still, they let the occasional star pupil live.

The mountains teach you to be prepared for change. Amongst the peaks the weather can shift from fair to foul quick as blinking. One moment you might be clambering up a forgiving slope and the next you could be clinging to it as though it were your mother, whilst an east wind tries to carry your frozen corpse off with it.

Climbing God's Finger I learned a lot about holding on by my fingertips. By the time I finally hauled myself weak and trembling onto the very top of the spire, I had come to realize that I've been holding on by my fingertips my entire life.

I flopped to my back. I lay there on the rock with nothing to see between me and a relentless blue sky. I had climbed light, taking nothing unneeded with me, no room on that narrow peak for anyone else, ghosts or otherwise, no Katherine, no William, my mother and father four hundred feet below, too far away to hear. Not even the shadow of a child on the rock or the glimmer of a copper box in memory. It isn't the danger or the challenge that keeps me climbing; it's the purity and focus. When you're a five-second drop from being a smear of guts and pulverized bone, when your whole weight is on eight fingers, then seven, then five, your choices are black and white, made on instinct without baggage.

When you climb hard and reach an impossible peak or ledge, you gain a new perspective, you see the world differently. It's not just the angle you're looking from that changes. You change too. They say you can't go back, and I learned that when I returned to the Tall Castle after four years on the road. I walked the same halls, saw the same people, but I hadn't gone back; I'd come to a new castle, seen with new eyes. The same is true if you climb high enough, only with climbing you don't need to stay away for years. Climb a mountain, see the world from its highest point, and a new man will climb down to a world of subtle differences the next day.

Metaphysics aside, there is plenty to be seen from a high point in the mountains. If you sit with your legs dangling over the biggest drop in the world, with the wind streaming your hair behind you, and your shadow falling so far it might never hit the ground . . . you notice new things.

On the road we have our sayings. "Pax," we say if we're caught with our hands in another man's saddlebags. "Visiting the locals," we say when a brother is off about dark business after a battle. Where's Brother Rike? Visiting the locals. In the Renar Highlands there's a saying that I didn't hear until I struggled up to the village of Gutting with Sir Makin in tow. "'E was taking a rock for a walk, yer worship." At the time I paid it no attention, a bit of local colour, a streak of green in the manure. I heard the expression a few more times in the years that followed, generally when somebody was off on mysterious business. Taking a rock for a walk. Once you've noticed a phrase or word it starts to crop up everywhere. "Lost his flock," was another one. I'd hear these things on the parade ground in main, from the local recruits. "That John of Bryn had my bowstrings while I was on wall watch." "What you gonna do about that?" "Don't you worry none, already happened. Lost his flock he did."

Up in a high place, especially one hard-reached, you gain a fresh perspective. Looking out over the peaks and cliffs and slopes I'd come to know, I noticed something new. The shadows gave it away, leading the eye here and there to places where the land didn't lie quite right. It took a time of empty watching, of idle legs dangling, and thought-stuff swirling behind my eyes before, like the snow in the globe, everything settled and I saw clear, the same scene but with new detail.

High on the sides of almost every valley, of all but the highest gorges, the loose rocks gathered too thickly, perched too precariously. At first the eye buys into the deception. It has to be natural. To move that much stone would take a thousand lifetimes, and to what end?

Taking a rock for a walk turns out to be a genuine national pastime in the Highlands, so deep grained, so known, that nobody seems to feel the need to say more. For generations the men going up to tend their goats have filled any idle moment with the business of carrying loose stones from one part of the slope to another higher part, slowly building up the same piles that their father and grandfather built upon.

If a Renar man takes the ultimate liberty and decides to graze his goats on another man's land, chances are that there'll be a sudden rockslide and the man will have lost his flock. If it weren't a Renar man then he might lose even more than that.

It's hard to tease out a thread when you're running, especially when that thread is a plan and you're teasing it from a memory box, and you're running uphill with thousands of soldiers in pursuit. But even our enemies call the Ancraths cunning, and I call us clever. So I pulled a little more and all of a sudden I saw the slopes we were running up with a whole new perspective. Or rather, an older one that I had forgotten.

FROM THE JOURNAL OF KATHERINE AP SCORRON

October 25th, Year 98 Interregnum
Ancrath. The Tall Castle. In my rooms again.
I'm always in my rooms.

I had that dream again. The one with Jorg. I have the knife as always, twelve inches and thin as a finger. He's standing there with his arms open and he's laughing at me. Laughing. I'm standing there in my torn dress with the knife and him laughing, and I thrust it into him, like he thrust . . . and I stab it into him. And old Hanna watches and she smiles. But her smile isn't right and when Jorg falls there are bruises on him too. On his neck. Long dark bruises. And I can almost see the fingers and the thumb print.

I'm running this torn satin through my fingers and it's me that feels torn. My memories fight my dreams. Every single day. And I don't know who is winning and who is losing. I don't remember.

November 7th, Year 98 Interregnum
Ancrath. The Tall Castle. Bell-tower—keep-top.

I've found a place to be alone, the tallest point on the Tall Castle, just me and the crows and the wind. The tower holds only one bell, huge and made of iron. They never ring it. At least now it's serving a purpose by sheltering me from the wind.

I find myself wanting to be alone. All the ladies grate on me, even the ones that mean well. There's no peace in the castle—only the feeling that something is wrong, something I can't name or touch.

I found initials up here, H.J.A, you can see them out on the far side of the tower where it leans over the outer wall of the keep. I can see no way to reach the spot. It says something about Honorous Jorg Ancrath that even his name is out of reach.

Sageous came to my chamber today. Just to the door. The Prince of Arrow has come again. The Prince and his brother, Orrin and Egan. Sareth said they would come back. She said they would come back to sniff around me again. That's just how she said it. As if they were dogs and I was a bitch in heat.

I don't think I am. In heat that is. I can be a bitch. I can be a bitch every day. I made Maery Coddin cry today and I hardly meant to.

Even so, there's something about Orrin and something else about Egan. Grandmother would say they both burn too bright. Too bright for regular folks, she'd say. But I've never counted myself regular. And if they do burn bright— if they do put heat in me—or me in heat—what of it? I fancy I put some heat in them. Or why would they both be back at the Tall Castle a moon after their first visit? I don't think it's for the pleasure of King Olidan's company. I don't think Orrin's charm or Egan's threat had much impact on that scary old man. I don't think the devil would make Olidan pause. I don't think he'd bow his head even if God himself sent an angel to his doors.

Sareth says both the Arrows are pointed my way. She has a dirty mouth. She says they'll both ask for my hand. Even though I'm not Scorron's first daughter and Father promised alliance and land to Olidan already. She says they'll both ask for my hand but it's not my hand they're interested in, or my dowry. She said more, but her mouth is dirtier than my quill, black with ink though it is. And if they did ask, what would I say? It hardly seems that they can be brothers, one as bright and good as my Sir Galen, the other as dark and tempting as Jorg who killed him.

I dreamed again last night. I woke up speaking the

words of that dream and now I can't even remember the shape of it. I can remember a knife, a long knife. I know I need to use it. I remember Jorg hurt me. I should go back and read my journal, but somehow my hands don't want to turn the pages back, only forward. I had a dream about that too.

Sageous is at the door again. The princes are waiting. I don't like that man's eyes.

Gorgoth is like no other. There is no mould for the leucrota. Twisted by the Builders' poisons they fall broken from the womb and follow strange paths as they grow. The ribs that pierce his flesh and reach from each side are black and thick, his hide more red than blood, and the muscle beneath surges as he moves. And though he is shaped for war and for horror, there are few men in Adam's image whose approval would mean as much to me—and most of them lie dead.

14

Four years earlier

A day after we left the sands of Thar and started to ride through the Thurtan grasslands I took the box from Makin. I felt the sharp edges of the lost memory through the copper walls and sensed the poison held there. Makin once told me that a man who's got no fear is missing a friend. With the thorn-patterned copper clutched uneasy in my fist I thought perhaps I had found that friend at last. I turned it one way, then the other. It held nothing good—only me. And a man should be a little scared of himself surely? Of what he might do. To know thyself must be terribly dull. I put the box at the bottom of my saddlebag and left it unopened. I didn't ask after Katherine. I took a new knife from Grumlow and rode toward our business in Heimrift.

We rode north across wide acres where the wind whipped the spring grass into a thrashing sea and green ripples raced one after the other. A land made for horse, for galloping, for chasing between the dark borders of one forest and the next. I let Brath have his head and exhausted both of us as if all hell were at our heels. The Brothers kept pace as best they could, all of us wanting to leave Thar many miles behind. Old fires still burned there, unseen. In a thousand years Mount Honas, the place where I lit a Builders' Sun, might be like Thar, a Promised Land that would return to man in time but for the now loved us not.

That night as we settled to sleep I saw the baby for the first time, lying dead in the long grass by our camp. I threw off my blanket and walked across to it, watched by Gorgoth, and by Gog who slept beside him now. The spot where the child had lain was empty. I caught a whiff of perfume, white musk maybe. With a shrug I returned to my bed. Some things are best forgotten.

We travelled the next day and the next along the banks of the River Rhyme that flows between Thurtan and its neighbours to the east. The Rhyme lands were once the Empire's garden, farmed with exquisite care. Push a nation's borders back and forth across a garden a dozen times and all that's left is mud and ruin.

At one point we rode through a field of old-stones, hundreds upon hundreds in marching lines, single blocks a little taller than a man, a little wider, all set on end, lichen covered, knee-deep grass swaying around them. Ancient before the Builders came, ancient before the Greeks, Lundist told me. An uncomfortable power throbbed between the monoliths and I led the Brothers faster than was prudent to clear the field.

On the fourth day a soft rain wrapped us and fell without pause from dawn till dusk. I rode for a while beside Maical, rolling gently in the grey's saddle. He always rode as if he were at sea, did Maical, slumping forward, rolling back, not an ounce of grace in him.

"Do you like dogs, Maical?" I asked him.

"Beef's better," he said, "or mutton."

I set a grin on my face. "Well, that's a new perspective. I thought you might like them on account of their stupidity." Why I was baiting Maical I had no idea. Part of me even liked Maical, almost.

I remembered a time when I came back to camp having scouted out the town of Mabberton down on the soft edge of the Ken Marshes. I'd come up from the bog path, with Gerrod picking his way through the tufts and cotton grass. At first I thought the shrieking was a village girl foolish enough to get snagged by the Brothers, but it turned out just to be two of the lads bent over a tied dog, poking it with something sharp to get a song out of it.

I had slipped off Gerrod and grabbed them by the hair, one black handful, one red, and hauled back, throwing my weight into the motion. Both took to shouting and one even reached for me in his anger. I sliced his palm open for him nice and quick.

"You shouldn't a-done that, Brother Jorg," Gemt said, cradling his cut hand with the blood dripping free and fast. "You shouldn't ah."

"No?" I had asked, as the Brothers started to gather around us. "And where have I been, Brother Gemt, whilst you hone your battle skills on this useless mutt?"

Jobe stood beside Gemt, rubbing at the spot I'd yanked his hair from. I looked pointedly at the dog and he knelt to cut it free.

"You been watching on that town," Gemt said, his face a hot red now.

"I've been scouting that town, Mabberton, yes," I said. "So we could come at it with what your idiot brother has been known to call the elephant of surprise. And all I told you lot to do was lie low."

Gemt had spat and used his left hand to hold closed the cut on his right.

"Lie low, I said, not wake the whole fecking marsh from tadpole to toad with a howling fecking dog. Besides," I'd said, making a slow turn to see the whole of my little band, "everyone knows that tormenting a dumb dog is bad luck. You'd all know that if you weren't too damn stupid to read."

Makin had been one of the first to join the show and a big grin he had on him. "I know my letters," he said, surprising not a few of the Brothers. "So which book is it that says that then, Brother Jorg?"

"The big book of Go Fuck Yourself," I told him.

"So hurting dogs is bad luck now, is it?" Still with that grin on him.

"It is near me," I had said.

Blinking now, I found the rain still rolling down my face on our long trek beside the Rhyme. I shook off the memory.

"Do you recall that dog your brother found before we hit Mabberton, Brother Maical?" I asked. He wouldn't of course. Maical recalled very little about anything.

He looked at me, lips pursed, spitting out the rain. "Putting the hurt on dogs is bad luck," he said.

"It was for your brother," I said. "Had himself an accident the next day."

Maical frowned, confused, and made a slow nod. "Everyone knows not to put the hurt on your food," he said. "It sours the meat."

"Another new perspective, Brother Maical," I sighed. "I knew I kept you around for a reason."

That dog came back the next morning, just before we hit Mabberton, as if I was its friend or something. Wouldn't leave until I gave it a good kicking, a free lesson in how the world works, if you like.

Maical just offered a vacant smile and kept on riding.

Heimrift lies in the dukedom of Maladon, a land where the hungry seas washed up what little of the Danelands they couldn't swallow. From the Renar Highlands it's a fair old trek by any standards, and given the tortuous routes we had to take, it would be a journey of weeks. On the road you fall into routine. Mine involved a hard hour at sword with Sir Makin every evening before the light failed. I took to the art with new interest. A fresh challenge is often the way to keep from brooding on the past.

I had seen the sword as a means of carrying death through a crowd. With the Brothers I often found myself amongst an unskilled foe, one more interested in running than fighting, and I used my blade for slaughter. I had met more skilful opponents of course, soldiers sent to stop us, well-trained mercenaries set to guard merchants' wagons, and other bandits with their own brothers on the road, wanting what we had.

When I saw Katherine's champion fight Sir Makin, and later when I set myself against the Prince of Arrow, I understood the difference between the workman and the artist. Of course there's time to be an artist when you're not having to worry about a farmer sneaking up behind you and sticking a pitchfork through your neck whilst you're showing off your feints and parries.

So I worked with Makin, day after day, building up the right kind of muscle, learning to feel the subtle differences through the blade even when it's being pounded so hard all you want to do is let go. And every time I got a bit better, he turned on the skill a little more. I started to hate him, just a piece.

When you swing a sword enough, put yourself through enough fights, there's a kind of rhythm you start to detect. Not the rhythm of your opponent, but a kind of necessary beat to the business of cut and thrust, as if your eyes read the very first hints of each action and lay it out as music to dance to. I heard just whispers of the refrain but every time I caught them it made Makin pay sudden attention and start to sweat to hold me back. I heard only murmured phrases of the song, but just knowing it was there at all was enough to keep me striving.

If you keep heading north and east from the Renar Highlands then eventually you have to cross the River Rhyme. Given that the river is at least four hundred yards across at all of the points where one might reach it without an invading army, the exercise of crossing it is one that normally requires a ferryman.

There is one alternative. A bridge at the free-town of Remagen. How any bridge could span such an expanse of water is a wonder and one that I decided to see for myself rather than dicker with the owner of some rickety barge farther upstream.

We closed on Remagen through the Kentrow hills, winding through endless narrow valleys—rock-choked gullies in the main of the kind where horses are apt to go lame. The boredom of the trail never bothered me when we used to range mile after mile in search of mischief or loot, or hopefully both. Since Thar though, I found the long silences a trial. My mind wandered along dark paths. I don't know how many ways there are to put Katherine together with a missing knife and a dead baby but I think I must have considered most of them, and at length. I knew where the answer lay, and kept finding that I didn't want to know it. At least not badly enough to open that box.

Brother Maical's wisdom lies in knowing he is not clever and letting himself be led. The foolishness of mankind is that we do not do the same.

15

Four years earlier

Gog had a bad dream in the dry canyons of the Kentrow hills. So bad a dream that it chased us out of there, tripping over our smouldering blankets as the fire guttered and spat around us. While we hunted the horses in the dark, stumbling over every rock and bush, the far end of the canyon glowed with a fierce red heat.

"Going to find us a crispy little monster when we go back up there," Rike said, the fire picking out the raw bones of his face in demonic tones.

"Never burned hisself before," Grumlow said, tiny beside Rike.

Ahead of us, closer than we wanted to get to the heat, closer than we *could* get to it, Gorgoth waited to return. His silhouette against the glow had a disturbingly arachnid shape to it, the splayed ribs like legs reaching from his sides.

Young Sim came back leading Brath and his own nag. "Be more use on a winter trip." He nodded toward the flames, shrugged, and led the horses off. Sim had a way with horses. He'd been a stable lad for some lord once upon a time. Spent time in a brothel too as a child, earning rather than spending.

We made a new camp and waited to see what was left of our old one.

When I went back with Gorgoth the sky had started shading into pearl. The rocks creaked as they cooled and I could feel the heat through the soles of my boots. Maical came with us. He seemed to like the leucrota.

We found Gog sleeping peacefully in a blackened area that resembled a burned-out campfire. I shone the only lantern we had left on the boy and he screwed his eyes tighter before rolling over. "Sorry to disturb." I snorted and sat down, standing up again sharpish with a scorched arse.

"He's changing," Gorgoth said.

I'd noticed it too. The stippled red-and-black of his skin had taken on fiercer scarlet-on-grey tones and a more flame-like form, as if the fire had somehow frozen into his hide.

We slept then, us back at the new camp and Gorgoth with Gog in the ruins of the old. In the morning they joined us and Gog ran to the breakfast fire as though it were a new thing he'd not seen before. The flames flushed scarlet as he approached and the water in Row's pots started to boil even though it was fresh from the stream.

"Can't you see them?" he asked as Gorgoth pulled him back.

"No," I said, following them away from the camp. "And best you don't see 'them' either. We'll be meeting with a man who knows all about these things soon enough. Until then, just keep . . . cool."

I sat with them farther down the canyon. We played throw-stones and cross-sticks. It seems that when you're eight you can shake anything off, at least for the short term. Gog laughed when he won and smiled when he lost. I can't remember a time when I didn't play to win but I didn't grate on him for his easy ways. When ambition gets its teeth into you it's hard to know how to just enjoy what's in front of you.

"Good boy." Maical passed Gog the cross-sticks he'd gathered back up, a small bundle in his callused hand. "Bad dreams."

I frowned at that. Gorgoth rumbled.

"We were all slow to wake . . ." I said. "Could have ended badly." I remembered feeling the heat, the smell of char, and the slow struggle free of my own nightmares.

Gorgoth and I found the answer in the same moment, but he spoke first: "Sageous."

I nodded, slow as the realization of just how stupid I'd been crept over me. Coddin had been right: many hands would seek to wield a weapon like Gog. Twice now the dream-witch had turned that power against me. He might not be able to kill me with my own dreams, but he'd had a good try with Gog's.

"All the more reason to press on." I might have said, *Third time's the charm*, but there's no point tempting the fates—unless you've got a big enough sword to kill them too.

After breaking fast we rode on, closing now on Remagen. There's a small fort on a ridge not far from the river as you come out of the Kentrow hills. It commands a view of the road approaching the town. We could see the Rhyme as a bright ribbon behind the fort, and a hint of the bridge towers.

Kent and Maical flanked me at the front of our band and we approached the fort at a trot, Gog clutching my back, Gorgoth jogging close by. Makin and Rike rode behind, chuckling. Makin could even get a laugh out of Rike when he put his mind to it. Then Grumlow, then Sim and Row. I guess it could have been Gorgoth that spooked the fort-men, though at that distance they couldn't have had a clear view of him. Either way, one moment I had Kent to my right and Maical to my left, and the next moment the grey had an empty saddle.

I pulled Brath in a tight circle and jumped down quick-smart even as the others rode past in confusion. It had to be a lucky shot. At the range between us and the fort walls a good archer would be hard-pressed to hit a house using a longbow. But there it was, one feathered end hard against his neck, the sharp end red and dripping and jutting a foot from the other side. Maical looked at me with unusual focus as I dropped to one knee beside him.

"Time to die, Brother Maical." I didn't want to lie to him. I took his hand.

He watched me, holding my eyes as the others wheeled their horses and started to shout.

"King Jorg," he said, only without sound, blood running from the corners of his mouth. He looked strange with his helmet off to one side and a light in him, as if what had been broken all his life was fixed by a simple fall off his horse. He'd never called me "king" before, as if "brother" was all he could get hold of.

"Brother Maical," I said. I've lost a lot of brothers but not many while I watched their eyes. The strength went from his hand. He coughed blood and went his way.

"What in hell?" Makin jumped down from his horse.

The glistening arrowhead kept my attention. A bead of blood hung from the point, a baby's reflection distorting across its curve. I saw a red knife and Katherine walking amongst the graves.

"Hello, Jorg," she had said.

"He dead." Kent joined me on his knees beside Maical. "How?" The arrow was plain enough but it didn't seem to answer the question.

I stood and walked past Makin's horse, pulling the shield from over his saddlebags. I kept walking. A coldness crawled through me, tingling on my cheeks. I took the Nuban's bow from its place on Brath's back, checked its double load.

"Jorg?" Kent clambered to his feet.

"I'm going in," I said. "Nobody gets out alive. Is that understood? Any man follows me, I'll kill them." Without waiting for answer I moved on.

I walked a hundred yards before another arrow fell, sailing far to the left. The shot that killed Maical had to have been a freak, loosed with no real hope of hitting its target. I slung the Nuban's crossbow over my shoulder. Thin ties held the bolts in their channels.

I could see four men on the battlements now. Fifty yards on and they loosed a volley. I raised the shield. One arrow hit it, the point just visible on my side, the others clattered on the rocks.

It wasn't a big fort, more of a watch point. Thirty men would have filled it elbow to elbow, and it looked to have been many years since it was fully garrisoned.

By the time I stood properly in range the men on the walls had found their courage. A single warrior approached them at a steady walk, and he didn't look much above sixteen. Three more joined them behind the battlements, not soldiers, no uniform, just a ragtag bunch, more of them looking out through the portcullis.

"You're not going to let me in then?" I called to them.

"How's your friend?" a fat one called from the wall. The others laughed.

"He's fine," I said. "Something spooked his horse and he fell. He'll be up and about as soon as he gets his breath." I peered over my shield and pulled the arrow from it. "Somebody want this back?" I felt utterly calm, serene, and yet at the same time with the sense of something rushing toward me like a squall racing across the grasslands beneath a darkening sky.

"Surely." One of the half dozen behind the gate snorted and started to turn the wheel, raising the portcullis notch by notch while the chain ratcheted through its housings. The thick muscle on his arms gleamed white through the dirt as he strained.

I saw two of those on the wall exchange glances. I don't think the arrow was all they planned to take from me. I started forward so that I would reach the gate just as it drew high enough for me to pass below without bending. The stink of the place after so many nights in the open made my eyes sting.

The storm that had been racing toward me across some hidden wasteland in my mind hit as I entered the fort. I offered the arrow to the closest man, a thin fellow with, of all things, a headman's axe in hand. He reached for it and I stuck it through his eye.

There's a still moment when something like that happens, when an arrow juts from a gleaming eyeball and the owner has yet to scream. The men who act in such still moments tend to live longer. Of the crowd behind the gate only one moved before the man's scream, and I moved quicker. I caught his wrist as he reached for me and drove Makin's shield against his elbow joint. With his arm held straight I pivoted him so his body struck another man before his head hit the wall. The quick men tend to live longer, but sometimes they just get themselves first in the queue.

I stepped back, almost to the portcullis that had started to fall, and shrugged the Nuban's bow from my shoulder, letting its weight swing it under my arm. Bringing it up I pulled both triggers without bothering to aim. Both bolts hit the same man, which was a bit of a waste, but of all of them he had the most armour on and the Nuban's crossbow put two big holes in it.

The portcullis slammed down behind me. The wind of it

tickled on my neck as it sliced past. Four left in view. The big man at the gate-wheel hunting for his sword, another unhurt on the floor climbing to his feet. Two who could be brothers, both wide with straggly hair and rotting teeth, reaching for me. They made the right choice. When the numbers are on your side, grapple your foe before he gets his steel clear.

I pushed off the gate, using it to accelerate my charge. The pair before me both had the weight advantage but if you hurl yourself hard behind a shield, especially if you ensure the iron edge of it hits somewhere useful, like the throat, you can get yourself a little advantage of your own, whatever you weigh.

I had no fear in me, just the need to kill, just something crawling on me, in me, that might be washed away with enough blood.

One of the two uglies went down beneath me, blood, spit, and teeth spattering my face. The other loomed above us as I pulled Grumlow's knife from my boot.

Knife-work is a red business, Brothers. With the knife you slice meat up close, lay it to the bone, and swim in what gushes out. The screams are in your ear, the hurting trembles through your short blade. I could say I remember all of it but I don't. A fury took me, painting the world in scarlet, and I howled as I killed. I have a vision of the moment I left the gate-yard, drawing my sword for the first time as the remainder of the garrison hurried down two sets of narrow stairs to the right and left. The men coming into view first tried to back off, with the others crowding behind, pushing.

It wasn't for Maical that I killed those men, or for the joy of slaughter, or the proud legend of King Jorg. Like Gog I have my own fires banked and burning, and on some days the right spark can set them blazing beyond my control. Perhaps that was the true reason I had come traipsing over half a dozen realms to find this fire-mage for my pet monster. Perhaps I wanted to know that such fires could be contained. That they didn't have to kill us both.

I survived my foolishness, though fourteen men did not, and I walked, half-drunk with exhaustion, from the gate once more. The Brothers left their posts on their perimeter around the fort and followed me back toward the horses.

"Jorg," Makin said.

I turned and they stopped.

"Red Jorg," said Red Kent, and he clapped his hand across his chest.

"Red Jorg," Rike grunted. He stamped.

Gorgoth stamped his great foot. Makin drew sword and clashed it against his breastplate. The others took up the chant. I looked down and saw that no part of me was without gore. I dripped with the blood of others, as red as Kent on the day we found him. And I knew then why he wouldn't speak of it.

I went to Maical and took his head-axe from the grey's harness. "We'll make him a cairn," I said. "And put the heads of the fort-men around to watch over it." I threw the axe to Rike. He caught it and set off for the fort without complaint. For once I believed the taking of loot was not at the front of his thinking.

We built the cairn. Gorgoth brought rocks that no single man would be able to roll away. I don't know that Maical would have wanted the heads, or cared, or have held any opinion on the matter, but we set them as his honour guard in any case. I don't know what Maical would have wanted. I never really met him until those last seconds when he lay dying. It surprised me that I cared, but I found that I did.

16

Four years earlier

You can cut seven shades from a man. Scarlet arterial blood, purple from the veins, bile like fresh-cut grass, browns from the gut, but it all dries to somewhere between rust and tar. Time for Red Jorg to take himself to a stream and clean off the fortmen. I watched the dirt swirl away, pinkish in the water.

"So what was that about?" Makin asked, striding up behind.

"They shot my idiot," I said.

A pause. It seemed that Makin always had that pause with me, as if I were a puzzle to him. "We told you he was dead back in Norwood and you didn't spare him a moment," Makin said. "So why now? The truth, Jorg."

"What is truth?" I asked, washing the last of the blood from my hands. "Pilate said that, you know? 'What is truth?'"

"Fine, don't tell me then," Makin said. "But we have to cross that bridge in a hurry now, before this gets out."

I stood, shaking water from my hair. "I'm ready. Let's go."

With the Brothers saddled and on the road I took a moment to revisit the cairn. Necromancy pulsed in my chest as I approached, an echo of the pain when Father's knife cut in. An echo of all the flavours of pain that filled me in that moment, stabbed, betrayed, the strength running from me, hot and red.

Ravens fluttered away from the heads as I drew close. I stood mute before the mound of dry rocks, mind empty, not knowing what I felt. My eye took in the spatters of yellowed lichen, a quartz vein through a large boulder, the black trickles of blood on stone. It seemed that the heads watched me, as if their raven-pecked eyes were turned toward me. And then, there was no "seemed" about it. As I made a slow circle of the cairn, each head in turn swivelled its gaze to follow me. I had killed the first man with an arrow in the eye. It twitched as he tried to turn that eye my way. I held the gaze of the single eye he could watch me with.

"Jorg." His lips formed my name.

"Chella?" I asked. Who else could it be? "I thought I buried you deep enough." For a moment I saw her toppling into that shaft, dragging the Nuban, after I'd shot them both with his bow.

The same smile twisted each man's lips.

"I'll find you, bitch," I spoke low. She had enough ears to hear me.

The heads broadened their smiles to show teeth. Lips moved. It looked like "Dead King" that they mouthed.

I shrugged. "Enjoy the ravens." And I left them. Whatever power worked here, I doubted it would trouble Maical under such a weight of stone.

We moved on, resupplied from the fort, with replacements for what Gog had burned in the night. Remagen huddled around both shores of the Rhyme, a modest walled town, smoke rising from scores of chimneys lined along well-ordered streets. The bridge held my attention though. I'd not thought of bridges as graceful before, but this one hung glittering between two silver towers taller than the Haunt, suspended on what looked like gleaming wire but must have been cables thick as a man.

Within half an hour we were lined at the town gates, waiting our turn behind pedlars, merchants with their wagons, farmers leading cows or carting ducks and hens. We stowed our weapons out of sight on the horses, but we still looked a rough crowd.

Gorgoth drew looks aplenty, but none of the normal screaming and the running.

"You'll be with the circus then," said the farmer with the ducks in wicker cages. He nodded as if agreeing with his statement.

"So we are," I said before Rike could grumble. "I juggle," I added, and gave him my smile.

The men at the gates were of the same rag-tag crowd that we found at the fort. The free-town had no soldiers, according to Row, just a loose militia drawn from the population, at the service of the mayor for a month or two then free to go back to their livelihoods.

"Well met." I clapped my hands to the shoulders of what should have been the gate captain in any decent town. I grinned as if we'd been best friends all our lives. "Jorg the Red and his travelling players, catching up with our colleagues at the circus. I juggle. Would you like to see?"

"No," he said, trying to shake free. A good answer in the main since I don't juggle.

"You're sure?" I asked, finally letting him go. "My friend here does knife tricks. And Little Rikey is famously ugly?"

"Move on," he said and turned to the tinker behind us.

I passed between the guardsmen—"Care to see some juggling? No?"—and through the gates.

"The bridge is that way," Makin said, pointing again as he did at the crossroads, as if it weren't two hundred feet tall and glittering in the morning sunshine.

"Indeed," I said. "But we're with the circus." And I led off to the right, not pointing at the multi-coloured pavilion rising above the rooftops. "I juggle!"

We had to start with the elbows to make a path before we got within clear sight of the pavilion. The people of Remagen were out in their hundreds, packing the streets around the circus, spilling from the taverns and crowding the smaller tents and stalls around the main attraction.

"Must be Sunday," Sim said, grinning like a boy, which I suppose he was by most accountings.

Rike moved to the front, pushing his way toward the big top. Like Sim he had an eager look on him, the kind of light that toy clown put in him back at the Haunt. I wasn't the only one who remembered.

"It's Taproot?" Makin asked, frowning.

I nodded. "Got to be."

"Excellent," said Kent. He'd swiped himself three sugar sticks from somewhere and was trying to get all of them in his mouth at once.

We got to the pavilion entrance, laced up all the way down and staked, with the smaller entrance to the side also tagged down. A man and a boy sat in the dust before the door, bent over a wooden board with black and white markers arrayed across it in various depressions.

"Show's not until sundown," the man said as my shadow fell across the board. He didn't look up.

"You've got mancala in three if you play from the end pit then the eye pit," I said.

He looked up sharp enough at that, lifting his bald head on the thickest of necks. "By Christ Jesu! It's little Jorg!"

He stood and took me under the arms, throwing me a yard in the air before executing a neat catch.

"Ron," I said. "You used to be strong!"

"Be fair." He grinned. "You've doubled in height."

I shrugged. "The armour weighs a bit too. Saved my ribs though!" I waved the others forward. "You remember Little Rikey?"

"Of course. Makin, good to see you. Grumlow." Ron caught sight of Gorgoth. "And who's the big fellow?"

"Show him the thing," said Rike, bubbling like a child, "show him the thing."

"Later." Ron smiled. "The weights are all stowed now. Besides, looks like your friend could put me out of business."

Ron, or to do him justice, the amazing Ronaldo, did the circus strongman act. He earned Rike's undying respect by the simple act of lifting a heavier weight than Rike could. It's true that nature treated Ron to an unreasonable helping of muscle, but I think that Little Rike might be the stronger even so. Certainly I'd bet on Rike before Ron in a tavern brawl. But with the lifting of weights there's grip and timing and commitment, and Rike faltered where Ron pressed on.

"So, where might we find the good Dr. Taproot?" I asked.

Ronaldo led us through the side flap, leaving the boy, who turned out to be a midget old enough to be going grey, to watch our horses. I took the Nuban's bow. I didn't trust the midget to be able to run down any thieves, and besides, I might want to shoot a circus clown or two. Just for laughs.

We skirted around the centre ring, kicking sawdust and watching three acrobats practice their tumbles out where the sun struck down through the high opening. Toward the back of the big-top, canvas divisions spaced out several rooms. Here the heavy stink from the animal cages reached in and you could hear a growl or two above the thumps and shouts of the tumblers.

Taproot had his back to me as I followed Ron in. Two of the dancer girls stood before him in slack poses, bored and rolling their eyes.

"Watch me!" Taproot said. "Hips and tits. That sells seats. And look as if you're enjoying it, for God's sake. Watch me."

He talked with his hands did Taproot, long-fingered hands always flying about his head.

"I am watching you," I said. They say Taproot got that habit from his days at the three cup game. *Watch me!* And the boy will dip your pockets.

He turned at that, hands plucking at the air. "And who have you brought to see me, Ronaldo? A handsome young fellow indeed, with friends outside."

Taproot knew me. Taproot never forgot a face, or a fact, or a weakness.

"Jorg the Red," I said. "I juggle."

"Do you now?" He drew fingers down his jaw to the point of his chin. "And what do you juggle, Jorg the Red?"

I grinned. "What have you got?"

"Watch me!" He fished a dark bottle from the depths of his cloak of many faded colours. "Come take a seat, bring your brothers in if they'll fit." He dismissed the dancers with a flutter of hands.

Taproot retreated behind a desk in the corner, finding glasses from its drawer. I took the only other chair as the others filed in behind Makin.

"I'm guessing you still juggle lives, Jorg," Taproot said. "Though in more salubrious surroundings these days." He poured a green measure into five glasses, all of a motion without a drop lost.

"You've heard about my change in circumstances?" I took the glass. Its contents looked like urine, a little greener.

"Absinthe. Ambrosia of the gods," Taproot said. "Watch me." And he knocked his back with a slight grimace.

"Absinthe? Isn't that Greek for undrinkable?" I sniffed it.

"Two gold a bottle," he said. "Has to be good at that price, no?"

I sipped. It had the kind of bitterness that takes layers off your tongue. I coughed despite myself.

"You should have told me you were a prince, Jorg; I always knew there was something about you." He pointed two fingers to his eyes. "Watch me."

More Brothers followed on in. Gorgoth ducked in under the flap, Gog scurrying in front. Taproot took his gaze from me and rocked back in his chair. "Now these two fellows I could employ," he said. "Even if they don't juggle." He waved to the three spare glasses. "Help yourselves, gentlemen."

There's a pecking order on the road and it helps to know how it runs. On the surface Taproot's business might be sawdust and somersaults, dancing girls and dancing bears, but he dealt in more than entertainment. Dr. Taproot liked to know things.

A beat passed. Most would miss it, but not Taproot. The beat let the Brothers know that Makin wasn't interested. Rike took the first glass, Red Kent the next, another beat, then Row snatched the last. Row threw his down and smacked his lips. Row could drink acid without complaint.

"Ron, why don't you take Rike and Gorgoth and show them the thing with the barrel?" I asked.

Rike gulped his drink, made a sour face, and followed Ron out, the leucrotas next, Gog tagging behind.

"The rest of you can lose yourselves too. See if you can't learn some new tricks in the ring." I sipped again. "It'd be foul at twenty gold a bottle.

"Makin, perhaps you could be finding out about that rather fine bridge for us," I said.

And they filed out, leaving me and Taproot watching each other across the desk in the dim glow of the sun through canvas.

"A prince, Jorg? Watch me!" Taproot smiled, a crescent of teeth in his thin face. "And now a king?"

"I would have cut myself a throne whatever woman I fell from," I said. "Had I been a carpenter's son, stable-born, I'd have cut one."

"I don't doubt it." Again the smile, that mix of warmth and calculation. "Remember the times we had, Jorg?"

I did. Happy days are rare on the road. The days we had ridden with the circus troupe had been golden for a wild boy of twelve.

"Tell me about the Prince of Arrow," I said.

"A great man by all accounts," Taproot said. He made a steeple of his fingers, pressed to his lips.

"And by your account?" I asked. "Don't tell me you've not met the man."

"I've met everyone, Jorg," he said. "You know that. Watch me."

I never knew if I liked Taproot.

"I've even met your father," he said.

I am rarely uncertain in such matters, but Taproot, with his "watch me" and his talking hands, with his whole life a performance, and his secret ways? It's hard to know a man who knows too much. "The Prince of Arrow," I said.

"He is a good man," Taproot said at last. "He means what he says and what he says is good."

"The world eats good men for breakfast," I said.

"Perhaps." Taproot shrugged. "But the Prince is a thinker, a planner. And he has funds. The Florentine banking clans love him well. Peace is good business. He is setting his pieces. The Fenlands fell to him before winter set in. He'll add more thrones to his tally soon enough. Watch me. He'll be at your gates in a few years if nobody stops him. And at your father's gates."

"Let him call on Ancrath first," I said. I wondered what my father would make of this "good man."

"His brother," said Taproot, "Egan?"

Taproot knew, he just wanted to know if I knew. I just watched him. He kept telling me to after all.

"His brother is a killer. A swordsman like the legends talk of, and vicious with it. A year younger than Orrin, and always will be, thank the Lord. More absinthe?"

"And how much support is there for the Good Prince among

the Hundred?" I waved the bottle away. You needed a clear head with Taproot.

"Well, they'd all murder him for half a florin," Taproot said.

"Of course."

"But he's merciful and that can be a powerful thing." Taproot stroked his chest as though he imagined a little of that mercy for himself. "There's not a lord out there who doesn't know that if he opened his gates to Arrow he'd get to keep his head and most of what was behind his gates too. By the next Congression his friends could vote him to the empire throne. And if he keeps going the way he is, he could vote himself to the throne at the Congression after next."

"It's a clever ploy," I said. Mercy as a weapon.

"More than that, watch me." Taproot sipped and ran his tongue over his teeth. "It's who he is. And he won't need too many more victories before more gates are opened to him than stand closed." He looked at me then, dark and shrewd. "How will your gates stand, Jorg of Ancrath?"

"We'll have to see, won't we?" I ran a wet finger around the rim of my glass and made it sing. "I'm a little young to be giving up on ambition though, neh?" Besides, sometimes an open gate just means you'd rather *they* did the walking. "What about the others?" I asked.

"Others?" Taproot's innocent look was a work of art, perfected over years.

I watched him. Taproot kept his frozen innocence a moment longer. I scratched my ear and watched him.

"Oh . . . the others." He offered a quick smile. "There's support for Orrin of Arrow there. He's foretold, the Prince of Arrow. Prophecy aplenty. Too much for the wise to ignore. The Silent Sister is of course—"

"Silent?" I asked.

"Even so. But others are interested. Sageous, the Blue Lady, Luntar of Thar, even Skilfar." He studied me as he spoke each name, knowing in a moment if I knew them. I put little enough on my face at such times, but a man like Taproot needs less than little to know your mind.

"Skilfar?" He already knew I didn't know.

"Ice-witch," Taproot said. "Plays the jarls off against each other. There are plenty of eyes on this Prince of Arrow, Jorg.

His star is not yet risen, but be sure it's in ascendance! Who knows how high and how bright it might be come Congression?"

If anyone knew, it would be the circus master before me. I turned Taproot's words over in my head. The next Congression stood two years away, four more again before the one after that. As lord of Renar I had my place booked, a single vote in hand, and the Gilden Guard would escort me to Vyene. I couldn't see the Hundred electing an emperor to sit over them though. Not even Orrin of Arrow. If I went, if I let the Gilden Guard drag me five hundred miles to throw my vote into the pot, I'd vote for me.

"I'm sorry about Kashta," Taproot said. He filled his glass and raised it.

"Who?"

Taproot dropped his gaze to the bow beside me. "The Nuban."

"Oh." Taproot knew stuff. Kashta. I let him fill my glass again and we drank to the Nuban.

"Another good man," Taproot said. "I liked him."

"You like everyone, Taproot," I said. I licked my lips. "But he was a good man. I'm taking the monsters to Heimrift. Tell me about the mage there."

"Ferrakind," Taproot said. "A dangerous man, watch me! I've had pyromancers that trained with him. Not magicians, not much more than fire-eaters, flame-blowers, you could do as much with this stuff and a candle." He raised his glass again. "Smoke-and-spark men. I don't think he lets the good ones go. But all the ones I had were terrified of the man. You could end any argument with them just by saying his name. He's the real thing. Flame-sworn."

"Flame-sworn?" I asked.

"The fire is in him. In the end it will take him. He used to be a player. You know what I speak of, a player of men and thrones. But the fire took too much from him and we no longer interest him."

"I want his help," I said.

"And this is your offer?" Taproot tapped his wrist. I hadn't seen him so much as glance at my watch but it seemed he knew all about it.

"Perhaps. What else might interest him?" I asked.

Taproot pursed his lips. "He likes rubies. But I think he'll prefer your fire-patterned child. He may want to keep him, Jorg."

"I may want to keep him myself," I said.

"Going soft in your old age, Jorg?" Taproot asked. "Watch me! I knew a twelve-year-old hard as nails and twice as sharp. Perhaps you should leave the monsters with me. There's a good enough living to be made in the freak tent."

I stood. I hefted up the Nuban's bow. "Kashta, eh?"

"Even so," Taproot said.

"I must be on my way, Doctor," I said. "I have a bridge to cross."

"Stay," he said. "Learn to juggle?"

"I'll look around once more for old times," I said.

Taproot raised his hands. "A king knows his mind."

And I left.

"Good hunting." He said it to my back.

I wondered if he'd taken enough from me to sell at profit. I wondered at what some men can fit between their ears.

I walked past the dancers. They hadn't gone far.

"Remember me, Jorg?" Cherri smiled. The other struck a pose. They both followed Taproot's advice. Hips and tits.

"Of course I do." I sketched a bow. "But sadly, ladies, I'm not here to dance."

Cherri I remembered, lithe and pert, hair lightened with lemon and curled around hot tongs every morning, a snub nose and wicked eyes. They both closed on me, half-playful, half-serious, hands straying, warm breath and that gyration in the pelvis that speaks of want. Her friend, dark-haired, pale-skinned, and sculpted from fantasy, I did not recall, but wished I did.

"Come and play?" the friend murmured. She smelled money. Sometimes, though, reasons don't matter.

It's hard to pass up an offer like that when you're young and full of juice, but fourteen heads around a rock cairn were telling me to get a move on and I had taken what I needed here, almost.

I left them and slipped through an exit to the rear of the tent. In a clearing to the left I could see Thomas swallowing a sword, watched by a scatter of circus urchins. He hardly needed the practice but that was Thomas, a crowd pleaser. An odd breed, the gypsies and the talent, needing to live in the torch ring, only alive in grease-paint. I swear, some of them would fade and die given a week without applause.

Rumbles from the cages drew me. A stack of them on the east side of the camp where the wind would take some of the stink away. They still had the two bears I remembered, pacing their madness in tight circles, dull shaggy fur, the bronze nose-rings big enough to fit an arm. The huge turtle—Taproot claimed it to be two hundred years old—statue-still and as interesting as a big stone, not caged but tethered to a stake. The two-headed goat was a new addition, a sickly-looking thing, but then again it should have been a still-birth, so it was more healthy than anyone had a right to expect. Every now and then the heads would sight each other and startle as if surprised.

"See anything you like?" A soft voice behind me.

"I do now." I turned to face her. She looked good.

"Jorg," Serra said. "My sweet Jorg. A king no less."

I shrugged. "I never did know when to stop."

She smiled. "No." Dark and delicious.

"I saw Thomas back there, putting on a show," I said.

Serra pouted at the mention of her husband. "It never stops amazing me, how people want to watch us."

"That's why the circus keeps on moving," I said. "Everything gets old quick enough. The swallowing of swords, the blowing of fire, they're wonders for an evening or two . . ."

"And did I get old quick enough?" she asked. "King Jorg of the Highlands?"

"Never," I said. If the sins of the flesh ever got old I didn't ever want enough years on me to know it. "I've not found a girl to compare."

"Girl" may have been pushing it but she was a good ten years younger than Thomas, and who better than a circus con-tortionist to deliver a boy's first lessons in carnality?

Serra stepped closer, shawl tight around her shoulders against the chill of the breeze. She moved in that fluid way that reminds every watcher she can cross her ankles behind her head. Even so, on her cheeks, here and there, the white powder cracked, and around her eyes the unkind morning light found tiny wrinkles. She wore her hair still in ribbons and bunches, but now it looked wrong on her and a thread or two of silver laced the blackness of it.

"How many rooms does your palace have, Jorg?" A husk in her voice. A hint of something desperate at the back of her smile.

"Lots," I said. "Most of them cold, stony, and damp." I didn't want her to go begging and dirty up my golden memories. I didn't know what I'd come looking for around the circus camp; Taproot's stories for sure, but not now, not here in the messy reality behind the show-ring mask. I didn't know what I'd come for, but not this, not Serra showing her years and her need.

A moment's silence, then a growl came, too deep and throaty for a bear, like a giant rasp drawn across timber.

"What the—"

"Lion," Serra said. She twirled, brightening, and took my hand. "See?"

And around the corner, at the bottom of the cage stack, Dr. Taproot did indeed have himself a lion. I hefted the Nuban's bow to see the ironwork around the trigger guard. The beast in the cage might be a bit threadbare, showing too many ribs, but his dirty mane remembered the one framing the snarling face on the Nuban's bow.

"Well, there's a thing," I said. The Nuban had told me in his youth he walked scorched grasslands where lions hunted in packs, and even though the Nuban never lied, I only half-believed him. "There's a thing." Words failed me for once.

"He's called Macedon," Serra said, leaning into me. "The crowds love him."

"What else has Taproot got caged? I expect a griffin next, then a unicorn and a dragon, a full heraldic set!"

"Silly," she husked. Old or not, that magic of hers had started to work on me. "Dragons aren't real." The twitch of a smile in her painted lips, her small and kissable mouth.

I shook it off—the circus was too full of distractions. Distractions I wanted to make a full and thorough examination of. But I had ghosts at my heels and Gog about to burst into flame at any moment . . .

"He looks hungry," I said. "The circus can't feed its main attraction?"

"He won't eat," Serra said. "Taproot's tearing his hair about it. Doesn't know how long he'll last."

The lion watched us, sat sphinx-like with his massive paws spread in the straw before him. I met his huge amber eyes and wondered what he saw. Probably a hunk of meat on two legs not meant for running.

"He wants to hunt," I said.

"We give him meat," Serra said. "Ron cuts him big hunks of cow, still bleeding. He barely sniffs it."

"He needs to take it," I said. "Not be given it."

"That's silly." Her fingers ran along mine, starting fires.

"It's in his nature." I looked away. I didn't think I could win a staring competition with Macedon even if I had time to try.

"You should let him go," I said.

Serra laughed, a note too shrill for comfort. "And what would he hunt? We should let him eat children?"

A distant scream saved me answering. A distant scream and a tongue of flame reaching up above the tent tops. A dead cook-fire close by suddenly lit. The flame flared, sucked in like a drawn breath, and became a little man made all of fire, a homunculus no taller than a chicken. It glanced around for a heartbeat then tore off in the direction of the scream, leaving the fire-pit black and smoking and a line of charred footprints behind it.

Serra opened her mouth, ready to scream or shout, decided on neither, and took off after the flame-man.

My gaze returned to the lion, who seemed wholly unmoved by the excitement.

"Do you think Taproot will still want Gog in his freak-show now?" I asked.

The lion gave no answer, just watched me with those amber eyes.

The lions the Nuban had told me of were magnificent beasts, lords of the plains. He understood why men who had never seen one might fight beneath their likeness on a banner. When he spoke of lions on cold nights camped along the roadside, I had sworn to walk those same sun-scarred plains and see them for myself. I hadn't imagined them caged, mangy, hopping with fleas beside a two-headed goat.

A single nail pinned the cage door, secured with a twist of wire.

I had pulled a single pin to set the Nuban free years ago, worlds ago. I pulled a pin and he took two lives in as many moments.

That Jorg would have pulled this pin too. That Jorg would have pulled this pin and not given a moment's thought to children clustered around a sword-swallower, to the livelihoods of dancers and tumblers. To townsfolk or to Taproot's revenge. But I'm not him. I'm not him because we die a little every day and by degrees we're reborn into different men, older men in the same clothes, with the same scars.

I didn't forget the children or the dancers or the tumblers. But I pulled the pin. Because it's in my nature.

"For Kashta," I said.

I swung the door open and walked away. The lion would stay or leave, hunt or die, it didn't matter, but at least he had a choice. As for me, I had a bridge to cross.

I set off after Serra to see what damage Gog had done.

Brother Sim looks pleasing enough, a touch pretty, a touch delicate, but sharp with it. Under the dyes his hair is a blond that takes the sun, under the drugs his eyes are blue, under the sky I know no one more private in their ways, more secret in their opinions, more deadly in a quiet moment.

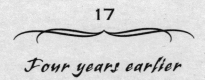

17

Four years earlier

When you journey north, past the River Rhyme, you start into the Danelands, those regions still unclaimed by the sea where the Vikings of old came ashore to conquer and then settle among the peoples who bowed before the axe. There are few Danes who will not claim Viking blood, but it's not until the sea bars your path that such claims take on weight and you start to feel yourself truly among the men of the wild and frozen north.

We crossed the bridge at Remagen leading our horses, for in places the metal weave of the deck had holes punched up through it, some the width of a spear, some wide enough to swallow a man. Nowhere did rust have a hold on the silver metal, and what had made the holes no one could say. I remembered the peasant in his house of gravestones back by Perechaise, unable to read a single legend from them. I shouldn't have sneered. We live in a world made from the Builders' graves and can read almost none of the messages they carry, and understand fewer still.

We left Remagen without trouble and rode hard along the

North Way so that trouble wouldn't catch us up if it followed. Farms, forests, villages untouched by war, good land to ride through with the sun on your back. It set me in mind of Ancrath, cottages golden with thatch, orchards in bloom, all so fragile, so easy to erase.

"Thank you for not burning up too much of the circus, Gog," I said.

"I'm sorry for the fire, Jorg," Gog said behind me.

"No great harm done," I said. "Besides, the stories they tell about it will bring more people to the show."

"Did you see the little men?" Gog asked.

"The midgets?" I asked.

His claws dug in. "My little men, from the fire."

"I saw them," I said. "It looked like they were trying to pull you in."

"Gorgoth stopped them," Gog said. I couldn't tell if he was happy or sad about that.

"You shouldn't go," I said. "You need to learn more. To know how to be safe. To know that you can come back. That's why we're going to Ferrakind. He can teach you these things."

"I think I've seen him," Gog said. At first I didn't think I'd heard right above the thud and clatter of hooves.

"I can look into one fire and see out of another," Gog said. "All sorts of things." He giggled at that and for a moment he sounded like William, laughing on the morning we climbed into that carriage.

"Did *he* see *you*?" I asked.

I felt him nod against my back.

"We'd best go on then," I said. "There's no hiding from him now. Best find out what he has to say."

We rode on and the rain started to fall, the kind of rain that comes and goes in the spring, cold and sudden and leaving the world fresh.

Heimrift lies in the Danelore, a hard ride from the Rhymelands. We made good speed and paced the season, caught in an unending wave of wakening, as if we carried the May with us.

Gorgoth ran beside me as often as not, tireless, pounding the road with great feet that seemed almost hooves. He spoke so seldom that it made you want him to, as if by storing each word he made it precious. I found him to be a deep thinker though he had never read a book or been taught by anyone.

"Why do you ask so much?" he asked once, his arms punching in and out like the great engine at York as he ran.

"The unexamined life is not worth living," I said.

"Socrates?"

"How in hell do you know that?" I asked.

"Jane," he said.

I grunted. She could have reached out from the dark halls of the leucrotas, that child, even without taking a step from the entrance caves. I had walked some of the paths she took, and the paths of the mind can take you anywhere.

"Who was she to you anyhow?" I asked.

"My eldest sister," he said. "Only two of us lived from my mother's line. The rest." He glanced at Gog. "Too strong."

"She was fire-sworn too?" I remembered the ghost-fire dancing across her.

"Fire-sworn, light-sworn, mind-sworn." Gorgoth's eyes narrowed to slits as he watched me. Jane died because of my actions, because of me, because I hadn't cared if she lived or not. Mount Honas had fallen on Jane and the necromancer both. The wrong one survived. I still owed Chella for the Nuban and other Brothers besides, but even my thirst for vengeance wouldn't see me digging in the burning wastes of Gelleth for her any time soon.

"Damnation!" It suddenly struck me that I should have asked Taproot about the Dead King. The excitement of the circus had somehow put him out of my mind. Given that a dozen and more severed heads had mouthed the Dead King's name at me, it's a tribute to the power of sawdust and grease-paint that they could push it out.

Gorgoth turned his head but didn't ask.

"Who's the Dead King?" I asked him. Gorgoth had enough dealings with the necromancers, and who better than necromancers to know about someone who speaks through corpses.

"*Who* he is I can't say." Gorgoth spoke in the rhythm of his running. "I can tell you something of *what* he is."

"Yes?"

"A new power, risen in the dry places beyond the veil, in the deadlands. He speaks to those that draw their strength there."

"He spoke to Chella?" I asked.

"To all the necromancers." A nod. "They did not want to listen, but he made them."

"How?" Chella struck me as a hard person to coerce.

"Fear."

I sat back in the saddle and chewed that one over. Gorgoth ran in silence, matching Brath's trot, and for the longest time I thought he wouldn't speak again. But then he said, "The Dead King talks to all who reach past death."

"So what should I do when he talks to me?"

"Run."

Gorgoth's sister had once given me the same advice. I resolved to take it this time.

We made good time and each evening I fought Makin, learning at every turn and occasionally teaching him a new trick. I taught him a new trick the very first day I met him, training squires in the Tall Castle. Since then, though, the process had seen a slow reversal. Somewhere along the line Makin turned from my rescuer, sent out by Father to recover me, into a follower, and ever since he decided to follow my lead the man had been teaching me. Not with books and charts like Tutor Lundist but in that sneaky, indirect way the Nuban had, the kind of way that gets under your skin and turns you slowly by example.

Four days out from Remagen a storm found us on the plains, a fierce cold squall carrying all the cruelty that spring can muster. Lashed by rain we found our way to the town of Endless by tracks turned to swollen streams. Some lordling undoubtedly calls Endless his own but whatever men he set to watch over it had found better things to watch that night. We clattered unopposed along the cobbled main street and found a stable by the glow of a single lantern hung behind the torrent spilling from its eaves. The stable-keep allowed that Gog and Gorgoth could stay with the horses. Taking the pair among the good folk of Endless would be an invitation to carnage.

"We'll be out of here at dawn," I told the stable-keep, a lean fellow, pockmarked, but along one side only, as if the pox had found no foothold on his right half. "Let me return to find gawkers here staring at my monsters and I'll have the big one twist your legs off. Understand?"

He understood.

We shed our sodden cloaks in some nameless tavern and sat steaming before a cold hearth while a serving girl fetched our ales. The place was packed with wet and sweating bodies, lumbermen in the main, some stinking drunk, others just stinking. We drew looks, not a few of them hostile, but none that lasted long when offered back.

Sim had his harp with him, a battered thing but quality, stolen from a very rich home once upon a time. He'd pulled it from his saddlebag and unwrapped it with the kind of care he usually reserved for weapons. As our drinks arrived he started to pluck a tune from it. He had quick fingers did Sim, quick and clever, and the notes rolled out fast enough to make a river.

By the time I left for my bed, in the inn across the road, the storm had passed. Sim and Makin had half the locals bawling out "Ten Kings," and Sim's voice, high and clear, followed me out of the door, rising over the deeper refrain and Makin's enthusiastic baritone. Strains of "The Shallow Lady" reached up through the window as I poked my way in under crawling blankets and let the bugs set to. At least it was dry. I fell asleep to the faint sounds of the nonsense doggerel "Merican Pie."

I woke much later in the calm dead hours of the night, still tangled in the song though all lay quiet save for the brothers' snoring.

Chevylevy was dry.

Moonlight reached across the room and offered me two figures in the doorway, one supporting the other. Makin stopped to close the door behind him. Sim hobbled on, something broken about his walking.

"Trouble?" I sat up, the ale still spinning in me.

My, my, missamerican pie.

Why two drunk brothers staggering in should spell trouble I couldn't have said, but I knew trouble was what we had.

Makin turned, pulling aside the hood on the lantern he'd brought up with him. "I found him in the street," he said. "Left him an hour ago with five locals, the last in the tavern."

Sim looked up. They'd given him a hell of a beating, lips

split and swollen, half a tooth gone, one eye full of blood. From the way he moved I guessed he'd be pissing pink for a week. In fact something in the way he moved suggested other kinds of hurt had been done to him.

"They took my harp, Brother." He turned out his empty hands. It had been a time and a half since Sim had called me Brother. I wondered what else had been taken.

I kicked Rike in the head. "Up!" Kent and Grumlow were already rising from the floor. "Get up," I said again.

"Trouble?" Kent asked, echoing my own question. He sat still in the dark, moonlight making black pits of his eyes. Always ready for trouble was Red Kent, though he never sought it out.

Grumlow found his feet quick enough and took Sim's arm. The boy flinched him off but Grumlow took firmer hold and led him to the window. "Bring the lantern, Makin, some stitches needed here."

"Five of them?" I asked.

Sim nodded as he passed me.

"I can't let this stand," I said.

Makin let the lantern drop an inch or two at that. "Jorg—"

"They took the harp," I said. "That's an insult to the Brotherhood." I let the pride of the Brotherhood take the slur: it would shame Sim to have this be for him.

Makin shrugged. "Sim cut at least one of them. There's a trail of blood in the street."

"Were they armed?" I asked. Know thy enemy.

Makin shook his head. "Knives. Probably have their wood-axes to hand by now. Oh, and the short one, he had a bow. Likes to do a bit of hunting he said."

My, my.

I threw the bundle of my blankets at Rike and made for the door. "Let's be about it then. You too, Brother Sim, you'll want to see this."

I let Rike go first into the street and followed, watching the dark windows, the lines of the rooftops. Makin found the trail of blood drops again, black in the cold light of the moon, and we followed, past the church, past the well, along the alley between tannery and stables, the dull rumble of Gorgoth's snore from within deeper than the snort of horses. Past a warehouse,

a low wall, and out into the rough pasture between town and
forest. We gathered with our backs to a barn, the last building
before the woods took over. No one had to be told—your enemy
has a bow, you keep a building at your back and don't let the
light silhouette you.

"They're in the forest," Grumlow said.

"They won't be far in." Makin set the lantern to one side,
its light hidden.

"Why not?" Grumlow asked, eyes on the black line of the
trees.

"The moon won't reach in there. Not a place to walk blind."
I lifted my voice loud enough for the men in the woods. "Why
don't you come out? We only want to talk."

An arrow hammered into the barn wall yards above my
head; laughter followed. "Send your girlfriend in after us if she
wants some more."

Grumlow took a step forward at that, but he wasn't dumb
enough to take another. Rike on the other hand took two and
would have taken more if I hadn't barked his name. It was Rike's
true brother, Price, who took young Sim from that Belpan
brothel in the long ago. Why he picked one child to save and
made red slaughter of the rest, along with the grown whores
and their master, none of the brothers could ever tell me, but it
seemed to matter to Rike that he had. And there it is, proof if
proof were needed, that though God may mould the clay and
fashion some of us hale, some strong, some beautiful, inside we
make ourselves, from foolish things, breakable, fragile things:
the thorns, that dog, the hope that Katherine might make me
better than I am. Even Rike's blunt wants were born of losses
he probably remembered only in dreams. All of us fractured,
awkward collages of experience wrapped tight to present a
defensible face to the world. And what makes us human is that
sometimes we snap. And in that moment of release we're closer
to gods than we know. I told Rike no, but hardly a part of me
didn't want to charge those woods.

"It'll have to keep for morning," Makin said.

I didn't like to admit it but he was right. I would have left
it there save for Gorgoth coming along the alley beside the
barn. A strange mix of clever and stupid, that one. He made a

nice target with the moon bright behind him, a big one too. I heard the hiss of an arrow and then his deep grunt.

"Here, idiot!" I called out to him and he lumbered to my side, Gog scampering around his legs. Makin lifted the lantern but I kept him from opening the hood. "He's not dead. He can wait."

"Take more than an arrow," Rike muttered.

Even so, light blossomed and we saw the shaft jutting from Gorgoth's shoulder, the head buried only an inch deep or so, as if the leucrota's flesh were oak.

"Makin! I said no—"

But it wasn't Makin. The light bled from Gog's eyes, hot and yellow.

I could have told Gog no, bundled him around a corner and left the woodsmen till morning, but the fire that burned in Gog at seeing Gorgoth harmed echoed a colder fire that lit in me when Sim hobbled through that door. I'd grown tired of saying no. Instead I took Gog's hand, though the ghosts of flame whispered across his skin.

He looked up at me, eyes white like stars. "Let it burn," I told him.

Something hot ran through me, up my arm, along the marrow of my bones, hot like a promise, anger made liquid and set running.

"What's cooking?" The taunt rang out from the tree-line, somewhere out past an old cowshed sagging in its beams.

Gog and I walked toward the sound, slow footsteps, the ground sizzling where his bare feet touched wet grass.

"The hell?" Voices raised in concern in the dark of the woods. An arrow zipped through the night, wide of its mark, the glowing child a disconcerting target, fooling the eye.

We heard the hissing before we'd gone ten yards, a thousand snakes hissing in the darkness . . . or perhaps just steam escaping the trees as their sap started to boil. A laugh bubbled from me in the same way, escaping my heat. The anger I brought with me ignited, becoming too large for my body, detaching from the men who hurt Sim and becoming an end in and of itself, all-consuming, a glorious laughing ecstasy of rage.

A skin of flame lifted from Gog, washing over me in a warm

wave. Back in the forest the first of the trees exploded, its fragments bursting into incandescent flame as they found air. Fire lifted around the intact trunks, rising through the spring foliage, making each leaf a momentary shadow. More trees exploded, then more, until the blasts became a continuous rumble of brilliant detonation. The cattle-shed ignited though it stood twenty yards back from the closest flame, one side of it just snapping into liquid orange fire. I saw a lone archer running from the edge of the forest, clothes alight. Farther back human torches staggered and fell.

That power, Brothers, is a drug. A fiercer joy than poppy-spice, and more sure to hollow you out. If Gorgoth hadn't knocked me aside and snatched up Gog we neither of us would have stopped until no tree remained, no board or beam of Endless. Maybe not even then.

Dawn found us still in the wet grass behind that barn, a smoking hole in the forest before us, acres wide. Gog went hunting amid the embers and returned with a twitching tangle, Sim's harp strings fused together and twisted by the heat. He took them with a curious smile, lopsided from his beating. "My thanks, Gog." He held them up and shook them so they rattled one against the next. "A simpler song, but still sweet."

And that was Endless.

We saw the smoke days from our goal, still skirting the borders of the Teuton kingdoms. A grey column reached miles into the sky, mountain high and higher still, as if Satan were trying to smoke the angels out of heaven.

The sight prompted Red Kent to curiosity. "What is a volcano, Jorg?"

"Where the earth bleeds," I told him. Sim and Grumlow rode in closer to hear. "Where its blood bubbles up. Molten rock, like lead melted for the siege, poured red and runny from the depths."

"It was a serious question." Kent turned his horse away, looking offended.

Days later we could smell the sulphur in the air. In places a fine black dust lay on the new leaves even as they unfurled, and stands of trees stood dead, acre after acre bare and brown, waiting for a summer fire.

You know you're entering the Dane-lore by the troll-stones. You start to see them at crossroads, then by streams, then in circles atop hills. Great blocks of stone set with the old runes, the Norse runes that remember dead gods, the thunder hammer and old one-eye who saw all and told little. They say the Danes choose one rock above another for troll-stones because they see the lines of a troll in some but not the next. All I can say is that trolls must look remarkably like chunks of rock in that case.

We hadn't seen so many troll-stones before a rider joined us on the road. He came from the south, setting a fast pace and slowing as he caught our band.

"Well met," he called, standing in his stirrups. A local man, hair braided in two plaits, each ending in a bronze cap worked with serpents, a round iron helm tight on his head and a fine moustache flowing into a short beard.

"Well met," I said as he drew level at the head of our column. He had a shortbow on his back, a single-bladed axe strapped to his saddlebags, a knife at his hip with a polished bone handle. He gave Gorgoth a wide berth. "You should follow me," he said.

"Why?"

"My lord of Maladon wishes to see you," he said. "And it would be easier this way, no?" He grinned. "I'm Sindri, by the way."

"Lead on," I said. A band of warriors probably watched us from the woods, and if not, Sindri deserved to be rewarded for his balls.

We followed him a couple of miles along a trail increasingly crowded with traffic, wheeled and on foot or hoof. Occasionally we heard a distant rumble, not unlike a giant version of the lion Taproot had caged, and the ground would tremble.

Sindri led us past two grey villages and brought us along the side of a narrow lake. When the mountains grumbled, the water rippled from shore to shore. The stronghold at the far end looked to be made of timber and turf with only the occasional block of stone showing above the foundations.

"The great hall of the Duke of Dane," Sindri said. "Alaric Maladon, twenty-seventh of his line."

Rike snorted behind me. I didn't bother to silence him. A voice was speaking at the back of my mind, just beyond hearing, a low moan or a howl . . . a stone face swam across my vision, a gargoyle face.

Men were gathered before the hall, some at work, others preparing for a patrol, each armed with axe and spear, carrying a large painted shield of painted wood and hide. Stable hands came to take our horses. As usual Gorgoth drew the stares. When we passed I heard men mutter, "Grendel-kin."

Sindri ushered us up the steps to the great hall's entrance. The whole place had a sorry look to it. The black dust coated everything with a fine film. It tickled the throat like a feather. The patrol horses looked thin and unkempt.

"The Duke wants to see us still wearing the road?" I asked, hoping for some hot water and a chair after so many miles in the saddle. A little time to prepare would be good too. I wanted to remember where I knew the name from.

Sindri grinned. Despite the beard, he hadn't too many years on me. "The Duke isn't one for niceties. We're not fussy in the northern courts. The summer is too short."

I shrugged and followed up the stairs. Two large warriors flanked the doorway, hands on the hafts of double-headed axes, their iron blades resting on the floor between their feet.

"Two of your party should be enough," Sindri said.

It never hurts to trust someone, especially when you've absolutely no other option. "Makin," I said.

Makin and I followed Sindri into the gloom and smoke of the great hall. The place seemed empty at first, long trestle tables of dark and polished wood, bare save for an abandoned flagon and a hambone. Wood-smoke and ale tempered the stink of dogs and sweat.

At the far end of the hall on a fur-strewn dais in a high oak chair a figure waited. Sindri led the way. I trailed my fingers along the table as we walked, feeling the slickness of the wood.

"Jorg and Makin," said Sindri to his lord. "Found heading north on your highway, Duke Alaric."

"Welcome to the Danelands," the Duke said.

I just watched him. A big man, white-blond hair and a beard down his chest.

The silence stretched.

"They have a monster with them," Sindri added, embarrassed. "A troll or Grendel-kin, big enough to strangle a horse."

In my mind a gargoyle howled. "You brought a snow-globe," I said.

The Duke frowned. "Do I know you, boy?"

"You brought a snow-globe, a toy of the ancients. And I broke it." It had been a rare gift, he would remember the globe, and perhaps the avarice with which a little boy had stared at it.

"Ancrath?" The Duke's frown deepened. "Jorg Ancrath?"

"The same." I made a bow.

"It's been a long time, young Jorg." Alaric stamped his foot and several of his warriors entered the hall from a room at the end. "I've heard stories about you. My thanks for not killing my idiot son." He nodded toward Sindri.

"I'm sure the tales have been over-told," I said. "I'm not a violent man."

Makin had to cover his mouth at that. Sindri frowned, looking rapidly from me to Makin and back at the Duke.

"So what brings you to the Danelands then, Jorg of Ancrath?" the Duke asked. No time wasted here, no wine or ale offered, no gifts exchanged.

"I'd like some friends in the north," I said. It hadn't been part of my thinking but once in a long while I like a man on sight. I'd liked Alaric Maladon on sight eight years earlier when he brought my mother a gift. I liked him now. "This place looks to have missed a harvest or two. Perhaps you need a friend in the south?"

"A plain speaker, eh?" I could see the grin deep in his beard. "Where's all your southern song and dance, eh? No 'prithees,' no 'beseeching after my health'?"

"I must have dropped all that somewhere on the way," I said.

"So what do you really want, Jorg of Ancrath?" Alaric asked. "You didn't ride five hundred miles to learn the axe-dance."

"Perhaps I just wanted to meet the Vikings," I said. "But prithee tell me what ails this land. I beseech you."

He laughed out loud at that. "Real Vikings have salt in their beard and ice on their furs," he said. "They call us *fit-firar*, land-men, and have little love for us. My fathers came here a long, long time ago, Jorg. I would rather they stayed by the sea. I may not have salt in my beard but it's in my blood. I've tasted it." He stamped again and a thickset woman with coiled hair brought out ale, a horn for him and two flagons for us. "When they bury me my son will have to buy the longboat and have it sailed and carted from Osheim. My neighbour had local men make his. Would have sunk before it got out of harbour, if it ever saw the ocean."

We drank our ale, bitter stuff, salted as if everything had to remind these folk of their lost seas. I set my flagon on the table and the ground shook, harder than any of the times before, as if I had made it happen. Dust sifted from the rafters, caught here and there by sunlight spearing through high windows.

"Unless you can tame volcanoes, Jorg, you'll not find much to be done for Maladon," Alaric said.

"Can't Ferrakind send them to sleep for you?" I asked. I'd read that volcanoes slept, sometimes for a lifetime, sometimes longer.

Alaric raised a hairy brow at that. Behind us, Sindri laughed. "Ferrakind stirs them up," he said. "Gods rot him."

"And you let him live?" I asked.

The Duke of Maladon glanced at his fireplace as if an enemy might be squatting there among the ashes. "There's no killing a fire-mage, not a true one. He's like summer-burning in a dry forest. Stamp out the flames and they spring back up from the hot ground."

"Why does he do it?" I knocked back the last of my salt beer and grimaced. Almost as bad as the absinthe.

"It's his nature." Alaric shrugged. "When men look too long into the fire it looks back into them. It burns out what makes them men. I think he speaks with the jötnar behind the flames. He wants to bring a second Ragnarök."

"And you're going to let him?" I asked. I cared little enough for jötnar, or any other kind of spirit. Push far enough past anything, be it fire or sky or even death, and you'll find the creatures that have always dwelt there. Call them what you will. "I heard tell there was no problem that a Dane couldn't cut through with an axe." It's a dangerous business questioning a man's courage in his own hall, especially a Viking's, but if ever a place needed shaking up then this was it.

"Meet him before you judge us, Jorg," Alaric said. He sipped from his ale horn.

I had expected a more heated response, perhaps a violent one. The Duke looked tired, as if something had burned out of him too.

"In truth I came to meet him," I said.

"I'll take you," Sindri said, without hesitation.

"No." His father, just as fast.

"How many sons do you have, Duke Maladon?" I asked.

"You see him." Alaric nodded to Sindri. "I had four born alive. The eldest three burned in the Heimrift. You should go home, Jorg Ancrath. There's nothing for you in the mountains."

18

Four years earlier

Sindri caught us up before we'd got five miles from his father's hall. I'd left Makin with Duke Alaric. Makin had a way with the finding of common ground and the building of friendships. I left Rike too, because he would only moan about climbing mountains and because if anyone could show the Danes true berserker spirit it was Rike. I left Red Kent also, for his Norse blood on his father's side and because he wanted a good axe made for him.

"Well met," I said as Sindri rode up between the pines. It had never been in doubt that he would give chase. He found us as we left the lower slopes and thick forest behind.

"You need me," he said. "I know these mountains."

"We do need you," I said.

Sindri grinned. He took off his helm and wiped the sweat from his brow, blowing hard from the ride. "They say you destroyed half of Gelleth," he said. He looked doubtful.

"Closer to a fifth," I said. "Legends grow in the telling."

Sindri frowned. "How old are you?"

I felt the Brothers stiffen. It can be annoying to always have the people around you think you're going to murder everyone who looks at you wrong. "I'm old enough to play with fire," I said. I pointed to the largest of the mountains ahead. "That one's a volcano. The smoke gives it away. What about the rest?"

"That's Lorgholt. Three others have spoken in my lifetime," Sindri said. "Loki, Minrhir, and Vallas." He pointed them out in turn. Vallas had the faintest wisps of smoke or steam rising from its western flanks. "In the oldest eddas the stories tell of Halradra being the father and these four his sons." Sindri pointed to the low bulk of Halradra. "But he has slept for centuries."

"Let's go there then," I said. "I'd like to watch a sleeping giant before I poke a woken-up one."

"These aren't people, Jorg," Makin had told me before we left. "They're not enemies. You can't fight them."

He didn't know what I thought I could achieve wandering the landscape. I didn't either but it always pays to have a look around. If I think back on my successes, such as they are, they come as often as not from the simple exercise of putting two disparate facts together and making a weapon of them. I destroyed Gelleth with two facts that when laid one atop the other, made something dangerous. There's a thing like that at the heart of the Builders' weapons, two chunks of magic, harmless enough on their own but forming some critical mass when pushed together.

The Halradra is not so tall as its sons, but it is tall. Its lower slopes are softened by the years, black grit in the main, crunching under hoof, the rocks rotten with bubbles so that you can crumble them in your hands, the fire so long gone that no sniff of it remains. Through the ash and broken rock, fire-weed grew in profusion, Rosebay Willowherb as they had it in Master Lundist's books. The first to spring up where the fire has been. Even after four hundred years nothing much else wanted to push its way through the black dirt.

"Do you see them?" Gorgoth rumbled at my shoulder. The depth of his voice took me by surprise as always.

"If by 'them' you mean mountains, then yes. Otherwise, no."

He pointed with one thick finger, almost the width of Gog's forearm. "Caves."

I still didn't see them, but in the end I did. Cave mouths at the base of a sharp fall. Not that dissimilar from Gorgoth's old home beneath Mount Honas.

"Yes," I said. "They are." I thought that sometimes perhaps Gorgoth should just keep holding on to those precious words.

We pressed on. Higher up and the going gets too steep and too treacherous for horses. We left our mounts with Sim and Grumlow, continuing on foot, trudging on through a thin layer of icy snow. The peaks of Halradra's sons look broken off, jagged, forged with violence. The old man could pass as a common mountain with no hint of a crater until you scramble up through snow-choked gullies and find the lake laid out before you, sudden and without announcement.

"Happy now?" Sindri climbed up beside me and found a perch where the wind had taken the snow from a rock. He looked happy enough himself despite his tone.

"It's a sight and a half, isn't it?" I said.

Gorgoth clambered up with Gog on his shoulder.

"I like this mountain," Gog said. "It has a heart."

"The lake is a strange blue," I said. "Is the water tainted?"

"Ice," Sindri said. "The water's just meltwater, a yard deep if that, run down off the crater slope. The lake stays frozen all year, underneath."

"Well now. There's a thing," I said. And I had two facts by the corners.

We hunkered down in the lee of some rocks a little way below the crater rim and watched the strange blue of those waters as we ate a cold meal from Alaric's kitchens.

"What kind of heart does the mountain have, Gog?" I threw chicken bones down the slope and licked the grease from my fingers.

He paused, closing his eyes to think. "Old, slow, warm."

"Does it beat?" I asked.

"Four times," Gog said.

"Since we started climbing?"

"Since we saw the smoke as we rode in from the bridge," Gog said.

"Eagle." Row pointed into the hazy blue above us. He reached for his bow.

"Good eyes as always, Row." I held his arm. "Let the bird fly."

"So," said Sindri, huddled, braids flailing in the wind. "What next?"

"I'd like to see those caves," I said. Gorgoth's observation felt more important all of a sudden. Precious even.

We started to make our way down, strangely a more difficult proposition than the climb, as if Halradra wanted to keep hold of us. The rock seemed to crumble under every heavy downhill step, with the ice to help any faller on his way. I caught Sindri at one turn, grabbing his elbow as the ground broke away under his heel.

"Thanks," he said.

"Alaric wouldn't be pleased to lose another son up here," I said.

Sindri laughed. "I would have stopped at the bottom."

Gorgoth followed, kicking footholds for himself at each step; Gog scampered free rather than risk getting squashed if the giant fell.

We found Sim and Grumlow sharing a pipe, sprawled on the rocks in the sunshine all at ease.

The caves were almost harder to see as we drew closer. Black caves in a black cliff with black interiors. I spotted three entrances, one big enough to grow an oak in.

"Something lives here," Gorgoth said.

I looked for signs, bones or scat around the cave mouth. "There's nothing," I said. "What makes you say there is?"

Expressions came hard to a face like Gorgoth's, but enough of the ridges and furrows moved to let a keen observer know that something puzzled him. "I can hear them," he said.

"Keen ears and keen eyes. I can't hear anything. Just the wind." I stopped and closed my eyes as Tutor Lundist taught me, and let the wind blow. I let the mountain noises flow through me. I counted away the beat of my heart and the sigh of breath. Nothing.

"I hear them," Gorgoth said.

"Let's go careful then," I said. "Time for your bow, Brother Row, good thing you didn't waste an arrow on that bird."

We tethered the horses and made ready. I took my sword in hand. Sindri unslung the axe from his back, a fine weapon with silver-chased scrollwork on the blade behind the cutting edge. And we moved in closer. I led in from downwind, an old habit that cost us half an hour traversing the slopes. From fifty yards the wind brought a hint of the inhabitants, an animal stink, faint but rank. "Our friends keep a clean front doorstep," I said. "Not bears or mountain cats. Can you still hear them, Gorgoth?"

He nodded. "They're talking about food, and battle."

"Curiouser and curiouser," I said. I could hear nothing.

We came by slow steps to the great cave mouth flanked by two smaller mouths and several cracks a man might slip through. Standing before the cave it seemed impossible that I had missed it from across the slopes. Apart from one shattered bone wedged between two rocks there was no sign of habitation. Except for the stink.

Gorgoth stepped in first. He carried a crude flail in his belt, just three thick chains on a wooden haft, set with twists of sharp metal. A leather apron kept the chains from shredding his legs as he ran. I'd never seen him take the weapon in hand, and somehow he seemed more scary unarmed. Gog walked behind Gorgoth with Sindri and me to flank him, then Sim and Grumlow, Row at the rear eyeing everything with suspicion.

"We can't go far," Row said. "Too dark." He didn't sound upset.

Gog lifted his hand and flames sprung from his fingertips. Row stifled a curse.

I looked back out across the mountain slopes. The fan of rocks and dirt spreading from the cave mouth reminded me of something. Random thoughts scratched each other at the back of my mind, fighting for form, for the words to say what they meant.

"We'll go on in," I said. "A little way. I want to hear what Gorgoth hears." He'd been right about the caves after all.

Toward the back of the cavern several tunnels led into the mountain. The larger passage led up at a shallow gradient. "That one."

We moved in. Underfoot the tunnel lay grit-floored, strewn with small rocks, but the walls were smooth, almost slick. The shadows moved and danced as Gog followed Gorgoth, his burning hand throwing a vast shadow-Gorgoth ahead of us. Fifty yards brought us to an almost spherical chamber with the tunnel leading on behind it, now heading up almost as steeply as the slopes outside. The fire glow gave the place memories of the cathedral at Shartres, our shadows processing over smooth rock on every side.

"Plato came to such a cave," I said. "And saw the whole world on its walls."

"Your pardon?" Sindri said.

I shook my head. "See here?" I pointed to a slick depression in the rock close by, as if a giant had sunk his thumb into soft mud and left his imprint.

"What is it?" Gog asked.

"I don't know," I said. But it looked familiar. Like a pothole in a riverbed.

I ran across to the tunnel at the back and stood at the entrance. Men didn't make these passages, nor troll or Grendel-kin, goblin, pixie or ghost. The air sat almost still, but moved even so, crawling from the tunnel. Cold air. Very cold.

"Jorg," Row said.

"I'm thinking," I said, not looking back.

"Jorg!" he said again.

And I turned. In the mouth of the tunnel through which we had come stood two trolls. I called them trolls to myself because they looked like the trolls of my imagination, not the rocky lumps the Danes decorated the landscape with, but lean dangerous creatures, dark-stained hide, muscles like knots in rope, laid along long limbs that ended in black talons. Crouched as they were their height was hard to judge, but I guessed eight feet, maybe nine. They moved with quick purpose, hugging the stone.

"Keep the arrow," I told Row. I couldn't see one arrow slow-ing either of them down unless it went in the neck or eye.

I would have called them monsters, leucrota, mistakes like Gorgoth, except that there were two of them. A pair speaks of design rather than accident.

"Hello," I said. It sounded stupid, one thin voice in that great chamber, but I could think of nothing else to say, and fighting them just didn't appeal. The only comfort to be taken was that both those pairs of black eyes were fixed on Gorgoth rather than me.

"Can't you hear them?" Gorgoth asked.

"No," I said.

The leftmost troll leapt forward without the preamble of feints or growling. He threw himself at Gorgoth, reaching for his face. Gorgoth caught the troll's wrists and stopped him dead. Both monsters stood, locked together, leaning in, muscles writhing and twitching. The troll's breath escaped in quick rasps. Gorgoth rumbled. I hadn't seen him struggle with anything since he held the gate up at the Haunt. Every task since then, be it unloading barrels, shifting rocks, anything, hadn't so much as raised a sweat.

Row lifted his bow again. For the second time I caught his arm. "Wait."

They held each other, straining, the occasional swift readjustment of feet. Troll claws gouging the rock. Gorgoth's blunt toes anchoring his weight. Muscle heaped against muscle, bones creaking with the strain, spit flecking at their lips as harsh breaths escaped. Moments stretched until they felt like minutes. My own nails bit into my palm, white knuckles on sword hilt; something had to give, something. And without warning the troll slammed into the floor, a beat of silence and Gorgoth let out a deep roar that hurt my chest and set Row's nose bleeding.

Gorgoth heaved in a breath. "They will serve," he said.

"What?" I said, then, "Why?

The troll on the floor rolled over and got to its feet, backing to its companion.

"They are soldiers," he said. "They want to serve. They were made for it."

"Made?" I asked, still watching the trolls, ready to try to defend myself.

"It has been written in their dena," Gorgoth said.

"By Ferrakind?"

"A long time ago," Gorgoth said. "They are a race. I don't know when they were changed."

"The Builders made them?" I asked, wondering.

"Maybe then. Maybe after." Gorgoth shrugged.

"They are Grendel's children," Sindri said. He looked as if he thought he was dreaming. "Made for war in the ashes of Ragnarök. They're waiting here for the final battle."

"Do they know what made these tunnels?" I asked. "And where they lead?"

Gorgoth paused. "They know how to fight," he said.

"That's good too." I grinned. "You're talking to them in your head, aren't you?"

Gorgoth managed surprise again. "Yes," he said. "I suppose I am."

"What now?" Sindri said, still looking from one troll to the other, testing the edge of his axe with his fingers.

"We go back," I said. I needed to muse and musing is more comfortable under a duke's roof than on a windswept volcano or buried in fetid caves.

"Gorgoth, tell the trolls we'll be back and to keep our visit to themselves." I looked the pair over one more time. I wondered what kind of havoc they'd wreak on a battlefield. The best kind, I thought.

"Let's go back," I said. *And see if our perspectives have changed any after our climb.*

19

Four years earlier

The forests in the Danelore have a character all their own, dense pines that make a perpetual twilight of the day and an ink-black soup of each night, moon or no. Old needles deaden every footfall and hoof, leaving the dry scratchings of dead branches the only sound. In such a place it takes no leap of imagination to believe every goblin tale of the long-hall. And in breaking clear once more into open air you understand that it was with the wood-axe man claimed these lands, not the battleaxe.

We came back to Duke Alaric's hall early with the cocks crowing and every shadow stretching itself out over the grass as if to point the way. A ground mist still hung in shreds around the trees, swirling where the horses stepped. A few servants were on the move, to and fro between the great hall and the kitchens, stable-boys getting horses ready to ride, a baker up from the nearby village with warm loaves heaped on his cart.

Two lads from the stables took our horses. I gave Brath a slap on his haunch as they led him off. A light rain started to fall. I didn't mind.

The rain made the stonework glisten, falling heavier by the moment. There's a word. *Glisten*. Silver chains on holy trees, the gloss on lips for kissing, dew on spiderwebs, sweat on breasts. Glisten, glisten, listen. Say it until the meaning bleeds away. Even without meaning it stays true. The rain made the grey stone glisten. Not quite a sparkle, not quite a gleam, but a glisten to the soaked cobbles, a gurgle from gutters where the dirt ran and leaves twirled in fleeting rapids, bound for dark and hungry throats, swallowed past stone teeth. A piece of straw ran by my feet, arrowing the straightest path; a kayak on white water, it bobbed, plunged, surged, reached the drain, spun twice, and was gone.

Sometimes the world slows and you notice every small thing, as if you stood between two beats of eternity's heart. It seemed to me I had felt something similar before, with Corion, with Sageous, even Jane. The air hung heavy with the metallic scent of rain. I wondered: if I stood out there, in the flood, would the rain wrap a grey life and make it shine? Should I stand, arms spread, and raise my face? Let it wash me clean. Or did my stains run too deep?

I listened to the fall of it, to the drumming, the drip, the pitter, and the patter. The others moved around me, handing over reins, taking saddlebags, the business of living, as if they hadn't noticed me step outside such things. As if they couldn't sense her.

Rike stumbled from the great hall, rubbing sleep from his eyes.

"Christ, Rike," I said. "We've been gone a day. How did you grow a beard?"

He shrugged, rubbing at stubble near deep enough to lose his fingers in. "When in Roma."

I ignored his bad geography and the fact that he even knew the phrase, and asked the more obvious question. "Why are you up?" On the road Rike always came last from his bed-roll and would never rise without some kind of threat or enticement.

He scratched his head at that. Sindri came back from the stables and clapped a hand on my shoulder. "He'll look good with a beard. We'll make a Viking of him yet!"

Rike frowned. "She said to meet her at the end of the lake."

"Who said?"

He frowned again, shrugged, and went back into the hall.

I looked out across the lake. At the far end, faint through the grey veils of rain, a tent stood, a yurt, yellowed with age, a thin line of smoke escaping through the smoke-hole. The strangeness came from there. That was where she waited.

Sindri looked too. "That's Ekatri, a völva from the north. She doesn't come often. Twice when I was young."

"Völva?" I asked.

"She knows things. She can see the future," Sindri said. "A witch. Is that what you call them?" He frowned. "Yes, a witch. You'd best go to her. Wouldn't do to keep her waiting. Maybe she'll read your future for you."

"I'll go now," I said. Sometimes you wait and watch, sometimes you walk right on in. There's not much to learn from the outside of a tent.

"I'll see you inside." Sindri nodded to the hall, grinned, and wiped the rain from his beard. He'd be waking his father before I got to the end of the lake, telling him about the trolls and Gorgoth. What would the good duke make of all that? I wondered. Perhaps the witch would tell me.

The ground trembled once as I walked along the lake, setting the water dancing. I could smell the smoke from the witch's tent now. It put an acrid taste in my mouth and reminded me of the volcanoes. The wind picked up, blowing rain into my face.

Old Tutor Lundist once taught me about seers, soothsayers, and the star-watchers who count out our lives by the slow predictions of planets rolling over the heavens. "How many words would be needed to tell the tale of your life?" he had asked. "How many to reach this point, and how many more to reach the end?"

"Lots?" I grinned and glanced away, out the narrow window to the courtyard, the gates, the fields beyond city walls. I had the twitchies in my feet, eager to be off chasing some or other thing while the sun still shone.

"This is our curse." Lundist stamped and rose from his chair with a groan. "Man is doomed to repeat his mistakes time and again because he learns only from experience."

He smoothed out an old scroll across the desk, covered in

the pictograms of his homeland. It had pictures too, bright and interesting in the eastern style. "The zodiac," he said.

I put my finger on the dragon, caught in a few bold strokes of red and gold. "This one," I said.

"Your life is laid out from the moment of your birth, Jorg, and you don't get to choose. All the words of your story can be replaced by one date and place. Where the planets hung in that instant, how they turned their faces, and which of them looked toward you . . . that configuration forms a key and that key unlocks all that a man will be," he said.

I couldn't tell if he was joking. Lundist was always a man for enquiry, for logic and judging, for patience and subtlety. All that felt rather pointless if we walked a fixed path from the cradle to whatever end was written in stars.

I'd reached the yurt without noticing. I made an abrupt stop and managed not to walk into it. I circled for the entrance and ducked through without announcement. She was supposed to know the future after all.

"Listen," she said as I pushed through the flap into her tent, a stinking place of hides and hanging dead things.

"Listen," she said again as I made to open my mouth.

So I sat cross-legged beneath the dangling husks, and listened and didn't speak.

"Good," she said. "You're better than most. Better than those bold, noisy boys wanting so much to be men, wanting only to hear the words from their own mouths."

I listened to the dry wheeze of her as she spoke, to the flap and creak of the tent, the insistence of the rain, and the complaints of the wind.

"So you listen, but do you hear?" she asked.

I watched her. She wore her years badly and the gloom couldn't hide it. She watched me back with one eye; the other sat sunken and closed in the grey folds of her flesh. It leaked something like snot onto her cheek.

"You should look better after ninety winters," she sneered. She needed just the one eye to read my expression. "The first fifty, hard ones in the lands of fire and ice where the true Vikings live."

I would have guessed two hundred just from looking at her, from the slide of her face, the crags, warts, and wattles. Only her eye seemed young, and that disappointed me for I'd come to seek wisdom.

"I hear," I said. I held my questions because folk only came to her with questions. If she truly knew the answers then perhaps I didn't need to ask.

She reached into the layered rags and furs around her waist. The stench increased immediately and I struggled not to choke. When her hand emerged, more a bone claw than supple fingers, it clutched a glass jar, the contents sloshing. "Builder-glass," she said, wetting her lips with a quick pink tongue, somehow obscene in her withered mouth. She cradled the flask in her hands. "How did we lose the art? There's not a man you could reach with five weeks of riding that could make this now. And if I dropped it a finger's width onto stone . . . gone! A thousand worthless pieces."

"How old?" I asked. The question escaped me despite my resolution.

"Ten centuries, maybe twelve," she said. "Palaces have crumbled in that time. The statues of emperors lie ruined and buried. And this . . ." She held it up. An eye made slow rotations in the greenish swirl. "Still whole."

"Is it your eye?" I asked.

"The very same." She watched me with her bright one and set the other on the rug in its Builder flask.

"I sacrificed it for wisdom," she said. "As Odin did at Mimir's well."

"And did you get wisdom?" I asked. An impertinent question perhaps from a boy of fourteen but she had asked to see me, not I her, and the longer I sat there, the smaller and older she looked.

She grinned, displaying a single rotting tooth-stump. "I discovered it would have been wise to leave my eye next to the other one." The eye came to rest at the bottom of the jar, aimed slightly to my left.

"I see you have a baby with you," she said.

I glanced to my side. The baby lay dead, brains oozing from his broken skull, not much blood but what there was lay shockingly red on his milk-white scalp. He seldom looked so clear, so real, but Ekatri's yurt held the kind of shadows that invited ghosts. I said nothing.

"Show me the box." She held out her hand.

I took it from its place just inside my breastplate. Keeping a tight grip I held it out toward her. She reached for it, quicker than an old woman has a right to be, and snatched her hand back with a gasp. "Powerful," she said. Blood dripped from her fingers, welling from a dozen small puncture wounds. The fact that there was blood to spill in those bony old fingers surprised me.

I put the box back. "I should warn you that I'm not taken with horoscopes and such," I told her.

She licked her lips again and said nothing.

"If you must know, I'm a goat," I said. "That's right, a fecking goat. There's a whole nation of people behind the East Wall who say I was born in the year of the goat. I've no time for any system that has me as a goat. I don't care how ancient their civilization is."

She gave the flask a gentle swirl. "It sees into other worlds," she said, as if I hadn't spoken at all.

"That's good then?" I said.

She tapped her living eye. "This one sees into other worlds too," she said. "And it has a clearer view." She took a leather bag from within her rags and set it by the jar. "Rune stones," she said. "Maybe if you go east and climb over the great wall you will be a goat. Here in the north the runes will tell your story."

I kept my lips tight shut, remembering my pledge at last. She would tell me about the future or she wouldn't. What she told me without questions to answer might be true.

She took a handful from the bag, grey stones clacking soft against each other. "Honorous Jorg Ancrath." She breathed my name into the stones, then let them fall. It seemed that they took a lifetime to reach the rug, each making its slow turns, end to end, side to side, the runes scored across them appearing and reappearing. They hit like anvils. I can feel the shake of it even now. It echoes in these bones of mine.

"The Perth rune, *initiation*," she said. "Thurisaz. Uruz, *strength*." She poked them aside as if they were unimportant. She turned a stone over. "Wunjo, *joy*, face down. And here, Kano, the rune of *opening*."

I set a finger to Thurisaz and the völva sucked a sharp breath over grey gums. She scowled and batted at my hand to move it, the stone cold to touch, the witch's hand colder, thin skin like paper. She hadn't spoken the rune's name in the empire tongue but I knew the old speech of the north from Lundist's books.

"The thorns," I said.

She flapped at me again and I withdrew my hand. Her fingers passed swiftly over the rest, counting. She swept them all away and poured them back onto the others still in the bag. "There are arrows ahead of you," she said.

"I'm going to be shot?"

"You will live happy if you don't break the arrow." She picked up the flask and stared one eye into the other. She shivered. "Open your gates." In her other hand the Wunjo rune stone, as if she hadn't put it into the bag. *Joy.* She turned it over, blank side up. "Or don't."

"What about Ferrakind?" I asked. I wasn't interested in arrows.

"Him!" She spat a dark mess into her furs. "Don't go there. Even you should know that, Jorg, with your dark heart and empty head. Don't go anywhere near that man. He burns."

"How many stones do you have in that bag, old woman?" I asked. "Twenty? Twenty-five?"

"Twenty-four," she said, and laid her claw on the bag, still bleeding.

"That's not so many words to tell the story of a man's life," I said.

"Men's lives are simple things," she said.

I felt her hands on me, even though one lay on the bag and the other held the flask. I felt them pinching, poking, reaching in to pick through my memories. "Don't," I said. I let the necromancy rise in me, acid at the back of my throat. The dead things above us twisted, a dry paw twitched, the black twist of a man's entrails crackled as it flexed, snake-like.

"As you please." Again that pink tongue flicking over her lips, and she stopped.

"Why did you come here, Ekatri?" I asked. I surprised myself by finding her name. People's names escape me. Probably because I don't care about them.

Her eye found mine, as if seeing me for the first time. "When I was young, young enough for you to want me, Jorg of Ancrath, oh yes; when I was young the runes were cast for me. Twenty-four words are not enough to tell all of a woman's story, especially when one of them is wasted on a boy she would have to grow old waiting for. I called you here because I was told to long ago, even before your grandmothers quickened."

She spat again, finding the floor-hides this time.

"I don't like you, boy," she said. "You're too . . . prickly. You use that charm of yours like a blade, but charming doesn't work on old witches. We see through to the core, and the core of you is rotten. If there's anything decent left in there, then it's buried deeper than I care to look and probably doomed. But I came because the runes were cast for me, and they said I should do the same for you."

"Fine words from a hag that smells as though she died ten years back and just hasn't had the decency to stop wittering," I said. I didn't like the way she looked at me, with either eye, and insulting her didn't make me feel better. It made me feel fourteen. I tried to remember that I called myself a king and stopped my fingers wandering over the dagger at my hip. "So why would your runes send you to annoy me if there's no chance for me then, old woman? If I'm a lost cause?"

She shrugged, a shifting of her rags. "There's hope for everyone. A slim hope. A fool's hope. Even a gut-shot man has a fool's hope."

I almost spat at that, but royal spit might actually have improved the place. Besides, witches can work all manner of mischief with a glob of your phlegm and a strand of your hair. Instead I stood and offered the smallest of bows. "Breakfast awaits me, if I can find my appetite again."

"Play with fire and you'll get burned," she said, almost a whisper.

"You make a living out of platitudes?" I asked.

"Don't stand before the arrow," she said.

"Capital advice." I backed toward the exit.

"The Prince of Arrow will take the throne," she said through tight-pressed lips, as if it hurt to speak plainly. "The wise have known it since before your father's father was born. Skilfar told me as much when she cast my runes."

"I was never one for fortune-telling." I reached the flap and pushed it aside.

"Why don't you stay?" She patted the hides beside her, tongue flicking over dry lips. "You might enjoy it." And for a heartbeat Katherine sat there in the sapphire satin of the dress she wore in her chamber that night. When I hit her.

I ran at that. I pelted through the rain chased by Ekatri's laughter, my courage sprinting ahead of me. And my appetite did not return for breakfast.

While others ate I sat in the shadows by a cold hearth and rocked back upon my chair. Makin came across, his fist full of cold mutton on the bone, grey and greasy. "Find anything interesting?" he asked.

I didn't answer but opened my hand. Thurisaz, the thorns. It's no great feat to steal from a one-eyed woman. The stone ate the shadow and gave back nothing, the single rune slashed black across it. The thorns. My past and future resting on my palm.

20

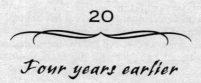

Four years earlier

Makin works a kind of magic with people. If he spends even half an hour in their company they will like him. He doesn't need to do anything in particular. There don't appear to be any tricks involved and he doesn't seem to try. Whatever he does is different each time but the result is the same. He's a killer, a hard man, and in bad company he will do bad things, but in half of one hour you will want him to be your friend.

"Good morning, Duke Maladon," I said as his axemen showed me into the great hall.

I squeezed the rain from my hair. Makin sat in a chair a step below the Duke's dais. He'd just passed a flagon up to Maladon, and sipped small beer from his own as I approached. You could believe they had sat like this every morning for ten years.

"King Jorg," the Duke said. To his credit he didn't hesitate to call me king though I stood dripping in my road-rags.

The hall lay in shadow, despite the grey morning fingering its way through high windows and the lamps still burning on every other pillar. On his throne Alaric Maladon cut an impressive figure. He could have been drawn from the legends out of dawn-time.

"I hope Makin hasn't been boring you with his tales. He is given to some outrageous lies," I said.

"So you didn't push your father's Watch-master over a waterfall?" the Duke asked.

"I may—"

"Or behead a necromancer and eat his heart?"

Makin wiped foam from his moustache and watched one of the hounds gnaw a bone. All the Brothers seemed to be hard at work on facial hair. I think the Danes made them feel inadequate.

"Not everything he says is a lie. But watch him," I said.

"So did Ekatri have warm words for you?" the Duke asked. No dancing around the issue with these northmen.

"Isn't that supposed to be between me and her? Isn't it bad luck to tell?"

Alaric shrugged. "How would we know if she was any use if nobody ever told what she said?"

"I think she passed on a hundred-year-old message telling me to lie down and let the Prince of Arrow have his way with my arse."

Makin snorted into his beer at that and some of the northmen grinned, though it's hard to tell behind a serious beard.

"I've heard something similar," Alaric said. "A soothsayer from the fjords, ice in his veins and a way with the reading of warm entrails. Told me the old gods and the white Christ all agreed. The time for a new emperor has come and he will spring from the seed of the old. The whisper among the Hundred is that these signs point to Arrow."

"The Prince of Arrow can kiss my axe," Sindri said. I'd not seen him in the shadows behind his father's guards.

"You've not met him, son," Alaric said. "I'm told he makes an impression."

"So how will your doors stand, Duke of Maladon, if the Prince comes north?" I asked.

The Duke grinned. "I like you, boy."

I let the "boy" slide.

"I've always thought that the blood of empire pooled in the north," Alaric said. "I always thought that a Dane-man should take the empire throne, by axe and fire, and that I might be the man to do it." He took a long draft from his flagon and raised a bushy brow at me. "How would your gates stand if the Prince came calling one fine morning?"

"That, my friend, would depend on quite how fine a morning it was. But I've never liked to be pushed, especially not by soothsayers and witches, not by the words of dead men, not by predictions based on the invisible swing of planets, scratched out on number slates or teased from the spilled guts of an unfortunate sheep," I said.

"On the other hand," Alaric said, "these predictions are very old. The new emperor's path has been prepared for a hundred years and more. Perhaps this Prince of Arrow is the one they speak of."

"Old men make old words holy. I say old words are worn out and should be set aside. Take a new bride to bed, not a hag," I said, thinking of Ekatri. "A fool may scrawl on a slate and if no one has the wit to wipe it clean for a thousand years, the scrawl becomes the wisdom of ages."

Nodding among the warriors, more grins. "Ekatri's message came from Skilfar in the north." That wiped the smiles away quick enough.

Alaric spat into the rushes. "An ice witch in the north, a fire-mage on our doorstep. Vikings were born in the land of ice and fire, and found their strength opposing both. Write your own story, Jorg."

I liked the man. Let the hidden players reach to move the Duke of Maladon across the board and they might find themselves short of several fingers.

The floor shook, a vibration that put a buzz in my teeth and held us all silent until it had passed. The lamps didn't swing but jittered on their hooks and the shadows blurred.

"And how did you find the Heimrift?" Alaric asked.

"I liked it well enough," I said. "Mountains have always pleased me."

In the wide hearth beside us the heaped ash of last night's fire smoked gently. It reminded me of Mount Vallas with the fumes rising from its flanks.

"And are you ready to seek out Ferrakind?" Alaric asked.

"I am," I said. I had the feeling that Ferrakind would be seeking me out soon enough if I didn't go to him.

"Tell me about the trolls," Alaric said. He surprised me this duke, with his dawn-time ways, his old gods, his axes and furs, so that you'd think him a blunt instrument built for war and little else, and yet his thoughts ran so quick that his mouth had to leap from one subject to the next just to keep up. "The trolls and your strange companions," he said. And as if on cue the great doors opened at the far end of the hall to admit Gorgoth, his bulk black against the rain.

The Duke's warriors took tighter hold of their axes as Gorgoth advanced toward us, the hall silent but for the heavy fall of his feet. Gog hurried on behind him, the rain steaming off him and each lamp burning brighter as he passed.

The ground shook. This time it jolted as if a giant's hammer had fallen close by. Outside something groaned and fell with a crash. And beside me a lamp slipped its hook and smashed on the flagstones, splashing burning oil in a wide bright circle. Several splatters caught my leggings and flamed there though the cloth lay too wet to catch. Gog moved fast. He threw one clawed hand toward me and the other at the hearth. He made a brief, high cry and the lamp oil guttered out. In the hearth a new fire burned with merry flames as if it were dry wood heaped there instead of grey ash.

Oaths from the men around us. Because of the fierceness of the tremor, or the business with the fallen lamp, or just to release the tension built as Gorgoth advanced through the shadowed hall, I didn't know.

"Now that was a clever trick." I crouched to be on a level with Gog and waved him to me. "How did you do that?" My fingers tested where the fire had burned, leggings and floor, and came away cold and oily.

"Do what?" Gog asked, his voice high, his eyes on the Duke and the glitter of the axes held around him.

"Put the fire out," I said. I glanced at the hearth. "Move the fire," I corrected myself.

Gog didn't look away from the Alaric in his high chair. "There's only one fire, silly," he said, forgetting any business of kings and dukes. "I just squeezed it."

I frowned. I had the edge of understanding him, but it kept slipping my grasp. I hate that. "Tell me." I steered him by the shoulders until our eyes met.

"There's only one fire," he said. His eyes were dark, their usual all-black, but his gaze held something hot, something uncomfortable, as if it might light you up like a tallow wick.

"One fire," I said. "And all these . . ." I waved a hand at the lamps. "Windows onto it?"

"Yes." Gog sighed, exasperated, and struggled to turn away for some new game.

I had the image of a rug in my head. A rug with a wrinkle in it. I remembered it from softer days. From days when I slept in a world that never shook or burned, in a room where my mother would always come to say good night. A rug with a wrinkle in it and a maid trying to smooth it down with her foot. And every time she squashed it flat a new wrinkle would spring up close by. But never two. Because there was only one fold in the rug.

"You can take fire from one place and put it in another," I said.

Gog nodded.

"Because there is only one fire, and we see pieces of it," I said. "You squeeze one corner down and pull up another."

Gog nodded and struggled to be off.

"And that's all you ever do," I said.

Gog didn't answer, as if it were too obvious for comment. I let him go and he ran beneath the nearest table to play with a red-furred hound.

"The trolls?" Alaric said, with the air of a man forcing patience.

"We met some. Gorgoth can talk to them. They seem to like him," I said.

Alaric waited. It's a good enough trick. Say nothing and men feel compelled to fill the silence, even if it's with things they would rather have kept secret. It's a good enough trick, but I know it and I said nothing.

"The Duke of Maladon knows about the trolls," Gorgoth said. The Danes flinched when he spoke, as if they thought him incapable of it and expected him to growl and snarl. "The trolls serve Ferrakind. The duke wishes to know why the ones we discovered were not in the fire-mage's service."

Alaric shrugged. "It's true."

"The trolls serve Ferrakind out of fear," Gorgoth said. "Their flesh burns as easily as man-flesh. A few hide from him."

"Why don't they just leave the Heimrift if they want to live free?" I asked.

"Men," he said.

For a moment I didn't understand. It's hard to think of such creatures as victims. I remembered their black-clawed hands, hands that could snatch the head off a man.

"They were once many," Gorgoth said.

"You told me they were made for war, soldiers, so why hide?" I asked.

Gorgoth nodded. "Made for war. Made to serve. Not made to be hunted. Not to be scattered and hunted alone across strange lands."

I pulled myself to my full height, topping six foot of late. "I think—"

"What do you think, Makin?" The Duke cut across me.

Makin caught my eye and offered the tiniest of grins. "I think all these things are the glimpses of the same fire," he said. "Everything here comes back to Ferrakind. The dead trees, the lung-flake in your cattle, your lost harvests, the knocking down of your halls one brick, one gable, one rafter at a time, the trolls, the chances of either of you ever making a play for the empire throne, all of it, with Ferrakind burning at the centre."

It's always a different thing that makes the magic happen. Today it was his cleverness. But at the end of it all, you wanted Makin to be your friend.

21

Four years earlier

The Danes are settled Vikings in the main. The blood of reavers mixed with that of the farmers they conquered. Every Dane counts his ancestry back to the north, to some bloody-handed warrior jumping from his longship, but in truth the wild men of the fjords scorn the Danes and call them fit-firar—*a mistake that has seen a lot of Vikings on the wrong end of an axe.*

"You're more use to me here, Makin."

"You're mad to go in the first place," Makin said.

"It's why we came," I said.

"Every new thing I hear about this Ferrakind is a new good reason not to go anywhere near him," Makin said.

"We're here because he's gone soft on the little monster," Row said from the doorway. He hadn't been invited to the conversation. None of them had. But on the road any raised voice is an invitation for an audience. Although strictly we weren't on the road. We were in chambers set aside for guests in a smaller hall paralleling the Duke of Maladon's great hall.

"Or *hard* on him." Rike leaned in under the door lintel, a

nasty leer on him. Since I took the copper box he seemed to feel he had license to speak his mind.

I turned to the doorway. "Two things you should remember, my brothers."

Grumlow, Sim, and Kent appeared as faces poking out behind Rike.

"First, if you answer me back on this I swear by every priest in hell that you will not leave this building alive. Second, you may recall a time when you and our late lamented brothers were busy dying outside the Haunt. And whilst the Count of Renar's foot-soldiers were killing you. Killing Elban, and Liar, and Fat Burlow . . . Gog had the whole of the count's personal guard, more than seventy picked men, either as burning pools of human fat, or too damn scared to move. And he was seven. So right now the kind of man he grows into, and whether he grows up at all, is a question of far greater interest to me than whether you sorry lot live to see tomorrow. In fact there are a lot of questions more important to me than whether you get a day older or not, Rike, but that one is top of the list."

"You still need me there," Makin said. Too many years guarding me had turned a duty into a habit, an imperative.

"If things go well I won't need you," I said. "And if they go badly, I don't think an extra sword or two will help. He has a small army of trolls at his beck and call, and he can set men on fire by thinking about it. I don't believe a sword will help."

I left Makin still arguing and the others slinking around like whipped dogs. Well, not Red Kent. He had his new axe. Not a new one in truth but a fine one, forged in the high north and traded from the long-ships off Karlswater. Kent raised the axe to me as I left, nodded, and said nothing.

Gorgoth and Gog waited for me at the Duke's storerooms, a sack of provisions between them and waxed blankets in case we needed shelter on the slopes.

We set off for the Heimrift with a fine spring morning breaking out all around us. We all walked. I'd grown used to Brath and had no desire to leave him untended on the side of a volcano. For all I knew trolls were partial to horsemeat. I quite like it myself.

Sindri caught us half a mile down the road, his plaits bouncing off his back as he cantered along.

"Not this time, Sindri, just me and the pretty boys here," I said.

"You'll want me until you're clear of the forest."

"The forest? We had no problems before," I said.

"I watched you." Sindri grinned. "If you had gone wrong I would have guided you. But you were lucky."

"And what should I be scared of in the forest?" I asked. "Green trolls? Goblins? Grendel himself? You Danes have more boogie-men than the rest of the empire put together."

"Pine men," he said.

"How do they burn?" I asked.

He laughed at that, then let the smile fall from him. "There's something in the forest that lets the blood from men and replaces it with pine sap. They don't die, these men, but they change." He pointed to his eyes. "The whites turn green. They don't bleed. Axes don't bother them."

I pursed my lips. "You can guide us. I'm busy today. These pine men will have to come to the Highlands and get in line if they want a part of me."

And so we walked, with Sindri leading his horse, along the forest paths he judged safe, and we watched the trees with new suspicions.

By noon the woods thinned and gave over to rising moorland. We marched through waist-deep bracken, thick with stands of gorse scratching as we passed, and everywhere heather, trying to trip us, clouds of pollen blazing our trail.

Sindri didn't have to be told to leave. "I'll wait here," he said, and nestled back in the bracken on a slope that caught the sun. "Good luck with Ferrakind. If you kill him you'll have at least one friend in the north. Probably a thousand!"

"I'm not here to kill him," I said.

"Probably for the best," Sindri said.

I frowned at that. If I'd had three brothers die in the Heimrift then I would have an account to settle with the man who ruled there. The Danes though seemed to think of Ferrakind in the same terms as the volcanoes themselves. To take issue with him would be the same as feuding against a cliff because your friend fell off it.

I took us back to Halradra, along the paths and slopes that we first followed. As we gained height the wind picked up and took the sweat from us. The sun stayed bright and it seemed a good day. If this was to be our last one then at least it had been pretty so far. We trailed along a long valley of black ash and broken lava flows, ancient currents still visible in the frozen rock. Far above us a lone herders' hut stood dwarfed by the vast heave of the mountains around it, built in days when grass must have found a way to grow here. Unseen in the blue heavens a cloud passed before the sun and its shadow rippled across the expanse of silent sunlit rock arrayed east to west. Gorgoth made a deep sound in his chest. I liked that about travelling with Gorgoth. He hoarded his words, so you wouldn't know his thoughts from one moment to the next, but he never missed anything, not even those rare occasions when the myriad parts of this dirty, worn-out world of ours come into some fleeting alignment that constructs a beauty so fierce it hurts to see.

Where Gorgoth held his silence, Gog normally provided enough chatter for two. In the most part I would let it flow over me. Children prattle. It is their nature and it is mine to let it slide. Climbing Halradra for the second time though, Gog said nothing. After so many weeks of, "Why do horses have four legs, Brother Jorg?" "What colour is green made from, Brother Jorg?" "Why is that tree taller than the other one, Brother Jorg?" you would think I'd appreciate a rest from it, but in truth it grated more when he said nothing.

"No questions today, Gog?" I asked.

"No." He shot me a glance then looked away.

"Nothing?" I asked.

We carried on up the slope without speaking. I knew it wasn't just fear that kept his tongue. As a child there's a horror in discovering the limitations of the ones you love. The time you find that your mother cannot keep you safe, that your tutor makes a mistake, that the wrong path must be taken because the grown-ups lack the strength to take the right one . . . each of those moments is the theft of your childhood, each of them a blow that kills some part of the child you were, leaving another part of the man exposed, a new creature, tougher but tempered with bitterness and disappointment.

Gog didn't want to ask his questions because he didn't want to hear me lie.

We came to the caves that I had failed to see before, wrinkled our noses at the troll stink, and passed on into the darkness.

"Some light if you will, Gog," I said.

He opened his hand and fire blossomed as if he'd been holding it in his fist all along.

I led the way, through the great hall of the entrance cave, along the smooth passage rising for fifty yards to the cathedral cave, almost spherical with its potholed floor and sculpted walls.

The trolls came quickly this time, a half dozen of them insinuating themselves into the shadowed circle around Gog's flame. Gorgoth stood ready to set his strength against any of the new ones who doubted him, but they crouched and watched us, watched Gorgoth, and made no attacks.

"Why are we here?" Gorgoth asked at last. I had wondered if he would ever crack.

"I've chosen my ground," I said. "If you have to meet a lion then it's better if it isn't in his den."

"You didn't look anywhere else," Gorgoth said.

"I found what I wanted here."

"And what's that?" he asked.

"A faint hope." I grinned and squatted down to be level with Gog. "We have to meet him sometime, Gog. This problem of yours, these fires, they're going to pull you down sooner or later, and there's nothing I can do, not even Gorgoth can help you, and the next time will be worse and the next worse still." I didn't lie to him. He didn't want to hear me lie.

A tear rolled down his cheek then sputtered into steam. I took his hand, very small in mine, and pressed the stolen rune stone into his palm, closing his fingers about it. "You and I, Gog, we're the same. Fighters. Brothers. We'll go in there together and come out together." And we were the same, all lying aside. Underneath it, brushing away the goodness in him, the evil in me, we had a bond. I needed to see him win through. Nothing selfless about it. If Gog could outlast what ate him from the inside out, then maybe I could too. Hell, I didn't come halfway across the empire to save a scrawny child. I came to save me.

"We're going to call Ferrakind to us," I said. I glanced at the trolls. They watched me with wet black eyes, no reaction to Ferrakind's name. "Do they even understand what I'm saying?"

"No," said Gorgoth. "They're wondering if you'd be good to eat."

"Ask them if there other ways out of here, ones that lead out higher up the mountain."

A pause. I strained to hear what passed between them and heard nothing but the flutter of Gog's flame.

"They can take us to one," Gorgoth said.

"Tell them Ferrakind is going to come. Tell them to hide close by but be ready to lead us out by one of these other paths."

I could tell when Gorgoth's thoughts hit them. They were on their feet in a moment, black mouths stretched in silent snarls and roars, black tongues lashing over their jagged teeth. Quicker than they appeared they were gone, lost in the darkness.

"Right, we're going to call Ferrakind. I'm going to try to get him to help us." I steered Gog's face away from the entrance and back to mine. "If things go badly I want you to do the trick we saw in the Duke's hall. If Ferrakind tries to burn us, I want you to take the fire and put it where I show you."

"I'll try," Gog said.

"Try hard." I'd been scared of burning all my life, since the poker, maybe before that even. I thought of Justice howling as he burned in chains. Sour vomit bubbled at the back of my throat. I could walk away from this. I could just walk.

"How will we make him come here, Brother Jorg?" Gog's first question of the day.

The vision of me walking down the slope still filled my eyes. I would whistle in the spring sunshine and smile. Sweat trickled from beneath my arms, cool across my ribs. If Makin were here he would say he had a bad feeling about this. He'd be right too.

I could just leave. I could just leave.

If Coddin were here he would call this too great a risk with no certain reward. He would say that but he would mean "Get the hell out of there, Jorg," because he wouldn't want me to burn.

And if my father were here. If he saw me stepping toward the sunlight. Taking the easy path. He would say in a voice so

soft that you might almost miss it, "One more, Jorg. One more."
And at each crossroad thereafter I would choose the easy path
one more time. And in the end what I loved would still burn.

"Make a fire, Gog," I said. "Make the biggest fucking fire
in the world."

Gog looked at Gorgoth, who nodded and stepped back. For
a long moment, measured by half a dozen slow-drawn breaths,
nothing happened. Faint at first, as if it were imagination, the
flame patterns on Gog's back started to flicker and move. The
colour deepened. Flushes of crimson ran through him and the
ash grey paled. The heat reached me and I stepped back,
then back again. The shadows had run from the cavern but I
had no time to see what they revealed. Gog pulsed with heat
like an ember in the smith's fire pulses with each breath of the
bellows. Gorgoth and I retreated into the tunnel that led up
from behind the cathedral cave. We stood with the heat of
Gog's fire burning on our faces and the air rolling down from
behind us icy on our necks.

The flames came without sound and the whole of the cathedral cave filled with swirling orange fire. We staggered back,
losing sight of the cavern but still blistered by the inferno. My
breath came in gasps as if the fire had burned out what I needed
from the air.

"How will this help?" Gorgoth asked.

"There's only one fire." I drew in a lungful of hot and useless
air. Black dots swam across my vision. "And Ferrakind watches
through it as if it were a window to all the world."

Gorgoth caught my shoulder and stopped me falling. It
seemed to take no effort and I managed a small pang of resent-
ment at that even as I began to slip into a darker place where
his hand could not support me. I could hear nothing but my
own gasps and the sound of my heels dragging as he pulled me
farther back, farther up. Most of me felt hot enough to ignite
spontaneously, but strangely my feet were freezing.

The fire that had made no sound as it came gave a distinct
whumpf as it went out. It ended before I passed out entirely,
and a shock of cold brought me round with a hoarse curse.

"What the hell?" I lay in a small stream of icy water. The
tunnel had been dry before, yet now a stream ran along it, rattling pebbles in its flow. I rolled in the freezing trickle for good

measure then used the wall to get myself vertical. Gorgoth led the way back. He'd spent a lifetime in the dark beneath Mount Honas and his cat's eyes found him good footing whilst I stumbled behind. The little stream followed us back into the cathedral chamber where it bubbled and steamed on the hot rocks.

Gog waited where we had left him, still glowing, and Ferrakind stood at the mouth of the tunnel that led to the entrance chamber.

I had thought to find a man with fire in him. Ferrakind was more of a fire with a touch of man remaining. He stood in the form of a man but as if fashioned from molten iron such as runs from the vats of Barrow and of Gwangyang. Every part of him burned and his whole shape flickered from one posture to another. When his eyes, like hot white stars, glanced my way his gaze seared my skin.

"To me, Gog!" It hurt to shout, but the steam from the melt water around my feet helped a little.

"The child is mine." Ferrakind spoke in the crackle of his flames.

Gog scrambled toward us. Ferrakind made a slow advance.

"And why would you want him?" I called. I couldn't get any closer without the skin melting off me.

"The big fire consumes the small. We will join and our strength will multiply," Ferrakind said.

It seemed to me as if he spoke from memory, using what parts of the man had yet to burn away.

"We came to save him from that," I said. "Can't you take the fire from him and leave the boy behind?"

Those hot eyes found me again and stared as if truly seeing me for the first time. "I know you."

I didn't know what to say to that. My lips felt too dry for the foolish words I might have found in other circumstances.

"You woke a fire of an old kind that hasn't burned for a thousand years," Ferrakind said.

"Ah, yes," I said. "That."

"You brought the sun to earth," Ferrakind's crackle softened as if awed by the memory of the Builders' weapon. Shadows ran across him.

Gog reached us, the heat gone from him leaving new markings, bright flames caught in orange across his back, chest, arms.

"So can you change him? Can you take the fire out of him, or enough so he can live with it?" I asked. It still hurt to breathe and the steam from the meltwater made it hard to see. Somewhere above and behind us the heat from Gog and Ferrakind was meeting the ancient ice at Halradra's core.

Ferrakind's fire guttered and spurted, flowing over the cavern floor. I realized he was laughing.

"The Builders tried to break the barriers between thought and matter," he said. "They made it easier to change the world with a desire. They thinned the walls between life and death, between fire and not-fire, whittled away at the difference between this and that, even here and there."

It occurred to me that Ferrakind's sanity had been one of the first things to be consumed in his own personal inferno. "Can you help the boy?" I asked, coughing.

"It's written in him. His thoughts touch fire. Fire touches his mind. He is fire-sworn. We can't change how we're written." Ferrakind stepped toward us, flames rising around him like wings readying for flight. "Give me the boy and you may leave."

"I've come too far for 'no,'" I said.

Fire isn't patient. Fire does not negotiate. I should have known these things.

Ferrakind reached toward us and a column of white flame erupted from his hands. I had considered myself quick, but Gog moved quicker than I could think and caught the conflagration in his arms, his body shading from orange toward white-heat, but none of it reaching Gorgoth or me.

"Behind us!" I shouted. "Send it back."

And Gog obeyed. The tunnel behind us filled with Ferrakind's white fire as Gog caught it on one hand and threw it away from the other. I could see nothing of the fire-mage, just the white inferno boiling off him, and nothing of the tunnel, just a fierce tornado of white fire swirling away through it, up. We stood in a cocoon with furnace heat on every side and one small boy keeping our flesh from charring to the bone.

For an age we saw nothing but blinding heat, heard nothing but the roar of fire. And each moment that I thought it could last no longer, the fury built. Gog blazed, first the bright orange of iron ready for the hammer, then the white of the furnace fire, then a pure white like starshine. I could see the shadows of his bones, clearer by the heartbeat, as if fire were burning though him, taking substance from muscle, skin, and fat. Leaving him brittle and ashen.

And in an instant the fire and fury fell away revealing Ferrakind, white-hot and molten, with Gog crouched, pale as silvery ash, unmoving.

A torrent of meltwater rushed around us now, hip deep, white, and roaring, pouring into the main chamber through a tunnel mouth that lay dry and gritty when we first scrambled through it to escape the fire. The waters divided around Gog and again around Ferrakind as if unable to touch the essence of fire. Gorgoth and I kept close to Gog and the water hardly reached us.

Ferrakind laughed again, new pulses of flame rising from him. "You thought to quench me, Jorg of Ancrath?"

I shrugged. "It's the traditional way. Fighting fire with fire doesn't seem to have worked." Already the flow around us had started to slacken.

"It would take an ocean!" Ferrakind said. He gathered fire into his hands and let it blaze white. "The child is done. Time to die, Jorg of Ancrath."

If it were time then so be it. I had a faint hope, but it had only ever been that. At least it wouldn't be a slow fire. I drew my sword. I always thought I would have a blade in hand when the time came.

I heard a roar, but not the roar of flame, somehow deeper and more distant.

It would take an ocean.

"How about a lake?" I asked and sighted along my sword at the burning mage.

"A lake?" Ferrakind paused.

The waters hit then, a black wall rushing down on the heels of the trickle around our feet. I dived at Gog, carrying him with me into the cathedral cavern, rolling to the side of the tunnel mouth. He broke as though he were made of glass. He shattered like a toy, into a thousand sharp and brilliant pieces. I felt the sudden flash of heat. Needles of fire pierced my cheek where I hit him, my jaw, my temple. I lay amongst the scintillating shards, Gog's remains, paralysed by a whole world of pain, curled on the gritty cavern floor with a flood of biblical proportions blasting its way out of the tunnel just yards behind me.

In Halradra's crater a thousand times a thousand tons of ice have lain for hundreds of years. But before that, in the distant long ago, waters flowed. How else would these tunnels be smooth, be strewn with grit and ancient mud, be scoured and potholed like the stone where rivers flow? With glacial slowness the ice has crept where underground streams carved hidden cathedrals and long galleries, and Halradra has slept, ice-choked and silent.

I couldn't expect any fire to melt enough ice to drown a fire-mage, least of all for the fire-mage's own fire to do the melting whilst he stood there patiently awaiting his own deluge. But I had a hope, a faint hope, that his fire and Gog's together might at least melt a passage through the ice, a passage where the tunnels led and where heat rises . . . a passage up.

In spring and summer Halradra's crater is a remarkable blue. The blue of a yard of meltwater lying on top of fathoms of ice. A twenty-acre lake, just a yard deep, sitting on all that ice.

When a hole wide enough to swallow a wagon is melted through that ice you discover that a yard times twenty acres is a lot.

The icy water hit Ferrakind in a thick column faster than the swiftest of horses, and swept him away without pause.

With the mage gone and the sparkles dying from Gog's fragments, darkness returned. I knew only pain and the roar of the waters. The knowledge that I would drown rather than burn held no interest. I only wanted it to be quick.

Somehow, in the darkness and the deluge, hands found me. Troll-stink mixed with the stench of my roasted flesh and I moved in their grasp. I cursed them, thinking only that the agony would last longer this way. I considered for a moment if they were still wondering whether I tasted good. Perhaps they liked their food part-cooked. I bit one at some point and I can say that trolls taste worse than they smell. I remember no more of it. I think they banged my head on a wall as they scrambled to escape the flood.

December 16th, Year 98 Interregnum
Ancrath. The Tall Castle. My bedchamber.
Maery Coddin sewing in the corner chair.
Rain rattling on the shutters.

"Madam, you send the winter running. We bask in the warmth of your smile."

That's what the Prince of Arrow said when I came down the stairway into the East Hall. "Madam," not "Princess," because that's how they have it in the land of Arrow. Madam. Pompous maybe, but it made me smile, for I'd been serious before, thinking of Sageous and the writing on his face. And even though a dead poet probably wrote Orrin's lines, it felt as though Orrin meant them and had spoken them just for me.

"Katherine, you look good."

Egan said that, while his brother bowed. Night and day those two. Or maybe morning and twilight. Orrin as blond as a jarl and handsome as the princes painted in those books to delight little princesses before they learn that it isn't kissing that turns frogs into princes, just the ownership of a castle and some acres. Egan with his hair short and blacker than soot, his skin still holding a stain from the summer sun, and his face that would be brutal, that would fit on a butcher or executioner, but for the fire behind it, the energy that sets the short hairs on your arms and neck on end.

And what were Jorg Ancrath's last words to me?

"*Perhaps, Aunt, you have a better hand?*" As he invited me to finish his father's work. As he stood there, more pale than Orrin, darker than Egan, his hair across his shoulders like a black river. He watched me and my knife, his face sharp and complicated, as if you could see there not the man he will become, but the men he might become.

And why am I writing of that boy here when there are men to speak of? That boy who hit me. I don't think he tore my dress. I think he considered it though.

They both asked for my hand. Orrin with sweet words that I can't capture. He made me feel perfect. Clean. I know he would keep me safe and would turn his mind toward making me happy. I paint him too . . . prissy. There's fire and strength in Orrin of Arrow. At his core he is iron and every part of him is wholly alive.

Egan asked with short words and long, dark looks. I think his passions would terrify Sareth, despite her dirty mouth. I think a weak woman would die in his bed. And a strong one might find it the only place she's been alive.

We walked in the rose garden that Queen Rowan had planted the year before she died, out between the keep and the curtain wall. I strolled first with Orrin, since he's the elder brother by a year, and then with Egan, with Maery Coddin a yard behind to chaperone us. The garden is overgrown now, not neglected but tended without care, the roses left withered on the stems, thorns and dead flowers all bearded with frost. Orrin walked without speaking to start, with only the crunch of feet in gravel to break the cold silence. His first words plumed before him: "*It wouldn't be easy to be my wife.*"

"*Honesty is always refreshing,*" I told him. "*Why should it be so difficult?*"

And he told me there among the roses, without bluster or pride, that he would be emperor some day but the path to Vyene would not be easy. God had not told him to do it, nor had he laid a promise to a dying father; he didn't paint it as destiny, only duty. Orrin of Arrow is, I think, that rarest of things. A truly good man with all the strengths to do what his goodness demands of him.

He was right of course. To love such a man might be easy, to marry him much more difficult.

Where Orrin first thought and then spoke about the future, Egan spoke without hesitation and about the now. All they shared was honesty. Egan told me he wanted me, and I believed him. He told me he would make me happy and how. I'm sure if I'd turned around Maery's face would have been as red as mine. Egan spoke of his horses, the battles he'd fought in, and the lands he would take me to. Some of it was boasting, sure enough, but in the end he spoke of his passions, killing, riding, travelling, and now me. It may be shallow of me, but to be counted among the simple primal pleasures of a man like Egan of Arrow is a compliment. And yes, he may see me as a prize to be won, but I think I would be equal to his fire and that he could find himself well matched.

I told them I would have to consider.

Sareth thinks I'm mad not to choose one and jump at the chance to leave Ancrath.

Maery Coddin says I should choose Orrin. He has more land, more prospects, and enough fire to melt her but not so much as to scorch her.

But I chose to wait.

February 8th, Year 99 Interregnum
Tall Castle. Library. Cold and empty.

Sareth has squeezed out her Ancrath brat. She howled about it, loud enough for half the castle to know more than they ever wanted about the business of pushing a big slimy head through a hole where even fingers feel tight. She sent me away after only a few hours. For my sulking she said. Truly, I was glad to go.

I should be happy for her. I should be thankful they both lived. I do love her, and I suppose I will come to love the boy. It's not his fault he's an Ancrath. But I'm scared.

It wasn't sulking. It was fear. She howled the rest of the day and into the night before she got it out of her. I knew she had a dirty mouth, but the things she shouted near the end. I wonder how the servants will look on her now. How the table-knights will watch their queen behind their visors.

I'm scared and this quill puts the fear wavering into each letter. I'm trembling and I have to write slow and firm just to be able to read what I've set down.

I missed my time last month, and again this month. I think before the year is out it will be me screaming and not caring what I say or who hears. And there won't be flags out and prayers in chapel for my bastard. Not like there were for little Prince Degran at midnight. Not even if my baby has the same black hair slime-plastered to its head and the same dark eyes watching out of a squashed up face.

I hate him. How could he? How could he spoil everything?

I dreamed of Jorg last night, coming to me, and my belly all fat, taut and hot and stretched, stretching like the bastard wanted out of me, little hands sliding beneath my skin. I dreamed Jorg brought a knife with him. Or it was my knife. The long narrow one. And he cut me open, like Drane guts fish in the kitchen, and he pulled the baby out scarlet and screaming.

I should tell somebody. I should go to Friar Glen with the story. How Jorg raped me. And seek forgiveness, though Christ knows why I should be the one to ask. I should go. They would send me to the Holy Sisters at Frau Rock.

But I hate that man, that stocky friar with his blank eyes and thick fingers. I don't know why but I hate him even more than Jorg Ancrath. He makes my skin want to drop off and crawl away.

Or I could ask someone to help me lose it. They had old mothers in the slum quarter in Scorron who could grind up a bitter paste . . . and the babies would fall out of the women who went to them, tiny and dead. But that was in Scorron. I don't know who to ask here. Maery Coddin maybe, but she's too good, too clean. She would tell Sareth and Sareth would tell King Olidan and who knows what he would do to me for spoiling his plans, for not playing his game of statehood like a good pawn, for falling off the board.

Better I should marry Prince Orrin or Egan. Quickly before it shows. Egan wouldn't wait for the wedding. He would be on me in a moment. He would never know it wasn't his. Orrin would wait.

22

Wedding day

"Where's Coddin, dammit?"

"Back down there." Watch-master Hobbs pointed down the valley. The grey rear-guard of the Watch sketched a ragged line ahead of the foremost of Arrow's troops.

"Should have left him in the castle, Jorg," Makin said, heaving a breath between every other word. "He's too old for running."

I spat. "Keppen's a hundred if he's a day, and he'd be up and down this mountain before you'd broke fast, Sir Makin."

"He might be sixty," Makin said. "A whack older than Coddin in any case, I'll grant you."

Watch-master Hobbs joined us on the ridge, with Captain Stodd beside him, his short beard white against a red face.

"Well?" Hobbs said.

I watched him.

"Sire," he added.

It's easy to lose faith on the mountain, but also to find it. Somehow being a few thousand feet closer to God makes all the difference.

Hobbs had good reason for his doubts in any case. Above

us the valley narrowed to a steep-sided pass, a choke point that would slow three hundred men to the point where the men of Arrow might finally get to blood their swords after their long chase. Above that, the snowline and the long climb to Blue Moon Pass, blocked at this time of year despite the promise of its name. Below us ten times our number and more filled the valley, a carpet of men in constant motion, the sun glittering off helms, shields, the points of sword and spear.

"Let's wait for Coddin," I said. Even Coddin needed his faith restored.

"Sire." Hobbs bowed his head. He took his bow in hand and waited, his breath heavy in his chest. A good man, or if not good, solid. Father picked him from the royal guard for the Forest Watch, not as punishment but to reward the Watch.

I looked away from the seething mass of men to the peaks, snow-clad, serene. The snowline waited for us not far above the choke point. The wind carried fresh snow, icy crystals in a thin swirl. None of us felt the cold. Ten thousand mountain steps burned in my legs, leaving them to tremble, and warming my blood close to boiling point.

To the west I could see God's Finger. The tiredness in me was nothing compared to what I felt the day I hauled myself onto the tip of that finger and lay as dead beneath the bluest sky. I lay there for hours and in the end I stood, leaning into the teeth of the wind, and drew my sword.

When you climb take nothing that is not essential. I took a sword, strapped across my back. There's a song behind the swinging of a sword. On God's Finger it can be heard more clearly. I had climbed chasing the memory of my mother's music, but the Spire had sung me a different song. Perhaps it's that heaven is closer, perhaps the wind brings it. Either way I heard the sword-song that day and I made my blade *kata*, slicing the gale, spinning, turning, striking high then low. I danced to the sword-song in that high place for an hour maybe more, wild play with an endless drop on every side. And then, before the sun fell too low, I left the blade on the rocks, an offering to the elements, and started down.

Standing on God's Finger I had first understood why men might fight for a place, for rocks and streams, no matter who calls themselves king there. The power of place. I felt it again at the head of the valley with the hordes of Arrow swarming toward me.

"What ho, Coddin," I said as my chancellor staggered to us. "You look half-dead."

He hadn't the breath for a reply.

"Do you have what I gave you?" I asked. At the time I hadn't known why I gave it to him, only that I should.

Still gasping, Coddin shrugged off his pack and dug into it. "Be glad I didn't drop it just to keep ahead of the enemy," he said.

I took the whistle from him, a Highland whistle such as the goatherds use, a foot long with a leather-washered piston.

"I always trust you to deliver, Coddin," I said, though I had Makin carry a second and had a third with Keppen. Trust is a fine thing but try not to build plans upon it.

"We're none of us local men," I said to my captains, voice raised for the Watch men starting to gather round. "Well, you are." I pointed to a fellow in the second rank. "But most of us were born and raised in Ancrath."

The last of the Watch were drawing in now, the men of Arrow a couple of hundred yards farther back, toiling over broken rock.

"You're here with me, men of Ancrath, because you're my best warriors, because you learned to fight in lands that are hard to defend and that others want to take. These Highlands of ours, however, are easier to protect, and hold bugger all save stones and goats." That got a laugh or two. Some of the Watch still had go in them.

"Today," I said. "We all become Highlanders."

I took the whistle, held it high, and drove the piston home, not too hard because that spoils the tone. It's a steady pressure gives the best results.

A goat-whistle will carry for miles across the mountains. It's pitched to let the wind take it and to bounce from rock to rock. One long blast would reach almost back to the Haunt. Certainly far enough to reach each and every Highlander I had hidden on the high slopes overlooking our path up the mountain. And not just any Highlanders these, but the men who had held these particular slopes from generation to generation. The men who like their fathers and grandfathers would take a rock for a walk. They kept their secrets well, the men of Renar, but from the tip of God's Finger, that day years before, it had all been revealed to me.

It took the blasts of seven trumpets to bring down the walls of Jericho, but they weren't stacked to fall. One blast of a herder's whistle set the mountainsides moving in the Renar Highlands. On both sides of the valley, along the full length, a dozen individual rockslides. The Highlanders know their slopes with an intimacy that puts lovers' knowing of each other's curves to shame. Big stones poised to fall, boulders on edge with levers set and ready, toppled with a shove and a grunt, rolling, colliding, cascading one into several into many into too many. We felt the ground tremble beneath our feet. The noise, like a millstone grinding, rattled teeth in loose sockets. In moments the whole valley had been set in motion and Arrow's thousands vanished as the dust rose and stone churned flesh into bloody paste.

"Well, thank you, Coddin. Much appreciated." I handed him back the whistle. "Hobbs," I said. "When the dust clears enough for a good shot, if you could have the men knock down anyone still standing."

"Christ Bleeding," Makin said, staring into the valley below us. "How . . ."

"Topology," I said. "It's a kind of magic."

"And what now, King Jorg?" Coddin asked, faith restored but still focused on the numbers, knowing our chances against seventeen or sixteen thousand were scarcely better than our chances against twenty thousand.

"Back down, of course!" I said. "We can't attack from up here now, can we?"

23

Wedding day

The journey back to the Haunt took us over fresh territory, a new and broken surface, littered with dead men turned into ground meat, and here and there along the way the cries of live ones trapped beneath us. We moved on, the grey of the Watch's tatter-robes renewed with rock dust, the men pale with powdered stone and with horror.

The Prince's army encircled the Haunt now, archers on the heights, siege machinery being hauled into place. All my troops at the castle crowded within the walls, space or not. There was no standing against the foe on open ground.

I could see units of bowmen descending in long files, presumably ordered east to meet our advance in light of the recent massacre. The Prince looked to be a fast learner. He anticipated my renewed attack. It didn't seem likely that he would consider my three hundred men a mere nuisance this time.

"He shouldn't be in a hurry," Makin said beside me.

"He'll reduce the walls and thin the ranks first," said Coddin.

"He doesn't need to get inside until the snows come, the big snows," said Hobbs. "Inside by the big snows. Winter by the fire. Over the passes when the spring clears them."

"He wants in today," I told them. "Tomorrow by the latest. He'll go through the front gate."

"Why?" Coddin asked. He didn't argue, but he wanted to understand.

"Why waste a good castle?" I said. "A big push. A surrender. A dose of mercy and he has a new stronghold, a new garrison, and a small repair to make on the entrance. He doesn't do half measures any more than I do. Go in hard, fast, get the job done."

"A dose of mercy?" Makin asked. "You think that famous Arrow mercy has survived recent events?"

"Maybe not," I said, my smile grim, "but I don't intend to offer any either. Mark me, old friend, nobody gets out alive, not this time."

"Red Jorg." Makin clapped his hand to his chest as he had at Remagen Fort years before.

"A red day," I said. I dipped two fingers into something that lived and laughed just hours ago and drew a crimson line down my left cheek then the right.

As we made our way back down the valley I fiddled with the copper box in its leather sack on my hip. All day I had felt Sageous trespassing through the edge of my imaginations, the half-dreams and daydreams to which he could find paths. My own sources, a spy network far less sophisticated than most of the Hundred maintained, told me the Prince of Arrow had a second army, far smaller than the one at my gates, headed for Ancrath and the Tall Castle, presumably to ensure my father kept his troops indoors. There seemed no reason for Sageous to be haunting my dreams unless he had joined Arrow when the balance of power became clear and now served as the Prince's advisor, seeking of course to own his mind rather than merely guide it.

Then again, the dream-witch might be keeping himself at the Tall Castle. It might be that Sageous sought to know my plans in order to sell them to Arrow and buy Ancrath's independence for my father. Either way, I wasn't going to show them to him.

I snagged the thread of memory that I'd been fishing for and pulled at it. The pre-laid plans that I stored in the box always emerged as sudden inspiration, moments of epiphany where disparate facts connected. I drew on the thread of my schemes but this time something went wrong. This time, despite my care, the box cracked open, a hair's breadth, and I saw in my mind's eye a dark light bleeding from beneath the lid. I hammered it down in an instant and it closed with a *schnick*.

For the longest moment I thought that nothing had escaped. Then the memory lifted me.

"Hello, Jorg," she says, and my clever words desert me.

"Hello, Katherine."

And we stand among the graves with the stone girl and the stone dog between us, and blossom swirls like pink snow as the wind picks up, and I think of a snow-globe broken long ago and wonder how all this will settle.

"You shouldn't be out here alone," I say. "I'm told there are bandits in these woods."

"You broke my vase," she says, and I'm pleased that her tongue has turned traitor too.

Her fingers return to the spot where I hit her, where the vase shattered and she fell.

I have put her loved ones in the ground, but she talks about a vase. Sometimes a hurt is too big and we skirt around the edge of it, looking for our way in.

"To be fair, you were about to kill me," I say.

She frowns at that.

"I buried my dog here," I tell her. She has me saying foolish things already, telling her secrets she has no right to know. She's like that knock on the head I took from Orrin of Arrow. She steals the sense from me.

"Hanna is buried there." She points. Her hand is very white and steady.

"Hanna?" I ask.

Thunder on her brow, green eyes flash.

"The old woman who tried to throttle me?" I ask. An image of a purple face floats before me, framed with grey wisps, my hands locked beneath her chin.

"She. Did. Not!" Katherine says, but each word is more quiet than the one before and the conviction runs from her. "She wouldn't."

But she knows she did.

"You killed Galen," she says, still glaring.

"It's true," I say. "But he was a heartbeat away from stabbing his sword through my back."

She can't deny it. "Damn you," she says.

"You've missed me then?" I say and I grin because I'm just pleased to see her, to breathe the same air.

"No." But her lips twitch and I know she has thought of me. I know it and I'm ridiculously glad.

She tosses her head and turns, stepping slowly as if hunting her thoughts. I watch the line of her neck. She wears a riding dress of leather and suede, browns and muted greens. The sun finds a hundred reds in her coiled hair. "I hate you," she says.

Better than indifference. I step after her, moving close.

"Lord but you stink," she says.

"You said that the first time we met," I say. "At least it's an honest stink from the road. Horse and sweat. It smells better than court intrigue. At least to me."

She smells of spring. I'm close now and she has stopped walking from me. I'm close and there's a force between us, tingling on my skin, under my cheekbones, trembling in my fingers. It's hard to breathe. I want her.

"You don't want me, Jorg," she says as if I had spoken it. "And I don't want you. You're just a boy and a vicious one at that." The line of her mouth is firm, her lips pressed to a line but still full.

I can see the angles of her body and I want her more than I have wanted anything. And I am built of wants. I can't speak. I find my hands moving toward her and force them still.

"Why would you be interested in the sister of a 'Scorron whore' in any case?" she asks, her frown returning.

That makes me smile and I can speak again. "What? I have to be reasonable now? Is that the price for growing up? It's too high. If I can't take against the woman who replaced my own mother . . . can't make childish insults . . . it's too high a price, I tell you."

Again the twitch of her lips, the quick hint of a smile. "Is my sister a whore?"

"In truth, I have no evidence either way," I say.

She smiles a tight smile and wipes her hands on her skirts, glancing at the trees as if looking for friends or for foes.

"You wouldn't want me reasonable," I say.

"I don't want you at all," she says.

"The world isn't shaped by reasonable men," I say. "The world is a thief, a cheat, a murderer. Set a thief to catch a thief they say."

"I should hate you for Hanna," she says.

"She was trying to kill me." I walk to the grave Katherine pointed out. "Should I apologize to her? I can speak to the dead, you know."

I stoop to pick a bluebell, a flower for Hanna's grave, but the stem wilts in my hand, the blue darkening toward black.

"You should be dead," she says. "I saw the wound."

I pull up my shirt and show her. The dark line where Father's knife drove in, the black roots spreading from it, threading my flesh, diving in toward the heart.

She crosses her own chest, a protection quickly sketched. "There's evil in you, Jorg," she says.

"Perhaps," I say. "There's evil in a lot of men. Women too. Maybe I just wear it more plainly."

I wonder though. First Corion, then the necromancer's heart. I could blame them for my excesses, but something tells me that my failings are my own.

She bites her lip, steps away, then straightens. "In any case, I have my heart set on a good man."

For all my cleverness I hadn't thought of this. I hadn't thought of Katherine's eyes on other men.

"Who?" is all I can find to say.

"Prince Orrin," she says. "The Prince of Arrow."

And I'm falling.

I hit the rocks with a curse and skinned a palm, saving my face. Makin pulled me to my feet sharp enough. "Kings fall in battle," he said, "not tripping up on the way."

It took me a moment to shake the memory off. Still, there's little better than a hard reunion with the ground and blood on your hands to haul a man back into the here and now. The mountains, impending snow, and an enemy many thousands strong. Real problems, not rogue memories best forgotten.

"I'm fine." I patted the sack on my hip. The box was still there. "Let's break this Arrow."

24

Wedding day

From the heights even Arrow's many thousands looked small, arrayed across the slopes before the Haunt and along the ridges to the east. The sight might have given me heart had not my castle looked smaller still, swamped on three sides by men and more men, the winter sun picking glimmers from spear and helm.

Whether the Prince of Arrow's plans were in line with my prediction of an overwhelming assault or with Makin and Coddin's siege wasn't yet clear. What was clear was that our second attack would cost us. On our line of approach the Prince's troops spread out before the main body of his army in a scattered buffer zone, foot-soldiers under the best cover the slopes could offer, with additional defences hastily cobbled from overturned carts and heaped supplies. They kept under cover whilst the Watch picked whatever targets they could. Our arrows were killing or wounding men in their scores but all the time the archer columns ordered down from the eastern ridges drew closer. Perhaps a thousand of the Prince's four thousand archers would be returning fire within five minutes.

"They're not happy," Makin said. He didn't look too happy himself.

"No," I said. The roar from the Prince's army waxed and waned as the wind rose and fell. No true warrior holds any love for archers or archery. Death wings in unseen from a distance and there is little that skill or training can do to save you. I remembered four years back, Maical sliding from the grey as if he'd just forgotten how to ride. I didn't relish the arrival of the Prince's archers myself. My little tale of wickedness and gambles could be cut short easily enough by the sudden arrival of the right arrow in the wrong place.

"We should leave now," Coddin said.

"They won't follow us until the archers join them," I said.

"And why do we want them to follow us? The rockslides, well that was impressive, I won't deny that, but it can't happen again," Coddin said.

"Can it?" Hobbs at my right, hopeful.

"No," I said. "But we need to draw as many men from the fight as we can. The castle can work for us, but not with these odds. And remember, gentlemen, the beautiful Queen . . . Mi-something?"

"Miana," Coddin said.

"Yes, her. Queen Miana. Remind the men who we're fighting for, Hobbs."

And that was Coddin for you. He watched and he remembered. The man had a mixture of decency and reserve in him that struck a chord with me, qualities I would never own but could appreciate nonetheless. He'd been the first man of Ancrath I met on my return four years back. I'd thought him tall back then, though now I overtopped him. I'd thought him old, though now he had grey amid the black and I thought him in his prime. I'd elevated him from a guard captain to Watch-master of the Forest Watch because something in him told me he wouldn't let me down. That same quality put the chamberlain's robe around his shoulders a year later.

Across the slope old Keppen had his archers lofting their flights high into the air, passing over the scattered foot-soldiers to rain down unaimed in the midst of the Prince's forces.

I could see the first of the archers emerging from the ranks, men of Belpan with their tall bows, and the Prince's own levies with the dragons of Arrow painted red on their leather tabards.

"Time to go." I slipped the purple ribbon over the end of my shortbow and held it high for the Watch to see.

In retrospect it would have been better to have somebody else do it. Somebody unimportant. Fortunately the Prince's archers were still finding clear ground to shoot from and the shafts aimed at me went wide, at least wide enough to miss me. A man ten yards ahead of us jerked back with an arrow jutting from under his collarbone.

"Damn," said Coddin.

I turned sharp enough toward him. Something down the slope held his gaze but I couldn't tell what.

"Problem?" I asked.

Coddin held up scarlet fingers. It didn't make sense at first. I tried to see where he was cut.

"Easy." Makin moved to support him as he staggered.

At last I saw the arrow, just the flights showing, black against the dark leather over his guts. "Ah, hell."

A gut-shot man doesn't live. Everyone knows that. Even with silks under the leathers to twist and wrap the arrow so it pulls out easy and clean, you don't live past a gut shot.

"Carry him," I said.

The others just looked at me. For a moment I saw the Norse witch, felt the intensity of her single eye and the mockery in her withered smile. "Even a gut-shot man has a fool's hope," she'd said. Had she been looking past me, at this day?

"Damn prophecy and damn prediction!" I spat and the wind carried it away.

"Sorry?" Makin looked at me, even Coddin stared.

"Get some men here, pick him up, and carry him," I said.

"Jorg—" Makin started.

"I'll stay here," Coddin said. "It's a good view."

I liked Coddin from the start. Four years with him at the Haunt just scored the feeling deeper. I liked him for his quick mind, for his curious honesty, and for his courage in the face of hard choices. Mostly though I liked him because he liked me. "It's a better view from up there." I gestured up the slope.

"This will kill me, Jorg." He looked me in the eyes. I didn't like that. It put a strange kind of hurt on me.

Arrows in the guts don't kill quick, but the wound sours. You bloat and sweat and scream, then die. Two days, maybe four.

Had a Brother once that lasted a week and then some. I never once met a man who could show me a scar on his belly and tell how it hurt like a bastard when they pulled the arrow out.

"You owe me, Coddin," I said. "Your duty to your king is the least of it. That arrow probably will kill you, but not today. And if you think I've a sentimental side that will give you a quick death here and lose several days of useful advice when I need it most, you're wrong."

I'd never met a man who lived after that kind of hurt. But I *heard* of one. It *did* happen.

"We carry him up to the rock fall. We send men ahead to make a hidey-hole in the loose stone. We put him there and cover him up. If he's lucky we come back for him later. If not, he's ready buried," I said.

Already men of the Watch were crowding around, linking arms to lift Coddin. No complaints. They liked him too.

25

Wedding day

None of the men who carried Coddin up the mountain breathed a word of complaint. They had no breath for it, but if they had still they would have held their peace. Coddin led men by example. Somehow he made you want to do it right.

"I love you, Jorg, as my king, but also as a father loves his son, or should."

There are some things two men can only say to each other when arrows are raining down and one of them lies mortally wounded, walled away in a rough void amid a mass of fallen rock, and thousands of enemy troops are closing in. Even then it's uncomfortable.

We carried Coddin, Captain Lore Coddin, formerly of Ancrath, High Chancellor of the Renar Highlands. We carried him ahead of the fresh and surging army of Arrow, fuelled as they were by the desire to avenge the thousands crushed beneath our rockslides. The archers of the Watch held every ridge until the last moment, loosing flight after flight into the oncoming soldiers, making them climb their dead as well as the mountain. And tired as they were, the men of my Watch still opened a lead on the enemy, even bearing Coddin in their arms.

The troops sent ahead to the loose rubble of the morning's rockslides found a suitable cavity between two large boulders freed amongst the general fall. They enlarged the void and set aside rocks suitable for sealing and hiding the space.

By the time we reached the cave, the men carrying Coddin were scarlet with his blood and he groaned at each jolt of their advance. Captains Keppen and Harold massed their commands at separate points across the slope and shot the last of their arrows to hold our enemies' attention. And to kill them.

With the narrow neck of the valley ahead of us, and the snowline glistening high above that, and the wind picking up, filching warmth with quick sharp fingers, and the men of Arrow panting and gasping as they closed the last few hundred yards, I lay on the rock and spoke through gaps to the dying man below.

"You shut your mouth, old man," I said.

"You'd need to dig me out to stop me," he gasped. "Or run away. And I've a mind you're not running, not just yet." He coughed and tried to hide a groan. "You need to hear such words, Jorg. You need to know that you are loved, not just feared. You need to know it to ease what poisons you."

"Don't."

"You need to hear." Again the cough.

"I'm coming back for you when this is done, Coddin. So don't say anything you'll regret, because I *will* hold it against you."

"I love you for no good reason, Jorg. I've no sons, but if I did I wouldn't want them to be like you. You're a vicious bastard at the best of times."

"Careful, old man. I can still stick a sword through this crack and put you out of my misery."

A Watch man screamed and fell to my left, an arrow through his neck. Just like Maical, but louder. Another shaft hit the rock behind me and shattered.

"I love thee for no good reason," Coddin said, falling back into some accent from wherever he was born, his voice weak now.

I could hear the thud of boots. Steel on steel. Shouts.

". . . but I do love thee well."

I looked up, blinking. Down the slope Makin cut into the first of the enemy to reach us, an expert sword against exhausted common swords. No contest. At least until the odds mounted.

"Do something about that girl." Coddin's voice with new strength.

"Miana?" I asked. She should be safe in the castle. For now at least.

"Katherine of Scorron." Another cough. "These things seem terribly important when you're young. Matters of the heart and groin. They fill your world at eighteen. But believe me. When you're the wrong side of forty-five and the past is a bright haze . . . they're more important still. Do something. You're haunted by many ghosts. I know that, though you hide it well."

The men of the Watch massed before our position now, in full melee against the first few dozen of the enemy, with more pressing in moment by moment. They knew the bow like lovers know each other, but they could fight hand to hand too. Fighting on a steep slope of broken rock is not a skill you want to learn for the first time when somebody is trying to kill you, and the Watch had had years to learn the art, so for now they held.

"Miss an opportunity like Katherine and it will haunt you longer and more deeply than any ghost you keep now," Coddin said.

Another arrow hit, closer than any before.

"Run!" I shouted.

Whatever other wisdom Coddin had been hoarding would have to keep. There's a time for sentimental chatter and none of it is on a mountain whilst being shot at.

"Run!" I shouted. But I didn't raise the purple ribbon on a shortbow, because I had a plan to carry out, and no part of it involved being hit by arrows.

26

Wedding day

I'd buried Brothers before, even friends, but never alive.

We left Coddin in his tomb, not dead but with his passage booked. We made a messy retreat, fighting across the ground where we'd buried him. I joined the fray and cut a path through the men of Arrow, as if I was planning to make my way right back to the Haunt. There's something about a fight that makes you forget your troubles. Mainly it's that all your troubles are suddenly very small in the face of the new problems swinging your way with sharp edges on them.

Perhaps there's something wrong with me. Perhaps it's part of those three steps I took away from the world of reasonable men, of good men. But there's little that is more satisfying to me than a well-blocked sword blow followed by a swift riposte and the scream of an enemy. God, but the noise and feel of a blade shearing through flesh is as sweet as any flute speaking out its melody. Provided it's not my flesh of course. It can't be right. But there it is.

I fought well but the enemy just kept coming, as if dying were the only thing on their list today. We fell back and left them slipping in blood, tripping on corpses. Most of us managed to find the space to turn and run. Many of us didn't.

About two thirds of the Watch made it through the neck of the valley and scrambled up the steeper slopes onto the broad shoulder of the mountain above. The rest, even if it were only a light wound that slowed them, were swallowed by the advancing army.

Wind is the cruellest cold. Exposed on the mountainside we felt those sharp fingers stealing our warmth. All the running and climbing didn't matter. The wind put a chill in you even so, taking your strength one pinch at a time.

We struggled on through the wind, a ragged bunch without ranks or squads, the snow blinding now, small flakes too cold to stick to the rocks. Not far above us the snowline glittered, the whiteness hiding the folds and hollows, making it all of a likeness. Whiteness, stretching up to Blue Moon Pass, snow-choked and useless for escape, stretching beyond to the peak of Mount Botrang, and past that, the sky.

I caught Makin up, grey-faced and staggering. He looked at me, just a glance as if he were too tired to do anything but hang his head. He hadn't the breath for words but his look, quick as it was, told me we were going to die on these slopes. Maybe on the next ridge, maybe farther up, on the snow with our blood making pretty crimson patterns against the white.

"Stick with me," I said. I had a little go left in me. Not much, but some. "I have a plan."

I hoped I had a plan.

The wind numbed my face. On the right where Gog had left me scarred it felt good. That twisted flesh had never stopped burning, as if shards of him found the bones in my jaw and cheek and lodged there with fire trapped inside. The wind made my face feel solid, like one block that would crack if I spoke again. I enjoyed the relief. I've become good at finding crumbs of comfort. Sometimes they're all you have to eat.

Screams behind us as the slowest men of the Watch met the fastest men of Arrow.

I had my head down, concentrating on one foot then the next, hauling in one breath and throwing it out to make room for the one after. Beside me Makin looked to have retreated into that closed and lonely place that we all reach if we keep digging. Dig a little deeper than that and you're in hell all of a sudden.

The snow took me by surprise. One moment *thump thump thump* over rocks and the next a silent wade through deep white powder. It took maybe four strides to go from bare rock to snow past my knees. Another hundred strides and my feet were as numb as my face. I wondered if I was dying piece by piece, a slow introduction rather than the traditional unexpected embrace.

The snowfield started to get us killed. Pushing a path through snow is hard work. Following in the beaten trail of two hundred men is easier. More men were caught. Natural selection had set the toughest of Arrow's men at our heels with the weaker troops still struggling through the neck of the valley below the snowline.

"Up there!" I pointed to a place with nothing to distinguish it from any other acre of white. I could feel the box hot against my hip. I picked up the pace and left Makin plodding. "Up there!" I didn't know why, but I knew.

I took the box in my hand and ran on, lungs filling with blood, or that's how it felt.

The thing that tripped me wasn't a rock. The snow had all the rocks covered, deep under our feet. What tripped me was something long and hard and near the surface. Broomstick came to mind as I fell. Then the box went *schnick* and my mind filled with entirely new things. Old things.

27

Wedding day

Schnick and the box opens. Memory drags me back to Rennat Forest to stand amongst gravestones and wildflowers in the spring sunshine.

"In any case, I have my heart set on a good man," Katherine says.

"Who?" I ask.

"Prince Orrin," she says. "The Prince of Arrow."

"No," I say. I don't want to say anything, but I speak. I don't want to admit any kind of interest, any form of weakness, but none of this is going as I planned, and plans are what I'm good at.

"No?" she asks. "You object? You'd like to offer a proposal? Your father is my guardian. You should go and discuss the matter with him."

It wasn't supposed to happen like this. None of the others made me this way. Not Serra leading me astray as a child almost, not Sally bought and paid for, nor Renar's serving maids, ladies-at-court, bored wives of nobles, comely peasant girls, not the ones on the road that the Brothers took and shared, none of them.

"I want you," I say. The words are hard, they have awkward shapes, they leave my mouth clumsy and ill-formed.

"How romantic," she says. Her scorn withers me. "You like me because I'm pleasing to your eye."

"You please more than my eye, lady," I say.

"Would you kill Sareth?" she asks. For a moment I think she's asking me to do it. Then I remember she's not like me.

"Maybe . . . does she please my father?" I don't say does he love her; he has never loved. And I don't lie. If it would hurt my father to lose her, then yes, maybe.

"No. I don't think anything pleases Olidan. I can't even imagine what would. Though he did laugh that day when you killed Galen," she says.

"I might kill Sareth in case you're wrong or trying to protect her," I say. I don't know why I can't lie to her. "But you're probably telling the truth. My father has found little in this world that doesn't disappoint him."

She steps towards me and although she's coming closer her eyes get more distant. I can smell her scent, lilacs and white musk.

"You hit me, Jorg," she says.

"You were going to stab me."

"You hit me with my mother's vase." Her voice is dreamy. "And broke it."

"I'm sorry," I say. And the strange truth is that I am.

"I wasn't made to be this way." She's reaching for something hidden in the folds of her riding dress, under fawn suede. "I wasn't meant to be the prize princes compete for, or the container to grow their babies in. Damn that. Would you want to be a token? Or made just to grow babies and raise children?"

"I'm not a woman," I say. It's just my lips filling the pause while the questions, or rather the new images they paint of her, bounce around my mind.

I see her pull the knife from her skirts. A long blade like those for slotting through chinks in armour when you have your foe pinned, only not so sturdy. This one would break if the man twisted and might not reach the heart. I'm not supposed to see it. I'm supposed to be watching her eyes, her mouth, the heave of her breasts, and I am, but often I see more than I'm supposed to.

"Can't I want something more?" she asks.

"Wanting is free." I can't stop watching her. My glance touches the knife only now and then. Her eyes don't see me. I don't think she knows what her hands are doing, the right gripping a hilt, the left on her belly, clawed like she wants to tear her way in.

"Do I have to be a monster? Do I have to be a new Queen of Red to—"

I catch her wrist as she drives the knife at me. She is stronger than I imagined. We both look down at my hand, dark on her white wrist, and the thin blade quivering with its point an inch from my groin.

"A low blow." I twist her arm but she drops the knife before I make her.

"What?" She stares at her hand and mine, mouth open.

"You're making a habit of trying to stab me," I say. The bitterness rises in me. I taste it.

"I killed our child, Jorg." Her laugh is too high, too wild. "I killed it. I swallowed a sour pill from Saraem Wic. She lives here." Katherine whips her head around, unfocused, as if expecting to see the crone among the trees.

I know of Saraem Wic. I've seen her gather her herbs and fungi. I crept to her hut once, almost close enough to look in, but I didn't want to go closer. It smelled of burned dog. "What are you talking about?" I ask. She looks beautiful. She curses being a woman but here I am forgetting even the knife on the ground, the knife she almost buried in me, forgetting it because of the curve of her neck, the tremble of her lips. Want makes fools of men.

"You hit me and then you took me. You put your seed in me." She spits. It misses my face but drips in my hair and wets my ear. "And I drove it out. With a sour pill and a paste that burned."

She grins and I can see the hatred now. She sees me clear for once, head down, hair framing her, eyes dark. She shows her teeth. She dares me.

I remember her lying there in the sapphire pool of her dress. Senseless. The voice from the briar, maybe mine, maybe Corion's, or something of both, told me to kill her. My father would give that advice. The hardest line. Want makes fools of men. But I didn't kill her. The voice told me to rape her too. To just take her. But I only touched her hair. What I wanted couldn't be taken.

"Nothing to say, Jorg?" She spits again. This time it's in my face. I blink. Warm spittle cools on my cheek. She wants me angry. She doesn't care what I might do. "I bled your baby out. Before he was even big enough to see."

And I don't know what to say. What words would serve? I wouldn't believe me. I have to believe my memory—things have been taken from it in the past, but never added—but who else would give Jorg of Ancrath the benefit of the doubt? Not me.

I fold Katherine's arm up behind her and walk her through the graveyard, back the way I came. There are white marks where my fingers touched her skin. Did I grip her that hard? Imagination has put my hands on her many times, but this feels as though I've broken something precious and I'm carrying the pieces, knowing they can't be reassembled.

"You're going to do it again?" The anger has leaked from her. She sounds confused.

"No," I say.

We walk on. Brambles catch at her dress. Her riding boots leave heel marks a blind man could follow. "I've left my horse tied," she says. This isn't the Katherine I left on the floor that day. That Katherine was sharp, clever; this one is dazed, as though just waking.

"I'm going to marry the Prince of Arrow," she says, twisting to look at me over her shoulder.

"I thought you didn't want to be a prize," I say.

She looks away. "We can't always have what we want."

I need her. I wonder if I can have what I need.

We walk in silence until Red Kent steps out of the under-growth before us. My sword is strapped over his shoulder. "King Jorg." He nods. "My lady."

"Take her to Sir Makin," I say. I let her arm go.

Kent gestures for Katherine to lead the way along the trail he's been guarding. "No kind of harm is to come to her, Kent. Watch Row and Rike particularly. Tell them you've my permission to cut from them any part that touches her. And move camp. We've left a trail from there to here." I walk away.

"Where are you going?" she asks.

I stop and turn, wiping her spit from my cheek. "Who found you?"

"What?"

"Who found you after I hit you?" I ask. "A man was with you when you recovered your senses."

She frowns. Her fingers touch the place where the vase shattered. "Friar Glen." For the first time she sees me with her old eyes, clear and green and sharp. "Oh."

I walk away.

Schnick and a heartbeat later the box closes again, snapped shut by numb fingers.

Back on the mountain, knee-deep in snow. My shin hurts. I tripped over a spade.

There are men to walk to the mountain with and then there are men that are the mountain. Gorgoth, though I may not call him brother, was forged from the qualities I lack.

28

Four years earlier

There are books in my father's library that say no mountain ever spat lava within a thousand miles of Halradra before the Thousand Suns. They tell it that the Builders drilled into the molten blood of the Earth and drank its power. When the Suns scorched away all that the Builders had wrought, the wounds remained. The Earth bled and Halradra and his sons were born in fire.

Gorgoth carried me to where Sindri waited. The sun still shone outside though I felt it should be dark. I came to my senses halfway down the mountain, bouncing on Gorgoth's broad back. They came one by one, my senses, first the pain and only the pain, then after an age, the smell of my own burned flesh, the taste of vomit, the sound of my moaning, and finally a blurred vision of Halradra's black slopes.

"God, just kill me," I whimpered. The tears dripped off my nose and lips, hanging as I was like a sack over Gorgoth's shoulder.

It wasn't Gog I was sorry for, it was me.

In my defence, having a hand-sized part of your face burned

crisp is ridiculously painful. It hurt worse hanging there, bumping with the monster's strides, than when it happened, and I had wanted to die back there in the cave.

"Kill me," I moaned.

Gorgoth stopped. "Yes?"

I thought about it. "Christ Jesu." I needed someone to hate, something to take my mind off the fire still eating into me. Gorgoth waited. He would take me at my word. I thought of my father with his young wife and new son, snug in the Tall Castle.

"Maybe later," I said.

I remember only snippets until Gorgoth laid me down in the bracken and Sindri leaned over me.

"Uskit'r!" He fell back into the old tongue of the north. "That's bad."

"At least I'm still half-pretty." I retched and turned my face to spit sour liquid into the ferns.

"Let's get him back," Sindri said. He looked around for a moment, opened his mouth then closed it.

"Gog's gone," I said.

Sindri shook his head and looked down. He drew a breath. "Come, we need to get you back. Gorgoth?"

The monster made no move.

"Gorgoth's not coming," I said.

Gorgoth bowed his head.

"You can't stay here," Sindri said, alarmed. "Ferrakind—"

"Ferrakind is gone too," I said. Each word hurt, almost enough to make them into one scream.

"No?" Sindri's mouth stayed open.

"We are not friends, Jorg of Ancrath," Gorgoth said, deeper than he'd ever spoken. "But we both loved the boy. You loved him first. You named him. That means something."

I would have told him what rubbish he was speaking but my face hurt too much for more words.

"I will stay in the Heimrift, in the caves."

I would have said, *I hope the troll-stink chokes you*, but the price for opening my mouth was too high. I just raised my hand. And Gorgoth raised his. And we parted.

Sindri closed his mouth, then opened it again. "Ferrakind's gone?"

I nodded.

"Can you walk?" he asked.

I shrugged and lay back in the bracken. Maybe I could. Maybe I couldn't. I wasn't going to, and that was the main thing.

"I'll get help. Horses," he said. "Wait there." He held out both hands as if to stop me standing, then turned on a heel and sprinted away. I thought the news drove him more than any of my needs. He wanted to be the one to tell it. Which was fair enough.

I watched the blue sky and prayed for rain. Flies buzzed about me, drawn by the raw pink, the skinless muscle and fat on offer. They wanted to lay their eggs. After a while I stopped trying to wave them away. I lay a-moaning, twisting one way and another as if there might be a way that helped. From time to time I fainted and in the afternoon a light rain did come and I prayed it would stop. Each drop burned like acid.

In the evening clouds of mosquitoes rose from wherever it is that mosquitoes hide. The Dane-lands were thick with the things. Probably why the folk are so pale. The blood's been sucked from them. I lay there, letting them eat me, and eventually I heard voices.

Makin came and I wanted to beg for death, but my face hurt too much. It would crack apart if I opened my mouth, all the wounds oozing. Then Rike stepped up, black against the deep blue of the sky and a little strength flowed into me. It doesn't pay to be weak in front of Rike, and there's something about Rike that makes me forget all about dying and want to do a bit of killing instead. "I knew I brought you along for a reason, Rike." Each word an agony, edged with murder.

We stayed five days in Alaric Maladon's hall. Not in the guest hall but in his great hall. They put a chair for me on the dais, nearly as grand as the Duke's own, and I sat there wrapped in furs when I shivered and stripped to the waist when I sweated. Makin and the Brothers celebrated with Maladon's people. Women appeared for the first time in any number, carrying the ale in flagons and horns from the storehouse, knives at their hips, eating at the long tables like the men, drinking and laughing almost as loud. One, near as tall as me, blond as milk and handsome in a raw-boned way, came up to my chair as I huddled in my furs. "My thanks, King Jorg," she said.

"I could be making it all up," I said. Feeling rotten and ugly made me want to sour the day.

She grinned. "The ground hasn't shaken since they brought you back. The sky is clear."

"What's that?" I asked. She had a clay pot in one hand, filled with black and glistening paste, a twist of hide next to it.

"Ekatri gave it to me. A salve for the burns, and a powder to swallow in water to fight the poison in your blood."

I managed half a laugh before the pain stopped me. "The old witch who keeps predicting my failures? There'll be poison in me if I take anything she sends all right. It's probably how the future turns out the way she says it will."

The woman—girl maybe—laughed. "That's not how völvas are. Besides, my father would take it in poor humour if you died here. It would reflect badly upon him, and Ekatri depends upon his favour."

"Your father?" I asked.

"Duke Maladon, silly," she said and walked away leaving the pot and wrap in my lap. I watched her backside as she went. I thought perhaps I wouldn't die if I could still find time to watch a well-crafted bottom.

She looked over her shoulder and caught me watching. "I'm Elin." And she walked on, lost in the crowd and the smoke.

I took Ekatri's powder and bit on a leather strap as Makin dabbed the ointment on my burns. He may have a light touch with a sword but as a healer he seemed to have ten thumbs. I nearly chewed through the strap but when he'd finished the pain had died to a dull roar.

The girl, Elin, said the völva depended upon her father's favour. I hoped that was so, rather than he on hers. Makin had been digging around, asking my questions in the right corners, doing that thing he does, the one that gets him answers. No one had said it, but if you stacked those answers up and looked at the pile from the right angle, it seemed the ice-witch, Skilfar, had a cold finger in every northern pie. I didn't doubt that many a jarl and north-lord danced to her tune without ever knowing it. Ekatri though, Makin said she was a smaller fish. I wondered on that one, sitting alone with my pain in the quiet of night. Alaric of Maladon should mind himself I thought—even the smallest fish can choke you.

I sat for five days, feeding on oat-mush whilst the Brothers gorged on roasted pig, ox heads, fat trout from the lake, sugar apples, and anything else that would be agony for me to chew. Each night more of the Duke's kith and kin arrived to swell the throng. Neighbours too. Men of the Hagenfast, beards plaited with locks from those who died under their axes, true Vikings tall and fair and cruel, out of Iron Fort and ports north, and a lone fat warrior from the marches of Snjar Songr, sour with seal grease and not parting with any of the furs that bundled him despite the hall's heat.

I watched Rike win the wrestling contest after ten drunken heats, finally throwing down a Viking with slab-muscled arms and a permanently florid face. I watched Red Kent come first in the throwing of the hand-axe at a wooden target board, and third in the log-splitting. A tall local with pale eyes beat Grumlow into second in the business of knife-throwing, but Grumlow was ever a stabber and better motivated to hit a target if it breathed. They told me Row acquitted himself well in the archery, but that took place outside and I didn't let them move me. Makin lost at everything, but then again Makin knows that winners may be admired but they are not liked.

The Duke and Sindri sat beside me often enough, asking for the tale of Ferrakind's end, but I shook my head and told it with a single word. "Wet."

The ale flowed, but I drank only water and watched the torch-flames more often than I watched the Danes at their feasting and sport. Flames held new colours for me. I thought of Gog, destroyed by fire, and of his little brother who bore the name I gave him, Magog, for only a few hours. I thought of Gorgoth among the silence of the trolls in the black caverns. I held the copper box in my hand and wondered if its contents would distract me from my pain.

Most of all, though, as boys do when they're hurt—and at fourteen I discovered I was still a boy if the hurt came fierce enough—I thought of my mother. I remembered how I twisted and moaned on the slopes after Sindri left me, the agony that held me and the thirst I had, nearly as large as the pain. I would have fitted well amongst the dying at Mabberton, amongst the wounded that I had watched with a smile, coiled about their hurts, calling for water. And when pain bites, men bargain. Boys too. We twist and turn, we plead and beg, we offer our tormentor what he wants so that the hurting will stop. And when there is no torturer to placate, no hooded man with hot irons and tongs, just a burn you can't escape, we bargain with God, or ourselves, depending on the size of our egos. I made mock of the dying at Mabberton and now their ghosts watched me burn. Take the pain, I said, and I will be a good man. Or if not that, a better man. We all become weasels with enough hurt on us. But I think a small part of it was more than that. A small part was that terrible two-edged sword called experience, cutting away at the cruel child I was, carving out whatever man might be yet to come. I promised a better one. Though I have been known to lie.

We were bound for Wennith on the Horse Coast that day, when Mabberton burned. Wennith, where my grandfather sits upon his throne in a high castle overlooking the sea. Or so my mother told me, for I had never seen it. Corion came from the Horse Coast. Perhaps he had aimed me there, a weapon to settle some old score for him. In any event, in Duke Maladon's hall in the quiet hours before dawn when the torches failed and the lamps guttered out, amid snoring Norsemen slumped over their tables, my thoughts turned once more to Wennith. I had friends in the north now, but to win this Hundred War of ours, of mine, I might need some family support.

Age set its hand on Brother Row and left him forever fifty, not wanting to touch him a second time. Grey, grizzled, lean, gristly, mean. That pale-eyed old man will bend and twist but never break. He'll hold where the better man would fail beneath his load. The shortest of our number, rank and filthy, seamed with forgotten scars, often overlooked by men who had scant time to reflect on their mistake.

29

Four years earlier

On the long journey south I questioned the motivation for my diversion more than once. More than a hundred times, truth be told. The fact of the matter was that I hadn't found what I needed yet. I didn't know what I needed, but I knew it wasn't in the Haunt. My old tutor, Lundist, once said that if you don't know where to look for something, just start looking where you are. For a clever man he could be very stupid. I planned to look everywhere.

We rode out on the sixth day. I sat in Brath's saddle stiff in every muscle, my face aching and weeping.

"You're still sick," Makin said beside me.

"I'm sicker of sitting in that chair watching you gorge yourself as if your only ambition were to be spherical," I said.

The Duke came to the doors of his hall with a hundred and more of his warriors to see us off. Sindri stood at his right hand, Elin at his left. Alaric led them in a cheer. Three times they roared and shook their axes overhead. They were a scary enough bunch saying farewell to friends. I didn't fancy the chances of any they deemed to be enemies.

The Duke left his men to come to my side. "You worked a magic here, Jorg. It will not be forgotten."

I nodded. "Leave the Heimrift in peace, Duke," I said. "Halradra and his sons are sleeping. No need to go poking them."

"And you have a friend up there." He smiled.

"He's no friend of mine," I said. Part of me wished he was though. I liked Gorgoth. Unfortunately he was a good judge of men.

"Good travels." Sindri came to stand beside his father, grinning as ever.

"Come back to us in the winter, King Jorg." Elin joined them.

"You wouldn't want to see this ugly face again." I watched her pale eyes.

"A man's scars tell his story. Yours is a story I like to read," she said.

I had to grin at that, though it hurt me. "Ha!" And I wheeled Brath to lead my Brothers south.

Back on the road, and with regular applications of Ekatri's black ointment, my face began to heal, the raw flesh congealing to an ugly mass of scar tissue. From the right you got handsome Jorgy Ancrath, from the left, something monstrous: my true nature showing through, some might say. The pain eased, replaced by an unpleasant tightness and a deeper burning around the bones. At last I could bear to eat. Now all the fine servings from the Duke's table were trailing farther and farther behind us, I discovered that I had an awful hunger about me. And that's a thing about the road. Out on a horse, trotting the ways of empire day after day with nothing to eat but what you can carry or steal, you discover that everything tastes good when your stomach is empty. If you look at a mouldy piece of cheese and your mouth doesn't water—you're just not proper hungry.

In the Haunt the cooks would honey-glaze venison and garnish it with baked, rosemary-sprinkled dormice just to tempt my palate. After days in the saddle I find that in order for food to tempt me it must be either hot or cold and preferably, though not essentially, if it is animal, that it should not be moving and should once have possessed a backbone.

Around the fire at camp on that first evening we made a subdued huddle, somehow more reduced by the absence of our smallest companion than by that of our largest. I stared at the flames and imagined a sympathetic tingling in the bones of my jaw, even under the deadening effect of the ointment.

"I miss the little fellow." Grumlow surprised me.

"Aye." Sim spat.

Red Kent looked up from the polishing of his axe. "Did he give good account of himself, Jorg?"

"He saved me and Gorgoth both," I said. "And he finished the fire-mage before he died."

"Sounds about right," Row said. "He were a godless bastard, that one, but he had a fire in him, God did he."

"Makin," I said.

He looked up, the flames reflected in his eyes.

"Since Coddin is at home . . ." I paused then, realizing that I'd called the Haunt "home" for the first time. "Since Coddin is at home, and the Nuban isn't with us . . ."

"Yes?" he said.

"I'm saying, if I set on a path that's . . . maybe a little too harsh. Just let me know. All right?"

He pursed those too-fleshy lips of his then sucked air in through his teeth. "I'll try," he said. He'd been trying all these years, I knew that, but now I gave him permission.

For a week we skirted villages, circled towns, and picked our way through the soft edges of the kingdoms we had passed on our journey north. We came to the settlement of Rye, too big to be a village, too recent and too random to be a town. On our trip out we had purchased provisions there and with our saddle-bags flapping empty we rode in to resupply. Paying for goods still feels odd to me, but it's a good habit to get into when you've the coin to spare. Of course you should steal every now and then, take something by force just for the wickedness of it, or how else will you keep your hand in the game? But aside from that, paying is recommended, especially if you're a king with a pocketful of gold.

The main square in Rye isn't square and it's only just about "main" as there are other markets and clearings in Rye almost as large. Rike had loaded the last sack of oats onto that great carthorse of his and Makin was trying to strap his saddlebag over four gutted hares in their fur when the crowd flowing around us seemed to part like the Red Sea for an old man. I had been leaning against Brath feeling rather faint. Summer had decided to give us a preview and the sun came beating down out of a faded sky. My face ached like a bastard and a fever had got its claws into me.

"Prince of Thorns!" the old fellow cried as he homed in on me, loud enough to turn heads.

"That'd be 'king' if it's anything," I muttered. "And if there's a Thorns on the map then I must have missed it."

He stopped about a yard in front of me, and drew himself up tall. A skinny fellow, dried like a prune, with white hair fluffing at the sides of a bald head. His eyes were milky, though not like cataracts but somehow pearly with a hint of rainbows. "Prince of Thorns!" Louder this time. People started to close in.

"Go away." I used my quiet voice, the one that recommends you listen.

"The Gilden Gate will open for the Prince of Arrow." Something electric crackled in the air around us, the white fluff stood out from the sides of his head. "You can only—"

There's an art to the quick drawing of a sword. Providing the scabbard strap is undone, and I always keep mine so, you can propel the whole blade several feet into the air just by hooking a hand loosely under one side of the cross-guard and literally throwing it upward. With good timing and a quick turn of the body you can snatch the hilt at the apex of the throw and as the sword falls you can turn that momentum into a sudden thrust into whatever is beside you.

I looked back over my shoulder. The man's eyes still had their milky sheen but he'd stopped prophesying on me. By stepping away I drew the blade from his chest. He looked down at the scarlet wound but, oddly, did not fall.

I waited a moment, then another. The crowd kept their silence and the old man kept standing, making a close study of the blood pumping down his stomach.

"Hey," I said.

He looked up at that, which helped. His chin had been in the way. I took his head with one clean blow. I'm not one to boast but it's not easy to decapitate a man in one swing. I've seen expert axemen take three blows to do it at an execution when their victim's neck is laid out for them on a block.

The seer had enough grace to let his body topple after his head landed by his feet. He kept looking at me though, with those pearly eyes. There's no magic in it, a severed head can watch you for close on a minute if you let it, but they say it's bad luck to be the last thing it sees.

I picked the head up by its tufts of hair and held it facing me at eye level. "Seriously? You can tell me what I am and am not going to sit on in years to come and you didn't see that one coming?" I kept my voice loud for the crowd. "This fake has been living off your misery and the misery of folk like you for years."

And in a quiet voice, just for the seer and any who watched me through his eyes, for all those who watched this moment across the span of years before I was born. "I will make my own future. Being dead doesn't make you right. Everybody dies."

The lips smiled. They writhed. "Dead King," they said, without sound, and where I touched him my skin crawled, as if a spider unfolded itself in my palm.

I dropped the head and kicked it into the crowd. I say "kicked" but in truth it's a bad idea to kick a head. I learned that years ago, a lesson that cost me two broken toes. What you want to do is shove the head with the side of your foot, like you're throwing it. It's going to roll anyhow so you don't need that much force. See, the thing about severed heads is the owner no longer has any interest in minimizing the force of the blow, or any ability to do so for that matter. When you kick somebody in the head as you do from time to time, they tend to be actively trying to move themselves out of the way and the contact is lessened. A severed head is a dead weight, even if it's watching you.

And that exhausts my insights into the kicking of severed heads. Admittedly it's more than most people have to offer on the subject but there were Mayans who knew a lot more than I do. That of course is a whole different ball-game.

Makin finished with his straps and stepped beside me. "That was probably too harsh," he said. "You did ask me to point these things out."

"Fuck off," I said.

I waved to the Brothers. "Let's ride."

For close on a hundred miles we retraced our path along the North Way, down through the duchies of Parquat and Bavar where most travellers are welcome so long as they don't plan to stay, and even our sort are tolerated so long as we don't get off our horses.

The town of Hanver greeted us with bunting. Among those peaceful huddles of thatched cottages that I had remarked upon whilst travelling north, Hanver lay equally untouched and unspoiled, a place not visited by war and cradled amidst idyllic farmland divided into tiny fertile fields.

"Looks like a holy day." Kent stood in his stirrups to see. For all that he was a dark and deadly bastard, Kent had himself a pious nature, the good kind of pious, or at least the better kind.

"Gah." Rike liked his celebrations louder, more wild, and more likely to end in a riot.

"There'll be chorals," Sim said, ever the music-lover.

And so without much more than a nod toward the fact I was king of Renar and that none of them were much more than scabby peasants at the end of it all, the Brothers led me into Hanver. We rode in down the main street, through the crowd, the locals with scrubbed faces, sporting their best rags, the children waving ribbon-sticks, some clutching sugar-apples kept sweet over winter. The Brothers set off on separate ways, Sim to the church, Grumlow to the smithy, Rike handing his reins to a boy outside the first tavern. Row, more particular, chose the second tavern and Kent veered off to a stables to get an expert eye on Hellax's front right foreleg.

"Looks like there'll be more than chorals." Makin nodded ahead to the main square. A wooden platform had been erected, fresh timbers, still weeping. A wide stage, a gallows frame, and three strangling cords dangling in the breeze.

We tied up at the public tether and Makin flicked the watch-boy a copper double.

"Church execution," Makin said. A white flag fluttered at the far corner of the platform, the holy cross and cup inked onto the linen.

"Hmmm." I had little enough enthusiasm for matters ecumenical in the Tall Castle. On the road the church spread Roma's poisons without moderation. And that perhaps is the only time I have considered my father to be a moderating influence.

We stood with the others in the sunshine, snagging skewers of roast mutton from a passing seller. An ale-boy sold us arac in pewter cups, a dark and bitter local brew, stronger than wine. He waited for us to throw it back then went on his way with his cups returned. I may not have any time for the church, but why miss a good execution? Once years back we'd watched them hang Brother Merron and Row had said, "A good execution don't need a good reason." Which is true enough.

We heard the singing first, four choirboys, probably none of them cut, not in a wattle-and-daub town like Hanver. Nothing to see to start with save a silver cross up high on a staff, then the crowd parting and the boys in white frocks, voices soaring. I saw Sim way back, mouthing the words, though he didn't know the Latin, just the sounds of it.

The priests then, two black crows with the holy purple showing at their breast, swinging censers. Blunt-faced, alike as brothers, no older than Makin. Following, drawn on a cart and bound at hand and foot, a mother and two daughters, ten, twelve, hard to say, white with terror. The senior priest brought up the rear, purple silks showing in diamonds through the black of his cassock, a stern man, handsome enough, silver hair in a widow's peak lending him gravitas.

"I need a decent ale." Makin spat. "That arac's left a sour taste."

It might be that a good execution doesn't need a good reason, but it seemed to me that no execution the church conducted could be called good. I'd held Father Gomst in contempt most of my life, as much for the lies he told as for his weakness. That night of thorns and rain had shown his lies, clear as if lightning found them in a dark room. But they would have surfaced in time either way. In fairness though, Gomst's brand of feeble optimism and talk of love had little of the Roma doctrine in it. Father wouldn't let the pope's hand inside his castle.

There were jeers among the crowd as the woman and her girls were manhandled onto the platform, though plenty kept silent, faces held tight and joyless.

"Do you know what the church of Roma has in common with the church that came before it, the faith the popes held in the time of the Builders, in the centuries before the Builders?" I said.

Makin shook his head. "No."

"Nobody else does either," I said. "Pope Anticus took in every bible that survived the Thousand Suns in deep vaults, all the books of doctrine, all the Vatican records. All of it. Could have burned the lot. Could be following every letter and footnote. The scholars can tell you nothing except that you're not allowed to know."

The priest up on the platform had found his stride, patrolling the edge before the crowd and bellowing about wickedness and witchcraft. White flecks of spit caught the sunlight as they arced over the heads of the peasants closest in.

"I never took you for a theologian, Jorg." Makin turned away. "Coming for that ale?"

I watched the executioners wrestle the first girl to the post. Not to be a straight hanging then, a little cutting first perhaps. She put up a struggle for a small thing: you could see the strain in the man's arms.

"Too early in the day for blood, Sir Makin?" I goaded him but the jibe was aimed inward at whatever was putting that same sour taste in my own mouth.

Makin growled. "Call me soft but I've no stomach for it. Not for children."

I don't think he'd ever a stomach for it, Makin, not for children, not for men, though he'd let himself be carried along in the darkness of the Brotherhood back in those early years when he counted himself all that stood to defend me.

"But they're witches." Another taunt meant for myself. They probably were witches. I'd met witches of many flavours and more magic seemed to leak into the world with each passing year, finding its way through this person or that as if they were cracks in the fabric of our days. I'm sure the priest would have had me up on his platform too if he knew I could talk to dead men, if he saw the black veins running corrupt across my chest—if he had the balls to take me. They might be witches, but just as likely the woman had dared to disagree, or invent. Roma hated nothing like it hated invention. A priest might order you burned for making free with some enchantment, but find the trick of a better steel, or rediscover some alchemy of the Builders, and they would have an expert spend all week killing you.

Makin spat again, shook his head, walked away. A judgment on me. On his damn king! I threw off the anger, it was an escape, I could hide in it, but it wasn't Makin that had made me angry.

Let people pray to God, it's nothing to me. Some good may even come of it, if goodness is something that matters to you. Trap him in churches if you must, and lament him there. But Roma? Roma is a weapon used against us. A poison flavoured sweet and given to hungry men.

Up on the platform the girl screamed as they stripped her. A man approached holding a cane all set with metal teeth, glittering and pretty.

"It's the bishop, isn't it?" I found Kent beside me, his hand on mine as somehow it worked to draw steel without asking my permission. With Kent's help I kept my sword in its scabbard.

"Murillo," I agreed. There were few men who would dare mention Bishop Murillo to me. I regret the nails still. I had hammered them slow enough into his head, but even so it was too quick an escape for him.

"A black day," Kent said, though I couldn't tell if he meant then or now. Pious or not, he had never once chided me for the pope's nephew.

I nodded. I had better reasons to hate the church of Roma than for Murillo, but the bishop had put the edge on it. "How's Hellax?" I asked.

"She'll be fine. They put a poultice on her leg," Kent said.

The girl howled like the damned though all they'd done was show her the cane.

"Fit to ride, is she?" I asked.

Kent gave me a look. "Jorg!"

We're built of contradictions, all of us. It's those opposing forces that give us strength, like an arch, each block pressing the next. Give me a man whose parts are all aligned in agreement and I'll show you madness. We walk a narrow path, insanity to each side. A man without contradictions to balance him will soon veer off.

"Let's get a better view." I moved through the crowd. Most got out of my way, some I had to hurt. Kent stayed close behind.

Makin walked away because his contradictions allowed him a compromise. Mine are not so gentle. I'll say it was hate that put me on that platform. Hate for Roma, for its doctrine of ignorance, for the corruption of its highest officials, perhaps for the fact it wasn't my idea. My Brothers would tell you the decision owed as much to contrariness, to my taking offence at the idea that the only things holding those prisoners save the binding cords were fear of the priest and the baying of the mob. Certainly my actions owed nothing to three months on the throne of Renar. When they set that crown on my head technically I accepted responsibility for the people of my kingdom, but the crown weighed more than the responsibility ever did, and I even took the crown off before too long.

Nobody tried to stop me clambering on stage. I swear there were even a few helping shoves. I took the cane from the executioner's hand as he drew back for his first swing. Sharp little twists of iron studded its length. The girl, naked against the post, watched that cane as if it were the only thing in the world. She looked too clean for a peasant. Perhaps the priests had washed her so the marks of her torture wouldn't be lost in the dirt.

Red slaughter was an option, my fingers itched for a sword hilt and I felt fairly sure I could kill everyone on the stage without breaking sweat. Hanver hadn't seen war in a generation—I was more than ready to change that. Instead I tried reason, or at least my brand of reason. Three strides brought me to within a yard of the silver-haired priest. The toothed cane twirling in one hand.

"I am King Jorg of Renar. I have killed more priests than you have killed witches, and I say you will release these three for no reason other than it pleases me." I spoke clear and loud enough for the crowd, which had fallen so quiet I could hear the flag's fluttering. "The next words out of your mouth, priest, will be 'Yes, Your Highness' or you'll be making a meal of this cane."

To his credit the priest hesitated, then said, "Yes, Your Highness." I doubt he believed my lineage, but he sure as hell believed my culinary predictions.

Armed men stood among the peasants, not so many but enough, bullies in helms and padded jerkins keeping order for whatever lordling held sway here. I met their eyes, beckoned to a group of three over by the horse trough. They shrugged and turned away. I can't say it pleased me. Makin stood just beyond the trio, his compromise not having taken him as far as the closest alehouse after all.

"Tell me no!" My sword cleared its scabbard so fast it almost rang.

Blood-hunger on faces in the crowd, the shock that they had been denied their due. I shared it too. Like a sneeze that goes unvoiced, a vacuum demanding to be filled. I waited, more than half of me wanting them to riot, to sweep forward in a wave of outrage.

"Tell me no." But they stood silent.

The prisoners' ropes gave before my sword's honed edge. "Get out," I told them, angry now as if it were their fault. The mother limped away pulling her girls behind her. Makin helped them down.

I wondered later if it would be enough to send my ghost away, if my good deed, whatever the reason for it, would keep that dead baby from my dreams. But he returned as ever with the shadows.

We stayed a full day in Hanver and left on a bright morning, our saddlebags full, and with the bunting still overhead. Such is the beauty of places untouched by war. And the reason they don't last.

30

Four years earlier

I had left my monsters in the North—Gog and Gorgoth—my demons I carried south with me as ever.

We made good time on our journey south. We crossed the Rhyme aboard one of those rickety barges I had been so dismissive of on the way north. I found it an interesting experience—my first journey *by* water rather than merely through it or over it. The horses huddled, nervous in the deck pen, and for the few minutes it took to haul the barge across by means of a fixed rope, I leaned over the prow and watched the river sparkle. I wondered at the captain, a sweat-soaked bulge of man, and the three men in his service. To live their lives on a broad river that would bear them to the sea in a few short hours. To haul their craft for mile after mile, hundreds in a month, and never get more than shouting distance from where they started.

"Remind me again," Makin said when we alighted on the far shore. "Why aren't we just going back to the Haunt where we, well you at least, can live like kings, instead of crossing half the world to see relatives you've never met?"

"I've met some of them. I've just not been to where they live."

"And the reason we're doing it now? Did you take the Highlands just so Coddin could rule it for you?" Makin asked.

"My family has always had a high regard for stewards," I said.

Makin smiled at that.

"But we're going because we need friends. Every soothsayer and his disembowelled dog is telling me that the Prince of Arrow is set for the empire throne. If that's even part true then he's going to roll over the Renar Highlands soon enough, and having met him I'd say we'd have a hard time stopping him. And despite the legendary friendliness of my nature it seems that these days I have to cross half the world to find someone who might be ready to help out in time of need," I said.

All that was true enough, but more than any move in the game of empire, I quite wanted to find a member of my family who didn't yearn to kill me. Blood runs thick they say, but what I have from my father is thin stuff. As I got older, as I started to examine the parts from which I'm made, I felt a need to see my mother's kin, if only to convince myself not all of me was bad.

We passed among the roots of Aups, mountains that put the Matteracks to shame both in size and number. Legion upon legion of white peaks marching east to west across nations— the great wall of Roma. Young Sim found them a fascination, watching so hard you might think he'd fall off his mare at any moment.

"A man could never climb those," he said.

"Hannibal took elephants across them," I told him.

A frown crossed him then passed. "Oh, elephants," he said.

Until that moment it hadn't occurred to me he hadn't the least clue what an elephant was. Even Dr. Taproot's circus didn't have elephants. Sim probably thought they climbed like monkeys.

For weeks we rode along the lawless margins of minor kingdoms, along the less worn routes. Seven is a dangerous number of men for travelling. Not so few that you can pass unnoticed. Not so many that safety is assured. Still, we looked hard-bitten. Perhaps not as hard-bitten as we were, but enough to dissuade any bandits who might have watched us pass. Looking poor helps too. We had horses, weapons, armour, true enough, but nothing that promised a rich prize, certainly not a rich enough one for taking on Rike and Makin.

The foothills of the Aups roll out along the margins of Teutonia in long barren valleys divided by high ridges of broken stone. Bad things happened here in the distant long ago. The Interdiction they called it, and little grows in the sour dust, even now. Amid the emptiness of those valleys, a week's march from anywhere you might want to be, we passed the loneliest house in the world. I have read that in the white north, beyond a frozen sea, men live in ice houses, sewn in their furs, huddled from a wind that can cut you in half. But this stone hut, dwarfed amongst abandoned boulders, its empty windows like dark eyes, it seemed worse. A woman came out of it and three children lined up before her to watch as we rode past. No words were spoken. In that dry valley with just the whisper of the wind, without crow call or the high song of larks, it felt as if words would be a sin, as if they might wake something better left sleeping.

The woman watched us from a face that looked too white, too smooth, like a dead child's face. And the children crouched around her in their grey rags.

Riding north, we had paced the spring. Now it seemed we galloped into summer. Mud dried to hardpan, blossoms melted away, the flies came. Rike turned red as he does in any hint of summer, even the dirt won't keep him from it, and the sunburn improved his temper not a bit.

We left the mountains and their grim foothills, finding our way across wild heathlands and into the great forests of the south.

At the end of a hot day when my face hurt less, not healed but no longer weeping, I drew my sword. We had set camp on the edge of a forest clearing. Row found us a deer and had a haunch spitting over the fire.

"Have at ye, Sir Makin of Trent!"

"If you're sure you've not forgotten how to use that thing." He grinned and drew. "My liege."

We sparred a while, parrying and feinting, stretching our limbs and practising our strokes. Without warning, Makin picked up the pace, the point of his blade questing for me.

"Time for another lesson?" he asked, still grinning, but fierce now.

I let my sword-arm guide me, watching only the plot of the fight, the advances and retreats, not the details of every cut and thrust. Behind Makin the sun reached through the forest canopy in golden shafts like the strings of a harp, and beneath the rustle of leaves, above the birds' calls, I caught the strains of the sword-song. The tempo of our blades increased, sharp harsh cries of steel on steel, the rasp of breath—faster. The burn on my face seemed to reignite. The old pain ran in me, acid and lightning, as if Gog's fragments were lodged in my bones, still burning. Faster. I saw Makin's grin falter, the sweat running on his forehead. Faster—the flicker of reflected light in his eyes. Faster. A moment of desperation and then—"Enough!" And he let the sword fly from his fingers. "Jesu!" he cried, shaking his hand. "Nobody fights like that."

The Brothers had stopped their various tasks and watched as if unsure what they had seen.

I shrugged. "Perhaps you're not such a bad teacher?"

My arms trembled now and I used my free hand to steer the point of my blade home into its scabbard. "Ouch!" For a moment I thought I had cut myself and raised my fingertips to my mouth. But there was no blood, only blistering where the hot metal scorched me.

We followed the curve of the mountain range and the sweep of one great river then another. The maps had names for them, sometimes the locals had their own, not trusted to maps. Sometimes those upstream called a river one thing and those farther down named it differently. I didn't much care as long as it led us where I chose to go. Lately though we had been blocked at each turn it seemed. Watchtowers, patrols, floods, rumours of plague, each of them turned us one way then another, as if funnelling us south along particular paths. I didn't much like the feeling but it was, as Makin said, just a feeling.

"Dung on it!" I jumped from Brath's saddle and approached the shattered bridge. On our side the stonework still held part of its original arc, spanning out across the white waters for several yards before ending like a broken tooth. I could see large chunks of the bridge just below the river's surface, making waves and troughs in the flow. The damage looked fresh.

"So we trek east a bit. It's not the end of the world," Makin said.

Of all of us Makin held the best mind for finding a path. Maps stayed with me. I could close my eyes and see each detail on the map scroll, but Makin had an instinct for turning ink on hide into wise choices in the matter of this valley or that ridge.

I grunted. Crouched at the side of the bridge I could smell something, just a hint, beneath that fresh metallic tang of fast-moving waters, something rotten. "East then," I said. And we turned toward the trail leading east, a thin line of darker green amid the verdant woods, overhung with willow and choked by brambles. The thorns scratched at my boots as we rode.

The thing about the path less travelled is that it is often less travelled for a good reason. When that reason is not the dangers that haunt the road then it is the road itself. Sometimes it's both. In Cantanlona the soft edge of civilization becomes very soft, so soft in fact that it will suck you down given a quarter-chance.

"We're going through?" Red Kent stood in his stirrups frowning at the reed-dotted marshland stretching before us into a greenish brown infinity.

"Stinks." Makin sniffed as if he weren't getting quite enough of the stink that offended him.

Rike just spat and slapped at the mosquitoes. He seemed to draw them as if they just couldn't tell how foul he was going to taste.

The Duchy of Cantanlona lies along what was once the border between two vast kingdoms, the bonding of which was the first step Philip took in forging the empire. It's said Philip's mother gave birth on that border, in Avinron, and being therefore a man of two lands he felt he had claim to both. It seemed fitting then that nothing remained of Avinron but a fetid swamp fed by a river aptly named "the Ooze."

Our route lay through the marshland. Good reasons for it

lay to either side. I led the way, on foot with Brath's reins in hand. The Brothers and I had spent long enough in the Ken Marshes to develop a sense for uncertain ground. The vegetation tells the story. Watch for cotton grass, the first whisper of deep mud, black bog-rush where the ground will bear a man but a horse will sink, sedge for clean water, pimpernel for sour, bulrush where the water is deep but the mud below is firm. Sharp eyes you need, and watchful feet, and the hope that the warm swamps of Cantanlona are not too different from the cold marshes that border Ancrath.

Makin was right about the stink. The heat made it a high summer. An all-pervading rot encompassed us, the reek of putrid flesh and worse.

We made slow progress that day though we covered enough miles to make the way we had come look pretty much identical to the directions ahead, pathless, uniform, and without hope of end.

I found a place to camp where we might be sure of a full complement in the morning. A series of grassy hummocks connected by strands of firm ground offered sufficient room for the men and horses, though we would all be keeping closer quarters than perhaps we would like.

Grumlow set to cooking, using sticks and charcoal that he'd had the foresight to bring with him. He brought out his iron tripod and hung a pot over the little fire and crouched over it, trickling in barley atop strips of smoked venison, the steam rising all about him and dripping off his moustache and back into the stew.

When night fell it dropped heavy and moonless, swallowing all the stars. The swamp, silent by day save for the squelching of our feet, came alive in the dark. A chorus of croaks, whirrs, chirps, and wetter, more disturbing sounds, flowed over us from sunset to sunrise. I set a watch, though the embers of our fire gave nothing to watch, and when my hour came I sat with closed eyes, listening to the darkness speak.

"Makin." I kicked him, wary lest he take off my foot. "You're on."

I heard him grunt and sit. He hadn't taken his breastplate off, or his gauntlets. "Can't see a damn thing. What the hell am I watching for?"

"Humour me," I said. The place just made me feel that if we all fell asleep together maybe none of us would wake up again. "And why are you still clanking if you think this place is safe?"

Dreams took me before Makin could find an answer. Katherine walked them, the dead child in her arms and accusations on her lips.

The morning sun drew a mist from the pools of standing water. At first it hung a foot or two above the cotton grass, but by the time we were ready to move, the mist boiled around our chests as if it were ready to drown us where the mud had thus far failed.

Some stenches you get used to. After a short while you can't say if they are gone or not. Not the stink of the Cantanlona Marsh though. That stayed as ripe after a day and a night as it did when the reluctant breeze first brought it to me.

The mist managed to make me sweat and give me chills at the same time. Wrapped in it, with my Brothers reduced to wraiths at the edge of vision, I thought for some reason of the woman and her brats at that remote cottage—the woman with her dead face and the children like rats around her calves. Isolation comes in many flavours.

"We could wait it out," Kent said.

A splash and Rike cursed. "Mud past my feckin' knee."

Kent had a point. The mist couldn't hope to hold out against the heat of the day as the sun climbed.

"You want to stay here a moment longer than you have to?" I asked.

Kent plodded on by way of answer.

Wherever the sun had got to, it was doing a piss poor job of keeping me warm. The mist seemed to seep into me, putting a chill along my bones, fogging my eyes.

"I see a house," Sim called.

"You do not!" Makin said. "What the hell would a house be doing in a—"

There were two houses, then three. A whole village of rough timber homes, slate-tiled, loomed about us as we slowed our advance.

"What the fuck?" Row spat. I think he invented spitting.

"Peat-cutters?" Grumlow suggested.

It seemed the only even half-sensible explanation, but I had it in my mind that peat bogs lay in cooler climes, and that even there the locals came to the bog to cut peat and then went home; they didn't build their homes on it.

A door opened in the house to our left and seven hands reached for weapons. A small child ran out, barefoot, chasing something I couldn't see. He ran past us, lost in the mist, just the splashing of his feet to convince me he was real, and the dark entrance to the house where the door lay open.

I approached the doorway with my sword in hand. It reminded me of a grave slot, and the breath of wet rot that issued from it did nothing to erase the image.

"Jamie, you forgot—" The glimmer of my steel cut the woman short. Even in the mist Builder-steel will find a gleam. "Oh," she said.

"Madam." I faked a bow, not wanting to lower my head more than a hair's breadth.

"I'm so sorry," she said. "I wasn't expecting company." She looked no more than twenty-five, fair-haired, pretty in a worn-thin kind of way, her homespun simple but clean.

Between the houses to our left a man in his fifties came into view, labouring under a wooden keg. He dumped it from his shoulder onto a pile of straw and raised a hand. "Welcome!" he said. He rubbed at the white stubble on his chin and stared up into the mist. "You've brought the weather with you, young sir."

"Come in, why don't you?" the woman said. "I've a pot on the fire. Just oat porridge, but you're welcome to some. Ma! Ma! Find the good bowl."

I glanced round at Makin. He shrugged. Kent watched the old man, his eyes wide, knuckles white on his Norse axe.

"I'm so sorry. I'm Ruth. Ruth Millson. How rude of me. That's Brother Robert." She waved at the old man as he went into the house he'd set the keg by. "We call him 'brother' because he spent three years at the Gohan monastery. He wasn't very good at it!" She offered a bright smile. "Come in!"

A memory tickled me. Gohan. I knew a Gohan closer to home.

"Does your hospitality extend to my friend?" I asked, opening a hand toward Makin.

Ruth turned and led on into the house. "Don't be shy. We've plenty for everyone. Well, enough in any case, and there's no sin like an empty belly!"

I followed her, Makin at my heels. We both ducked to get under the lintel. I had half-expected the interior to be dripping with the mire but the place looked clean and dry. A lantern burned on the table, brass and polished to a high shine as if it were a treasured heirloom. The place lay in shadows, the shutters closed as though night threatened. Makin sheathed his sword. I was not so polite.

I cast about. Something was missing. Or I was missing something.

Rike stood outside, looming over the Brothers who pressed about him. Foolish enough they looked, bristling with weaponry as two young girls ran past laughing. An old woman hobbled up with a bundle under her arm, oblivious to Grumlow's daggers as she grumbled on by.

"Ruth," I said.

"Sit! Sit!" she cried. "You look half-dead. You're a just a boy. A big lad, but a boy. I can see it. And boys need feeding. Ain't that right, Ma?" She put her hand to her neck, an unconscious gesture, and stroked her throat. Pale skin, very pale. She'd burn worse than Rike in the sun.

"They do." The mother put her head around the entrance from what must be the only other room. Grey hair framed a stern face, softened by a kind mouth. "And what's the boy's name then?"

"Jorg," I said. As much as I like to roll out my titles there is a time and a place.

"Makin," said Makin, although Ruth only had eyes for me, which is odd because even if I were handsome before the burns, it's Makin that has a way with . . . everyone.

"And is there a Master Millson?" Makin asked.

"Sit!" Ruth said. So I sat and Makin followed suit, taking the rocker by the empty fireplace. I leaned my blade against the table. The women gave it not so much as a glance.

Ruth picked up a woollen jerkin from behind my stool. "That Jamie would forget his head!"

"You have a husband?" I asked.

A frown crossed her like a cloud. "He went to the castle two years back. To take service with the Duke." She brightened. "Anyhow you're too young for me. I should call Seska over. She's as pretty as the morning." She had mischief in her eye. Blue eyes, pale as forget-me-not.

"So what are you doing out here?" I asked. I'd taken a shine to Ruth. She had a spark in her and put me in mind of a serving girl named Rachel back at the Haunt. Something about her made me unaccountably horny. Unaccountable if you don't count eight weeks on the road.

"Out here?" Distracted she put her fingers to her mouth, a pretty mouth it has to be said, and wiggled at one of her back teeth.

"Ma" came from the kitchen with an earthenware pot, carried in a blackened wooden grip to keep the heat from her fingers. Makin got up to help her with it but she paid him no heed. She looked tiny beside him, bowed under her years. She laid the pot before me and set her bony hand to the lid, hesitating. "Salt?"

"Why not?" I would have asked for honey but this wasn't the Haunt. Salt porridge is better than plain, even when you've eaten salt and more salt at Duke Maladon's tables for a week.

"Oh," said Ruth. Her hand came away from her mouth with a tooth on her palm. Not a little tooth but a big molar from far back, with long white roots and dark blood smeared around it, so dark as to be almost black. "I'm sorry," she said, holding her hand at arm's length as if horrified by the tooth but unable to look away, eyes wide and murky.

"No matter," I said. It's strange how quickly impersonal lust can slip into revulsion. It probably crosses the tail end of that thin line the poets say divides love and hate.

"Perhaps we should eat?" Makin said.

My stomach rolled at the thought of food. The marsh stink, that had yet to fade, invaded the room with renewed vigour.

Ma returned with three wooden bowls, one decorated with carved flowers, and a chair that looked too fine for the house. She set the bowls on the table, the fancy one for me, one before the new chair. The third she held on to, casting about for something, confusion in her eye. She put her hand to the side of her head, rubbing absently.

"Lost something?" I asked.

"A rocking chair." She laughed. "A place this small. You

wouldn't think you could lose a thing like that!" Her hand came away from her head with a clump of white hair in it. Pink scalp showed where it came from. She looked at it with as much bewilderment as her daughter, studying her tooth.

"The Duke's castle you say, Ruth?" Makin said from the rocker. "Which duke would that be?" Makin could take the awkward edge off a moment, but neither woman looked at him.

Ma stuffed the hair into her apron and shuffled back into the kitchen. Ruth set the tooth on the window ledge. "Is it supposed to be lucky?" she asked. "Losing a tooth. I thought I heard that once." She opened the shutters. "To let the dawn in."

"What duke rules here?" I asked.

Ruth smiled, the smallest smear of black blood at the corner of her mouth. "Why you *are* lost, aren't you? Duke Gellethar of course!"

In that moment I realized what was missing. The dead baby, the box-child, he would lie in any idle shadow. But not here. These shadows were too full.

The front door banged open and little Jamie charged in. Boys of a certain age seem only to go flat out or not at all. He grazed the doorpost as he passed and lost a coin-sized patch of skin to a loose nail.

He ran up to me, grinning, snot on his upper lip. "Who're you? Who're you, mister?" Oblivious to the missing skin where dark muscle glistened like liver.

"So this would be the land of . . ." I ignored the boy and watched Ruth's muddy eyes.

"Gelleth of course." She opened the shutters. "Mount Honas is west of us. On a clear night you can sometimes see the lights."

Makin may have been the man for maps, but I knew we were five hundred miles and more from Gelleth and the dust I had made of its duke. You would need the eyes of the god of eagles to see Mount Honas from any window in the Cantanlona . . . and yet Ruth believed what she said.

She turned from the window, the right half of her as scarlet as if she'd been dipped in boiling water.

31

Four years earlier

I stood up sharp enough, beating Makin out of his rocker. "Ladies, my thanks but we have to leave."

"We?" the mother asked from the kitchen doorway, half-scarlet like her daughter but on the left rather than the right, as if together they might make an untouched woman and a wholly scalded one.

"There's only you, Jorg," Ruth said, the side of her face starting to blister and weep. "There's only ever been you for us." She spat two teeth—incisors, one upper, one lower—making a slot in her smile.

Makin slipped past me, out into the mist. I backed after him, sword held ready to ward the women off. Ruth's smile held my gaze and I forgot her child. He clamped himself to my leg, the skin falling off him like wet paper. "Who're you? Who're you, mister?"

"Only you, Jorg," said the mother, her head bald now but for random white tufts. "Since the sun came." She lifted her hand to the window.

The mist lit with a yellow glow then shrivelled back, drawn across the marsh as if it were a tablecloth whipped away fast enough to leave everything in place.

Out across the marsh it seemed that a second sun rose, too terrible and too bright to look at, too awful to look away from. A Builders' Sun.

In horrible unison both women started to scream. Ruth's hair burst into flame. Her mother's scalp smouldered. I shook Jamie from my leg and he crashed against the wall, pieces of his skin left adhering to my leggings. I backed away from the house. I recognized the screams. I had made the same sounds when Gog burned me. Justice made those screams when Father lit him up.

Once upon a time perhaps I might have thought two women running around on fire was a free show. Rike would laugh that laugh of his even now. Row would bet on which one would fall first. But of late my old tastes had gone sour. I had grown to understand this kind of pain. And whatever enchantments might have staged this show for me, these people had felt real. They had felt kind. A truth ran through this lie and I didn't like it.

Outside the sun shone, watching us from a midmorning angle, and the screams sounded fainter, farther off.

"The hell?" Red Kent swung his head. "Where'd the mist go?"

"Ain't that a thing." Row spat.

The buildings dripped with mud. They looked rotted. The roofs were gone.

"What did you see in there, Makin?" I asked, watching the doorway. No fire. No smoke. It looked dark. As if the sun wasn't reaching in even though the roof had gone.

He shook his head.

"They're sinking," Rike said.

I could see it. Inch by inch each of the houses sunk into the foulness of the marsh. The sound of it put me in mind of sex though nothing had been more distant from my thoughts.

"They're going back," Sim said. He kept his distance from the walls.

He had it right. If we were seeing true now the mist had gone, then those buildings sunk long ago and something had made the marsh vomit them up again just for us.

"What happened?" Makin asked, although his face said he'd rather not know.

"They were ghosts," I said. "Summoned for my benefit." Some tortured re-enactment of the suffering at Gelleth. People who died because of me. "They can't hurt us."

Within minutes the buildings were swallowed and no trace remained above the mud. I scanned the horizon. Nothing but stagnant pools for mile after mile. The retreating mist had cleared more than my sight though. A second veil had been drawn away. A more subtle kind of mist that had been with us since we first scented the marsh. The necromancy tingled in me. We stood on the surface of an ocean and the dead swam below. Something had been overwriting my power, blinding me. Something or someone.

"Show yourself, Chella!" I shouted.

The weight of her necromancy pulled me around to stare at the mire where she rose. She emerged by degrees, black slime sliding from her nakedness, her hair plastered around her shoulders, over the tops of her breasts. Ten yards of dark and treacherous mud stood between us. Row had his bow across his back, the Nuban's bow lay strapped to Brath's saddle. Grumlow at least had a dagger in hand. In both hands actually. But he didn't seem tempted to throw either. Perhaps he just didn't want to draw her attention to him.

None of us spoke. Not one of us reached for a bow. The necromancer had a magic to work on the living as well as the dead. Or at least a magic to work on men. The mire had tainted the flesh that I remembered so well, leaving it dark but still firm. The slime that ran from her, that dripped and clung, seemed to guide the eye, to gild each dark curve and point.

"Hello, Jorg," she said.

She used Katherine's words from the graveyard. Maybe what is spoken in such places is always heard by those who have married Death.

"You remember me." I wondered how long she had been leading me to this point. I had no doubt now that her creatures had torn down the bridge we hoped to cross.

"I remember you," she said. "And the marsh remembers you. Marshes have long memories, Jorg, they suck down secrets and hold them close, but in the end, in the end, all things surface."

I thought of the box at my hip and of the memories it held. "I suppose you've come to tell me not to stand against the Prince of Arrow?"

"Why? Do you think I have my hooks in him?"

I shook my head. "I would have smelled you on him."

"You didn't smell me here and this place reeks of death," she said, always moving, slow gyrations and stretches, demanding the eye.

"To be fair, it reeks of so much more beside."

"The Prince of Arrow has enough defenders, enough champions, he doesn't need me. In any case, you don't want to believe everything you read, and the older a book is the less reliable its stories."

There were written prophecies too? That made me snarl. It was bad enough that every turn of the tarot card and toss of the rune sticks put Arrow on the throne. Now books, my oldest friends, had turned traitor. "So why are we here?" I asked. I knew, but I asked in any case.

"I'm here for you, Jorg," she said, husky and seductive.

"Come and take me, Chella," I said. I didn't lift my sword but I turned it so the reflected light slid across her face. I didn't ask what it was she wanted. Revenge doesn't need explanation. "And *how* are you here?" A mountain had fallen on her in Gelleth and buried her deeper than deep.

She frowned at that. "The Dead King came for me." And for a moment, just a moment, I swear I saw her shudder.

"The Dead King." This was new. I had thought I understood—that she was after revenge, pure and simple, emotions I could appreciate. After all, I had dropped Mount Honas on her. "Did he send you?"

"I would have come anyway, Jorg. We have unfinished business." Again the seduction, stilling the Brothers who had started to move.

"So who wants me more, Chella? You or this king of yours?"

A hint of a snarl in Chella now, the Brothers starting to shake her influence as irritation wore it thin.

"Or did he want me more than he wanted you, Chella? Is that it? Your new king only dug you up to find me for him?" I showed her my best smile. I had the truth of it: she couldn't hide the annoyance that flickered across her brow. All to the good, an angry enemy is the best kind to have, but why this Dead King should have taken against me so I'd no idea.

"Come and take me." I invited her again, beckoning, hoping to goad her into range. With my free hand I shoved Makin. "I know there's a naked woman and everything, but if you could point the Brothers in more useful directions then we're less likely to be eaten by her friends."

"Come and take you?" Chella smiled, composure returned. She wiped her hand across her mouth, flicking mud aside, her lips blood-red. "I do want you. I do. But not for breaking. I know your heart, Jorg. Join with me. We can be more than flesh."

The creature put an ache in my groin, true enough, as if that line between lust and revulsion had been erased as completely as the village. Part of me wanted to take her dare. *Embrace what you fear,* I had told Gog. *Hunt your fears.* And what is death if not the ultimate of fears, the final enemy? I had eaten the cold heart of a necromancer. Perhaps I should take Chella, take death by the throat, and make it serve me. I thought of the women burning in their house. "You are less than flesh," I said.

"Cruel words." She smiled. She stepped closer. The fluid motion of her held my eyes. The jounce of breasts, the jut of hips, the redness of her mouth. "There's a magic between us, Jorg. Surely you must have felt it? Does it not echo in your chest? Doesn't it underwrite the very beating of your heart, dear one? We were meant to be together. The Dead King has told me I can have you. Told me to bring you to him. And I will."

"You'll have a long wait for me in hell," I said. "Because I intend to send you there right now." A weak line perhaps but mention of the Dead King knocked me out of my stride.

She smiled and made a kiss with crimson lips. "Are you angry because I showed you your ghosts? It wasn't me who made them, Jorg."

That stole the certainty from me. I saw Ruth again, and her mother, scalded by the hot light of the Builders' Sun. "I didn't know—"

"You didn't know a sun would burn them. You thought a cloud of poison would roll out and devastate the land. Isn't that right? So, if Ruth and her mother and her child were choking on their own intestines, bleeding from eyes and anus, screaming different screams, that would be all right? That would be fine because that was the plan?" Chella stepped closer. Relentless.

I couldn't answer that. I had thought to poison the Castle Red, and I had known it would be everyone in it, not just the warriors. And if the toxins had spread? I had no idea how far they might go. And I hadn't cared.

"You know what men are really afraid of, Chella?" I asked.

"Tell me." She ran her hands up her thighs, across her belly, smearing dark skin with darker mud.

Makin pressed the Nuban's bow into my palm. I grasped it. The thing nearly too heavy to hold in one hand.

"Men are afraid of dying. Not of death. Men want it to be quick, clean. That's the worst thing, the wound that lets you linger. Ain't that right, Makin?"

"Yes," he said. Makin isn't a man of few words, but it's difficult to break into a necromancer's spell.

"Linger," I said. "That's a word that frightens the Brothers. Don't let me linger, they say. And you know what undeath is, Chella? It's the ultimate in lingering. A coward dies a thousand times, the Bard told us. And what about you? You've died just once but you've lingered a thousand times longer than you should."

"Don't mock me, child," Chella said. Her ribs stood out now, her cheeks hollowed. "I hold more power—"

"You can show me my ghosts, Chella. You can try to scare me with death and with dead things, so that I'll choose your path. But I have my own road to follow. My ghosts are my own and I will deal with them alone. You are a thing of rot and fear and you should find a grave that will take you."

The time when nothing could put fear in me had passed. It seems terror is a companion in the soft years when everything is new, and returns to us with age, as we acquire things to lose. Perhaps I didn't have my full share of old man's cowardice just yet, but Gelleth's ghosts and knowing how many dead things swam beneath the mud, ready for the necromancer's call, had set a coldness in my bones. I had a prince to defeat, perhaps Katherine to woo, a comfortable throne to warm. Being drowned in slime by dead men didn't fit into those plans.

"It wasn't just ghosts I brought with me from Gelleth, Jorg." Chella raised her arms high, a languid motion.

Other forms started to emerge from the mire, human forms. I stuck my sword into the ground and lifted the Nuban's bow.

"I've been collecting," Chella said.

The shape rising in front of her held familiar lines, a broad and powerful build, darkest in the places where the mud lay thin. A hole in his chest.

"I think he wants his bow back," Chella said.

To her left a bloated form, guts hanging like black sausage from his slit belly. Others around us, clawing and shaking the mud from their faces. One stood head and shoulders above the rest, flesh hanging from his bones in tatters.

"I've walked where you walked, Jorg, taken what you tried to burn, and dug where you buried. Even in the shadow of your walls."

I knew them all. The Nuban between Chella and my bow . . . his bow, Fat Burlow to her left. Gemt with patches of dull red hair showing through the muck, head stitched back on, Brother Gains, Brother Jobe, Brother Roddat. Old Elban who always prayed for a quiet grave, Liar whose body we never found to bury even though he fell at the Haunt, and Brother Price all bones and tatters from four years in the ground. And more rising in the deep mire or hauling themselves onto firmer ground from the standing pools.

Chella watched me over the Nuban's shoulder, using him as her shield. Another lesson in the value of attacking without hesitation.

"Join with me." Her voice fluttered from corrupt lungs. Her eyes glittered, sunken in their sockets as if lifting my Brothers from the depths had sucked vitality from her. "My brother's strength runs in you, all but unused, fading, wasted."

Brother? The necromancer I cut down was her brother?

"My thanks, lady, but I've had my fill of necromancers." I fired both bolts from the Nuban's bow. One punched a hole in his shoulder. The other passed through Chella's neck just to one side of her throat.

The Nuban, almost turned around by the impact, straightened and faced me again, no expression on his grey lips. Chella put a hand to her neck and twisted her head with a noise like popping cartilage.

"We're family, Jorg. Families argue. But I forgive you, and when I've taken you down into the marsh with me . . . when we're together in the cold deep places . . . embracing like family do . . . you'll forgive me too."

Brother Sim holds himself close and you will never know him no matter what words pass between you. He whispers something to each man he kills. If he could speak it to a man and let him live, then I might have lost a killer.

32

Four years earlier

In the hot and endless swamp of the Cantanlona many things are lost, secrets swallowed, lives drawn down into blackness. And sometimes, slow currents return what was better kept hidden.

It's never a good idea to run in a bog. Slow steps are called for when a place is littered with sucking pools, deep mire, and tufted hummocks perfect for the breaking of ankles. However, there are times when a bad idea is the best you have.

"Follow me!" I shouted, and I ran out between the pools and the tussock-grass to my left. Chella let herself slide under the mud whilst the Nuban moved to intercept.

Whatever necromancy I'd gained from Chella's brother would have made only a drop in the ocean of Chella's strength. However, secrets hold power. The secret I had in mind had slipped from Dr. Taproot's lips, and he would never have given the information away for free if he thought it still held value.

"I release you, Kashta!" I slapped my palm to the wound in his chest, careless of his grasping hands.

When a name is held secret its power multiplies. The Nuban

toppled without hesitation and I felt that he would never rise again. As he fell my anger rose.

I splashed on with the live Brothers behind me and the dead Brothers behind them. Back and to my right, Fat Burlow moved to block Rike. I raced on, finding a low ridge of firmer ground. Turning, I saw Rike's broadsword shear through Burlow's arm. Burlow grabbed him with his remaining hand, but Makin cut that off and both men charged on, slowing as they hit softer ground and starting to wade. Makin lost a boot to the sucking mud but he made it to my side. Our panicked horses ran in various directions; some cantered after us, Brath among them, but I saw two horses hit the mud and start to sink, rearing and plunging as if they thought they might win through.

Some yards away a mud-pit began to boil with activity. Corpse after corpse clambered from it as if they had been stacked fathoms deep and with unsettling intimacy.

I led on. It seemed that whilst the undead lacked fear and would literally need to be hacked apart before they stopped trying to kill us, they were at least slow. On an open field we would have left them in our dust. In the swamp the match turned out to be more even. A pervasive aura of lingering death infects the mud in the Cantanlona bogs. Somehow the mire itself is half-alive, or half-dead depending on your perspective, and it supported the undead, vomiting them up, keeping them from sinking.

The corpses from the mud-pit managed to intercept us when the firm ground swung to the left.

"Keep moving!" I shouted.

Makin sliced one across the chest, his training misleading him for once. The creature didn't notice the wound and grappled him with muddy arms. Rike didn't bother with his sword. He set his boot to the stomach of the corpse-man in his path with such force that he threw it yards back, felling another before it reached us. Of all the Brothers, Red Kent proved best suited to the work. His Norse axe sheared off grasping limbs, weaving a savage pattern that left the bog scattered with hands, arms, and heads.

We raced on with the creatures at our heels, silent in their determination to catch and dismember us, just the noise of their splashing and our panting. At one point a mud-grey army of undead hunted our trail, but each mile left them farther behind us until at last they dropped from sight.

I called a halt on a low mound that offered a firm footing and an elevated view of the bogs. A ring of weathered stone indicated the place had once been a burial, some local chieftain perhaps, but the grave looked to have been emptied years ago and I felt no more death there than in any of the surrounding mire. My anger had kept pace with me during the long chase. Chella had kept the Nuban's corpse as her plaything for more than half a year. I didn't know if anything of the man remains when necromancy animates his flesh, but the possibility of his suffering, and the horror of it if he did, made me swear revenge. I had only made one such vow before and then as now I made it without words and with every intention to tear the world apart if that were needed to see it through.

"I don't want to spend another night in this place," Makin said.

"Really?" Rike growled, sitting on the largest of the stones. I'd never heard him use sarcasm before. I guessed he must have been saving it for extreme circumstances.

"Stand a moment, Rike," I said.

And he did. I lifted the point of my sword to his side. With a stab and a twist I took Burlow's severed hand away, tearing off the patch of tunic it had a grip on, and flicked it into the swamp.

"We've wandered into hell," Grumlow said with conviction. "We got lost and now we're in hell." He had mud plastered up one side of his face and blood clotting in his moustache, trickles of it making crimson trails from nose to lip.

"Hell smells better," I said.

With the horses around us the mound was crowded and our sightlines blocked. I pushed the grey aside, slapping her rump. Of the five horses left to us she was the only one relaxed enough to crop at the short grass.

"We should go," Makin said.

We should, but where to? The horizon offered nothing. Except, perhaps . . .

"Is that the sea?" I pointed. To the east a hint of black or blue lined the farthest reaches of the marsh.

A sharp cry cut off anyone inclined to answer. I spun toward the sound. Just behind us, thigh-deep in water, chest-deep in rushes, Chella held Young Sim by the throat and head. She took another step back away from the mound, dragging Sim. It seemed that she had done something to him, to his neck maybe, for his arms hung limp at his side though he watched us with wild eyes. We called him Young Sim and he had perhaps sixteen years, but when it came to killing he was an old hand and he would not have gone easy without good reason.

"Jorg, you shouldn't run from me," Chella said. The water had washed away the mud though it couldn't take the bog-stain from her skin, the colour of old teak. The Celtic patterns scrolling across her were deep-set too, not the paint I had once thought them. A needle must have placed those swirls and knots along her arms, reaching across her sides.

"I don't want any part of you, necromancer." I still held the Nuban's bow, though I hadn't reloaded it. I aimed at her, assuming she wouldn't pay close attention to the number of bolts in place. "Whatever power I consumed is fading from me. Slower than I would like it to fade, but it will be gone and I won't be sorry. I want no part of you or your dirty trade."

She smiled. "The Dead King won't let you go, Jorg. He's gathering all our kind to him. Black ships wait to take us to the Drowned Isles."

I made no reply. My anger had subsided once I vowed to destroy Chella. Vengeance is patient when it needs to be and she sought to use the Brothers against me to enrage me, to set me chasing her into the drowning pools. I didn't let her know how deep her hooks had sunk.

"You're not going to ask me to release your brother, Jorg?" She dragged Sim a yard farther back.

Row had an arrow trained on her and Grumlow looked ready to throw his knife this time. Grumlow had a soft spot for Sim: fear wouldn't stay his hand.

"So, you have my brother. Eat his heart and we will be even. Back to where we started," I said. I knew she wouldn't be letting go of Sim. She just wanted me to ask.

"Oh, you can't go back, Jorg. You should know that. You can never go back. Not even if every trace of necromancy left you. Look!" She made a quick change of grip and jerked Sim's head to the right. Far too far to the right. The grating of bone set my teeth on edge. "Annnnnd . . ." She rotated his head slowly back to face us. "He's back. But he's not the same now, is he?"

"Bitch!" Row released his arrow. Whether his hand trembled or Chella moved faster than I could see I don't know, but the arrow ended up jutting from Sim's eye.

"Now see what you've done." Her red mouth smiling, her eyes seductive, and she whispered in Sim's ear.

Grumlow threw his knife but Chella was already falling. It may have cut her, but the waters closed over her before I could tell.

Sim, despite his arrow and his broken neck, remained standing. And then he took an uncertain step toward us. The clear water between the rushes clouded as the mud below began to stir.

"The sea," I shouted. I pointed for good measure. The Prince of Arrow had advised me to see the ocean and it looked as though it might be the last thing I did. The Brothers needed no encouragement. We set off running, hoping that Brother Sim would prove as slow as the other dead men and not as fast as we remembered him.

Brother Row you can trust. Trust him to lie, trust him to cheat, perhaps to betray. Most of all trust him to be true to what he is, a weasel, a killer in the dark, handy in the fight. Trust in all that and he will not disappoint.

33

Four years earlier

The sea air added no more than a salt tang to the rankness of the Cantanlona bogs. I could see a grey expanse of water now, still miles off.

"At least they're slow," Kent said. He splashed along beside me, axe in hand. He risked a backward glance. Running in a marsh with a sharp axe whilst looking over your shoulder is not to be advised. But then again, nothing we had done for two days was advisable.

The sea breeze carried a low moaning with it. I tried not to worry about that.

We pressed on, unwilling to rest after the last time. Four horses followed us, Row's having taken a broken ankle after putting its leg down a mud-hole. I made Kent cut its legs off once Row had slit its throat. "I'm not having Chella stand him up again and have her dead men ride after us."

The sea kept looking bigger by the minute. We'd soon be in the salt marsh.

"Jesus please us." Row stopped dead ahead of me. Of all the Brothers he was the one least likely to call on divine aid.

I came to his shoulder. The tufted marshland we'd been

crossing ended without warning and a long stretch of mudflats reached out before us, eventually giving over to reed-beds after two hundred yards or so. The heads were what stopped Row, not the mud.

Every five yards, like cabbages in a field, a head stuck up from the flats. The closest ones stopped moaning and swivelled their eyes to watch us.

The one by Row's feet, a woman of middle years, slightly jowly, strained to see our faces. "God save me," she said. "Save me."

"You're alive?" I knelt beside her on one knee, the mud firm beneath me, like wet clay.

"Save me!" A shriek now.

"They're underneath." A man to our left, Makin's age maybe, black-bearded, the mud only in the lower parts of his beard as if rain had washed him clean.

I reached out with the necromancy lurking in my fingertips. I could sense no more death in this mud than in any other part of the bog. Except around the people themselves. I could feel the life leaching out of them—being replaced by something less vital, but more durable.

"They're tearing my skin off!" The man's voice rose to a howl.

To our right, a younger woman, black hair flowing down into the mud. She raised her face to us, the skin mottled with dark veins like those on my chest. She snarled. A deep throaty sound, full of hunger. And behind her another woman who might have been her sister. "They come at night. Dead children. They give us sour water and feed us awful things. Awful things." She hung her head again.

"Kill me." A man farther out on the mudflats.

"And me." Another.

"How long . . ." I said.

"How long have you been here?" Makin asked.

"Three days."

"Two weeks."

"Nine days."

"Forever!" The moaning and the snarling grew in volume.

I stood, cold in my limbs and sick in my stomach. "Why?" I asked Makin. He shrugged.

"I know," Rike said.

"You don't know anything, Rike," I told him.

But he did. "The quick and the dead," he said. "She's making them here. Letting them stew. She's turning them slowly and they'll be fast. Heard of this kind before."

Out on the flats another head watched us with new hunger and screeched. Several more took up the call.

"Give them what they want, Kent," I said.

"No! Please mercy." The woman at Row's feet begged. "I have children."

"Or if they don't want it, give them what they need," I said.

Kent set to cropping the field. Red work and hard on the back. The others pitched in, Rike with rare enthusiasm.

We moved on at a trot, eager to be quit of the place.

"That won't be the only field," Makin said. He'd lost his other boot along the way and ran barefoot now.

I wasn't so much worried about what else Chella had growing. Rather I worried about what she had already grown.

We moved through a green sea to reach a grey one. The reeds came chest high and higher, dark mud around them that took you calf-deep before your next step. Broad swathes of open mud divided the reed banks, each with a tiny stream trickling at its middle. I started to hear the distant waves as we broke out onto yet another of these divisions.

"No." Grumlow put a hand on my shoulder before I stepped onto the mud.

Out toward the middle, where the stream made a bright ribbon, the mud heaved.

Row took out his bow. I wound the Nuban's crossbow.

The mud flexed again, mounded, and began to flow in reluctant waves as something black emerged.

"It's a fucking boat," Rike said.

Clearly it was Rike's day for being right. A fishing boat of black and rotting timber emerged as if surging from beneath a rogue wave, its crew lifting themselves from the deck, shedding mud and clumps of decayed flesh as they rose. I thought of the fat captain on his barge crossing the Rhyme. Perhaps he'd made the wise choice to stick to the route he knew after all.

"Back!" And I led them into the reed-beds again.

We ran, carving our path through reeds that overtopped me, reed-heads beating at my face.

"Something's coming," Rike shouted. He could still see above the green.

"From the boat?" I called.

"No. The other side."

We veered away and ran harder.

I could hear them. Gaining on us, beating a path through the stems.

"What is it?" I shouted.

"Can't see," Rike said, panting now. "I just see the reeds falling."

"Stop!" And I followed my own order. I threw the Nuban's bow down and whipped out my sword, scything through reeds. "Cut a clearing!" I shouted.

There's no point running if you're going to be caught.

Three dead men tore into our clearing as we cut it. They moved at a blinding pace, howling the moment they saw us. Without hesitation all three launched themselves at us, hands reaching for throats. Row went down. I skewered the one that chose me. He literally swallowed my sword, his split cheeks reaching the hilt whilst the point dug between his lungs and down into his stomach. An image of Thomas at the circus flashed to mind.

Having his vital organs divided by four foot of steel only seemed to enrage my foe. He almost tore the sword from my grip as he struggled to take hold of my throat. I held on and he pushed me back through the reeds, him nearly on all fours, lunging at me as if to take more of the sword. If he could have opened his jaws wider he would have taken the hilt and my hands too. Vital organs seemed to be a misnomer.

The dead man pushed on, gargling dark blood as he forced me back, splashing into a sucking pool. I dug in, twisted my blade, and ripped it down, carving a path out through his neck, chest, and stomach. His guts flooded out and he pitched into the pool, clawing at me as I tore free and drove my sword into the firmer ground. Kicking in wild fear and hauling on my sword I managed to drag myself out of the pool. I lay on my back, panting and gasping. I could hear the howls and snarls of the other dead men and the Brothers cursing as they fought. The reeds rose about my head like forest giants, swaying gently against the blueness of the sky.

By the time I found my breath and returned to the cut clearing, the fight had ended.

"Row's dead." Makin scrubbed at rips on his cheek with a handful of reeds. They seemed to make matters worse, but maybe he wanted to bleed it clean.

"I never liked him," I said. We said that sort of thing on the road. Also it was true.

"Make sure there's nothing left for Chella to play with," I told Kent.

He set to beheading the first of our attackers. Someone had already taken its arms off and mud filled its mouth, but it still wriggled and glared.

Seeing Makin tend his wounds I thought to pat myself down. Sometimes it's hours before you notice an injury taken in battle.

"Fuck," I said.

"What?" Makin looked up.

"I've lost the box." I ran my hands over my hips as if I could have missed it the first time.

"Good riddance," Makin said.

I walked back along the path of flattened reeds where the dead man had pushed me. Nothing. I reached the sucking pool.

"It's sunk here," I said.

"Good." Makin came up behind me.

I turned away. It didn't feel right to lose it. It felt like something I should keep. Part of me.

"Kent!" I shouted. He stopped with his axe poised overhead, Row's corpse at his feet.

"Leave him," I said.

I walked back and knelt beside Row. Death isn't pretty close up. The old man had fouled himself and stunk even worse than usual. Red-and-pink tatters of his throat hung down over his collarbones; loose ends of white cartilage reached out to frame the dark hole to his lungs. Trails of snot and purple blood had run from his nose, and his eyes had rolled to the left at a painfully sharp angle.

"I've not finished with you, Brother Row," I said.

I took his hands in mine. Dead men's hands are not intrinsically unpleasant but in truth it did make my skin crawl as I laced fingers with him. He lay limp, the hard skin at the top of his palms scratched against me.

"What're you doing?" Grumlow asked.

"I have a job for you, Brother Row," I said.

I searched for him. He couldn't have gone far in just a few minutes. I felt the pulse of necromancy in the unhealed wound in my chest. A dark hand closed around my heart and a chill wrapped me.

I knew I had very little power, just a trickle, like the ribbon of water in those wide avenues of mud. But Row still held warmth. His heart didn't beat but it twitched and quivered, and more important—I knew him blood to bone. I'd never liked him, but I knew him.

To make a dead man walk you have to wear his skin. You have to ease under it, to let your heartbeat echo in him, to run your mind along his thoughts.

I spat like Row did. I lifted my head and watched the Brothers with narrowed eyes, seeing them with Row's likes, dislikes, jealousy, old grudges, remembered debts.

"Brother Row," I said.

I got up. We got up. He got up.

I stood face to face with his corpse and he watched me from a distant place through eyes he once owned. The Brothers said nothing as I walked back to the pool and Row followed me.

"Find it," I said.

I didn't have to explain myself. We wore the same skin.

Row walked into the pool and let it take him. I crouched to watch.

Row had sunk from view before I felt the steel at my neck. I looked around, up along the blade.

"Don't ever do that to me," Makin said. "Swear it."

"I so swear," I said.

I needed no convincing.

34

Four years earlier

It seemed that we had been running in the marshes for most of our lives. Mud spattered each of us to the tops of our heads. The Brothers showed white skin only where they had scraped the filth from around their eyes. Now as the sun lowered red toward the western horizon it gave them a wild look. Soon, when the sun drowned in the marsh and left us in darkness, we would drown too.

"More of the bastards," Rike shouted. Once again he was the only one who could see over the reed-sea.

"How many?" I asked.

"All of them," he said. "It's like all the reeds are falling."

I could hear the snarls, faint but clear on the evening air. I patted the box at my hip. It took Row two hours to find, two hours before his hand finally broke the surface to give it to me. The Brothers had not liked waiting, but two more hours would not have got us out of Chella's muddy hell. We left him in the pool. I told Makin I had set him free. But I didn't.

"Can you see any clear ground?" I asked.

Rike didn't answer but he set off with purpose so we followed.

The snarling grew louder, closer behind us. We ran hard,

the splashing of quick dead feet closer by the second, and the shredding of reeds as they tore their path.

One moment I ran through a rushing green blindness and the next I broke clear onto a low mound. It felt like a hill though it rose no higher than three feet above the water level.

"Good work," I told Rike, then gasped in breath. It's better to die in the open.

Chella's army converged on us from all sides. The quick ones, mottled and mire-stained, undying rage on their faces and an unholy light in their eyes, dozens of them, flowing out to surround the mound. Behind them, minutes later, shambling in through the flattened reeds, came the grey and rotting dead, and amongst them the bog-dead from the depths, cured to the toughness of old leather and of a similar colour. I saw Price's tall bones and tattered flesh overtopping all others. Chella walked at his side wearing a white dress, all lace and trains such as might be worn at a royal wedding. Hardly a touch of mud on it.

"Hello, Jorg," she said. She stood too far away for me to hear but every dead mouth whispered her words.

"Go to hell, bitch." I would rather have said something clever.

"No harsh words on our wedding day, Jorg," she said, and the dead echoed her. "The Dead King is risen. The black ships sail. You'll join with me. Love me. And together we will open the Gilden Gate for our master and set a new emperor on the throne."

The dead of Gelleth came then, wandering through the marsh as if lost, ambling one way and the next. Ghosts these, but looking real enough, with their burns and their sores, teeth missing, hair and skin falling away. Hundreds of them, thousands, in a great ring of accusation. They pressed so hard that at the back some of the bog-dead were pushed aside and trampled under.

"So," said Rike. "Marry the bitch."

"She's going to kill you all either way, Rike. She'll have your corpse walking beside her. Price on one side, you on the other, the brothers back together again."

"Oh," he said. "Fuck that then."

"Come now, Jorg, don't be a baby," Chella said, and the dead spoke with her. She spoke again, echoed this time by just one voice, from a corpse woman close by the edge of our mound. A muddy corpse, one arm chewed to the bone, her skin stained, lips grey and rotting, but something of Ruth's lines in her face. "The Dead King is coming. The dead rise like a tide. They outnumber the living, and each battle makes more corpses, not more men." The dead woman's tongue writhed, black and glistening, Chella's words slipping from it. "Join with me, Jorg. There's a place for you in this. There's power to be taken and held."

"There's more to this," I said. Even the high esteem in which I held my own charms didn't allow me to believe her so smitten as to cross nations for this. And if vengeance drove her then she could take it easily enough now without this charade. "The Dead King scares you." She sounded too eager, desperate even. "What does he want with me?"

Even with so many yards between us I could read her. *She didn't know.*

I made to step forward but something caught my foot. Looking down I saw teeth, a dog's skull half-buried, half-emerged, gripping my foot. Another ghost, but it pinned me even so.

I looked out across the dead horde, scanning the packed crowds of ghosts behind them. Chella couldn't know about my dog, Justice. She couldn't have gathered all the dead of Gelleth or learned their stories. Somehow this came from me. Somehow Chella was pulling the ghosts of my past out through whatever hole it was I made in the world. And not even the ghosts I knew of but the ghosts of those whose end I caused. I felt the corner of an idea, not the whole shape of it, but a corner.

The skull brought my gaze back to the ground at my feet. "You shouldn't have done that," I said. I tore free. I felt him rip me but Justice's teeth left no marks upon my boot. It was just pain, no blood. It was just my mind that trapped me. The ghosts couldn't harm us or we would have died in Ruth's house, we would have burned with them when the Builders' Sun lit. Chella brought them only to torment me.

"Let's get married, dear-heart," Chella said. "The congregation is assembled. I'm sure we can find a cleric to perform the ceremony."

And pushing from the other ghosts came Friar Glen, a shade

wavering in the daylight, less clear than the other spirits, as if something tried to keep him back. At my hip the box of memories grew heavy. I hadn't known Friar Glen to be dead, but perhaps I knew it once and chose to forget. He came with a slow step, hobbling, though I could see no wound upon him, and he didn't look well pleased. In one hand he held a knife, a familiar knife, red with blood. When a dead man shambled into his path the friar stabbed him in the neck. The creature toppled with the knife still in him. Ghosts couldn't hurt the living, but apparently they could hurt the dead plenty. Friar Glen hobbled on until he stood at Chella's side.

I wondered how the friar's ghost came to be here, watching me with such hatred. I could feel it from fifty yards. But more than that—more than I wondered about Friar Glen—I circled around the words Chella spoke before she called him.

The congregation is assembled.

The quick-dead moved closer though I heard no instruction. They took slow steps, their hands ready to grab and twist and tear. Against so many we would last moments.

"It's no kind of wedding if my family can't attend." I sheathed my sword.

"Some ghosts I can't summon. The royal dead are buried in consecrated tombs and lie with old magics. If I could have made your mother dance for you I would have done so long ago," Chella said. The whisper reached me through the crowd, writhing on the lips of the quick-dead as they stepped ever closer.

The congregation is assembled, but some ghosts she can't summon.

The remaining horses nickered behind me, nervous, even the grey.

"I was thinking of my Brothers," I said. I opened a hand to the left and right to indicate Makin, Kent, Grumlow, and Rike.

"They can attend," Chella said. "I will leave them their eyes."

"Will we have no music? No poets to declaim? No flowers?" I asked. I was stalling.

"You're stalling," she said.

The congregation is assembled. Aside from those she can't summon. And those she does not wish to.

"There's a poet I'm thinking of, Chella. A poem. A fitting one. 'To his coy mistress.'"

"Am I coy?" She walked closer now, swaying through the dead. The wisdom of poets has outlived that of the Builders.

"The poem is about time, at least in part. About how the poet can't stop time. And in the end he says, 'For Thus, though we cannot make our sun; Stand still, yet we will make him run.'"

Ghosts can't hurt men. They can drive them mad. They can torment them to the point at which they take their own lives, but they cannot wound them. I felt this to be true. My stolen necromancy told me it was so. But they can hurt the dead, it seems. I had seen it with my own eyes. The corpses that Chella set to walking could be felled by spirits because they stood closer to their world, close enough to the gates of death for a ghost to reach out and throttle them.

"Very sweet," Chella said. "But it won't stop me."

"So I'll make you run." And with every fragment of my will I summoned my ghosts. I pulled them through the gates that Chella had opened. With arms spread wide I returned each shade and phantom, each haunt and spirit that had trailed me these long years. I bled them through my chest, let them pulse through me with each beat of my heart. I couldn't stop Chella drawing forth those she wanted but I could make damn sure they all came, each and every one. At a run.

And they came. The congregation Chella had chosen not to invite. The burning dead of Gelleth, those that the Builders' Sun took first, not victims from the outskirts of the explosion like Ruth and her Ma, but those who burned in the Castle Red at the heart of the inferno. They poured from me in an endless torrent. Ten of them to every child of Gelleth that Chella had brought forth. And my dead, the burning dead, brought with them a fire like no other. They burned as candles in the hearth, flesh running, flames leaping, each man or woman screaming and racing or staggering and clutching. And behind them, with measured pace, a new kind of ghost, each glowing with a terrible light that made their flesh a pink haze and shadows of their bones.

I saw nothing but fire without heat, heard only screams, and after forever we stood alone on our mound with no sign of Chella or her army save for blackened bones smouldering on damp reeds.

"Wedding's off," I said, and taking my bearing from the sunset I led the Brothers away to the south.

Brother Makin has high ideals. If he kept to them, we would be enemies. If he nursed his failure, we would not be friends.

35

Wedding day

"A spade?" Hobbs said.

If there was ever a man to call a spade a spade, Watch-master Hobbs was that man. I was just impressed a man of his age had any breath left at this point, for stating the obvious or otherwise.

I kicked about in the snow. Spades lay everywhere, covered by a recent fall.

"Get Stodd and Keppen's squads shooting down the slope. Harold's men I want using these spàdes to dig," I said.

"Stodd's dead." Hobbs spat and watched the snowfield. The gap between the Watch and our pursuit had vanished. Here and there men stopped running. Few managed to draw a blade, let alone swing, before they were cut down.

Blood on snow is very pretty. In the deep powder it melts its way down and there's not much to see, but where the snow has an icy crust, that dazzling white shines through the scarlet and makes the blood look somehow richer and more vital than ever it did in your veins.

"Get men shooting down the slope. I don't much care what they hit. Legs are good. Put more bodies in the way. Slow them down."

An injured man is more of an obstacle than a dead one. Put a big wound in a man and he often gets clingy, as though he thinks you can save him and all he has to do is hold on so you won't leave. The fresh-wounded like company. Give them a while and they'd rather be alone with their pain. For a moment I saw Coddin, odd chinks of light offering the lines of him, curled in his tomb. Some folk bury their dead like that, curled up, forehead to knee. Makin said it makes for easier digging of a grave, but to my eye it's more of a return. We lay coiled in the womb.

"Shoot the bastards down!" I yelled. I waved my hands toward the men that I wanted using their bows. "Don't pick targets."

Makin staggered up and I slapped a spade across his chest. Captain Harold and I started to collar other men and set them digging. None of them asked why. Except for Makin, and truthfully I think he just wanted the chance to rest.

"We came here once," he said.

"Yes." I threw another load of snow behind me. It felt odd having climbed for what seemed like forever, to now be desperately digging back down with the last of my strength.

"We were on our way to some village . . . Cutting?"

"Gutting," I said. Another load of snow. The cries and clash of blades on the slopes closer now.

"This is insane!" Makin dropped his spade and drew his sword. "I remember now. There are caves here. But they don't lead anywhere. We searched them. The men we have here—they'd barely fit in."

My spade bit into nothing and slipped from numb fingers into the void below. "I'm through! Dig here!"

The melee reached to within fifty yards of our position, a bloody, rolling fight, men slipping in the snow, a pink mush now, screaming, severed limbs, dripping blades. And beyond the carnage, like an arrowhead pointing directly at me, more and more and more soldiers, the line of them broadening to a mass several hundred men wide as they crossed the snowline far below.

"I may have left it too late," I said. I knew I'd left it too late. I spent too long with Coddin. And Arrow's men had been faster than I thought they would be.

"Too late?" Makin shouted. He waved his sword at the army converging on us. "We're dead. We could have done this back down there! At least I would have had the strength to fight then."

He looked strong enough to me. Anger always opens a new reserve, a little something you'd forgotten about.

"Keep digging!" I shouted at the men around me. The entrance to the caves stood wide enough for three men. A black hole in the snow.

"How many men died in avalanches in the Matteracks last year, Makin?" I asked.

"I don't know!" He looked at me as if I'd asked to have his babies. "None?"

"Three," I said. "One the year before that."

Some of the enemy were trying to flank us, spreading out around the melee to come at us from the side. I unslung my bow and loosed an arrow at the men on the left.

"We're done," Hobbs laboured across the slope, avoiding the diggers. To his credit he managed to add, "Sire."

My arrow had hit a man just above the knee. Looked like an old fellow. Some old people just don't know when to quit. He pitched forward and fell, rolling down the mountainside. I wondered if he'd stop before he reached the Haunt. "There's a reason we lost four men in two years to avalanches," I said.

"Carelessness?" Makin asked. One of the Prince's more enterprising men had found his way uninjured around the edge of the battle below us. Makin made a quick parry then cut him down. A second soldier on the heels of the first took an arrow through his Adam's apple.

The clash of metal on rock. The diggers had found the cave's edges. The hole stood wide enough for a wagon to pass but it wouldn't be getting any wider.

When the world is covered in snow it turns flat. All the hollows, all the bumps, are written into one unbroken surface like the white page ready for the quill. You may place on a snowfield whatever your imagination will produce, for your eyes will tell you nothing.

"Well?" Makin asked. The men of Arrow were pushing ever closer. He seemed in want of distraction and irritated that I'd drifted off into a daydream.

"You have to see the shades," I said.

"Shades?"

I shrugged. I had time to waste: the cave was no use to us yet. "I thought that the power of being young was to see only black and white," I said. I looked on as a man I knew among the Watch fell with the red point of a sword jutting from his back, hands locked on the neck of the blade's owner.

"Shades?" Makin asked again.

"We never look up, Makin, we never raise our heads and look up. We live in such a vast world. We crawl across its surface and concern ourselves only with what lies before us."

"Shades?" Makin kept stubbornly to his purpose. His thick-lipped mouth knew a thousand smiles. Smiles for winning hearts. Smiles for making friends. Smiles for tearing a laugh from the unwilling. Now he used his stubborn smile.

I shook my arms, willing life back into them. The line buckled here and there: soon enough there'd be call for my sword. "Shades," I told him. When all you have to look at is white, given time you will see a symphony in shades of pale. The peasants in Gutting told me this—though in their own words. There are many types of snow, many shades, and even in one shade, many flavours. There are layers. There is granularity, powder. There is power and there is danger. "When I stabbed Brother Gemt I pre-empted something," I said. "You understand, 'pre-empt,' Brother Makin?"

A thousand smiles; and one frown. He gave me the frown.

"I killed him for the hell of it, but also because it would only be a matter of time before he came against me. Before he tried to slit my throat in the night. And not just for the cutting of his hand."

"What does bloody Gemt have to do with—" He cut down another man who slipped the line and I loosed an arrow at the men flanking our right side.

"There were four deaths in two years rather than forty because the Highlanders pre-empt avalanches," I said. "They set them off."

"What?"

"They watch the snow. They see the shades. They see the ups and downs, not the flat page. They dig and test. And then they pre-empt." I waved my bow overhead, purple ribbon cracking in the wind. "In the caves. Now!"

When a slope looks dangerous the Highlanders take themselves above it by ridge and pass and cliff. They take with them straw, stones, a crude bowl of fired clay, kindling, charcoal—often from the burners in Ancrath's woods—a glazed pot and a sheep's bladder. They dig themselves a hole at the very top of the most treacherous layers, setting the bowl on top of several inches of packed straw. In the bowl they put kindling and charcoal, and set stones so that the pot will be held above the bowl. They fill the pot with snow and inflate the bladder, blowing into it as hard as they can and tying it off with a strip of guthide. They light the kindling and leave.

The men of the Watch started to pack into the caves. I had thought it would be crowded, once upon a time, back when I ordered the spades to be left there. I had wondered if we would all fit. Fewer than a hundred men made it in. We had space aplenty.

So much in life is simply a matter of timing.

I took my place at the cave mouth, eager to cross swords with the men of Arrow. I had the timing wrong. Plain and true. I should have said what mattered to Coddin days ago, months ago. My timing had been off.

Tired men die easy, as if they relish the prospect of infinity. My legs had the trembles but my arms were ready enough. I held my blade two-handed and took the first man in the eye with its point. Makin came to fight beside me. Beyond the enemy I could see forever. I could see the wildness and wideness of the mountains. Beyond them, the day moon, white like the memory of bone. Faint strains of the sword-song reached me as I crossed blades again, shearing partway through a man's neck. My sword felt lighter, twitching to the song as if it held a life of its own and pulsed with its own blood. *Snicker-snack, snicker-snack*, and men fell away in pieces. The sun flashed crimson on my uncle's sword as if heliographing a message to the Prince of Arrow.

"I'm sorry!" I shouted, for Makin and the others.

Timing.

We weren't far enough ahead. The men of Gutting would

have lit the fires in their bowls as they saw us emerge from the neck of the valley onto the mountain's shoulder. I had thought we would reach the caves with a clear margin. That we would dig in and rake the slope with bow-fire. I was wrong. Just a few minutes' error but plenty long enough for the enemy to fill the caves with our corpses.

Makin gave an oath and fell back, throwing himself beyond a swinging blade.

I nearly said "Sorry" again—but a mountain is a good place to die. If you're going to die, try to make it somewhere with a view.

For moments without time I fought, enfolded with a fierce joy, the heat rising in me until the burns on my face blazed and the wind had no hold on me. Each part of that fight played out to a secret score and the timing that had eluded me returned in the scream of steel against steel. A wildness infected me and I thought of Ferrakind incandescent and consumed, whatever made him human abandoned to the inferno.

A block, a sway, step to the side, the ring and scrape of my sword as it slid from the foe's sheared flesh. When a heavy blade meets the head of a man who has discarded his helm in the long climb, a red ruin is wrought. Worse than the neat butchery of the slaughterman in his abattoir is this destruction. Brain, skull, and hair follow the swing of your sword in a wet arc of crimson, white, and grey. Pieces of a face hang for a frozen moment: an accusing eye, its juices leaking, then everything falls and the next man stumbles through to battle, wearing scraps of the last.

Fire wrapped me, or so it felt, hot lines of it snaking from Gog's burn, scorching, fierce.

A swordpoint traced its path within a hair of my brow, whispering across the bridge of my nose as I jerked back. Lunging, I thrust out both arms, my blade a bar held at hilt and end, the point hard against the iron plate in the palm of my leather glove. The Builder-steel divided the man's face horizontally between nose and lip. The grip of his bone tried to take the sword with him as he fell but I kept the hilt and let the motion swing the blade out right, catching a spear thrust and angling it over my shoulder. That man I kicked down the slope and the roar that burst from me rippled the air like a furnace breath. If I'd had the time to look down I would not have been surprised to see the snow shrink back from the heat pulsing off my skin.

Much of me, very nearly all of me perhaps, wanted to surrender to the battle-madness, to be consumed, to throw myself down among the foe and paint the mountain with their blood no matter the cost. But surrender of any kind comes hard to me. Instead I drew back and the fury left me, blown out as swiftly as it ignited. I had a plan to follow and I'd follow it even though all hope seemed lost. And following plans requires a clear head.

More men pressed at me. My arms started to feel as tired as my legs. We just needed a few more minutes, but sometimes you don't get what you want, or what you need. My eyes flickered to the view. Time to die.

In the past I have been saved by a horse. Not borne to safety by a noble steed, but saved by the wild kick of a panicked horse. That had been unexpected. It probably surprised Corion even more. To be saved by a sheep's weak bladder though . . . that takes the biscuit. It takes all the biscuits.

High above us slow fires burned, melting the snow in the pots, heating the inflated bladders now floating in the steaming water. The process gives the Highlanders time to retreat to a point of safety. You have to place the pots in the danger zone. You do it as high up as you can for your own preservation, but not so high that it won't have the desired effect.

The hot air expands. The bladders swell further. Stretching beyond the point a man could inflate them. It's just a matter of time. A matter of timing. The water starts to boil. The pressure builds. And bang!

The Highlanders play the bladder-pipe. The things had screeched at my wedding that morning, similar to the bagpipes found farther north, less complex but just as raucous. You wouldn't think an exploding bladder would be so loud. The sound is as if every squeal and howl a bladder-pipe might make in its long and unfortunate life has been squeezed into half a moment. It's a noise to wake the dead. But this was a case of a noise to make the dead.

One of the six sheep that donated the six bladders to the six avalanche pots, that the men of Gutting lit on the slopes when we came into view, must have been a particularly incontinent beast for its bladder exploded several minutes earlier than expected.

You feel an avalanche before you hear it. There's a strange build-up of pressure. It presses into your ears. Even with men trying to slice me into bloody chunks I noticed the pressure. Then there's the rumble. It starts faint and builds without end. And finally, just before it hits, there's the hissing.

My timing came good at the right moment. I threw myself into the cave. Before the men attacking me could follow, the world turned white and they were gone.

36

Wedding day

The cave lay blind dark and silent although it held close on a hundred men.

The last rumbles of the avalanche stilled. In my fall I had bruised my arse on an unforgiving rock and my curse was the first sound.

"Shitdarn!" I'd learned that one from Brother Elban and felt a duty to roll it out from time to time since no one else ever used it.

Still no noise, as if a gang of trolls had ripped the head from each man as he entered.

"There's lanterns at the back, and tinder," I called.

Scuffling now.

More scuffling, the scritch of flint on steel and then a glow cutting dozens of men from the darkness.

I looked at the silver watch on my wrist for the first time in an age. A quarter past twelve. The arm for counting seconds *tick tick tick*ed its way in yet another circle.

"I know my spade made it in here," I said, standing, careful not to brain myself on the low ceiling. "Find some more and dig us out."

"We should take a roll-call," Hobbs said, moving to the front. More lanterns were lit and the wall of snow behind him glistened.

"We could," I said. I knew his wasn't just a bureaucratic interest. He had lost friends, protégés, the sons of friends, and he wanted to know what remained of the Watch, of *his* Watch. "We could, but it's not the snow that kills men in an avalanche," I said. "None of those soldiers out there are dead."

I had their attention now.

"They're all busy suffocating whilst the snow has them trapped. And that, my friends, is exactly what's happening to us. Whilst I explain it to you I'm using up the strictly limited supply of air in this cave. Whilst you're listening to me you are breathing in the good air and breathing out the bad. Each of those lanterns that lets you see me, is eating up the air." Silent thanks to Tutor Lundist and his lessons in alchemy—I might not outlive my wedding day but I had no desire to exit by snuffing out like the candle in the bell-jar.

They took my point. Three men who had found spades hurried to the snow, others searched for more. Soon all the space at the exit was occupied. I could have just told them to dig, but better they know the reason, better they not think I didn't share Hobbs's interest in the Watch's sacrifice.

I saw Captain Keppen leaning against a boulder, clutching his side. Makin had set himself against the rear wall of the cave on his backside with his knees drawn up to his forehead.

"Get the wounded seen to," I told Hobbs. I clapped a hand to his shoulder. Kings are supposed to make such gestures.

I found my way to Makin's side. The cave floor lay strewn with men but whether they had been felled by exhaustion or injury I couldn't tell. I slid my back down the icy wall and sat beside him. We watched the diggers dig and tried to breathe shallow. He smelled of clove-spice and sweat.

A strange path I had followed to end trapped in a snow-locked cave, buried in the highest of places. From the Tall Castle to the road, from the road to Renar's throne, a year and more roaming the empire until at last the Highlands called me back. And in the Highlands finding the prize less rewarding than the chase, growing into manhood on a copper crown throne, wrestling with the mundane from plague to famine, building an economy like a swordsman builds muscle, recruiting, training, and for what? To have some preordained emperor trample it beneath his heel on his march to the Gilden Gate.

I closed my eyes and listened as my aches and pains announced themselves into the first pause since Father Gomst married me to Miana that morning. The weight of the day settled on me, squeezing words out.

"There's men dead out there because I spent too long talking with Coddin," I said. "Renar men and Ancrath men."

"Yes." Makin didn't lift his head.

"Well, here we are, both dying in a cave like Coddin is. Got anything you need to unburden, Sir Makin? Or do we need more extreme circumstances and even less time?"

"Nope." Makin looked up, his face in shadow with just the curve of a cheekbone and the tip of his nose catching the lamplight. "Those men chose to follow you, Jorg. And they'd all be dead if it weren't for your tricks."

"And why did they choose to follow me? Why do you?" I asked.

I could hear rather than see him lick his teeth before answering. "There are no simple answers in the world, Jorg. Every question has sides. Too many of them. Everything is knotted. But you make the questions simple and somehow it works. For other men the world is not like that. Maybe I could have found a way to drag you back to your father years before you took yourself back—but I wanted to see you do what you promised to. I wondered if you really could win it all."

"It seemed simple when I had Count Renar to hate," I said.

"You were . . ." He smiled. "Focused."

"It's about being young too. I hardly recognize myself in that boy."

"You're not so different," Makin said.

The snow around the diggers had a glow of its own now, the daylight reaching down through what remained to clear.

"I was consumed by me, by what I wanted. Nothing else mattered. Not my life, not anyone's life. All of it was a price worth paying. All of it was worth staking on long odds just for the chance to win."

Makin snorted. "That's a place everyone visits on their way from child to man. You just went native."

I reached into the pouch on my hip and slid my fingers around the box. "I have . . . regrets."

"We're all built of those." Makin watched the diggers. A spear of daylight struck through into the cave.

"Gelleth I am sorry for . . . My father would think me weak. But if it were now—I would find another way."

"There was no other way," Makin said. "Even the way you took was impossible."

"Tell me about your child," I said. "A girl?"

"Cerys." He spoke her name like a kiss, blinking as the daylight found us. "She would be older than you, Jorg. She was three when they killed her."

We could see the sky now, a circle of blue, away to the east beyond the snow clouds.

"I follow you because I'm tired of war. I would see it stopped. One empire. One law. It doesn't matter so much how or who, just being united would stop the madness," Makin said.

"Heh, I can feel the loyalty!" I pushed up and stood, stretching. "Wouldn't the Prince of Arrow make a better emperor?" I set off toward the exit.

"I don't think he'll win," said Makin, and he followed.

In the long ago, in the gentle days, Brother Grumlow carved wood, worked with saw and chisel. When hard times come carpenters are apt to get nailed to crosses. Grumlow took up the knife and learned to carve men. He looks soft, my brother of the blade, slight in build, light in colour, weak chin, sad eyes, all of him drooping like the moustache that hangs off his lip. Yet he has fast hands and no fear of a sharp edge. Come against him with just a dagger for company and he will cut you a new opinion.

37

Wedding day

A hundred and twelve men climbed out of the cave below Blue Moon Pass. I let Watch-master Hobbs take his roll-call as they gathered on the new snow. It amazed me that the avalanche which had broken like a wave on the rocks below, and had run like milk into and around the cave, could now support my weight, letting my feet sink no more than an inch or two with each step. I listened to the names, to the replies, or more often to the silence that followed a name.

The new snow glittered below us, perfect and even, no trace of the blood, of the carnage strewn there only minutes before. And as Hobbs made his tally a thousand and a thousand and a thousand men died unseen beneath that fresh white sheet, held motionless, blind, struggling for breath and finding nothing.

Sometimes I feel the need of an avalanche within me. A clean page with the past swept away. Tabula rasa. I wondered if this one had wiped the slate for me. And then I saw a shadow beneath the whiteness at my feet, a child buried so shallow that the snow could not hide him. Not even the force of mountains could clean the stains from my past.

While Hobbs droned on I took the copper box from its place at my hip and sat on the slope, heels dug in.

A man is made of memories. It is all we are. Captured moments, the smell of a place, scenes played out time and again on a small stage. We *are* memories, strung on storylines—the tales we tell ourselves about ourselves, falling through our lives into tomorrow. What the box held was mine. Was me.

"What now then?" Makin slumped beside me.

Down beyond the farthest reach of the avalanche I could see movement, tiny dots, the remnants of Arrow's force retreating to join his main army.

"Up," I said.

"Up?" Makin did the surprised thing with his eyebrows. Nobody could look surprised like Makin.

It didn't seem right to die incomplete.

"It's not a difficult concept," I said, standing. I set off walking up the slope aimed a little to the left of the peak, where Blue Moon Pass scores a deep path across Mount Botrang's shoulder.

Hobbs saw me go. "Up?" he said. "But the pass is always blocked in—" Then he looked around. "Oh." And he waved at the men, who had come forward to answer their names, to follow.

I still held the box in my hand, hot and cold, smooth and sharp. It didn't seem right to die without knowing who I was.

The child walked beside me now, barefoot in the snow, his death resisting even the light of day.

With the nail of my thumb I opened the box.

Trees, gravestones, flowers, and her.

"Who found you after I hit you?" I ask Katherine. "A man was with you when you recovered your senses."

She frowns. Her fingers touch the place where the vase shattered. "Friar Glen." For the first time she sees me with her old eyes, clear and green and sharp. "Oh."

I walk away.

I leave the Rennat Forest behind me and walk toward Crath City. The Tall Castle stands behind and above the city. It's a still day and the smoke rises from the city chimneys in straight lines as if making bars for the castle. Perhaps to keep it safe from me.

From the fields I see the sprawl of the Low City reaching out to the River Sane and the docks, and behind it the land steps upward to the Old City and the High City. The Roma Road cuts my path and I follow it to the Low City, gateless and open to the world. I have a hat stuffed in my tunic, a shapeless thing of faded checks such as the bravos at the river docks wear. I tuck my hair into it and pull it low. I won't be noticed in the Low City. The people who might know my face do not go there.

I walk through the Banlieu, nothing but slum dwellings and waste heaps, a boil on the arse of the city. Even a fine spring day cannot make these streets bloom. Children root through the mounded filth left by poor folk. They chase me as I make my way. Girls of ten and younger try to distract me with big eyes and kiss-mouths whilst skinny boys work to pull something from my pack, anything they can snatch free. I take my knife in hand and they melt away. Orrin of Arrow might have given them bread. He might have resolved to change this place. I just walk through it. Later I will scrape it from my shoes.

Where the Banlieu shades into the Low City the worst of the taverns crowd around narrow streets. I pass the Falling Angel where I first plotted Gelleth's end, where I first thought to pay for affection. I know better now. Affection is always paid for.

I choose another alehouse, the Red Dragon. A grand name for a dim and reeking place of shadows.

"Bitter," I say.

The barkeep takes my coin and fills a tankard from the barrel spigot. If he thinks I look young to drink here, among the broken old men with their red noses and watery eyes, he says nothing.

I take a table where I can put a corner at my back and watch the windows. The ale is as bitter as my mood. I take slow sips and wait for the night to come.

I think of Katherine. I make a list.

She said I was evil and that she hates me.
She has set her heart on the Prince of Arrow.
She tried to kill me.
She destroyed the child she thought was mine.
She was defiled by another man.

*   *   *

I run through it again and again as the sun sinks, as the drunkards come and go, carts and whores and dogs and labourers pass in the street, and still I cycle through my list.

Love is not a list.

Full dark, and my tankard has stood empty for hours. I walk into the street. Here and there a lantern hangs, too high for thieves, casting a parsimonious light that struggles to reach the ground.

Despite all my waiting, despite my resolve, still I hesitate. Can I tread the paths of childhood again without taint? Overhead the stars turn, a slow revolution about the Pole Star, the Nail of Heaven. Part of me doesn't want to go back to the Tall Castle. I push that part away.

I cross the river by the New Bridge and find a quiet corner where I can watch the High Wall. Crath City and its parts have been named with the same lack of imagination the Builders put into the architecture of its castle. As if the box-like utilitarianism of the castle has leached into the language of the city. If I had the power to build for the ages, to know that what I set in stone would stand for millennia, I would put at least some measure of beauty into the mix.

The High Wall is indeed high, but it is not well lit, and some way west of the Triple Gate the stonework is broken by the remnants of a second wall that once led off at right angles and is now gone. I practised my climbing here when I was little. It seems easy now. Handholds that I struggled to reach can be bypassed entirely in favour of the next. My hands know this surface. I don't need to see it. This is memory. I gain the top well before the next guard makes his rounds. On the far side ill-advised ivy makes the descent a simple matter.

Young Sim taught himself the ways of the assassin. He made a hobby of it, the short knife, drop-leaf in powder or tincture, or once in a while a harp string used to garrotte. Of all my Brothers it is Sim that is the most deadly in the long haul. In a battle I could surely cut him down. But lose sight of the boy and he will not come at you in the next moment, or the next day, but in his own time. When you have forgotten the wrong you did him, he will find you again. Sim taught himself the long game and he passed a little knowledge on to me.

Disguise is not a matter of clothes and artistry with paints and kohl. Disguise lies in how you move. Of course the right uniform, a chin made of putty, a well-applied scar, all these can be of great help in the proper circumstances, but the first step, Sim taught me, the most important step, is exactly that . . . how you step. Move with confidence, or at least confidence in your role. Believe you have every right to be where you are. Step with purpose. Then even a prop as small as a hat can furnish a full disguise.

I stride through the streets of Old City, aiming directly for the East Gate, the gate where deliveries are made to the Tall Castle, supplies unloaded, messages handed to runners for carriage to distant quarters. A patrol of my father's soldiers, ten strong, passes the head of Elm Street as I walk it. They spare me a first glance but not a second.

Three torches burn above the East Gate. They call it a gate but it is a door, five yards high, three yards wide, black oak with iron banding, a smaller door set into the middle of it for when it is simply men seeking entrance rather than giants. An armoured knight stands duty before the door. If he wished to see anything he should stand in the dark.

I turn aside and come to the base of the castle wall close to the corner of the great square keep.

A man seeking to protect himself from the assassin's knife concentrates his defence. You cannot stop a single anonymous enemy entering your realm. You cannot stop him entering your city. Unless he is unskilled you would be lucky to stop him finding a way past your castle wall. Your keep may hold him out if it is secure and well guarded—but it is unwise to bet your life on it. To defeat the assassin you don't spread your defences over your whole estate, you focus them around you. Ten good men tight around your bedchamber can do more to preserve you than ten thousand spread across a kingdom.

My father's keep is secure and well patrolled, but by the time I reached seven I knew the outside of it better than the inside. In the dark of the moon I climb the Tall Castle once more. Builder-stone rough under my fingers, my toes hunting familiar holds through the soft leather of my boots, the scrape of the wall on my cheek as I hug it. I see my knuckles white in the starlight as I grip the corner of the Tall Castle and move up.

I hold still just beneath the battlements. A soldier pauses and leans out watching some distant light. The battlements are new additions, dressed stone atop the Builder-stone. The Builders had weapons that made mockery of castles and of battlements. I don't know what the Tall Castle was when the Builders made it, but it was not a castle. In the deepest part of the dungeons under layers of filth an ancient plaque declares "No Overnight Parking." Even when the Builders' words make sense alone, they hold no meaning together.

The soldier moves on. I climb up, cross the thickness of the wall, and shin down one of the wooden supports for the walkways.

In a dark corner of the courtyard I take off my bravo's hat and return it to my pack. I pull out a tunic, blue and red in the Ancrath colours. I had a woman called Mable tailor it for me at the Haunt, in the style of my father's servant garb. With the tunic on and my hair tucked into it, I enter the Printers' Door. I pass a table-knight about his rounds. Sir Aiken if I remember rightly. I keep my head up and he takes no notice of me. A man with his head bowed is hiding his face and worthy of close inspection.

From the Printers' Door it is left then right along a short corridor to reach the chapel. The chapel door is never locked. I look in. Only two candles still burn, both little more than stubs and making scant light. The place is empty. I move on.

Friar Glen's quarters are close to the chapel. His door is latched but I carry a short strip of steel thin enough and flexible enough to fit between door and frame, strong enough to lift the latch.

His room is very dark but it has a high window that opens onto the courtyard where Makin used to school the squires in the arts of combat. A borrowed light filters in and I let my eyes learn its ways. The place stinks like cheese left too long in the sun. I stand and listen to the friar's snore whilst my eyes hunt him.

He lies hunched in his bed, an inchworm frozen in mid-crawl. I can see little of the room, just a cross on the wall with the saviour absent as if he'd taken a break rather than watch this night's business. I step forward. I remember how Friar Glen dug in my flesh for those hooks the briar left in me. How he hunted them. What pleasure he took in it, with his man, Inch, holding me down. I pull my knife from its sheath.

Crouched beside his bed, my head level with his, the snores are loud. So loud you would think he should wake himself. I can't see his face so I remember it instead; flat I would call it, too blunt for deep emotion but well suited to the sneer. At service with Father Gomst holding forth from the pulpit, Friar Glen would watch from the chair by the chapel door, hair like wet straw around a tonsure that needed little shaving, his eyes too small for the broadness of the forehead above.

I should slit his throat and be gone. Anything else would make too much noise.

You raped Katherine. You raped her and let her think I had done it. You made her pregnant and made her hate me so much she poisoned the child from her womb. Made her hate me enough to stab me.

Katherine's blow was for Friar Glen, not me.

My eyes have learned the darkness and the room lies revealed in night shades. I trim a long strip from the edge of his sheet. I make only a whisper below the roar of his snoring but he stirs and complains even so. I cut a second strip, a third, a fourth. I bundle the last strip into a tight ball. A candle stand and small table are set near the bed. I move them farther back so they will not fall and make a racket. I count his snores and get their rhythm. When he breathes in I stuff the wadded cloth into his mouth. I tie another strip around his head to hold it in place. Friar Glen is slow to wake but surprisingly strong. I snatch the remains of the sheet from him and hammer my elbow down into his solar plexus. The air hisses from him past his gag. I see the gleam of his eyes. He coils, foetal, and I bind his ankles tight with the third strip. The fourth is for his wrists. I have to punch his throat before I can manage to secure them.

I've lost my taste for the work by the time he is properly trussed. He is an ugly naked man whimpering in the dark and I only want to be gone from here. I take my knife from the table that I moved aside.

"I have something for you," I say. "Something that was very nearly misdelivered."

I drive my knife in low, at the base of his scrotum. I leave it there. I don't want it back. Also, if I pull it free he will bleed to death quickly. I think he should linger.

Also, I have a spare.

I am almost at the door, with Friar Glen wheezing and hissing behind me. He makes a loud thump as he falls from the bed, but it isn't that which stops me.

Sageous appears. He doesn't step through the doorway, he doesn't rise from behind a chest, he is just there. His skin glows with its own light, not bright enough to illuminate even the floor at his feet, but enough to make silhouettes of the endless script tattooed across every inch of him. His eyes and mouth are dark holes in the glow.

"I see you are making a habit out of the clergy. Are you working your way down the list? First a bishop, now a friar. What next? An altar boy?"

"You're a heathen," I say. "You should applaud me. Besides, his sins cried out for it."

"Oh well, in that case . . ." His smile makes a black crescent in the light of his face. "And what do your sins cry out for, Jorg?"

I have no answer.

Sageous only smiles wider. "And what were the friar's sins? I would ask him but you appear to have gagged him. I do hope the dreams I gave young Katherine have not caused trouble? Women are such complex creatures, no?"

"Dreams?" I say. My hand searches in my pack, hunting my second knife.

"She dreamed she was with child," Sageous says. "Somehow the dream even fooled her body. I think they call it a phantom pregnancy." The writing on his face seemed to move, words pulsing as if spoken. "Such complex creatures."

"There was a child. She killed it." My mouth is dry.

"There was blood and muck. Saraem Wic's poisons will do that. But there was no child. I doubt there ever will be now. That old witch's poisons are not gentle. They scrape a womb bare."

I find the blade and I'm moving toward him. I try to run but it's like wading through deep snow.

"Silly boy. You think I'm really here?" He makes no move to escape.

I try to reach him, but I'm floundering.

* * *

Schnick.

Makin's hand on the box. The closed box.

I found myself cold, short of breath, hands tight around each other instead of Sageous's neck. He gone. Just a memory. And I'm in the mountains. Still running.

"What the hell are you doing?" Makin panted.

I looked around. I stood waist-deep in powder snow. Rock walls loomed on either side. The men of the Watch marched behind me . . . a hundred yards behind me.

"You can't open that. Not now, not ever. Certainly not now!" Makin shouted. He retched and sucked his breath back. He must have run hard to catch me. I snatched the box back from him and buried it in a pocket.

It's rare for Blue Moon Pass to be open in the winter. Very rare. A good avalanche will clear it out though, and for a few days before new snow chokes it again, a man can escape across the back of Mount Botrang and then, by a series of lower passes that parallel the spine of the Matteracks, that man can leave the range entirely and the empire is his to wander.

"Run."

A whisper in my ear. A familiar voice.

"Run."

"Sageous?" I asked, voice low to keep it from Makin.

"Run."

Drops of pure nightmare trickled down the back of my neck. I shivered. "Don't worry, heathen. I'll run."

38

Wedding day

So, will we go to Alaric?" Makin asked.

I kept walking. The sides of the Blue Moon Pass rose sheer around us, caked in ice and snow, the black rock showing only where the wind scoured it clean.

"I guess the roads to the Dane-lore will be difficult in winter. But she did want you to come in winter, that girl of his. Ella?"

"Elin," I said.

"Your grandfather would offer you sanctuary," Makin said.

He knew we'd lost. The dead men stretched out behind us on the mountain, under stone and snow, didn't change that.

I kept walking. Underfoot the snow left by the avalanche lay firm, creaking as it recorded my footprints.

"Is it good there? On the Horse Coast? It'd be warm at least." He hugged himself.

There are two paths up into the Blue Moon Pass; it's like a snake's tongue, forked at the tip. The avalanche had opened both of them. I'd had the Highlanders place their boom-pots to ensure it.

"What?" said Makin. "You said 'up.'"

I carried on making the hard right that led back down the

second fork of Blue Moon Pass, picking up the pace. "Now I'm saying 'down.' I had Marten hold the Runyard for a reason, you know."

And so with the surviving third of the Watch trailing me I led the way down through the Blue Moon into the high valley above the Runyard. And when the slope lessened and the ground became firmer . . . we ran.

We saw the smoke before we heard the cries, and we heard the cries before we saw the Haunt. At last, far below, the Haunt came in view, an island of mountain stone in a sea of Arrow's troops. His forces laid siege on every side, attacking with ladders and grapple ropes, siege engines hurling rock at the front face of the castle, a covered ram pounding the gates, a legion of archers on the high ridge sending their shafts over the walls.

To my mind siege machinery is more an act of show and determination than it is a well-judged investment of time. Look! We hauled these huge bits of wood and iron to your castle—we mean business, we're here to stay. The Renar Highlands were perhaps that rare place where there really were enough big rocks lying around for a castle to be reduced to rubble by trebuchets, though it would take forever. But the ram! The ram is the queen of sieges, especially where walls may not be undermined. No mechanics, no counter-weights and escapements, just a simple direct force applied with vigour to the weakest point so that you may set your men against theirs, and that after all is the aim of it all. If you didn't outnumber the foe you wouldn't have marched to their castle and they would not be hiding behind walls.

Marten's men sheltered at the margins of the Runyard, as long and gentle a gradient as could be found in the Highlands, running down from our valley to the left of the Haunt. The ridge from which the Prince's archers gained their vantage broke the Runyard at its far end.

We could see Marten's troops, but from lower down the slope they were almost invisible, sheltered by rocks and hidden in their mountain greys. Marten posed little threat to the enemy, though. His hundred men would make no impression on the three thousand occupying the ridge, even if they weren't shot down as they advanced.

"Why?" Makin asked.

"Why is it called the Runyard?" I chose to answer the wrong question. "Because it's the only place for miles that you can actually have a horse run without breaking its legs. I've seen you at the gallop there many times."

Makin shook his head. Hobbs and Keppen joined us.

"We're going through the east port?" Hobbs asked.

Not many men knew about the sally ports, one to the east, one to the west. I didn't recall ever telling Hobbs about the east port but I supposed it was his business to know. We had, after all, led his Watch out of the west port that morning.

"Yes," I said.

We covered the last of the ground with great care, hugging the valley walls and being in no hurry. The archers proved intent on their targets within the Haunt, crouched behind its battlements. We reached Marten without attracting any attention.

"King Jorg." Marten had kept his country accent despite four years at court. He stood in the entrance to the sally port, a crack just wide enough for a single rider. The rocks above the crack looked natural but an experienced eye could tell they had been set to fall with only slight encouragement, a sufficient number of them to seal the portal with some permanence. A peculiar stink hung around the entrance. I saw Makin wrinkle his nose and frown as if he recognized it.

"Captain Marten," I said. "I see you've held the Runyard against all odds!"

He didn't smile at that. Marten had never smiled to my knowledge. It would look odd on his face, long like the rest of him, grey like the short crop above his eyes.

"The enemy have shown no interest in trying to take it from us. I don't believe they know we're here," he said.

"All to the good," I said. "Keppen, lead the Watch back to the castle."

Keppen slipped into the crack and the Watch started to file after him. They had a journey of three or four hundred yards ahead of them, most of it through natural caves carved by ancient streams, the last hundred yards through a tunnel hacked out by men with picks in hand and candles to light their work.

I glanced at the timepiece on my wrist, starting to get the habit again. A quarter past two.

"Come with me," I told Marten. Makin and Captain Harold followed too.

We crept across to the rocks that hid us from the slopes below, and edged out to a position that offered a view of the archers on the ridge. I pushed the watch up my wrist so my sleeve hid it. It never pays to sparkle when you're hoping to be unobserved.

"There are a lot of them," Makin said.

"Yes." In fact even without a single foot-soldier, just with archers, the Prince of Arrow had brought with him four men for every man I had under arms.

We watched. They weren't raining arrows on the Haunt, just picking targets of opportunity and making sure the men at my walls kept their heads down. They could raise an arrow storm if the need arose, but why waste arrows?

We kept watching.

"Fascinating," Makin said.

"Wait," I said. I looked at my watch again.

"For—" Makin stopped asking. A black stain spread from beneath the ridge.

"What is it?" Harold asked.

The archer ranks started to break. A wave of confusion rippling through the order.

"Trolls," I said.

"What?" Makin cried. "How? Who? How many?"

At our distance it was hard to see the detail but it looked messy. The rocks ran red.

Makin slapped fist to palm. "I smelled them back there at the entrance. The same stink you had on you when Gorgoth brought you down that day." He frowned again. "I guess this explains all those goats we kept buying in—that stuff about holding out for a long siege never made much sense."

"Gorgoth brought them south," I said. "I've offered them sanctuary in the Matteracks, though possibly it was the promise of goats that sealed the deal . . . He has a hundred and twenty with him. They've been tunnelling. Making covered exits below that ridge."

Marten almost smiled. "That would be why you refused to listen when I begged you to defend it."

"They can't win," Makin said. "Not with a hundred. Not even trolls!"

"No. But look at them. What a mess they're making, neh? As Maical would say, it helps to have the elephant of surprise on your side." I slid back down into the shadow of the rock. "Right, let's go."

Marten joined me. "Why now though, and how did you know?"

"Ah. What you should ask is how Gorgoth knew. An hour after the avalanche I told him. And he agreed—but how in hell did he know when the avalanche happened?"

At the sally port the last of the Watch were stepping into the dark.

"I need you to hold here, Marten," I said. "Come what may."

"We will hold. I don't forget what you did, and my men will follow where I lead," Marten said.

It seemed a small thing that I had done. A toy and something for the pain, to ease a little girl's passing from the world. I hadn't even done it for good reasons.

Makin set a hand on Marten's shoulder as he moved by. They shared a bond these two. Two lost daughters. I saw how deep that ran—so deep I'd known Makin half my life before he even spoke of it. I wondered if I were made for such emotions or if I were just the clever, shallow boy most people saw. These men carried dead daughters through the years. I had a dead child whose name I had lost, who dogged my trail because I would not shoulder the burden of my guilt. For a small box it surely held a weight of memory. Perhaps more than I could carry.

We trekked the cave trails, worn smooth by years of use. I held a lantern taken from a store just inside the entrance. It flared brighter as I took it, and my cheek pulsed. I'd had me a touch of that magic ever since Gog burned me. I took Ferrakind as an object lesson in not pursuing those paths.

I paused from time to time to gaze upon galleries of stone

forests that stretched away left and right. Stalagmites and sta-
lactites Lundist had called them, though he only had pictures
in books, and frankly those looked dull as hell. I'm not sure
what the difference is—maybe the big ones are stalagmites.
Lundist said they grow, but I've never seen it happen. I do know
that in the light of flames, beneath immeasurable weight of
rock, they hold a beauty that cannot be communicated.

For long moments the wonder of the living rock held me
and when it let me go I found myself alone, an island of light
in the ancient dark. Quick glances along the path confirmed it.
No men of the watch, no Brothers, not even footsteps in the
distance.

Something is wrong.

"Jorg." And Sageous stepped from behind a pillar of stone,
the light within him writing his tattoos across the walls in
shadow, sliding, moving, wrapping over every fold and curve
of the cavern.

"Heathen." I kept my eyes on his. "You have more church-
men you need killed perhaps?"

He smiled. "You've been so hard to reach, Jorg. A hedge of
thorns around all your dreams." A frown. ". . . or a box? Is it a
box, Jorg? There's another hand in this. Someone has been
keeping you from me."

I kept my hands still, my eyes on his, but I felt the weight
at my hip and his gaze wandered there.

"Interesting," he said. "But no matter. Now we're so close
I can touch you again."

"Have you come to play me, heathen? To set me on the path
of your choosing?" I drew steel but he seemed unimpressed.
"Don't tell me—you're not here again?"

Again the smile. He inclined his head a fraction. "I'm
beyond your reach, Jorg, and you still walk the path I placed
you on long ago. All you have left to choose is the manner of your
death. I took Katherine from you. She would have made you
strong. Yin to your yang, if you like. And now you are weak,
and she serves instead to place in my hands an Arrow I can
point where I will."

"No." I shook my head and took a step toward him, careful
of my footing.

In the caves a wrong step can leave you broken at the bottom of a long fall. Yet however I chose my steps the heathen had always made me doubt my footing. He carried doubt with him, doubt of self, doubt of motives, the kind of uncertainty that eats at a man like cancer.

"No." I repeated myself, hunting confidence. "Gloating is for fools. If I were playing your game you would leave me to play it." I quested toward him with the point of my sword. "Perhaps those gentle touches didn't work quite so well as you had hoped and you come in desperation to turn me more boldly from the path I'm walking. Gloating is for fools, and I have never counted you a fool."

The light flickered across his skin. "You can't win, boy. You can't win. So why are you still here? What are you planning? Where are you hiding your secrets?" His eyes fell to the box again, though it made but the slightest bulge at my hip.

A quick step and I thrust at him. He hissed as the blade bit in, with no more resistance than if only his robe hung before me.

"I'm not here!" Through gritted teeth, as if insistence made it true. And he was gone.

"Jorg?" Makin at my side, a frown on his brow, his hand on my arm. "Jorg?"

"Heh. Dreaming on my feet." I shook my head. "Lead on!"

The sally tunnels connect to separate cellars beneath the Haunt, their exits disguised as huge wine barrels. I elbowed my way among the Watch and found Hobbs.

"Do what you can about the ram," I said. "It looks to be well covered but it needs fresh men to swing it, so shoot a few of the bastards as they come up to take a turn. Also, you'll find there's not much incoming at the moment. At least not of the pointy kind. They'll still be slinging rocks at us. So take advantage and just kill as many of his men as you can."

Next I took myself to the courtyard where my levies, subjects, and bannermen waited, crowded rank upon rank before the gatehouse. Knights from Morrow to the left of the portcullis, armour gleaming, swords in hand. To the right more knights, plate-armoured, the noblest sons of Hodd Town, my capital down in the valleys to the north. No doubt they had come to win the king's favour and honour for their houses.

Young men in the main, soft with gold and more used to lance and tourney than blood and ruin. I saw Sir Elmar of Golden among them, his armour radiant as his name implied. A warrior, that one, despite his finery.

They had some strength among them. Crowded on the gallery and stairs, crossbow men from the Westfast under Lord Scoolar, hard-eyed and wind-burned. Packed before the splintering gate, men of the Hauntside, tough fighters from the hills, in leather and iron, axes honed, round wooden shields layered in goat-hide. Behind these, warriors from Far Range, their iron helms patterned with silver and tin, each man armed with hammer and hatchet. And to the rear, ranked before the keep wall, Cennat shield dancers, their warboards taller than a man.

I walked among them, Makin at my shoulder, amid the stink and heave of bodies, the tension a taste in the air at once both sour and sweet. I hadn't words for them, no kingly gestures, no speech to shout above the screams from beyond the wall and the crash of the ram. When you fight alongside Brothers you bind them with word and deed. When you fight among subjects you are a figure, a form, an idea. Men will die for many things; lives hoarded with care can be spent for the strangest of reasons. What bound us here, we men of the Highlands, was defiance. All men will dig their heels in if pushed enough. All men will reach the point that they say "no" for no reason other than opposition, for no reason other than the word fits their mouth, and tastes as good as it sounds. And in the Highlands, among our mountains, the heights breed men who will give no single inch without defiance.

I walked between the men of the Highlands, the old and young, some bearded, others clean-cheeked, some pale, some red, the trembling and the steady, and came to stand before the portcullis, iron-bound timbers splintered, the rush of the ram beyond, the savage cries of the hundred wrestling it toward me. My fingers found my knife hilt and I pulled it clear. Laid against my unburned cheek the metal felt like ice. The portcullis shuddered and groaned before the ram. Men of Arrow screamed and died as missiles rained upon them. The knife blade cut skin soft as a kiss. I took the blood on scarlet fingers and wiped it over the gate timbers. I turned my back on the gate, crouched before my men, and smeared a line of blood across the flag-stones. As I returned to the keep I set my hand to a score of warriors, the eager ones, the ones in who I saw an echo of the same hunger that made me want that gate open every bit as much as those men on the ram.

"King's blood!" Sir Elmar of Golden raised his axe, the crimson smear of my fingers left across his shining helm.

"King's blood!" A hairy Hauntside warrior pressed the heel of his hand to the red imprint I set across his brow.

"King's blood!" A Cennat dancer twirled the huge shield where my handprint sat scarlet across the white moon of his house.

"King's blood!"

The roar pulsed back and forth, following us within the keep. A king is a sigil, not a man but an idea. I thought they had the idea now.

I took myself up to my throne-room with Makin at my side, and called for my table-knights, Red Kent, and the captain of the contingent from the House Morrow, Lord Jost.

Lord Jost arrived last, with a second knight and Miana. Queen Miana I supposed I should call her. She still wore her wedding dress, though with the train and veils taken off and a shawl set with pearls added against the cold. Lord Jost looked rather embarrassed by her presence at my council of war.

"Gentlemen," I said. "My lady."

I sat in the throne. Slumped would be more accurate. It felt good to take the weight off my feet. I'd done more running and climbing and descending than I wanted and was ready to sleep for a week.

"How many of the enemy did you kill, and at what loss?" Miana asked. The men had been waiting for me to speak. She felt no such need. I would have asked the same question.

"About six thousand for the loss of two hundred," I said.

"A thirty to one ratio. Better than the rate of twenty to one needed." To hear her high sweet voice recite the statistics of our body count seemed wrong.

"True. But they were two hundred of my very best, and I have played the aces from my hand."

"And Chancellor Coddin has not returned," Miana said. She was remarkably well informed for a little girl.

A pang of something ran through me at that. I saw Coddin once more in the tomb we made for him. "He's safer than we are," I said. He would probably live longer too. He would linger.

I took a goblet of watered wine from a page and a plate with crusted bread and goat cheese.

"And your plans?" she asked.

I blew through my lips. "We will have to place our faith in stone and mortar, and hope that in the time they buy us, fortune decides to smile our way." The wine tasted like heaven and made me dizzy after one sip.

"Perhaps my new father-in-law will send us aid?" Miana said, her smile faint and years too old for her.

"I was hoping something similar myself," I said.

More than in muscle heaped on bone, Brother Rike's strength springs from the ability to hate the inanimate.

39

Four years earlier

"She's gone, yes?" Makin shaded his eyes against the sunrise and squinted back across the marsh. We stood on rolling scrubland now with yellow rock breaking through in sandy patches here and there.

"I hope so," I said. Part of me wanted Chella to find destruction at my hands, the personal touch, but perhaps she ended there in the marsh amongst the burning dead. I hadn't felt it. No sense of satisfaction, but my uncle's death had taught me that revenge is far less sweet than it promises to be. An empty meal, however long you take over it.

We took to horse for the first time in what seemed an age. Rike on Row's roan since his own plough-horse proved too heavy for its own good in the bogs. Kent and Makin on their horses. Grumlow riding double with me since he and I were the lightest of the Brothers and Brath the strongest of the nags.

The sour stink of the marshes followed us for miles. Black mud caking on our clothes, drying grey and flaking away. More persistent than stink or mud, the image of Chella as the flames rose around her, and the echo of her last words. *The Dead King sails.*

In three days we came by moorland and scrub, then by forgotten roads, and finally by country tracks, to the free port of Barlona. Rike made ceaseless complaint about his sunburn until I convinced him to smear pig-shit over the worst affected areas. For some reason it seemed to help though I hadn't intended it to. Suggestion can be a powerful thing.

The ancient walls shimmered in the summer heat as we approached. They must have been impressive a thousand years ago. Now only the base of the walls remained, twenty foot high and just as thick, spilling black stone in great heaps for the peasants to raid to make huts and boundary walls for their fields.

I liked the city from the moment we rode in. The air held exotic scents, spices and cooking smoke that made my stomach growl. The people thronged, loud in voice and clothing, bright silks, garish jewellery made of glass and base metals, flesh of all colours on display in wide swathes. Men and women as light as me, as dark as the Nuban, and all shades in between. None as pale as Sindri and Duke Alaric though. Those, I think the sun would melt.

Music came from almost every corner in as many shades as the people. It seemed that the citizens walked in time to the beat and pulse of a thousand drums, horns, voices. I'd not heard such sounds before, so many strange melodies, some reminding me of the marching beats the Nuban used to slap against his thigh as we walked and which he elaborated on around the campfire. Others held remembrances of the curious atonal humming Tutor Lundist lapsed into in empty moments.

A port is an open ear to the world, a mouth ready for new flavours. Approaching my fifteenth year I felt more than ready to explore the wideness of the world that Barlona offered up.

"You know, Makin, you can take ship from here to almost any place you've ever heard of and a thousand that you haven't," I said.

"Ships make me hurl." Makin looked as if he were remembering the taste.

"You don't like them?"

"It's the waves. I get seasick. I vomit from one shore to the next. I was nearly sick crossing the Rhyme."

"Well, that's good to know." With Makin you can keep digging and find a new fact year on year. I hadn't known he'd ever crossed an ocean, or even travelled under sail.

"How is that good to know?" He frowned.

"Well, the only way to get to the Horse Coast is by sea and I'm going alone. Knowing what a bad sailor you are just makes it easier to send you back to the Haunt."

"We can ride there," Makin said. "It's less than a hundred miles."

"Through the Duchy of Aramas and then the lands of King Philip the nine hundredth," I said.

"Thirty-second," Makin corrected.

"Whatever. The point is that those are not places men like us can pass unnoticed, whereas a ship will sail me right to my grandfather's doorstep in a day or two."

"So we take a ship and I coat the decks in vomit. What's the problem?"

"The problem, dear Makin, is that I don't want Rike there, or Grumlow, or Kent. I don't even want you there. I want to make my own introductions in my own time. This is family business and I'll do it my way."

"That tends to mean everyone dies." Makin grinned.

"Maybe, but I don't need you there for that either. Just get them back to the Haunt. We've lost too many on this trip. I won't say we've lost good men, but ones that I would rather have kept. Though if you misplace Rike on the way back, that would be fine."

"This is a bad idea, Jorg." Makin had that stubborn look of his, lips pressed tight, a vertical line between his brows.

"I need you in Renar," I said. "I needed you there from the start. If you recall I did my damnedest not to have you come in the first place. Coddin's a good man but how long can he hold a kingdom together for? Go back, crack any heads that need cracking, and let my people know I'll be returning."

"Oi!" Grumlow's cry. A man running away through the crowd. I saw Grumlow's arm flick back and throw. The man fell without a sound twenty yards off, shoving his way through the crowd.

I walked with Grumlow to where he lay. People got out of our way, except for the children who ran everywhere as if we were part of a show. Grumlow pulled his saddlebag from the man's limp hands.

"Cut the bloody strap! That'll cost!" he said.

"I told you to secure it better," I said. The few bits and pieces Grumlow had managed to bring through the bogs were tied randomly around Brath's tack.

Grumlow grunted and bent to retrieve his knife. It had hit the man hilt-first in the back of the head. A pool of blood glistened beneath the man's face, but it must have come from his nose or mouth hitting the cobbles. We didn't bother turning him over to find out.

"I love this city," I said, and we went back to the others.

We stabled the horses and sat at a tavern by the docks. I call it a tavern but we sat outside, around tables in the sun if you please, with wine in bottles shaped like tear drops with baskets woven around them. Makin with his bare feet, traces of dried mud still visible. Rike complained of course, about the sun, about the wine, even about the chairs which seemed unable to support his weight, but I paid more attention to the seagulls' chatter. I sat and watched the ships moored at the quayside, bigger than I had thought they would be, and more complex, with rigging and spars and deck ropes and a multitude of sails. I felt better than I had in an age. Even my burns hurt less fiercely, as if the hot sun soothed their anger. For the first time in a long time we relaxed, smiled, and spoke of the dead. Of Brother Row, who I would remember, and Brother Sim, who I would miss for his harping and for his promise. We raised our bottles to them both and drank deep.

Only Kent put up any resistance to the idea of returning without me. I let him protest a while until he ran out of things to say and in the end convinced himself that my plan was the best one. Red Kent's like that. Give him a little space to turn and he'll come around.

I stood, rolled my neck, and stretched in the sunshine. "Catch you on the road, Brothers."

"You're going now?" Makin asked, putting down his bottle-in-a-basket.

"Well, unless you want to drink till we're all sunburnt and maudlin and then declare undying love for each other and part with drunken hugs?" I said.

Rike spat. He seemed to have inherited the role of spitter from Row.

"In that case, your path lies that way." I pointed north. "I should note that the first quarter mile of that path is on a street that boasts several fine-looking whorehouses. So take your time. As for me—I'm going to find out about ships."

I set off at an amble, following my shadow across the bright flagstones.

"Look after Brath for me," I called back.

They picked up their bottles and drank to me. "Catch you on the road," they replied. Even Rike.

And if Makin hadn't been there I think I really could have ditched them that easily.

40

Four years earlier

In a great port like Barlona there are hundreds of ships at harbour. Most belong to merchants, or collectives of merchants, and hug the coastline loaded with things that are cheap where the ships set out and that command a higher price where they are bound. It's a simple equation and the devil lies in the details. There are warships too, owned in name by the Prince of Barlona and in the service of his people. In reality it is the wealthiest of the merchants who put new princes on the throne, and the warships serve to protect their trade routes. And among the merchant cogs and the Prince's warships, a scattering of ocean-going ships, triple-masted and more, deep-hulled, from the strangest and most distant shores. Even one great vessel of sickwood, twice the size of her largest rival, her grey planks grown one into the next, half-living despite the lumberman's saw. Her hull, crusted with barnacles large as dinner plates even above the wave-line, bore many scars, and on her decks men with copper skin worked at repairs.

I spent a few hours watching the great ships with their foreign crews, yellow men from Utter, black crews from the many Kingdoms of Afrique, turbaned sailors with curling beards, sun-stained, strutting the decks of pungent spice-boats. The

Prince of Arrow's words returned to me. His observations on the smallness of my world and the largeness of my ignorance. Even so, every man amongst these travellers knew of the empire, even though it stood in pieces. And so we had us some common ground.

I saw Makin and the others trailing me almost from the start. He'd had the sense to leave Rike behind, most likely in one of the whorehouses I'd suggested. Rike's not one to be missed, even on a crowded street. Makin would have done better to leave himself and Red Kent in the whorehouse too. Grumlow I might not have spotted. Grumlow has quiet ways about him.

The smaller and more shabby of the merchant cogs stood at anchor on the margins of the great harbour. They moored along sway-backed quays that abutted semi-derelict warehouses separated by dangerous alleys where the stink of rotted fish made my eyes water. I followed two bare-chested men carrying a barrel up the gangplank onto the *Sea-goat*.

"You! Get off my ship." The man shouting at me was smaller and dirtier than the other men on deck but loud enough to be the captain.

"A ship now, is it?" I looked around. "Well, I suppose if you set a sail in a rowboat you can call it a ship. But you were unwise to throw away the oars."

"I was going to let you choose which side you left by. But that offer is now void," the little man said. The mass of black curls framing his ugly face looked to be a wig, but why anyone would want to set ten pounds of stolen sweaty hair on their head in this heat I couldn't fathom.

I magicked a silver coin into my hand, an Ancrath royal stamped with my father's head. "Customer," I said.

The fat man advancing on me stopped. He looked relieved.

"I want to get to the Horse Coast," I said. "Somewhere around the ear would do."

The Horse Coast isn't named for the stallions that make it famous these days. Apparently the peninsula coastline resembles a horse's head. I've studied the map scrolls in my father's library and I can say with surety that it looks like a horse's head in the same way that troll-stones look like trolls, or that the constellation of Orion looks like a belted giant holding a club. They could have called it the Happy Pig Coast or the Crooked

Thumb Coast just as well. To give the ancients the benefit of the doubt I will note that the sea has risen twice the height of the Tall Castle since the time of Building and the old maps had to be rewritten many times. Even so, I'd stake a bag of stolen gold on the fact that there was never a time that "horse" was the first thing to spring to mind when contemplating the run of the Horse Coast.

I had plenty of time to think while the little captain favoured me with a sour stare and chewed his lip. I could have picked a ship at random. Any small vessel actively loading would be departing for ports up the coast from Barlona or down the coast. I'd bought a couple of ales for a sailor earlier in the day. He'd gone through his share from his previous trip and was delaying a new signing until the last possible moment. In return for my keeping him from sobriety for a few more hours he'd run off a list of the best bets for a trip south. The *Sea-goat*'s name had taken my fancy. Who wants to sail on the *Maria*, or the *God's Grace*, when there's a *Sea-goat* to be ridden?

"Two silver and you haul rope when told," he said.

"One silver and I get fed with the crew," I said and started walking toward the gangplank. I could ride the *Maria* just as well. In fact it sounded better each time I said it.

"Done," he said.

And so I sailed on the *Sea-goat* with Captain Nellis.

Before the *Sea-goat* hoisted sail I took a last walk around the seafront and stopped in at the Port Commander's office long enough to place a bribe of sufficient weight to considerably lighten my gold supply. Ideally the Brothers would be steered onto a ship that would take them north up the coast and abandon them in a minor port. Makin would be too busy vomiting to notice which side of the boat the land lay off. Failing that, they need only arrest Makin and hold him a week or two—long enough for my trail to grow cold and to remind him that in the end when your king tells you to do something, you do it.

I like the sea. Even with a gentle swell, with the coast in plain view just ten miles to starboard, it sets me in mind of mountains in motion. I like the nautical phrases. Splice this, belay that. If Lundist proves right and we are all reborn, I'll go once more round life's wheel as a pirate. Everything about the ocean puts me in a good mood. The smell and the taste of it. The cry of seagulls. God jammed some kind of magic down their throats. No wonder the crows want to murder them and the ravens are unkind.

Captain Nellis didn't like me being on the quarterdeck, or so he said, but I spent my time there, legs dangling through the rail with him behind me, dwarfed by the wheel. He could have roped it off for all the steering he did, but he seemed to like to hold it while he shouted at his men. To my eye he steered them as little as he did the ship. His curses and instructions rolled off the crew and they went about their tasks oblivious.

"I'll buy me a ship one day," I said.

"Surely," Captain Nellis spat something thick and unpleasant onto the deck. Without men like him and Row, decks probably wouldn't need swabbing at all.

"A big one, mind. Not a barge like this. Something that cuts the waves rather than wallows about in them."

"A young sell-sword like yourself shouldn't set his sights so low," Nellis growled. "Buy a whole fleet."

"A valid point, Captain. Very valid. If my kingdom ever gets a coastline I will buy a fleet. I'll be sure to name one of them the *Spitting Nellis*."

And so for the rest of that day, and most of the next, the *Sea-goat* wallowed its way sedately around the shore, stopping once in a small port to unload a huge copper pot and to fill the space with red-finned fish called . . . red-fin. I slept a night in a hammock, below decks, rolling in the gentle arms of coastal waters and dreaming of absolutely nothing. I can only recommend hammocks if you're at sea. On dry land there seems no point to them. And sleep above deck if you have the chance. The *Sea-goat* had an appropriately animal smell to it in the stale heat of its hold.

My grandfather's castle is called Morrow. It overlooks the sea, standing as close to a high cliff as a brave child might, but not so close as a foolhardy one. It has an elegance to it, being tall and slender in its towers, and sensibly tiled on its many roofs, having fought fiercer and more prolonged battles with ocean storms than with any army trekking to it overland.

The port of Arrapa lies just two miles north of Castle Morrow and I disembarked there, taking some pleasure in unsettling Captain Nellis with enthusiastic thanks for his services. I left the crew unloading red-fin and taking on crates of saddles destined for Wennith Town. Why the fishermen of Arrapa couldn't catch their own red-fin I never did find out.

A well-maintained cart track winds up from the port to Castle Morrow. I walked, enjoying the sunshine, and turned down the offer of a ride in a charcoal man's cart.

"It gets steep," he said.

"Steep's fine," I said. And he flicked his mule on.

I wanted to come incognito to Castle Morrow, wanted it bad enough to see Makin thrown in a cell rather than risk him spoiling my cover. It has to be said that my experience with relations has been a mixed bag. Having a father like mine breeds caution in these situations. I needed to see these new family members in their element, without the complications of who I was or what I wanted.

Add to the mix the fact that my grandfather and uncle were said to hate Olidan Ancrath with a passion for the way he sold the absolution for Mother's death—as if his brother had merely inconvenienced him by sending assassins to kill her. I might be my mother's son but I have more than my fair share of Father's blood and with the tales Grandfather was like to have heard of me it would not be unreasonable for him to see me cast in the image of Olidan rather than the child of his beloved Rowen.

I had a sweat on me by the time I reached the castle gates, but the cliff tops caught a sea breeze and I let it cool me. I stepped up to the archway. Double portcullis, well-crafted merlons topping the gatehouse, arrow slits positioned with some thought—in all a nice bit of castle-building. The smallest of three guardsmen stepped to intercept me.

"I'm looking for work," I said.

"Nothing for you, son." He didn't ask what kind of work. I had a big sword on my belt, a scorching hot breastplate over my leathers, and a helm at my hip.

"How about some water then? I've sweated my way up from the beach and it's a thirsty mile."

The guard nodded to a stone trough for horses by the side of the road.

"Hmmm." The water looked only marginally better than the stuff in the Cantanlona swamp.

"Best be on your way, son. It's a thirsty mile back to Arrapa too," the guard said.

I started to dislike the man. I named him "Sunny" for his disposition and his repeated claims of fatherhood. I reached inside my breastplate, trying not to touch the metal and failing. My fingers discovered the corner they were hunting and I pulled out a sealed letter, wrapped in stained linen. "Also, I have this for Earl Hansa," I said, unfolding it from the cloth.

"Do you now?" Sunny reached for it and I pulled it back at the same speed he moved his hand. "Best let me see that, son," he said.

"Best read the name on the front before you grubby it up too much, Father." I let him take it, and used the linen to mop sweat from my forehead.

To Sunny's credit he held the letter with some reverence by the very corners, and although we both knew he couldn't read, he played out the pantomime well, peering at the script above the wax seal. "Wait here," he told me and set off into the courtyard beyond.

I smiled for the two remaining guards then took myself off to a patch of shade where I slumped and let the flies have their way. I set my back to the trunk of the lone tree providing the shade. It looked to be an olive. I'd never seen the tree before but I knew the fruit, and the stones littered the ground. It looked old. Older than the castle perhaps.

Sunny took almost an hour to return and by that time the horse trough had started to look tempting. He brought two house guards with him, their uniform richer, chainmail on their chests rather than the leathers of the wall guard who had to endure the heat.

"Go with them," Sunny said. I think he would have given a day's wages to be able to send me back down the hill, and another day's to be able to send me on my way with the toe of his boot.

In the courtyard a marble fountain sprayed. The water jetted from many small holes in the mouth of a fish and collected in a wide circular pool. I had seen illustrations of fountains in Father's books. Reference was made to the team of men needed to work the pump in order to maintain pressure. I pitied any men sweltering away in darkness to make this pretty thing function . . . but the fine spray made a cool heaven as we walked past.

Many windows overlooked the courtyard, not shuttered but faced with pierced veils of stone, worked with great artistry in intricate patterns that left more air than rock. I couldn't see into the shadows behind but I felt watched.

We passed through a short corridor, floored with geometric mosaic, into a smaller courtyard where on a stone bench in the shade of three orange trees, a nobleman waited, plain dressed but with a gold band on his wrist and too clean to be anything but highborn. Not Earl Hansa; he was too young for that, but surely someone of his family. Of my family. He kept more of my father's features but this man shared some of my lines, high cheekbones, dark hair cropped close, watchful eyes.

"I am Robert," he said. He had the letter open in his hand. "My sister wrote this. She speaks well of you."

In truth I spoke well of myself when I set quill to parchment some months ago. I called myself William and said that I had proven a loyal aid to Queen Rowen, honest, brave, and gifted in both letter and number. I copied the slant and shape of the writing from an older letter, a crumpled scrap I kept close to my heart for many years. A letter from my mother.

"I'm honoured." I bowed deeply. "I hope that the Queen's recommendation, God rest her, will find me a place in your household."

Lord Robert watched me, and I watched him. It felt good to find an uncle that I didn't long to kill.

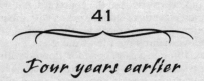

41

Four years earlier

"You look very young, William. How many years are you? Sixteen? Seventeen?" Robert said.

"Nineteen, my lord. I look young for my age," I said.

"And my sister has been dead nearly five years. So that makes you fourteen or fifteen when she wrote this?"

"Fifteen, my lord."

"Early in life to have made such an impression. Honest, brave, numerate, literate. So why are you wandering so far from home in such poor circumstances, William?"

"I served in the Forest Watch, my lord. After Queen Rowen was slain. And when the Watch-master led us against Count Renar who took your sister's life, Queen Rowen I mean, I fought in the Highlands. But I have family in Ancrath, so when justice was served on the Count, I took to the roads so that I would be thought killed in the battle at the Haunt, and no punishments would fall on my relatives to make me surrender to King Olidan. Since then I have been making my way here, my lord, hoping to continue in service to Queen Rowen's family."

"That's quite a tale," Robert said. "To be told in one mouthful without pause for breath."

I said nothing and watched the shadows of the orange trees dance.

"So you fought alongside my nephew, Jorg?" Robert said. "Did you come by your injury that way?" He set his hand to his cheek.

"I didn't fight by his side, my lord. But I was on the same battlefield. He wouldn't know my name and face," I said. "Not even with this scar. That came more recently. On my travels."

"That must be the honesty Rowen wrote of. Many would be tempted to say they fought at his left hand in order to lay stronger claim on my generosity." Robert smiled. He rubbed at the small dark triangle of beard on his chin. "Can you use that sword?" he asked. He wore plain linens, a loose shirt, his chest and arms tanned and hard muscled. Perhaps more a horseman than a swordsman but he would know blades.

"I can."

"And read. And write?"

"Yes."

"A man of many talents," Robert said. "I'll have Lord Jost find a place for you in the house guard. That will do for now. I should introduce you to Qalasadi too—he always likes to meet a man who knows his numbers." He smiled as if he'd made a joke.

"My thanks, Lord Robert," I said.

"Don't thank me, William. Thank my sister. And be sure to show us all how good a judge of character she was." He looked up through the orange-tree leaves at the dazzling blue sky. "Take him to Captain Ortens," he said, and house guards led me away.

I slept that night in a bunk in the west tower guardhouse. Ortens, a man with more scars on his bald head than would seem reasonable or even possible, had grumbled and cursed, but he had a chain surcoat brought up from the armoury and sent for the seamstress to fit me with a uniform in the blues of House Morrow. I also got a service blade, a longsword from the same forge as the other guards, assumed to be superior to the one in my dirt-caked scabbard and certainly more aesthetically pleasing, completing the house guard ensemble as it did.

The older men of the guard offered the traditional doubts about my ability to use a sword, concerns that I would miss my mother, and bets about how long it would be before the captain threw me out. In addition, my foreign heritage allowed for the airing of low opinions of the northern kingdoms in general and Ancrath in particular. Ancrath proved an especially sore point since their Princess Rowen had met a foul end there. I owned that I did miss my mother but it wouldn't cause me to go running home. I further admitted that I was a citizen of Ancrath, but one who had fought at the gates of the man who killed its queen, and who had seen him pay for his crimes. As to my fighting skills I invited any man who felt overburdened with blood to come and test them for himself.

I slept well that night.

The House Morrow wakes early. Most of it pre-dawn so that some progress can be made before the summer descends and any sensible man retreats into the shortening shade. I found myself in the practice yard with four other recent recruits. Captain Ortens came from his breakfast to watch in person as an elderly sergeant put us through our paces with wooden swords.

I resisted the urge to put on a show and kept my swordplay basic. An experienced eye is hard to deceive though, and I suspected that Ortens left with a higher opinion of recruit William than the one he brought to the yard with him.

After a couple of hours it grew warm for sword-work and Sergeant Mattus sent us to our assignments. I had always imagined the duties of the guard at the Haunt and at the Tall Castle to be tedious. Not until I tried them myself for half a day did I fathom quite how dull service is. I got to stand at the Lowery Gate, an iron door affording access to what was little more than an extended balcony garden where the noble ladies cultivated sage grass, miniature lemon trees, and various flowering plants that had lost their blooms months earlier and set to seed. If any intruder were to gain the balcony then I was to refuse him entrance to the castle. An unlikely event since they would need to fall off a passing cloud to reach the balcony. If any lady of the house were to wish to visit the garden, then I was empowered to unlock the door for them and to lock it again when they had taken their leave. I'm bored even scratching it out on this page. I stood there for three hours in an itchy uniform and saw nobody at all. No one even passed down the adjoining corridor.

Another recruit from the morning's training exercise relieved me at noon and I set off to find the guards' refectory. I now know why it's called relief.

"A moment of your time, young man."

I stopped just a yard from the refectory door and let my stomach complain for me. I made a slow turn.

"I'm told you are numerate." The man had stepped from the shade of a lilac bush that swarmed up the inner wall of the main courtyard. A Moor, darker than the shadow, wrapped in a black burnoose, the burnt umber of his skin exposed only on his hands and face.

"Count on it," I said.

He smiled. His teeth were black, painted with some dye, the effect unsettling. "I am Qalasadi."

"William," I said.

He raised an eyebrow.

"How may I help you, Lord Qalasadi?" I asked. He held himself like a noble, though no gold glittered on him. I judged him by the cut of his robe and the neat curl of his short beard and hair. Wealth buys a certain grooming that speaks of money, even when the rich man's tastes are simple.

"Just Qalasadi," he said.

I liked him. Simple as that. Sometimes I just do.

He crouched and with an ivory wand, drawn from his sleeve, he wrote numbers in the dust. "Your people call me a math-magician," he said.

"And what do you call yourself?" I asked.

"Numbered," he said. "Tell me what you see."

I looked at his scribbling. "Is that a root symbol?"

"Yes."

"I see primes, here, here, and . . . here. This is a rational number, this one irrational. I see families." I circled groups with my toe, some overlapping. "Real numbers, integers, imaginary numbers, complex numbers."

He sketched again, flowing symbols that I remembered only dimly. "And this?"

"Some part of the integral calculus. But it goes beyond my lessons." It panged me to admit defeat though I should have held my tongue after recognizing prime numbers for him. Pride is my weakness.

"Interesting." Qalasadi scuffed the dust to erase his writings as if they might prove dangerous to others.

"So do you have me figured out?" I asked. "What's my magic number?" I had heard tell of mathmagicians. They seemed little different from the witches, astrologers, and soothsayers from closer to home, obsessed with casting futures, handing out labels, parting fools from their coin. If he told me something about the glories ahead for the Prince of Arrow I would have trouble restraining myself. If he suggested I might be born in the year of the goat then there would be no restraint!

Again the black smile. "Your magic number is three," he said.

I laughed. But he looked serious. "Three?" I shook my head. "There are a lot of numbers to choose from. Three just seems a little . . . predictable."

"Everything is predictable," Qalasadi said. "At its core my arts are the working of probability, which produces prediction, and that leads us to timing, and in the end, my friend, everything comes down to a matter of timing does it not?"

He had a point. "But three?" I waved my hands, groping for outrage. "Three?"

"It's the first of your magic numbers. They form a series," he said. "The second of them is fourteen."

"See, now you're talking. Fourteen. I can believe in that." I crouched beside him since he seemed unwilling to rise. "Why fourteen?"

"It is your age is it not?" he asked. "And it is the key to your name."

"My name?" An uneasiness crept up my back, chill despite the heat.

"Honorous, I should say. With some certainty." He scratched in the dust and erased it just as quick. "Ancrath, quite likely. Jorg, maybe."

"I'm fascinated at how you would calculate all that from fourteen," I said. I considered breaking his neck and leaving for the docks. But that wasn't the man I wanted to show my mother's father, or her brother. It wasn't the Jorg she had known.

"You have the look of a Steward to me. The right lines. Particularly around the eyes, nose, the forehead too. And you've declared yourself from Ancrath which would fit with your accent and colouring. Almost all Stewards are named after Honorous. You could be a bastard, but who teaches a bastard to even recognize calculus? And if you're legitimate then as a Steward from Ancrath you would be named Ancrath. And what members of that household are young men? Jorg Ancrath springs to mind. And how old is he? Close on fifteen but not yet there."

I didn't yet know if I was right to like the man but his store of facts and talent for deduction impressed me. "Spectacular," I said. "Wrong, but spectacular."

Qalasadi shrugged. "I try." He nodded to the refectory. "Your lunch awaits, no doubt."

I stood and started across the courtyard. Then paused. "Why three?"

Qalasadi frowned as if trying to recall a lost sensation. "Three steps outside? Three in the carriage? Three women that will love you? Three Brothers lost on your journey? The magic lies in the first number, the mathematics in the second."

The "three steps" put a cold finger down my spine, as if he had rummaged in the back of my skull and pulled out something I would rather keep hidden. I said nothing and walked away, a wild night running through my mind, cut by lightning and glimpses of the empty carriage as I hung in thorns.

I found myself at the refectory table without memory of getting there. I wondered how long it would be before Qalasadi laid his deductions at my uncle's feet. He might spoil my game but it presented no danger.

"Not hungry?" The short guardsman from the gates sat across from me. Sunny.

I looked down at my lunch and tried to make sense of it. "What's this stuff? Did someone throw up in my bowl?"

"Spicy squid." The guardsman kissed his fingertips and spread them. *Mwah.*

I skewered a tentacle, a difficult feat in itself, and set to chewing. The experience wasn't dissimilar from chewing shoe leather. Except that to fully replicate it you would have to set the leather on fire. Spices are all well and good. Salt to taste, a little pepper, a bay leaf in soup, a clove or two in an apple pie. But on the Horse Coast they seem to favour chillies that will take the skin off your tongue. Having been burned on the outside and not liked the experience, I saw no reason to burn on the inside. I spat my mouthful back into the bowl.

"That is truly vile!" I said.

"I would have had it off you," the guardsman said. "But you went and spat in it. I'm Greyson by the way."

"William of Ancrath," I said. I picked up my hunk of bread and nibbled it, wary that the cook might have mixed a bag of chilli dust in with the flour.

"What's the deal with the Moor?" I asked, and ran my fingers over my teeth as if "Moor" were not sufficient description.

"You've met Qalasadi now have you?" Greyson grinned. "He keeps the castle accounts. Works wonders with the local merchants. Gets Earl Hansa the good contracts. Best of all he's in charge of paying the guards and he's never a day late. Five years back we had Friar James keeping the books. We could go a month without coin." He shook his head.

"He's close with the Earl and his son, this Qalasadi?" I asked.

"Not especially. He's just the bookkeeper." Greyson shrugged.

I liked the sound of that, but wondered at a man of such talent occupying a relatively minor role without complaint.

"I like him well enough," Greyson said. "Plays cards with the wall guard sometimes. Always loses, never complains, never drinks our ale."

"You'd have thought he'd be good at cards," I said.

"Terrible. Not sure he even knows the rules. But he seems to love it. And the men like him. They don't even give him a hard time about being the castle's only Moor. And by rights they should. What with his countrymen set on invading the mainland and turning us all to heathens or corpses."

"Moors, is it?" I asked. "Should I be expecting to kill some soon?"

Others of the guard leaned in, listening to the conversation as they chewed their squid. I thought perhaps the chilli dissolved the tentacles in the end, because chewing seemed insufficient.

"You might yet," Greyson said. "Ibn Fayed, he's caliph in

Liba, has sent his ships three times this year. We're due another raid."

Without warning the rumble of conversation died and Greyson put his head down. "Shimon, the sword-master," he hissed. "He never comes in here."

A man loomed behind me. I focused on the squid but refrained from actually putting it in my mouth.

"You, boy," Shimon said. "Ancrath. Out in the yard. I'm told you have promise."

42

Four years earlier

I knew of Sword-master Shimon. Makin told me stories about him. About his exploits as a young man, champion to kings, teacher of champions, legend of the tourney. I hadn't expected him to be so old.

"Yes, Sword-master," I said, and I followed him out into the courtyard.

To say he moved like a swordsman would be understatement. He looked as old as Tutor Lundist, with the same long white hair, but he stepped as if he heard the sword-song beating through each moment of the day.

Qalasadi had gone from the shadows and the courtyard lay empty but for a serving girl crossing with a basket of washing, and the men on guard at the gate. Other guards crowded the door of the refectory behind us, but they didn't dare follow us out. Shimon had not extended them an invitation.

The sword-master turned to face me. The bookish look of him surprised me. He could have passed as a scribe, but for the dark burn of the sun and a hawkishness about the eyes. He drew his sword. A standard-issue blade the same as mine.

"When you're ready, young man," he said.

I slid my sword out, wondering how to play this. Qalasadi

was probably telling my uncle who I really was right now, so why not make full use of the opportunity?

I slapped at his blade, and he did that rolling-wrist trick the Prince of Arrow used, only better, and took my sword out of my hand. I heard laughter from the doorway.

"Try harder," Shimon said.

I smiled and picked my sword up. This time I moved in quick with a thrust at his body. He did the trick again but I rolled my wrist with his and kept my blade.

"Better," he said.

I attacked him with short precise combinations, the moves I had been working on with Makin. He fended me off without apparent effort, replying at the end of each attack with a counter-attack that I could barely contain. The rapid clash of metal on metal echoed around the courtyard. I felt the music of steel rise about me. I felt that cold calm sensation rolling out over my arms, cheeks, the skin of my back. I heard the song.

Without thought I attacked, slicing high, low, feinting, deploying my full strength at precisely the right moments, all of me moving, feet, arms, hips, only my head still. I increased the tempo, increased it, and increased it again. At times I couldn't see my blade or his, only the shape of our bodies, and the necessity of the dance let me know how to move, how to block. The sound of our parrying became like the *clickety-click* of knitting needles in expert hands.

Shimon's hard old face didn't look made for smiling, but a smile found its way there. I grinned like an idiot, sweat dripping off me.

"Enough." He stepped away.

I found it hard not to follow him, to press the attack, but I let my sword drop. There had been a joy in it, in the purity, living on the edge of my blade without thought. My heart pounded and sweat soaked me, but I had nothing of the anger that normally builds even in practice sessions. We had made a thing of beauty.

"Could you beat me?" I asked, pulling in a breath. The old man seemed hardly winded.

"We both won, boy," he said. "If I'd taken a victory we would have both lost."

I took that as a yes. But I understood him. I hoped that I

would have had the grace to step back if I saw him weaken.
Not to do so would have spoiled the moment.

Shimon sheathed his sword. "Enjoy your lunch, guardsman," he said.

"That's it?" I asked as he turned to go. "No advice?"

"You don't try hard enough at the start, and you try too hard
at the end," he said.

"Hardly technical."

"You have a talent," he said. "I hope you have other talents
too. They will probably bring you more happiness."

And he went.

"Unreal," Greyson said when I returned to the table. "I've
never seen a thing like that."

And that was all the time I had to bask in my glory. The
bell sounded to let us know lunch had ended and I got to go
back to guarding the Lowery Gate.

The Lowery Gate nearly broke me. I gave deep consider-
ation to naming myself to my grandfather. In the end though,
I wanted to see how this court worked from the inside, how
my relatives went about their lives, who they really were. I
guess I wanted a window into my past and not to mucky it up
with my own surprises.

I slept again in the guardhouse and woke to new duties.
Qalasadi didn't appear to have gone to my uncle. I suspected
that he thought I would wield some influence once my identity
was known and he didn't want to make an enemy of me. If he
didn't let my secret slip, who would know that he ever knew
it? And so he would face no censure for not revealing me.

My new assignment was as personal guard to Lady Agath,
a cousin of my grandfather's who had been living at Castle
Morrow for some years. A fat old lady, getting to the point
where the weight started to slip from her as it does with the
very old. Live long enough and we all die skinny.

Lady Agath liked to do everything slowly. She paid me no
attention other than to moan that my scar was ugly to look at
and why couldn't she have a presentable guard? To the wrinkles
brought by her advanced years she added those that fat people
acquire as they start to deflate. The overall effect was alarming,
as if she were a shed skin, discarded perhaps by a giant reptile.
I followed her around Castle Morrow at a snail's pace, which

afforded me the time to look the place over, at least the part of it lying between the privy, the dining hall, Lady Agath's bed-chamber, and the Ladies' Hall.

"Be still, boy, you're never still," Lady Agath said.

I hadn't moved a muscle for five minutes. I continued the habit and held my tongue.

"Don't be smart with me," she said. "Your eyes are always flitting from one thing to the next. Never still. And you think too much. I can see you thinking right now."

"My apologies, Lady Agath," I said.

She harrumphed, jowls quivering, and settled back in her black lace. "Play on," she told the minstrel, a dark and hand-some fellow in his twenties who had a sufficient combination of looks and talent to hold the attention of Agath and three other old noblewomen at one end of the Ladies' Hall.

The Ladies' Hall appeared to be where Horse Coast women came to die. For certain there weren't any ladies there on the right side of sixty.

"You're doing it again," Lady Agath hissed.

"My apologies."

"Go to the wine-cellar and tell them I want a jug of wine, Wennith red, something from the south slopes," Lady Agath told me.

"I'm not supposed to leave you unattended, Lady Agath," I said.

"I'm not unattended, I have Rialto here." She waved toward the minstrel. "I always have my wine from the cellar. I don't know what they do to it in that kitchen but they ruin it. Leave it open to the air I guess. And the girls always dawdle so," she remarked to the other ladies. "Go, boy, quick about it."

I had my doubts as to whether Rialto could protect Lady Agath from an angry wasp, let alone any other threats, but I didn't feel her to be in any danger, and I didn't much care if she was, so I left without complaint.

It took me a while to find my way down to the right cellar, but after a few wrong turns I located the place. You can gener-ally tell a wine-cellar by the sturdiness of the door, second only to the treasury door in the majority of castles. Even the most loyal servants will steal your wine given a quarter of a chance, and they'll piss the evidence over the wall.

I had another trip to find the day cook and get him to unlock for me. He sat on a chair positioned by the door and set to chewing on the leg of mutton he'd carried down with him in his apron.

"Jugs are by the door. Go find what you want. Don't leave the spigot dripping. Wennith reds are at the far end, left corner, marked with a double cross and crown."

I lit a lantern from his and ventured in.

"Watch out for spiders," he said. "The smaller brown ones are bad. Don't get bit." When he said "small" he made a circle with his finger and thumb that didn't look particularly small.

The cellar stretched on for dozens of yards, the wine casks stacked on shelves, most unbroached, the occasional one set with a spigot. I wound a path along the narrow alleys, squeezing past a loading truck and several empty casks left to trip me.

The Wennith red caskets were all sealed save for an empty one. I suspected most of its contents had swilled through the Lady Agath on their way to the privy. The tools and spare spigots for broaching a new cask weren't apparent. I noted a door, almost concealed beneath a build-up of grime and mould, behind a stack of emptied barrels. It looked too disused to be a store cupboard, but the need of a mallet and spigot provided a good excuse to have a look behind. I'm an explorer at heart and I'd come to nose around in any case. What noble folk keep in their cellars and dungeons can tell you a lot about them. My father kept most of my road-brothers for torture and execution in his dungeon. I won't say that they didn't deserve it. Harsh but fair, that's what my father's dungeon said about him. Mostly harsh.

I had to lift and heave at the same time to get the door to judder across the flagstones, pushing the empties aside. When a gap had opened large enough to admit me, I went in. A spiral staircase led down. The stairs themselves were carved stone, the work of the castle masons, but the shaft down which they led was poured, Builder-stone. The shaft led down fifty feet or so, into the bedrock. At the bottom an archway led into a rectangular chamber dominated by a grimy machine of cylinders, bolts, and circular plates. Glow-bulbs provided a weak light, three of maybe twenty still working, though not as bright as those in the Tall Castle.

I crossed to the machine and ran a hand along one of its many pipes. My fingers came away black, leaving gleaming streaks of exposed silver metal. The whole machine shook with a faint vibration, little more than heavy footfalls echoing in a stone floor.

"Go away." An old man stood there, sketched rapidly by an invisible hand. The ghost of an old man I should say, because only light fashioned him. I could see the machine through his body, and he had no colour to his flesh, as if he were made from fog. He wore white clothes, close fitting, of a strange cut, and from one moment to the next his whole form would flicker as if a moth had passed before whatever light was projected to create him.

"Make me," I said.

"Ha! That's a good one." He grinned. In looks he could have been brother to Sword-master Shimon. "Most folk just run screaming when I say 'boo.'"

"I've seen my share of ghosts, old man," I said.

"Of course you have, boy," he said. He looked as though he were humouring me. Which was odd given that he was a ghost himself.

"How long have you haunted this place, and what manner of machine is this?" I asked. It pays to be to the point with ghosts and spirits. They tend to vanish before you know it.

"I'm not a ghost. I'm a data echo. The man I am copied from lived another fourteen years after I was captured—"

"How long?"

"—and died more than a thousand years ago," he said.

"You're the ghost of a Builder?" I asked. It seemed far-fetched. Even ghosts don't last that long.

"I am an algorithm. I am portrayed in the image of Fexler Brews, my responses are extrapolated from the six terats of data gathered on the man during the course of his life. I echo him."

I understood some of the words. "What data? Numbers? Like Qalasadi keeps in his books of trade?"

"Numbers, letters, books, pictures, unguarded moments captured in secret, phrases muttered in his sleep, exclamations cried out in coitus, chemical analysis of his waste, public presentations, private meditations, polygraphic evidence, DNA samples. Data."

"What can you do for me, ghost?" His gibberish meant little to me. It seemed that they had watched him and written his story into a machine—and now that story spoke to me even though the man himself was dust on the wind.

Fexler Brews shrugged. "I'm an old man out of my time. Not even that. An incomplete copy of an old man out of his time."

"You can tell me secrets. Give me the power of the ancients," I said. I didn't think he would, or my grandfather would already be emperor, but it didn't hurt to try.

"You wouldn't understand my secrets. There's a gap between what I say and what you can comprehend. You people could fill that gap in fifty years if you stopped trying to kill each other and started to look at what's lying around you."

"Try me." I didn't like his tone. At the end of it this thing before me was nothing but a shadow-play, a story being told by a machine of cogs and springs and magic all bound by the secret fire of the Builders. "What does this do?" I tapped the machinery with my foot. "What is it for?"

Fexler blinked at me. Perhaps he had often blinked so and the machine remembered. "It has many purposes, young man, simple ones that you might understand—the pumping and purification of water—and others that are beyond you. It is a hub, part of a network without end, a tool for observation and communication, bunkered away for security. For me and my kind it serves as one of many windows onto the small world of flesh."

"Small?" I smiled. He lived in a metal box not much bigger than a coffin.

Fexler frowned, peevish. "I have other things to do: go and play elsewhere."

"Tell me this," I said. "My world. It's not like the one I read about in the oldest books. When they talk about magic, about ghosts, it's as if they are fairy-tales to frighten children. And yet I have seen the dead walk, seen a boy bring fire with just a thought."

Fexler frowned as if considering how to explain. "Think of reality as a ship whose course is set, whose wheel is locked in place by universal constants."

I wondered if a drink would help with such imaginings. All that wine seemed very tempting.

"Our greatest achievement, and downfall, was to turn that wheel, just a fraction. The role of the observer was always important—we discovered that. If a tree falls in the wood and no one hears it, it both does and doesn't make a sound. If no one sees it, then it is both standing and not standing. The cat is both alive and dead."

"Who mentioned a fecking cat?"

The ghost of Fexler Brews sighed. "We weakened the barriers between thought and matter—"

"I've heard this before," I said. Ferrakind had told me something similar. Could this ghost of a Builder share that same madness? The Nuban had spoken of barriers thinning, of the veil between life and death wearing through. "The Builders made magic? Brought it into the world with their machines?"

"There is no magic." Fexler shook his head. "We changed the constants. Just a little. Strengthened the link between *want* and *what is*. Now not only is the tree both fallen and unfallen— if the right man wills it so, with sufficient focus, the fallen tree will stand. The zombie cat will walk and purr."

"What's a zombie?"

Another sigh. Fexler vanished and all the lights went out. Even my lantern.

I climbed back up the stairs in the dark, got bitten by a spider, and was very late with Lady Agath's wine.

43

Four years earlier

I came to the Castle Morrow refectory with a swollen hand and a sore head. Spider venom makes your insides crawl and puts illusions at the edge of your vision, illusions as nasty as you can imagine. And I've been cursed with a good imagination.

The house guards and the wall guards tend to agree on very little, but they all agreed I was a dumb northerner and that I probably wouldn't swing a sword quite so fancy for a while.

It being Sunday, the cook prepared a special treat for us. Snails in garlic and wine, with saffron rice. The snails came from the local cliffs. A big variety as thick as a child's arm. But let's face it, snails are just slugs with a hat on. The main dish looked like large lumps of snot in blood. Why the Horse Coast is obsessed with eating things that squish I'm not sure. Already feeling queasy, I tried the rice. Apparently Earl Hansa had bestowed a great honour upon us, saffron being the spice of kings and trading at silly prices. All I can say is that it tasted of bitter honey to me and turned my stomach. I took the smallest nibble and decided to go hungry.

I slunk off to bed with a heel of bread and fell into vivid dreams.

The fact that I was caught sleeping, or rather that I was

caught whilst sleeping, I put down to the spider bite and the truth that if you jumped up swinging at every passer-by in a guards' dormitory you would soon kill off half the castle.

I woke with strong hands clasped around my wrists and ankles, and discovered that no amount of struggling was going to stop them dragging me through several corridors, down a flight of stairs, and into a dungeon cell. They had a healthy respect for my ability to do them harm, so in order to retreat in safety, one of them hit me in the stomach as hard as he could whilst the others stretched me wide for the blow. I heard them running out, and the slam of the door boomed over my retching.

Shouting to be let out always seemed rather silly to me. It's not as if you're going to help the people who put you there to realize that they hadn't meant to do it after all. So I didn't shout. I sat on the floor and wondered. Perhaps Qalasadi had told his secret and my family weren't amused. Or more likely my excursion to the Builder machine below the wine-cellar had been discovered and judged poorly.

It took an hour. A face appeared at the small window in the cell door. A foolish move in my opinion, since if I had been so minded I could have done serious harm to that face with the knife they had left on me.

"Hello, Lord Jost," I said. I'd met him only for moments before he passed me on to Captain Ortens for the house guard, but he had a pinched face and small dark moustache that was easy to remember.

"William of Ancrath," he said. He spoke the words slowly as if having trouble giving them credit.

The floor was uncomfortable and quite cold. I felt I might get out of there more quickly if I let him have his say. So I said nothing.

"What poison did you use, William?" he asked.

I looked at my hand in the half-light. The spider bite had turned purple. "Poison?" I asked.

"I'm not here for games, boy. I'll leave you to rot. If they die before you're ready to talk, then the Earl will hire in Moorish torturers to make an example of you."

The face drew back.

"Wait!" I got to my feet sharpish. I didn't like the sound of

Moorish torturers. In fact it's hard to put any word in front of "torturers" that doesn't sound unsettling. "Tell me what happened and you'll have the whole truth from me. I swear by Jesu."

He turned and walked away.

I threw myself to the door, face at the window. "I can save them," I lied. "But I have to know who was affected."

Lord Jost turned and I thanked whoever it was that invented lying. "Every guard on the day shift is falling into delirium," he said. "Several have gone blind."

"And I'm the only one not showing symptoms, so that makes me guilty?"

"You're some kind of assassin, clearly. Probably Olidan of Ancrath's man. If you provide an antidote I can promise you a quick death."

"I don't have an antidote," I said. Who would want to poison a whole shift of guards?

"What poison did you use? You promised the truth," Lord Jost said.

"If I'm an assassin why would you expect me to keep my promise? And if I'm not, then I can't, can I? Because I didn't do it."

Lord Jost spat in an unlordly fashion and started to walk off again.

"Wait. It's got to be Moors, hasn't it? Why would King Olidan want to poison a few guards? He not going to march an army a thousand miles to knock at your door. The Moors are planning a raid."

He turned the corner.

"I'm not sick because I didn't eat the meal!" I shouted after him.

The echoes of his footsteps faded away.

"Because all your food tastes like shit that somebody set fire to!" I shouted.

And I was alone.

The dead baby came to me in the dark, solemn eyes watching, head lolling on a broken neck. For the millionth time I wondered if I had killed Katherine back there in that graveyard. Was this my child, that could never be because I'd murdered his mother, or just one of the many children whose blood stained my hands? Gelleth's children. It had taken a monster to make them real to me. Not a monster in shape. I'd called Gog and Gorgoth monsters. But Chella and I were the real item, foul in deed if not form.

Why poison the guards? It could be the Moors, but they could hardly take the castle in a single raid, and they couldn't poison all her defenders. And it's not wise to give such warning if you're hoping for a fast strike on outlying towns and churches.

An iron fist clenched around my stomach, taking me by surprise, and I hurled watery vomit across the cell. I fell forward onto my hands.

"Shit."

The darkness kept spinning on me, so I pressed my cheek to the cold stone floor. My scar still burned, as if the splinters lodged in my flesh were kept hot.

Maybe I had been poisoned after all. But why would it take longer with me? Not my hardy northern constitution, surely? And I ate almost nothing. A piece of bread. A mouthful of bitter rice.

I had to get out. And that's the trouble with dungeon cells. Somebody took trouble to make sure you're not going anywhere, and no amount of wanting will change that.

I stood and went to the door. With Lord Jost and his lantern gone there was almost no light, but something filtered down, perhaps a whisper of the sun dazzling in the courtyards above if day had swung around, perhaps an echo of torchlight farther down the corridors they'd dragged me along. In any event it proved enough for night-tutored eyes to find edges and the occasional detail. I examined the little window in the door. I could fit an arm through it if it weren't for the bars. The wood was three fingers thick, hardwood. It would take a week of whittling with my dagger to make much of a hole.

Something scurried behind me. A rat. I can tell rat noises in the dark. I threw my dagger. It used to be a game amongst the Brothers. Nail a rat in the dark. Grumlow proved a master of that particular game. We would often wake to find a rat skewered to the sod by one of his blades. Sometimes uncomfortably close to my head.

"Got you."

Being as there was no morning to wait for, I hunted my victim down by hand and retrieved my knife.

I went back to the window and its bars. I pushed against them, trying to imagine how they would be fixed to the wood. There was no give in them. It's funny how often our lives shrink down to a single obdurate piece of metal. A knife edge, a manacle, a nail. Gorgoth might have reached out and twisted those bars off in that blunt hand of his. Not me. I pulled and pushed until my hand bled. Nothing.

I sat back down. I thought, thought, and then thought some more. In the end I went to the window and started hollering for them to let me out.

It took a while. Long enough for my throat to grow raw and my voice to crack, but in the end a glow approached. The swinging glow of a lantern.

"You get one chance to shut your mouth, boy. After that—"

"You're going to shut it for me?" I asked, pressed close to the door.

"Oh, you'd like that, wouldn't you? For me to open the door. I heard about you and Master Shimon. I wouldn't open that door for a gold coin. No. You shut your mouth or you'll discover you've taken your last drink of water on God's earth."

"Hey, don't be like that. I'm sorry." I reached up and dropped my watch so that it fell into the basket made by the window cage. "Look, take this, it's worth a hundred coins. Just bring me something good to eat would you?"

I crouched low. Listening. Listening.

The gaoler stepped in to take the bait and bang, I slid my arm out through the feeding slot at the base of the door, skinning my elbow, and caught him behind his ankle. A sharp yank and he fell. I took a firmer grip hauling his foot toward the slot, but he didn't struggle.

"Damn."

The bastard had hit his head and knocked himself senseless. I'd been planning to reduce the number of his toes with my knife until he offered me his key. It's hard to intimidate an unconscious man.

I picked up my dead rat. Still warm.

There are quite a few uses for a dead rat. I'll go into them at another time. The use I had in mind proved difficult. It turned out to be harder to make a dead rat scurry again than it did to set Brother Row diving in the mud. It's hard to understand a rat, to wear its skin. I almost gave up but when I focused on hunger, it twitched in my hands. It turns out that being dead doesn't stop a rat thinking about its next meal. Before too long I had the creature marching to my tune, and I pushed it out through the food slot.

In the light of the gaoler's lantern, which helpfully he had hung on a hook before reaching for my watch, I sent the rat out searching.

I sat in the small blob of rat brain telling it to gnaw on the thong holding the ring of keys to the gaoler's belt. When the key ring came loose I had the rat drag it to me. In a truly secure cell you wouldn't be able to unlock from the inside, but all systems have their flaws. I let the rat die again and stepped out into the corridor, a free man after my long hours of incarceration!

My stomach clenched but it didn't feel as if I was dying; a touch lightheaded, a touch unclean, but necromancy will do some of that for you in any case. If I had been poisoned then whoever did it had done a bad job.

I gagged the gaoler with strips of cloth and locked him in my cell. Glancing into the other cells along the corridor it appeared that my grandfather was not the locking-up sort. That meant he was either very keen on executions or that he ruled with a light touch.

Slow steps took me to the gaoler's desk where the ceiling port let the moonlight in. It was late but perhaps not midnight. I had had some time to think and I kept thinking. If I were going to poison my enemies I wouldn't waste my efforts on thirty guardsmen, I'd try to empty the throne and throw the whole place into confusion. But any kind of poisoning is hard to do. Castle kitchens are well watched, the cooks as trusted as the men who shave the royal throat. Fresh provisions are hard to taint, potatoes, carrots, and the like. Dry provisions are bought incognito and escorted to locked pantries.

I left the dungeons. I still wore the household uniform and the single guard at the exit had been obliging enough to let me knock his head against the wall. Unfortunately a burned face is hard to hide. You can't present your good side to the whole world. I found a window and took to the rooftops.

Sitting against the main chimney stack, legs stretched out across the terracotta tiles of the great hall's roof, I pondered.

Not the slugs—sorry, snails. I didn't partake. So the rice. But poisoning rice? The water and boiling and draining would soak it all away. So the saffron. But that would be purchased from whatever ship next turned up at harbour with stocks on board. How often does a household run out of a spice that costs more per ounce than gold? How many ships carry it? What households other than those of the Hundred would buy such luxury in any case? Bundle all those factors together . . . what would the odds be . . . what probabilities would emerge? Just thinking about the necessary calculations made my head hurt.

Qalasadi!

I slid down the slope of the roof, hoping no tiles would come with me. I reached the wide stone gutter and edged across it, looking for a place where it was well supported. Ending my reign as king in a gory splat at the bottom of a seventy-foot drop was no part of my ambitions. I could hear muffled voices from several quarters, the sigh of the ocean, waves lapping the foot of the cliffs, and the relentless buzz and chirp of the night insects that haunt the Horse Coast.

Castle Morrow bakes in the southern sun much of the year. The winters can be ferocious but are rarely cold. There may well be old men in the region who have never seen snow. In consequence the windows are large and unscreened, the storm-shutters heavy and locked open from early spring to late autumn. With a firm grip on the gutter's edge and my left ankle locked under the bottom row of tiles, I hung upside-down and looked through a high window into the great hall.

The far end of the single long table had been set with silver and crystal. Wall lamps burning smokeless oil gave a welcoming glow. A servant brought in three decanters of wine, two white, one red. Elite house guards in plumed finery stood watch at six points around the hall.

The servant left. Minutes passed. The blood ran to my head, my eyeballs began to prickle and itch, my fingers grew numb where they gripped the stonework. I heard noise down in the courtyard below. A quick commotion. I decided not to move. Silence returned.

At last the black oak doors opened and two servants stepped through to hold them wide as my uncle walked in, escorting Lady Agath. They took their seats, maids now attending to pull the chairs out and settle the nobility. Two more ladies followed in. Old biddies I recognized from the Ladies' Hall. A young man with a fat gut strode in, wrapped in blue velvet despite the heat. My grandmother, who I saw once at the Tall Castle, came escorted and supported by a pageboy. She looked unsteady, her hair very white, her skin pale, thin, drawn. Then my grandfather, taking his high-backed chair at the head of the table. Earl Hansa surprised me; he looked only a little older than my father, a solidly built man with a short grey beard and long thick hair still streaked with black.

More servants now, bearing covered silver platters.

A drop of sweat left my nose and fell away into the darkness. My head felt fuzzy and full of blood.

The covers came away in a choreographed move, flourished overhead by the servants, and revealing today's delicacies. No snails. No rice.

I slid with less grace than I had hoped and swung clumsily into the window, sitting on the ledge and steadying myself with both hands. I very nearly ended up in the unplanned splat. Hanging upside-down before attempting acrobatics is not to be recommended.

I had hoped to go unnoticed a while longer but perhaps Lady Agath was the only person in the great hall not to look up.

To his credit, while the fat boy jumped to his feet, and several of the ladies shrieked, Lord Robert called for the house guard to shield the Earl. The Earl Hansa himself took a sip from his wine then called out, "I had a grandson named William Ancrath."

"And I had a brother of that name," I called back.

My uncle stood up at that.

I released the edges of the window. With a quick motion I threw my dagger. It struck the centremost platter and yellowed slices of potato sprinkled with sea-salt and crushed black peppercorns leapt across the table. The spider bite had left my finger joints sore and swollen and the knife went far closer to one of the old women's ears than I had intended.

More shrieks. "It's that damnable boy!" Lady Agath cried, having finally laid eyes on me.

"You don't approve of our meal arrangements . . . Nephew?" Lord Robert asked.

"I think if you ate the contents of that platter I might soon be lacking relatives in the south. In fact, I could even be legal heir to the earldom!"

"You'd better come down here, Jorg," my grandfather said.

To my shame I had to be helped down with a ladder. The drop would have broken my legs and the inner walls of the great hall were plastered smooth. Clambering down a ladder arse first to the room wasn't the most impressive of entrances, but I *had* just saved their lives.

"You think our food is poisoned?" Grandfather asked.

I took a silver fork and speared a slice of the potato. "Have Qalasadi brought here and see if he would like a taste."

Lord Robert frowned. "Just because we're at odds with Ibn Fayed doesn't mean all Moors are out to get us."

Earl Hansa nodded to the guardsman at his shoulder and the man set off on an errand.

"Even so, he is guilty," I said. "And in such a manner that there is no proof other than to see if he will sample a little of your saffron."

"The saffron?" the Earl asked.

"You'll find you've recently had a new consignment come to the kitchens, properly sealed and kept safe both for its intrinsic value and for your protection. It is probably part of a larger supply that is busy killing rich folk up and down the coast. A seemingly random act of pointless destruction. But I know a man capable of calculating that part of this same consignment would end up on your table, Earl Hansa. A man who also knew my identity and thought I'd make a perfect villain, and that I would accept the blame with the good graces of my line."

"Dig a deeper hole with your sword, you mean?" Lord Robert asked, a slight smile on his lips.

For a moment I wondered if Qalasadi had factored in even my arrival, wondered if I were not some chance victim to pin his crime on but part of some larger calculation. I pushed that thought aside as both unlikely and unsettling. "Our mathmagician made only one mistake. It's unfair perhaps to even call it a mistake. I expect he considered the possibility and decided it remote enough to chance. He didn't think it likely you would let the cooks waste such fine ingredients on mere guards."

The man who left on Grandfather's errand returned. "Qalasadi is not in his quarters, Earl Hansa, and neither is he in the observatory."

It turned out Qalasadi left the castle as soon as news of the guards' sickness reached him.

FROM THE JOURNAL OF KATHERINE AP SCORRON

March 26th, Year 99 Interregnum
Rennat Forest. Late afternoon.

*I had thought I might write about Hanna at her graveside.
Sareth says I take this journal everywhere, that I have too
little in my life if I can't be without it. People who are truly
living, she says, don't need to write about it every minute—
they're too busy getting on with real things. But Sareth
hasn't left the Tall Castle in a year, and whilst that baby is
sucking the milk out of her I'm sat in Rennat Forest with
monsters!*

*There's an ogre at least ten foot tall with a mouthful of
sharp teeth and slit-eyes. It glanced my way at first but now
it just stands carving a chunk of deadfall, not with a knife
but with the black nail on a finger as thick as my wrist.*

*The second monster is just a little boy really. A skinny
one but nearly naked and marked with patterns in red and
black, like ripples or flames. He scampers from bush to
bush, trying to keep hidden, watching me with big black
eyes. When he runs you can see his claws.*

*I'm distracting myself. I don't want to think about what
Jorg said.*

*The monster-child is called Gog. He says Jorg named
him, after those giants in the bible. I told him there should
be a Magog too. He looked so sad at that and the forest felt
too hot all of a sudden as if it were the highest of high
summers.*

*"And what will you be when you grow up, Gog?" I asked
him to take his mind from whatever had upset him.*

"I want to be big and strong," he said. "To make Jorg happy. And I want to be happy, to stop Gorgoth being sad." He looked at the ogre.

"And what do you want for you?" I asked him.

He looked at me with huge black eyes. "I want to save them," he said. "Like they saved me."

Jorg's men look as though they've never left the road. They're bandits, not a king's retinue. Sir Makin, who they say is a proper knight, is as filthy as the rest. There's dried muck all over his armour and he stinks like a sewer. He has a way with him though, even with the dirt. Sir Makin has manners at least.

The one they call Red Kent tries to be polite, my lady this and my lady that, bowing at every turn. It's quite comical. When I thanked him for the water he brought me he blushed from neck to hairline. I think I know how he got his name.

When he's not waiting on me Kent spends most of his time whittling, carving away with his back against a tree and a black knife in hand. It's a wolf he's working on. It looks as though it's climbing out of the wood, snarling at the world. He said he was a woodsman once. A long time ago.

And there's a boy, Sim. Very delicate features like that stage player who performed in court last week. He looks kind, but shy. He won't speak to me but I see him looking when he thinks I can't see. He's the cleanest of all of them. I can't think he would be much of a warrior. Surely he's too slight to swing that sword of his.

I know Sir Makin can fight. I remember that he put Sir Galen to the test when Jorg's father set them against each other, though I think my Galen would have beaten him. Perhaps that's why Jorg pushed over Sageous's tree. To save Sir Makin.

The other two, the two Jorg warned Red Kent to watch, are killers through and through. You can see it in their eyes. There's a giant called Rike who's nearly as tall as the ogre and as broad as a Slav wrestler. He just looks angry the whole time. And there's an old man, maybe fifty, skinny, gristly, with grey stubble on his chin and as wrinkled as

Hanna was. They call him Row and he has kind eyes, but there's something about him that says his eyes are lying.

And I'm sitting here scratching the paper with my quill to record rogues and vagabonds because my hand doesn't want to follow where Jorg has gone, or to write what he might be doing, or to frame the words that are pounding through my head.

I tried to stab Jorg but it was like a dream. I both knew and did not know what my hand was doing. I didn't want to hear his pain or see him bleed. I don't recall picking up the knife to take with me. I told myself to stop. But I didn't stop.

And now. If I had Friar Glen here. I would want to hear his pain and see him bleed. I would not tell myself to stop. But I would stop. Because for the first time in a long while my head feels clear, my thoughts are all my own, and I am not a killer.

March 27th, Year 99 Interregnum
Rennat Forest. Before noon. A high wind in the trees.

Sir Makin has been pacing. He doesn't say it but he's worried about Jorg. We saw a patrol ride by earlier, between the fields. They'll be looking for me. Sir Makin says the more of them looking for me, the fewer for Jorg to worry about in the castle.

The big one. The huge one, really. Rike. He's been saying they should go. That Jorg is captured or dead. Kent says Jorg helped them all escape the dungeons and if he's stuck there in those same dungeons himself, they should go free him. Even Sir Makin says that's madness.

The night was cold and noisy. They gave me their cloaks, but I'd rather be cold than under those stinking, crawling things. Everything moves in the forest at night, creaking, or croaking, or rustling in dead leaves. I was glad to see the dawn. When I woke up, the boy, Sim, was standing against the tree beside me, watching.

Breakfast was stale bread and bits of smoked meat. I

*didn't like to ask what animal it came from. I ate it. My
stomach was grumbling and I'm sure they could hear.*

*Jorg has come back. His men are more scared now than
when they thought he was lost. He's a wild thing, his hair
torn and spiky with blood, he won't look at anything, his
eyes keep sliding, he can hardly stand. He's got blood on
his hands, past his elbows, his nails are torn, two of them
missing.*

*Makin told him to sleep and Jorg just made this terrible
sound. I think it might have been laughing. He says he won't
sleep again. Ever. And I believe him.*

*Jorg keeps moving, fending off trees with his hands,
colliding with whatever's in his way. He says he's been
poisoned.*

*"I can't clean them," he said. And he showed me his
hands. It looks as though he's rubbed the skin off.*

*I asked him what was wrong and he said, "I'm cracked
through and filled with poison."*

*He scares his men and he scares me too. Of all of us
I am the one his eyes avoid the most. His eyes are red
with crying but he doesn't cry now, just a kind of dry
hacking sob.*

*My great aunt got a madness in her. Great Aunt Lucin.
She must have been sixty, a small woman, plump, we all
loved her. And one day she threw boiling water over her
handmaid. She threw the water and then went wild, spout-
ing nursery rhymes and biting herself. Father's surgeon sent
her to Thar. He said there was an alchemist there whose
potions might cure her. And failing the potions, he had other
methods. The surgeon said that this man, Luntar, could take
out pieces of a person's mind until what remained was
healthy.*

*My great aunt Lucin came back in a carriage two
months later. She smiled and sang and could talk about
the weather. She wasn't my great aunt Lucin any more but
she seemed nice enough, and she didn't scald any more
maids.*

I don't want that for Jorg.

Jorg has told his men to kill me, and some of them seem ready to do it. Rike looks keen. But Sir Makin has said Jorg doesn't know his mind and they are to leave me alone.

Jorg is saying he needs to kill Sareth too. He says it's a kindness. He's insistent. Kent and Makin had to wrestle him to the floor to stop him running back to the castle to do it. Now he's lying in the dirt watching me. He keeps telling me what they do to men in his father's dungeons. It can't be true, any of it. It makes me sick to hear. I can taste vomit at the back of my throat.

Jorg soiled himself. Half the time he seems to see something other than the forest about us. He watches nothing, stares with great intent, then screams, or laughs without warning.

He's been talking about our baby. I still call it ours. It feels better than saying it was Friar Glen who violated me. He's been saying he killed it, even though it's me that carries that sin, me that will burn for it. He says he killed the baby with his own hands. And now he's crying. He still has tears then. He's bawling, snot and forest dirt stuck to his face.

"I held him, Katherine, a soft baby. So small. Innocent. My hands remember his shape."

I can't hear him speak of this.

I have told Sir Makin about Luntar and how to reach Thar.

This is what Jorg said when they dragged him away and tied him to his horse:

"We're not memories, Katherine, we're dreams. All of us. Each part of us a dream, a nightmare of blood and vomit and boredom and fear. And when we wake up— we die."

When they led his horse off, he shouted at me, but it seemed more lucid than what he said before.

"Sageous has poisoned us both, Katherine. With dreams. He puts his hands into our heads and pulls the strings that make us dance, and we dance. None of it was true. None of it."

I walked across the fields to the Roma Road and followed

it toward the Tall Castle until soldiers found me and escorted me back. I'll say back. I won't say home.

As I walked, Jorg's words ran through my head, again and again, as if some of his madness had got inside me. I kept thinking of the dreams I've been having. It seems to me I've heard Sageous called the dream-witch before, but somehow that fact faded away, became unimportant. It wasn't that I forgot it, but I stopped seeing it. Just as I stopped seeing that knife I took to stab Jorg with.

I'm seeing it now.

The heathen has been in my head. I know it. He's been writing stories there, on the inside of my skull, on the backs of my eyes, like he's written on his skin. I will need to think on this. To unravel it. Tonight I am going to dream myself a fortress and sleep within its walls. And woe betide anyone that comes looking for me there.

The soldiers brought me in through the Roma Gate into the Low City, across the Bridge of Change, the river running red with sunrise. I knew something awful had happened. All of Crath City held quiet as if some terrible secret were spreading through the alleys like poison in veins. Shutters—opened for the dawn—closed as we passed.

Up in the Tall Castle the dull tone of a bell rang out over and over. The iron bell on the roof tower. I've been up to see it, but it's never rung. I knew it had to be that one though—no other bell could make such a harsh, flat toll. And in answer a single deep voice from Our Lady.

I asked the soldiers but they would say nothing, wouldn't even guess. I didn't recognize the men, only their colours, not castle guards but army units drafted in for the search.

"Has he killed his father?" I asked them. "Has he killed him?"

"We've been hunting for you all night, my lady. We've heard nothing from the castle." The sergeant bowed his head and pulled off his helm. He was older than I had imagined, tired, swaying in his saddle. "Best let the news wait to tell itself."

A cold certainty gripped me. Jorg had killed Sareth. Throttled her for taking his mother's place at Olidan's side.

I knew they would take me to her body, cold and white, stretched out in the tomb vaults where the Ancraths lie. I bit my lips and said nothing, only let the horses walk away the distance that kept me from knowing.

We came through the Triple Gate, clattering, hooves on stone, grooms on hand to take the reins and help me dismount as if I were some old woman. The iron bell tolled all the while, a noise to make your head ache and jaws clench.

In the courtyard someone had lit a myrrh stick, a thick wand of it smoking in a torch sconce by the windlass. If sorrow had a scent it would be this. We burn them in Scorron too, for the dead.

From the window arch high above the chapel balcony, between the pulses of the bell, I heard keening. A woman's voice. My sister had never made such cries before, but still I knew her, and the fear that had sunk its teeth into me back at the Roma Gate now twisted cold in my gut. The sounds of hurt, as raw and open as any wound, could not be for Olidan.

44

Four years earlier

I went to see my grandmother in her chambers. Uncle Robert had warned me that she wore her years less well than Grandfather.

"She's not the woman she was," he told me. "But she has her moments."

I nodded and turned to go. He caught my shoulder. "Be gentle with my mother," he said.

Even now they thought me a monster. Once I'd sought to build a legend, to set fear among those who might stand against me. Now I dragged those stories behind me into my mother's home.

The maid showed me in and steered me to a comfortable chair opposite the one Grandmother occupied.

Of all of them, my grandmother had the most of Mother in her. Something in the lines of her cheekbones and the shape of her skull. She sat hunched with a blanket over her knees despite the heat of the day. She looked smaller than I remembered, and not just because I was no longer a child. It seemed she had closed on herself after her daughter's death, as if to present a smaller target to a world grown hostile.

"I remember you as a little boy—the man before me I don't

know at all," she said. Her eyes moved across me, seeking something familiar.

"When I see my reflection I feel the same thing myself, Grandmother." And the box at my hip, in a velvet pocket now, felt too heavy to carry. *I don't know me at all.*

We sat in silence for a long minute.

"I tried to save her." I would have said more but words wouldn't come.

"I know, Jorg."

The distance between us fell away then, and we spoke of years past, of times when we were both happier, and I had my window onto the world that I'd forgotten, and it was good.

And by and by when I sat beside her feet, knees drawn to my chest, hand clasping wrist before them, that old woman sang the songs my mother had played long ago, as she had played them in the music room of the Tall Castle on the black keys and the white. Grandmother put words to music I remembered but couldn't hear, and we sat as the shadows lengthened and the sun fell from the sky.

Later, when comfortable silence had stretched into something that convinced me she had fallen asleep, I stood up to go. I reached the door without creak or scrape, but as my hand touched the handle Grandmother spoke behind me.

"Tell me about William."

I turned and found her watching me with sharper eyes than before, as if a chance wind had stirred the curtains of age and showed her as she once was, strong and attentive, if only for a moment.

"He died." It was all I could find to say.

"William was an exceptional child." She pursed wizened lips and watched me, waiting.

"They killed him."

"I met you both, you're probably too young to recall." She looked away to the hearth as if staring at the memory of flames. "William. There was something fierce in that one. You have a touch of it too, Jorg. Same mix of hard and clever. I held him and I knew that if he let himself love me or anyone else, he wouldn't ever give it up. And if someone crossed him, that he would be . . . unforgiving. Maybe you were both bound to be a bit like that. Maybe that's what happens when two people so strong, and yet so utterly different from each other, make children."

"When they broke him . . ." The lightning had shown him to me in three quick flashes as they carried him. One frozen moment had him staring at the thorns, into the heart of the briar. Looking at me. No fear in him. The second and he was scooped up by his legs. The third, dashed against that milestone, scarlet shards of skull among blond curls. "My little emperor" Mother used to call him. The blond of that line in a court filled with Steward-dark Ancraths.

"Broke who, dear?"

"William," I said, but the years had settled on her again and she saw me through too many days.

"You're not him," she said. "I knew a boy like you once, but you're not him."

"Yes, Grandmother." I went and kissed her brow then and walked away. She smelled of Mother, the same perfume, and something in her scent stung my eyes so I could hardly find the door in the gloom.

They gave me a chamber in the east tower, overlooking the sea. The moon described each wave in glimmers and I sat listening to the sigh of the waters long into the night.

I thought again of the music my mother played, and that I remembered in images, and never heard. I saw her hands move across the keys as always, the shadow of her arms, the sway of her shoulders. And for the first time in all the years since we climbed into that carriage, the faintest strain of those silent notes reached me. Fainter and more elusive than the swordsong, but more vital, more important.

Two days passed before the Earl Hansa summoned me to his throne-room, a chamber built against the hind wall of the castle where a great circle of Builder-glass offers the Middle Sea to gaze upon in all its ever-changing shades. I faced the old man, my back to the distant waves, the setting sun edging each with crimson, and with the faint crash of their breaking ready to underwrite any silence.

"We stand in your debt, Jorg," my grandfather said.

Actually it was my uncle who stood, at the right hand of Grandfather's throne, whilst the old man sat ensconced in his whalebone seat.

"We're family," I said.

"And what is it your family can do for you?" Earl Hansa may have been my mother's father but he was shrewd enough to know young men don't cross half a continent just to visit old relatives.

"Perhaps we can do things for each other. In troubled times being able to call on military help can make the difference between life and death. It may be that this Ibn Fayed becomes more of a threat and the day comes when the men of the Highlands stand side to side with the House Morrow to oppose him. It may be that my own position is threatened and my grandfather's troops or horse could be of aid."

"Are you threatened now?" Grandfather asked.

"No," I said. "I'm not here in desperation, begging. I'm looking for a strategic alliance. Something to span years."

"Our lands are very far apart," he said.

"That may not always be so." I allowed myself a smile. I had plans for growth.

"It seems strange that you come so far when your father's armies stand mere days from your gates." The Earl ran his tongue over his teeth as if he tasted something rotten.

"My father is an enemy I will face in the field of battle in due course," I said.

The Earl slapped his thigh. "Now that's the kind of alliance I could get behind!" He watched me for a moment, the laughter leaving him. "You are your father's son, Jorg. I won't lie. It's hard to trust you. It's hard for me to speak of sending my people to fight and die on foreign soil for Olidan's boy."

"It would pain him to hear you call me that," I said.

Lord Robert leaned in and whispered in his father's ear.

"If you would bind your fate with mine, Jorg, then we need stronger bonds. Lady Agath is dear to your grandmother and me. Her son rules in Wennith, and he has two daughters. Small girls now, but they'll be ready for marrying soon enough. On the day you wed one of them, my soldiers will be ready to fight in your cause." The Earl settled back in his throne with a grin.

"What say you, Jorg?" Uncle Robert asked, also smiling.

I spread my hands. "I do?"

Robert nodded to a knight at the door who drew it open and spoke to a servant beyond. The jaws of the trap closed around me. Birds had flown in the two days since Qalasadi fled. Replies returned, carriages had set out.

"Kalam Dean, Lord of Wennith, third of the name!" the herald called out, sweating in his silks. "And the Lady Miana."

A stout man, short with thin grey hair, marched in. Near as old as Grandfather, he wore a plain white robe and might have passed as a simple monk but for the heavy-linked chain of gold looped about his neck and down across his chest. A ruby bigger than a pigeon's egg hung from the chain. Lady Miana trailed in his wake, a child of eight years, bundled into crinoline and crushed velvet, wide-eyed, red-faced in the heat, a rag doll clutched tight in both hands.

The Lord of Wennith strode right up to me without preamble, craning his neck to look me up and down as if examining a suspect horse. I resisted the urge to show him my teeth. Plump and grey and old he might have been but he had a look about him that said he knew his business, he knew men well enough and the notion of putting his child in my marriage bed pleased him as little as it did me. He leaned in close to share some confidence or threat not meant for any ears but mine. As he moved forward the ruby swung out on its chain, catching the dying rays of the sun. It seemed to hold them, burning at its heart, and that light woke something in my blood. Heat rose through me as I fought to keep my hands from reaching for the gem.

"Listen well, Ancrath," Kalam Dean of Wennith said, and the ruby swung back against his chest ending further conversation. He gave a cry of pain and jerked away, a charred patch smouldering on his robes beneath the stone.

While guards hastened to Wennith's side and Grandfather called for servants, the child approached me. "King Jorg?" she said.

"Lady Miana?" I went down on one knee to be level with her, turning my face so as not to scare her with my burns. "And how is your dolly called?" I'd little enough experience with children but it seemed a safe enough opening. She looked down in surprise as if she hadn't known the toy was there.

"Oh," she said. "That's not mine. I'm near grown. It's Lolly's, my sister's." The shape of her mouth told the lie: it tasted sour to her. Her first words to me and already I'd made a liar of her. If we ever wed it would be the least of my crimes. I would be the ruination of her life, this little girl with her rag doll. If she had any sense she would run. If I had any decency I would make her. But instead I would lie to her father, smile, be for the moment whatever man he needed me to be, and all for the promise of heavy horse, of five hundred riders on the Horse Coast's finest steeds.

A friar from the Morrow chapel helped Lord Wennith from the throne-room with the aid of a guardsman. Miana trailed after them. She paused and turned. "Remember me," she said.

"Oh, I will." I nodded, still kneeling. A proud day like this would stay with me forever if I let it. I gave her my smile. "I won't let your memory go, Miana. I've somewhere to keep it in, nice and safe."

On the next day Kalam Dean and I finished our negotiations. He didn't bring his ruby to the discussion but promised it as Miana's dowry. And on that very same evening I found out how to squeeze an unwanted memory from my mind and set it into Luntar's copper box. All I kept of Miana was her name, the fact I was to marry her, and that half a thousand cavalry would one day come in answer to my call.

The remaining time I spent at Castle Morrow, and my journey back to the Highlands, are tales best kept for another day. Before I left though, in fact on the day after my engagement, I took myself back to the room beneath the wine-cellar, this time with permission.

My uncle called it the "grouch chamber." The machine appeared to have only three tasks. Firstly, to keep alive a number of glow-bulbs dotted around the oldest parts of the castle.

Secondly, to suck seawater from beneath the cliffs and turn it into pure drinking water for the fountains around the court-yards. And finally, to allow the grouch, Fexler Brews, to enjoy a kind of half-life in which he generally poured scorn on the ignorance of the living, pitied our existence, and moaned about the things he left unfinished in his own.

"Go away."

Fexler appeared the moment I entered the chamber and repeated his previous greeting.

"Make me," I said again.

"Ah, the young man with the questions," Fexler said. "I was a young man with questions once upon a time, you know."

"No, you weren't. You're the echo of a man who was. You were never young—only new."

"And what is your question?" he asked, scowling.

"Can you end your existence?" I asked.

"Not everyone seeks an end, boy."

"You think I seek my end?"

"All young men are a little in love with death."

"I would be more than in love with it if I'd spent a thousand years in a cellar."

"It has been trying," Fexler admitted.

"Are you even allowed to want to end yourself?" I asked.

"You're obsessed with death, child."

"You didn't answer the question," I said.

"I'm not allowed to answer the question."

"Complicated!" I stepped back and sat on the bottom stairs. "So. What can you do for me?"

"I can give you three questions."

"Like a genie," I said.

"Yes, but they give wishes. Two left."

"That was an observation, not a question!" I cried.

I chewed my lip. "Do you swear to give full and honest answers?"

"No. Two left."

Dammit. "Tell me about guns," I said.

"No. One left."

"Point me at the single most useful and portable piece of Builder-magic in this chamber," I said.

Fexler shrugged and then pointed to what looked to be one of the valves on the blackened machine. I moved to examine it. Not a valve, something else. A ring set in a depression.

"It's hardly portable."

"Twist it," he said.

I cleaned the area with my sleeve. A silver ring about three inches across topped a stubby cylindrical projection. Shallow grooves around the edge offered some traction. I twisted it. It proved extremely stiff but with the bones in my hand creaking I managed to turn the ring.

Nothing happened.

I twisted again. Easier this time. Again. I spun it several times and the ring came loose in my hand.

"Pretty," I said.

"Look through it," Fexler suggested.

I held it to my eye. Nothing for a second, then an image over-wrote my vision, a blue circle swirled with white patterns, intricate, infinitely detailed. For some reason it put me in mind of Alaric's snow-globe. "It's wonderful," I said. "What is it?"

"Your whole world. Seen from a little over twenty thousand miles above the ground."

"That's a ways to fall. What are all the white swirls?"

"Weather formations."

"Weather?" It seemed incredible that I might be seeing clouds from above rather than below, and over such reaches that their whole cycle and design lay revealed. "Weather from when? From your day?"

"From today. From now."

"This isn't just a painting?"

"You're seeing the world as it happens. Your world," Fexler said.

I shifted my grip on the ring and I plunged, or felt that I did, racing down and to the left, like an eagle diving. A small curl at the end of one vast cloud swirl now filled my vision and I could see land far below, a sparkling thread wove across the greens and browns. I stumbled but managed to keep my feet.

"I can see a river!" An old instinct bit in. Suspicion drew the ring and its visions from my eye. "Why?"

"Why?" he asked.

I spun the ring between finger and thumb. "Beware of ghosts bearing gifts, they say."

"You'll find that's Greeks, but the principle is sound." Fexler frowned. "You're carrying something that interests me. And as it turns out you're more than you seem. It's not every day a battleground walks down my stairs."

"Battleground?"

"You're a nexus for two opposing forms of energy, young man—one dark, one light. I have technical terms for them, but dark and light serve well enough. Given a little more time they'll tear you apart. Quite literally. It's an exponential process, the end will be sudden and 'violent.'"

"And you know this because?" My gaze returned to the ring.

"A lesson in life, Jorg. Whatever you look into can look back into you. The ring has scanned your brain in quite minute detail."

My jaw clenched at that. The idea of being measured, being classified, did not appeal. "But that's something unexpected you discovered, not what you were looking for?"

"You know what I was looking for." Fexler smiled. "Perhaps you'd be good enough to set the ring to it for me?"

I pulled out my little box of memories. Today it seemed to tremble in my hand. The view-ring clunked against it as if both were lodestones drawn by mutual attraction. For a moment Fexler's image pulsed more brightly.

"Interesting," he said. "Crude but clever. Remarkable even."

Box and ring fell apart—done with each other. Fexler fixed me with an intense stare.

"I can help you, boy. Fire and death have their hooks deep in you. Call it magic. It isn't but this will go easier if we say it is. Your wounds anchor the enchantments, both of them trying to pull you into the domains from which they spring. Alone either one would draw you down in time, make something different of you, something no longer human. You understand me?"

I nodded. Ferrakind and the Dead King waited for me in separate hells.

Fexler's gaze settled on the box, clenched tight in my hand. "All that saves you is that these forces are in opposition. Soon enough, though, that opposition will rip you open."

He waited for me to speak, to beg or entreat his aid. I held my tongue and watched him.

"I can help," he said.

"How?"

He flashed a nervous grin. "It's done. I've bound both forces through that interesting little box of yours. It's far stronger than you are. It may hold indefinitely. And while it holds the process should be halted; neither power should be able to get a better grip on you or able to pull you any further into their domain."

"And what is it you want for this . . . gift?" I asked.

Fexler fended the question off with an irritable wave. "Just remember this, Jorg of Ancrath. Do not open that box. Open it and my work is undone. Open it and you're finished."

The box glinted as I turned it in my hand. "Pandora had one of these."

I looked up for Fexler to share the joke, but he had gone. Several silent minutes passed, alone in the cellar, weighing box and ring in my hands. I had tickled far more than three answers from the ghost, but had a thousand more questions than when I started.

"Come back." I sounded foolish.

The ghost did not return.

I put the ring in my pocket. Interesting or not it seemed odd that the grouch had favoured me above the others that visited him. Uncle Robert never mentioned a gift of any kind, nor any really meaningful answers to questions. Fexler wanted something from me. Something personal. That last nervous grin of his said it. He might be dead a thousand years, might be a Builder, or just the story of a Builder in a machine of cogs and magic, but before all that he was a man, and I knew men. He wanted something—something he couldn't take but that he thought I could give.

I wondered, despite his mocking, if death held an allure for the ghost too. We aren't meant to live forever, nor dwell in solitude. A life without change is no life. The spirit beneath Mount Honas agreed with me. Maybe the only way Fexler Brews had to tell me so was to offer me his gift. And to hope that I would help him. He wanted something, that much was sure. Everyone wants something.

I would have to think on it. The machine made Fexler.

Grandfather would not thank me for destroying his source of fresh water, and neither would the men who would have to pump the fountains thereafter. Gone or not though, Fexler Brews and I were not finished with each other.

I spoke with my uncle on the night of that visit to Fexler's cellar. We sat in the observatory tower with an earthenware jug of wine that looked old enough to have been excavated from a pharaoh's tomb, and two silver goblets chased with rearing horses. A cool wind sighed through the arches and a bright dust of stars covered the black sky.

"Your mother used to come here when we were children," Robert said.

"She taught us the star names," I said. "Though William was young for it. He could only ever find the dog star and the Pole Star." I saw Will pointing, arm stretched out as if to touch each star, finger questing.

"Sirius and Polaris." Robert sipped his wine. "I can't remember much more. Rowen had the mind for it. In some twins the gifts are not shared out evenly. She got the brains and the looks. I got . . . a knack with horses."

"I got a knack with killing." The wine ran over my tongue, its flavour dark and layered.

"More than that, surely." Robert pointed out a constellation through the window arch. "What's that one?"

"Orion." I stood and stepped to look out. "Betelgeuse, Rigel, Bellatrix, Mintaka, Alnilam, Alnitak, Saiph." I named the giant's parts. "Did you feel her die? Are twins like that?"

"No." He stared into his goblet.

"Perhaps." He set the wine before him. "Perhaps it was like that for her. When I got trapped against Crab Cliff by the spring tide Rowen knew where to bring the guard with ropes. We were just children, not even ten years old, but she knew somehow. Another talent that didn't split even between us."

I watched him, half-resentful that he had so many years with her. She was my mother and yet everything about her escaped me, a little more each day, sand through fingers. I couldn't draw her face, tell you the colour of her eyes, or any concrete thing, just angles, glimpses, moments, the scent and softness of her. The security she gave—and the night when I learned it to be a lie.

"I went to the grouch chamber this morning," I said.

The Builders' view-ring hung on a thong about my neck, under the tunic Robert's dresser had given me. I considered drawing it out to show him, but didn't. Habits learned on the road die hard. I had laid hands on it and it was mine; I would keep my advantage hidden. The metal weighed heavy over my heart. Perhaps guilt feels like that.

"All that dust and spiders just to have an old ghost tell you to go to hell." My uncle sipped his wine. "I used to go down a few times a year. But the grouch never changes, and in the end I did."

"Do you know what the machinery does?" I asked.

"Who knows what any of that devilry is for? It pumps water—I understand that much—but they say everything the Builders made did ten different things. My father has left it alone for sixty years, his father left it untouched, and his father before him. It's from a world best forgotten. Gelleth should have taught you that."

My wine tasted sour. The light of that Builders' Sun reached even here into a summer's night on the Horse Coast. He was wrong in any case. The Builders weren't gone, we couldn't forget them. Their ghosts echoed in machinery buried in our vaults, their eyes watched us from above clouds, we fought our little wars in their shadow. Perhaps we even waged those wars at their instigation, something to keep us busy, to have us too focused on the now to think about the then.

"Gelleth taught me a lot of things. That we're children in a world we don't own or understand. That we stand alone and whether I fail or succeed depends on the strength of my will. On how far I will go. And that no one will come to help us in our hour of need." And that some things can't be fixed even if you bring the sun to earth and crumble mountains.

I thought of Gelleth, of the ghosts Chella drew from me. Since the night of storm and thorns I'd been haunted by what others had done to me. Gelleth taught me I could also be haunted by what I'd done to others.

The dead child watched me, broken against the tower battlements, blood and hair, a reminder of William and the milestone, his eyes two bright points of starlight. Another ghost, another misfortune seeking a home.

"You never came. I thought you would come for me." In my mind I had seen Uncle Robert ride to the Tall Castle a hundred times, with the cavalry of the House Morrow streaming behind him, to demand an accounting for his sister's death, to claim his nephew and take him home. "If Morrow had ridden to avenge Mother's death there would have been no Gelleth." No years on the road. No rivers of blood. No dead child watching.

Robert studied his goblet. "You fled Ancrath before news of Rowen's death even reached us here. Olidan was slow to send word, and the word was slow to find its way."

"But you didn't come." Old anger ignited within me and I went quickly to the stair in case it boiled out. I had climbed the steps a king, a man pressing fifteen years, and now a hurt and wrathful child shouted through me, through the years.

"Jorg—"

"No!" The hand I raised to keep him in his seat shook with the fierceness of what I held back and the air seemed to shimmer with heat. I hadn't known the memories would seize me like this.

I ran from the tower, scared that I might find the blood of a second uncle on my hands.

We calmed the hurt between us the next morning, but with pleasantries and empty words of the kind that are layered over rather than used to scour clean. I didn't let him speak of it again. Instead I spoke of Ibn Fayed and of Qalasadi. I had been to considerable lengths to get an accounting for Mother's death and for William's, and yet here were two men who had come within moments of taking Mother's whole family from me— Uncle, Grandmother, Grandfather. What's more, the mathmagician had, with a cool head, seen through my secret and chosen to take them all before they even knew I was amongst them, to kill with poison all my mother's kin and to see me die for it under horrible restitution. There seemed no malice in it, only calculation, but I couldn't leave such an equation unbalanced. It wouldn't be proper.

Robert tried to turn me from revenge. "Ibn Fayed will come to us in time and break his strength here. That will be the time for his accounting." But I had more immediate plans. Revenge can be the easy path to follow though I have often painted it as the hardest.

I left for the last time months later, suntanned, taller, provisioned, and laden with gifts. My saddlebags bulged with them, tempting enough for any bandits I might meet. I kept what mattered most about my person. The thorn-patterned box, the Builders' view-ring, and the weapon that killed Fexler Brews more than nine hundred years previously, a hard and heavy lump strapped beneath my arm. I've always seen "no" as a challenge rather than an answer.

Above those treasures though I left with a message, a mantra if you like. *Do not open that box. Open it and my work is undone. Open it and you're finished.*

Never open the box.

You won't see Brother Grumlow try to knife you, only the sorrow in his eyes as you fall.

45

Wedding day

The crash of a rock against the keep wall drowned me out. A shield fell off its hook and clattered to the floor; dust sifted down from above.

"The gate will not hold," I said again.

"Then we will fight them in the courtyard," Sir Hebbron said.

I chose not to mention that he had surrendered to me in the same courtyard four years earlier, with just Gog and Gorgoth at my back rather than the Prince of Arrow's fourteen thousand men.

If Coddin were present he would have spoken of surrender himself. Not out of fear but compassion. Perhaps he might say that when we fell back to the keep he would call out for terms, so that the common folk sheltering at the Haunt might be spared.

But Coddin wasn't present.

The dead child watched me from a shadowed corner, older and more sad with each passing year. At the corner of my vision he seemed to speak, but if I looked his way he said nothing, blue lips pressed tight. What man can hope for victory when his doom watches from every shadow? He was nothing but mine, this ghost, no trick of Chella's, no sending of the Dead King, just a sad and silent reminder of a crime even Luntar's little box couldn't keep entirely secret.

Another crash and I looked away from the corner, shaking off the moment.

The knights and captains watched me, the light from high windows gleaming on their armour. These men were built for war. I considered how many of them I would sacrifice to stop the Prince of Arrow. How many I would sacrifice just to wound Arrow, just to put a bigger hole in his army.

The answer turned out to be all of them.

"When they come we will fight them in the courtyard. And through the doors of the keep, and up each stair, and to this very room if need be." My cheek throbbed where I'd sliced it, aching at each word. I ran my fingers across the line of black and clotted blood.

"Sir Makin, Sir Kent, I want you leading the defence at the gate. I want everyone in this room out there."

They started for the door. Kent stopped.

"Sir Kent?" he said.

"Don't let it go to your head," I said. "And don't expect a ceremony."

Kent made a slow shake of his head. I could see his eyes shine. I hadn't thought it would mean much to him.

"Take the scorpions from the walls and set them in the yard. Put them front and centre. You'll get one shot and then they'll just be a barricade," I said. "And, Makin, get some armour on."

The Haunt had five scorpions, giant crossbows on wheels that could send a spear four hundred yards. Line enough men in front of them and you might get something like the chunks of meat on skewers served at table in Castle Morrow.

"Not you, Miana. Stay," I said as she made to follow the knights. "And Lord Jost!" I added. "I am depending on your help. Everything is in place."

Lord Jost set his conical helm on his head and flicked the chainmail veil out over the back of his neck. He looked from me to Miana. "Our alliance requires that the union be sealed, King Jorg."

I threw my hands up. "Christ bleeding! You saw us married. It's the middle of the day and we're fighting a pitched battle."

"Even so." No room for negotiation on that pinched face. He turned to follow Sir Makin. "Your grandfather knows the blood of both your parents runs in you, sire. I cannot act until the alliance is complete."

And that left me on my throne in an echoingly empty room with Miana in her wedding whites and two guards at the door watching their feet.

"Crap." I jumped up and took her hand. Leading her to the door. It felt like taking a child for a walk.

I brushed past the guards and hurried to the east tower staircase. Miana had to hitch her skirts and half run to keep up as I took the steps two and three at a time.

A hefty kick sent my chamber doors slamming open. "Out!" I shouted and several maids ran past me, clutching cloths and brushes. I think they had been hiding rather than cleaning.

"Lord Jost requires that I remove your virginity from you," I said to Miana. "Or the House Morrow can't support me." I hadn't meant to be quite so blunt but I felt angry, awkward even.

Miana bit her lip. She looked frightened but determined. She reached for the dress ties at her side.

"Stop," I said. I've never liked being pushed. Not in any direction. Miana looked well enough, and twelve isn't so young. I was killing at twelve. But some women bloom early and some late. She may have had the mind of a she-pirate but she looked like a child.

"You don't want me?" She faltered. Now she added hurt and angry to frightened and determined.

I've observed on the road that it's old men who like young girls. Brother Row and Brother Liar would chase the young ones. Younger than Miana. Brother Sim and I had always admired experience. The fuller form. So, no, I didn't want her. And being told to have something you don't want, rather like being told to eat spiced squid when what you want is beef and potatoes, will kill your appetite. Any kind of appetite.

"I don't want you right now," I said. It sounded more politic than calling her spiced squid.

I put my hand to the back of my left thigh. It was throbbing like a bastard after the run up the stairs. I'd opened a wound I didn't remember taking. I think perhaps I did it falling into the cave just before the avalanche. Six thousand men dead for a morning's work, and I come away with a self-inflicted wound in the arse. My fingers came back bloody.

Four quick steps took me to the bed. I threw back the covers. Miana flinched like I'd hit her. I wiped my hand over the clean linen; squeezed my leg wound again and repeated the process.

"There," I said. "Does that look like enough?"

Miana stared. "I never—"

"It will have to do. It looks like enough to me. Damned if I'm bleeding more than that."

I ripped the sheet from the bed and thrust it out through the window bars, noting two spent arrows on the floor that must have looped in from the ridge earlier in the day. I tied the sheet to one of the bars and let the wind flutter it out so all the world could see I'd made a woman of Miana.

"Speak a word of this to anyone and Lord Jost will insist we do it on the high table in the feast hall with everyone watching," I said.

She nodded.

"Where are you going?" she asked as I made for the door.

"Down."

"Fine," she said. She sat on the bed with a slight bounce. Her feet didn't touch the floor.

I set my hand to the doorhandle.

"But they'll sing songs about Quick Jorg for years to come. Fast with one sword, faster with the other," she said.

I took my hand off the doorhandle, turned, and walked back to the bed. Defeated.

"What would you like to talk about?" I asked, sitting beside her.

"I've met Orrin of Arrow and his brother Egan too," she said.

"So have I." Remembering how that swordfight ended still gave me a headache. "And where did you meet them?"

"They came to court in my father's castle in Wennith, on one of their grand tours of the empire. Orrin had his new wife with him." She watched me for a reaction. Someone had been talking to her.

"Katherine." I reacted anyway. It wasn't as if being married to a child would end my fascination with women, this one in particular. "And what did you think of the Prince?" I wanted to ask about Katherine, not Orrin and his brother, but I bit down on the urge, not to save Miana's feelings but in disgust at the weakness even mention of Katherine put in me.

"Orrin of Arrow struck me as the finest man I'd ever met," Miana said. Clearly she had no compunction to save my feelings either! "His brother Egan, too full of himself, I felt. Father said as much. The wrong mix of weak and dangerous. Orrin though, I thought he would make a fine emperor and unite the Hundred in peace. Didn't you ever consider just swearing to him when the time came?"

I met her gaze, shrewd dark eyes that had no place in a child's face. The truth was that I'd thought many times what I would do if Orrin of Arrow came back to the Haunt, regardless of whether he brought an army with him or not. I didn't doubt not one person would find me better suited to the emperor's throne than Orrin, and yet without my say-so thousands had been prepared to bleed to stop him. To get somewhere in life you have to walk over bodies, and I'd paved my way with corpses and more corpses. Gelleth burned for my ambition. It still does.

"I considered it."

Miana started, surprised when I spoke. She had thought I wasn't going to answer.

"There might have been a time I could have served as steward to Orrin's emperor, might have let my goatherds and his farmers go about their lives in peace. But things change, events carry us with them, even when you think you're the one leading, calling out commands. Brothers die. Choices are taken away from us."

"Katherine is very beautiful," Miana said, lowering her gaze for once.

Screams from outside, the hiss of arrows, a distant roar. "Have we been at this long enough?" I hadn't asked about Katherine and I had a battle to fight. I made to stand from the bed but Miana put her hand to my thigh, half-nervous, half-bold.

She reached for her dress again, and I thought that there might have been more determination than fear in her, but she wasn't unlacing. She pulled out a black velvet bag, dangling from its drawstring. Big enough to hold an eyeball.

"My dowry," she said.

"I hoped for something bigger." I smiled and took it.

"Isn't that my line?"

I laughed out loud at that. "Somebody poured an evil old woman into a little girl's body and sent it to me with the world's smallest dowry."

I tipped the bag's contents into my hand. A single ruby, the size of an eye, cut by an expert, and with a red star burning at its heart. "Nice," I said. It felt hot in my hand. It made my face burn where the fire had scarred me.

"It's a work of magic," Miana said. "A fire-mage has stored the heat of a thousand hearths in there. It can light torches, boil water, heat a bath, make light. It can even make a spot of heat sufficient to join two pieces of iron. I can show you—"

She reached for the gem but I closed my hand around it. "Now I know why fire-sworn like rubies," I said.

"Be gentle," Miana said. "It would be . . . unwise to break it."

In the moment that my fingers met around the gem a pulse of heat ran through me, like a shock, burning up my arm. For an instant I saw nothing but the inferno and it seemed I felt Gog's sharp hands on my sides, as if he sat behind me on Brath once more as he had for so many days in that spring long ago. I heard his high voice, almost, like Mother's music, trying to reach me from too far away. Something lit at my core, and the flow of fire reversed, raging unseen down my arm into the gem. A sharp splintering noise sounded from the ruby and I released it with a cry. Miana caught it: quick hands this one. I expected her to scream and drop the gem, but it lay cool in her palm. She placed it on the bed.

I stood. "It's a worthy dowry, Miana. You will be a good queen for the Highlands."

"And for you?" she said.

I walked to the window. The ridge where the Prince's archers had arrayed themselves was still in confusion. The trolls would have retreated to their cave defences, but no man wants to be lining up a shot whilst worrying that a black hand is going to twist his head off any second.

"And for you?" she repeated.

"That's hard to say." I took the copper box from my hip pouch. I had sat before this window the previous night and watched the box. A goblet, the box, a knife. Drink to forget, open to remember, or slice to end. "It's hard to answer you if I don't know who I am."

I held the box before my eyes. "Secrets. I filled you with secrets, and there's one last secret left, blacker than the rest." Some truths should perhaps be left unsaid. Some doors unopened. An angel once told me to let go of the ills I held too close, to let go of the flaws that shaped me. What remained of me might have been forgiven, might have followed her into heaven. I told her no.

The rockslide, avalanche, the trolls, none of them mattered. Arrow's army would still crush us. To fight so hard and not even come close to victory. That had a bitter taste.

I'd faced death before with odds as slim but never as a broken man, some piece of me locked away in a little box. Luntar in his burning desert had done what the angel couldn't. He'd taken me from me, and left a compromise to walk about in Jorg Ancrath's shoes.

Do not open that box.

The dead boy watched me from the corner of the room as if he had always stood there, waiting silent day after silent day for this moment, to meet my eyes. He stood pale but without wounds, unmarked save for handprints fish-belly white on his skin, like the scars Chella's dead things left on Gog's little brother long ago.

Open it and my work is undone.

I turned the box, letting the thorn pattern catch the light. Damn Luntar and damn the dead child too. When I faced Arrow's legions for the last time I would do it whole.

Open it and you're finished.

My hands didn't shake on the metal. For that I was grateful. I opened it wide, and with a quick motion twisted the lid off, flicking it out past the crimson flutter of the sheet.

Never open the box.

Friar Glen's chamber once again, lit by the heathen's glow. The need to kill him fills my hands immediately.

"There was blood and muck," Sageous says. He smiles.

"Saraem Wic's poisons will do that. But there was no child. I doubt there ever will be now. That old witch's poisons are not gentle. They scrape a womb bare."

I find the blade and I'm moving toward him. I try to run but it's like wading through deep snow.

"Silly boy. You think I'm really here?" He makes no move to escape.

I try to reach him, but I'm floundering.

"I'm not even in this city," he says.

Peace enfolds me. A honeyed dream of sunlight, fields of corn, children playing.

I wade through it, though each step feels like betrayal, like the murder of friends.

"You think I'm like you, Jorg." He shakes his head and shadows run. "Thirst for revenge has dragged you across kingdoms, and you think me driven by your crude imperatives. I'm not here to punish you. I don't hate you. I love all men equally. But you have to be broken. You should have died with your mother." Sageous's fingers stray to the lettering on his throat. "It was written."

And as I reach him he is gone.

I stumble into the corridor. Empty. I close the door, using my metal strip to drop the latch. Friar Glen will have to pray for help. I don't have time for him now and even through the layers of Sageous's lies and dreams I hold the suspicion that he is guilty of *something*.

Katherine didn't bring me to the Tall Castle, and certainly neither did Friar Glen. I didn't turn right where the road forked from the Ken Marshes just to visit my dog's grave. I came to see family. And now I need to be quick about it. Who knows what dreams Sageous might send this way?

Sim taught me about moving quietly. It's not so much about noise. The art is to be always on the move, heading somewhere with purpose. Any hesitation invites a challenge. On the flip side, if there can be no possible reason for your presence, then utter stillness can hide you, even in plain sight. The eye may see you but if you are stone, the mind may discount you.

"You there. Hold fast."

Eventually all tricks will fail and someone will challenge

you. Even at this point they will find it hard to believe you're an intruder. The minds of guards are especially dull, blunted by a career of tedium.

"Your pardon?" I cup a hand to my ear.

If you are challenged, pretend not to hear. Move closer, lean in. Be quick as you set your hand over their mouth, palm flat to lips so there's no edge to bite. Press them back against a wall if there is one. Stab in the heart. Don't miss. Hold their eyes with yours. It gives them something to think about besides making a noise, and nobody wants to die alone in any case. Let the wall help them to the ground. Leave them in shadow.

I leave the dead man behind me. A second dies at the end of the next hall.

"You!" This one rounds a corner with sword in hand. Almost knocking me down.

Sharp hands. That's what Grumlow said to me. Sharp hands. It's his tutorial in knife-work. A sword's all about the swinging, the thrust, the momentum, timing your move against that of your foe—a man with a knife is a man with sharp hands, nothing more. A knife-fight is a scary thing. That's why men jab and feint, posture, run. Grumlow says the only thing to do is go in fast, go in first, kill him quick.

I go in fast. His sword falls on the long rug and doesn't clatter.

Around the corner is the door I'm seeking. Locked. I take the key from the guard's belt. The door opens on oiled hinges. Silent. The hinges never squeak on a nursery door. Babies fight sleep hard enough as it is.

The wet-nurse is snoring in a bed by the window. A lantern glows on the sill, its wick trimmed low. The shadows of the cot bars reach for me.

I should kill the nurse, but it looks like Old Mary who chased after Will and me in the long ago. I should kill her, but I let her sleep. She would be ill-advised to wake.

I drag the guard into the room and close the door. For a long moment I pause, picturing my escape routes. There is a second exit from the room, leading to the nurses' quarters. As long as I have two ways to run I feel safe enough. There are passages that lead from the castle. Secret tunnels that lead to hidden doors in the High City. I couldn't open those doors from the outside, but I can leave by them.

I take a deep slow breath. White musk—his mother's scent. Another. I step to the cot and look upon my brother. Degran they call him. He's so small. I hadn't thought he would be so tiny. I reach in and lift him, sleeping. He barely fills my hands. He gives a gentle sigh.

The assassin's work is dirty work.

I vowed to take the empire throne, to take the hardest path, to win the Hundred War whatever the cost. And here in two hands I hold a key to the Gilden Gate. The son of the woman who replaced my mother. The son my father set me aside for. The son on whom he has settled my inheritance.

"I came to kill you, Degran." I whisper it.

He is soft and warm, his head big, his hands tiny, his hair so very fine. My brother.

The lamp glow catches the white scars along my arms as I hold him up. I feel the briar's hooks in me.

I should twist his neck and be gone. In the game of empire this is not a rare move, not even unusual. Fratricide. So common there is a word for it. Oft times carried out in person.

So why do my hands shake so?

Do it and be done.

You are weak, Jorg. Even my father tells me to do it. *Weak.*

I feel the hooks so deep, finding the bone as I struggled to save William. The blood runs down me. I can feel it. Streaming down my cheeks, blinding me. The thorns hold me.

DO IT.

No.

I will burn the world if it defies me, carry ruin to every corner, but I will not kill my brother. Not again. I came here to make that choice. To show that I could have chosen to. To weigh the decision in my hands.

And I set Degran back down among his covers. The nurse has put a woolly sheep there with stubby legs and button eyes. Sleep brother, sleep well.

He rolls limp from my hands, white where my fingers have touched him. I don't understand. Ice forms across me, a sick hollowness fills me until I am nothing but a brittle shell. I prod him.

"Wake up."

I shake the covers under him. Shake the cot. "WAKE UP."

He flops, limp, with the white prints of my hands on his soft flesh like accusations.

"Wake up!" I scream it but not even the nurse wakes.

Sageous is there, in the corner of the room, all aglow. "Necromancy, Jorg. How many edges does that sword have?"

"I didn't kill him. He was mine to kill and I didn't."

"Yes, you did." Sageous's voice is calm where mine is shrill.

"I didn't want this!" I shout.

"The necromancy listens to your heart, Jorg. It listens to what you can't say. Does what the secret core of you wants and needs. It isn't fooled by posturing. You have the death of small things in your fingers. A small thing died."

"Take it back." I'm begging. "Bring him back."

"Me?" Sageous asks. "I'm not even here, Jorg. I can't do much more than keep that fat slattern asleep. Besides, I wanted you to do it. Why do you think I brought you here in the first place?"

"Brought me?" I can't look at him, or Degran. Or even the shadows, in case Mother and William are watching me from the corner.

"With dreams of Katherine, to bring you to the castle, and dreams of William to lure you inside. Really, Jorg, I thought a clever child like you would have understood how I work by now. It's not the killing dreams that are my best weapons—the most subtle tools have the most profound effect. A nudge here, a nudge there."

"No." As if shaking my head will make it a lie.

"I bleed for you, Jorg," he says, all compassion and mild eyes. "I love you, but you have to be broken, it's the only way. You should have died, and now only breaking you will restore equilibrium, only that will allow matters to take their course as they should."

"Matters?"

"The Prince of Arrow will unite us. The empire will prosper. Thousands upon thousands that would have died will live. Science will return to us in the peace. And I will guide the emperor's hand so that all might be well. Isn't that worth more than you, Jorg? Isn't that worth the life of a single baby?"

I scream and hurl myself at him, as if anger might wash away grief, but what I've done has put a crack right through me and into that crack Sageous pours madness, a torrent of it. I stagger blind and howling.

I see nothing more. Nothing until this moment finds me staring into an empty and lidless box.

So much madness and regret poured into me that it left no room for memory, nothing for the box. What instincts, luck, or guidance led me from the castle without discovery, or how many more corpses I left in my wake, I can't say.

"Jorg?"

I turned and looked at Miana. My cheeks wet with tears. Sageous's magics crawled under my skin, but it wasn't his spells that emptied me. *I killed my brother.*

His ghost lay on the bed, stretched behind Miana. Not the soft babe, but the little boy of four he would have been. For the first time ever he smiled at me, as if we were friends, as if he were pleased to see me. He faded as I watched and I knew he wouldn't return, wouldn't grow, wouldn't heal.

Someone hammered on the door. "Sire, the gate has given!"

I backed against the wall and slid to the floor. "I killed him."

"Jorg?" Miana looked concerned. "The enemy are within our gates."

"I killed my brother, Miana," I said. "Let them come."

March 28th, Year 99 Interregnum
Tall Castle. Chapel.

Degran is dead. My sister's boy is dead. I can't write of it.

March 29th, Year 99 Interregnum

Jorg did this. He left a trail of corpses to and from Degran's door.

    I will see him die for it.

    There is such anger in me. I cannot unlock my teeth. If Friar Glen were not dead. If Sageous were not absent. Neither of them would live to see the morning.

March 31st, Year 99 Interregnum

We put him in the ground today. In the tomb where Olidan's family lie. A small white marble casket for him. Little Degran. It looks too small for any child to fit in. It makes me cry to think of him in there, alone. Maery Coddin sang the Last Song for him, my nephew. She has a high, pure voice that echoed in the tomb and it made me cry. My sister's ladies placed white flowers on the tomb, Celadine lilies, one each, weeping.

    Father Eldar had to come up from Our Lady in Crath City to say the words, for we have no holy men in the castle. Jorg has stolen or killed them all. And when Father Eldar was done, when he'd read the passages, spoken of the Valley of Death and Fearing No Evil, we all walked away. Sareth didn't walk. Sir Reilly had to carry her, screaming. I understood. If it were my baby, I couldn't leave them. Dear God, I can just poison them from my belly, let them fall in blood and slime, but if I had held my child, seen his eyes, touched his lips ... it would take more than Sir Reilly to drag me from him.

April 2nd, Year 99 Interregnum

I've gone back through this journal and followed the track of my dreams through its pages. At least the ones I wrote about, but I seem to have written about a lot of them, as if they were troubling me. I've no memory of them. Maybe they left me while I scratched them down.

I don't want to turn the page back either. It feels as if another's hand is on mine, holding it down. But I won't be kept back.

I can see now—how the heathen played me, steered me like a horse with light flicks of a whip, just a turn here and there to set the path across a whole map. I don't believe this magic is beyond me. I can't accept that a thing like Sageous should be allowed such power and that I should not.

I can't rule a kingdom like Jorg or Orrin. No soldiers will follow my orders and fight and die on foreign soils at my say-so. These things are forbidden me. Because of my sex. Because I can't grow a beard. Because my arm is not so strong. But generals do not need a strong arm. Kings don't need a beard.

I may never rule or command, but I can build a kingdom in my mind. And armies. And if I study what the heathen did to me. If I take it apart piece by piece. I can make my own weapons.

April 8th, Year 99 Interregnum

Orrin of Arrow called upon my brother-in-law today. I said that I would marry him. Though first he had to promise to take me far from this castle, from this place that stinks of the murderer Jorg Ancrath, and never to bring me back.

Orrin says he will be emperor and I believe him. Jorg of Ancrath will try to stop him, and on that day I'll see him pay for his crime. Until that time I will work on unpicking the heathen's methods and learning them for myself. It's fear that keeps such power from the common man, nothing more. I don't believe that creature Sageous capable of something I'm not, I won't believe it. Fear keeps us weak, fear of what we don't know, and fear of what we do know. We know what the church will do to witches. The Pope in Roma and all her priests can go hang though. I've seen what happens to holy men in such times. Here's a power a woman can gather into her hands as well as any man, and the time will come when Jorg will find out how it feels to shatter with his dreams.

June 1st, Year 99 Interregnum
Arrow. Castle Yotrin.

We are married. I am happy.

July 23rd, Year 99 Interregnum
Arrow. New Forest.

We've ridden out from Castle Yotrin to the New Forest. They call it that because some great-great-grandsire of Orrin's had it planted just after pushing the Brettans back into the sea. It's my first real chance to see Arrow though mostly we're going to be seeing trees. Egan practically demanded Orrin go hunting with him and Orrin wanted me to come. I don't think Egan did. Egan said Orrin had promised a private hunt, no courtiers, no fuss. Orrin said the richer he got the fewer luxuries like that he could afford but promised to keep the hunting party small.

Arrow is a lovely country. It might lack Scorron's mountains and grandeur but the woodland is gorgeous, oak and elm, beech and birch, where Scorron has pines, pines, and more pine. And the woods are so light and airy with room to ride between the trees, not the dense dark valley-forests of home.

We've made camp in a clearing, the servants are setting up pavilions and cooking fires. Orrin invited Lord

Jackart and Sir Talbar along, and Lady Jackart too, and her daughter Jesseth. I think Lady Jackart is supposed to keep me happy while the men kill things in the woods. She's kind but rather dull and she seems to think she needs to shout in order for me to understand her accent. I have no problem hearing her, I only wish she would just pause for breath and let one word finish before starting the next. Little Jesseth is a darling girl, seven years, always sprinting into the undergrowth and having to be retrieved by Gennin, the Jackarts' man.

I'd like girls, two of them, blonde like Orrin.

Orrin came back with Egan riding double behind him, Jackart and Talbar flanking. I stood to ask after the deer but thought better of it, all of them grim-faced save Egan who looked ready for murder. Little Jesseth didn't know any better though and ran in shouting to her father, did he bring her a doe or a buck? Lord Jackart practically fell out his saddle and scooped her up before Egan jumped down. The way Egan stared after the man I thought Jackart might burst into flame. And then I saw the blood, dark and sticky on Egan's hands, like black gloves, and drying splatters up his forearms.

"I'll cut some wood." That's all Egan said and he stalked off shouting for an axe.

Lord Jackart carried his daughter to their pavilion, Lady Jackart hurrying on behind. Dull she might be but sharp enough to know when to lie low.

"Egan ran Xanthos into a stand of hook-briar," Orrin told me. He spread his hands. "I didn't see it either."

"But you told him to go slow—said to watch for it." Sir Talbar rubbed at his whiskers and shook his head.

"It's not in Egan to give up the chase, Talbar. That stag must have been an eighteen pointer." Orrin has a way of showing a man's weakness as strength. Perhaps it's the goodness in him. In any case it makes men follow him, love him. He may work the same magic on me too—I don't know.

"Poor Xanthos." The stallion had been a marvellous beast, named for Achilles' horse, black like rock-oil with muscle rippling under a slick hide. I had been wanting to

ride him myself but Egan is so hard to talk to, he manages to make me feel as though I've angered him with each word. "We don't have so many horses in Scorron but I've never heard of one killed by a briar." Then I understood, or thought I did. "Did he break his leg? Poor Xanthos."

Orrin shook his head, Sir Talbar spat.

"Hook briar is foul stuff," Orrin said. "It was a miracle he didn't break a leg, but he got torn up along his flanks."

"The horsemaster . . . the chirurgeon could have sewn him up?" I couldn't see that such wounds would be fatal.

Orrin shook his head again. "I've seen it before, and the surgeon Mastricoles speaks of it in his masterwork, even the footnotes of Hentis's Franco Botany say so. The thorns of the hook briar are barbed, what they leave in the wound sours, the blood is poisoned, the animal dies. Even men can die. Sir Talbar's uncle caught two thorns in the palm of his hand. The wound was cut and cleaned and packed with salve and still it went black with rot. He lost the hand, then the arm, then the rest of his days."

I understood the blood. "At least Egan offered a quick ending."

Orrin bowed his head. "Xanthos didn't linger."

Sir Talbar glanced at Orrin then looked away and said no more.

I walked with little Jesseth later on, letting her babble as we followed the edge of the glade. Axe blows rang out from somewhere among the trees. Egan had split a mountain of logs and the cooks already had ten times the firewood they needed. Now he was felling trees. He came out from a stand of elm an hour later close by where Jesseth and I were playing board-checks. The blood had gone from his arms and sweat ran down a body as muscled and lithe as Xanthos's. He barely nodded our way and strode past, axe on his shoulder.

"I don't like him," Jesseth whispered.

"Why not?" I asked, bending in with a conspiratorial smile.

"He killed his horse." Jesseth nodded as if to prove it no lie.

"But that was a kindness."

"Mother says he cut its head off with his sword because the deer got away."

July 25th, Year 99 Interregnum
Yotrin Castle. Library.

I've found certain scrolls in Orrin's library that speak of dreams in terms of tides and currents. There's a woman in the village of Hannam who tells fortunes for her living, but she has more to say than that, to the right person. In a small room at the top of her house she has spoken to me of sailing on the seas of dream.

August 18th, Year 99 Interregnum
Yotrin Castle. Royal bedchamber.

Orrin has left to command his armies in the west. I will miss him. I will make good use of the rest though. It seems we've spent a month in the bedchamber. If it takes more than that to make a baby then I'll be worn out by winter and an old lady by spring.

July 18th, Year 100 Interregnum
Castle Yotrin. Library.

Orrin is a good man, probably a great man. All the oracles say he will be emperor and wear the all-crown. But even great men need to be disobeyed now and again.

When Orrin is here he spends at least half of his days in this library. The knights and captains who hunt him down walk into the reading hall furtively, out of place, eyeing the walls with suspicion as if the knowledge might just leak out of all those books and infect them. They find us, Orrin in one corner, me in another, and he'll look at them over the top of one of those great and worthy leather-bound tomes of his. "General So-and-so," he'll say. He lets the kingdoms he's taken keep a general each. He says it's important to let the people have their pride and their heroes. "General So-and-so," he'll say. And General So-and-so will shuffle from foot to foot, awkward among so many written words, and not expecting the future emperor to look so scholarly, as if he should be wearing reading lenses.

Orrin reads the great books. The classics from before the Builders' time, stretching back to the Greeks and Homer. It's not that he chooses the biggest and most impressive books for show, but that's what he always ends up with. He likes to read philosophy, military history, the lives of great men, and natural history. He's always show-ing me plates of strange animals. At least when he's here he is. Creatures that you'd think the author just made up on a hot afternoon. But he says the pictures were captured not painted, as if an image were frozen in a mirror, and these things are real. Some of them he's seen. He shows me a plate of a whale and puts his fingernail beside its mouth to give the size of a horse next to it. He says he saw the back of one from a ship off the coast of Afrique. Says it rolled through the water, an endless grey sheen of whaleback, broad enough for a carriage and longer than our dining hall.

I read the small forgotten books. The ones found behind the rows on the shelves. In locked chests. In pieces to be assembled. They look old. Some are—a hundred years, three hundred, maybe five, but Orrin's are more ancient. Mine though, they look older, as if what is written in them takes its toll, even on parchment and leather. Mine were set down after the Burning, after the Builders ignited their many suns.

The ancient books tell a clear story. Euclid gives us shape and form. Mathematics and science progress in an ordered fashion. Reason prevails. The newer stories are confusion. Conflicting ideas and ideologies. New mythologies, new magics offered with serious intent but in a hundred variants, each wrapped in its own superstition and nonsense, but with a core of truth. The world changed. Somewhere along the line of years it changed and what was not possible became possible. Unreason shaded into truth. To assemble it all into some pure architecture, some new science that delivers control in this present chaos, would be a work of lifetimes. But I am making a start. I find it more to my liking than sewing.

Orrin says I should leave it alone. That such knowledge corrupts and if he must make use of it then it will be through others, as Olidan used Sageous, as Renar used Corion. I tell him he mistakes the puppet and the puppeteer. He smiles and says maybe, but if the time comes he will be pulling the strings, not pulled by them. Orrin tells me he is sure I could draw from the same well as

Sageous, but such waters would make me bitter and he likes me sweet.

I love Orrin, I know I do. But sometimes it's easier to love someone who has flaws you can forgive in return for their forgiving yours.

In the red ruin of battle Brother Kent oft looks to have stepped from hell. Though in another life he would have tilled his fields and died abed, mourned by grandchildren, in combat Red Kent possesses a clarity that terrifies and lays waste. In all else he is a man confused by his own contradictions—a killer's instincts married to a farmer's soul. Not tall, not broad, but packed solid and quick, wide cheekbones, dark eyes flat with murder, bitten lips, scarred hands, thick-fingered, loyalty and the need to be loyal written through him.

46

Wedding day

"Jorg! The Prince's men are through the gates!"

Miana didn't have to shout it at me. I could hear them through the windows, the deep resonances of the scorpions as they fired their spears, the screams, the crash of swords, the strum of bowstrings from the men on my walls, firing down into their own castle now. And the drums! The furious pounding of Uncle Renar's battle-drums. A beat so loud and fierce that it picks up even the meekest of men and makes them part of the beast. They drum courage into you.

Uncle should have played them that day I came a-calling.

None of it mattered. Sageous's poison dreams bubbled through me, but all their work only played variations around a nightmare of my own making. I killed my brother. After years defined only by the quest for revenge—years consumed by the need to reach William's murderer—I took the life of my brother, a baby who could barely fill my hands.

"Jorg!"

I ignored her. I held my hands before my face, remembered the feel of him, remembered the realization that he was dead. Degran. My brother.

Tutor Lundist showed me a drawing once. An old woman's

face. Look again, he said, it's a young girl. And it was. Just a trick of the mind. Nothing had changed, not one line of the drawing, and yet everything was different. The box gave me Degran back and he had spoken to me across the years. Look again, he had said to me. Look at your life—now look again. And suddenly nothing mattered.

She slapped me, the little bitch slapped me, and for a second that mattered. She'd put her whole body into it. But the anger died quicker than it came.

Then a siege rock hit the window to our right. Fragments of stone flew across the room, smashing on the far wall. Dust rose around us.

"I'm not going to die here," Miana said.

She had her hand in my hair. She turned my head to the window and its torn bars. Part of the wall below the window had fallen away and we could see the courtyard, where the peasants had gathered to cheer us that morning. A wedge of Arrow's men, marked by their scarlet cloaks, had driven in through the ruins of the portcullis that Gorgoth had once held open for me. My soldiers, half of them goatherds with the swords I'd given them, hemmed the enemy in. I saw the blue of Lord Jost's small contingent and the gleam of their plate armour. The odds were against the intruders, but the weight of numbers behind drove them forward as they died. The Prince of Arrow poured his men into the killing field, my archers and troops reducing them but not stopping them. And under it all, pulsing through it, the throb of the battle drums.

"Do something!" Miana shouted.

"It doesn't matter," I said. "Everyone dies." My past, my ghosts, danced around me, the dead, the betrayed. I considered diving through the shattered wall into the foe over the heads of my men. Could I make such a leap? With a run maybe. A short run, and a long drop into eternity.

She slapped me again. "Give me the ruby."

I fished out the bag and put it in her hand. "You deserved a better husband."

Miana gave me a look of contempt. "I deserved a stronger one. There's no victory without sacrifice. My mother taught me that. You have to raise the stakes and raise them again."

"She was a warrior?" I shook my head hard. Dreams showered from me. The dead held me with cold hands, tearing my insides.

"A card player," Miana said.

Miana went to the fireplace and picked up one of the two fire screens, an exotic tapestry in an ebony frame. She beat it into splinters against the wall and repeated the process with the second one. Outside the wedge of scarlet developed into a semi-circle around the broken gates. Beyond the walls a blood-red sea would be surging forward.

Miana picked the two heavy stone bases from the wreckage of the fire screens and placed the ruby between them. She tried to tear strips from the tapestries, and finding them too resistant she tore lengths from the hem of her wedding dress.

Despite the emptiness pulsing inside me, a tickle of curiosity scratched at the back of my mind.

A stray arrow struck up through the window on the left and buried itself in the ceiling.

Miana bound both the stone bases together, good and tight, with the ruby between them.

"Is Lord Jost still fighting?" she asked.

I crawled to the broken wall, blinking to clear my sight. "I can see knights from the House Morrow. I think one of them is Jost."

Miana bit her lip. "Sometimes you can only win if you're prepared to sacrifice everything," she said.

I started to wonder if I didn't get my darkest streak from my mother's side of the family.

Her eyes grew bright. Tears for the dead.

"Miana, what—"

She ran at the gap, feet falling to the drumbeat, and hurled the stone bases out. I wouldn't have thought she could throw so hard or so far. The package sailed over the heads of the men, fighting, dying, pressing in the crush to be at each other. It flew over the Highlanders, over Jost, over Arrow's red-cloaked foot-soldiers, bounced once in a clear spot to the left of the gates, and smacked against the outer wall.

I remember only light and heat. The boom was heard as far away as Gutting, but I heard nothing. A hot fist knocked the air from me. I saw Miana thrown back toward the fireplace. The burn on my face ignited as if it were on fire again and I howled. A moment before nothing had mattered, but we are made of flesh before we are made of dreams, and flesh cares about pain.

When I rolled to my hands and knees I could smell my own charred skin, as if the burn really had reignited. I crawled to the hole and looked out. For long moments I saw only smoke. There was no sound, none at all. Then the mountain wind hauled the smoke off-stage and the ruination lay before me. The front walls of the Haunt were gone. All the tanneries, taverns, abattoirs, animal pens before them . . . gone. Just smoking rubble. And out beyond that, the Prince's huge army, tattered, wide avenues of destruction carved through it by chunks of masonry the size of wagons tumbling down the slope.

The damage appeared to have been wrought by the walls exploding. Although most of the force seemed to have been directed away from us, the heat and fire had been confined within the courtyard. Rank upon rank of blackened corpses radiated from the spot where the ruby broke and released, in one moment, the flame magics hoarded inside it over many years. The bodies closest to the release looked crisp. Those farther back still burned. The dead where Lord Jost and his men had fought looked red and melted. Farther back still and men rolled in horrific agony. Back farther their lungs hadn't been seared and they could scream. And back farther still, closer to the base of the keep, survivors struggled up from under the dead who had shielded them.

The timbers supporting the walkways for the archers burned. The shutters on the windows facing the courtyard burned. The remnants of my scorpions burned. Something lodged in the bone of my cheek burned with its own heat and in every flame possibilities danced. I could see them. As if the fire were a window into hot new worlds.

I guessed I had lost three hundred of my remaining eight hundred men. In two heartbeats a twelve-year-old girl had destroyed the prime fighting men of Renar.

I looked out across the slopes. The Prince of Arrow had lost five thousand, maybe seven thousand. In two heartbeats the Queen of the Highlands had cut her foe in half.

I shouted down into the courtyard. I could barely hear

myself over the ringing in my ears. I tried again. "Into the keep! Into the keep."

My face hurt, my lungs hurt, everything hurt, the air was full of smoke and the screams of the dying, and suddenly I wanted to win again. Very much.

I went over to the fireplace and picked Miana out of the rubble. Dust fell from her hair as I hauled her onto my shoulder, but she coughed, and that was good enough.

47

Wedding day

I laid Miana on my bed and left her there. She had proved tougher than expected so far and it looked as if she'd just been knocked out. Habit put the lidless box back in my hip pocket.

Although I couldn't see the fires in the courtyard, I could feel them. When I woke the Builders' Sun beneath Mount Honas its power had ignited Gog's talent. It seemed that releasing the ruby's fire-magic in one blast had woken in me what echoes of Gog and his skills had lodged in my flesh when he died beneath Halradra. I pushed back against the feeling. I remembered Ferrakind. I would not become such a thing.

The Haunt's keep has four towers, my bedchamber being at the top of the eastmost one. I went to the roof. A young guardsman sat hunched on the top steps just below the trapdoor. A new recruit by the look of him, his chainmail shirt too big for his slight frame.

"Waiting here in case giant birds land on my roof and try to force an entry?" I asked.

"Your Majesty!" He leapt to his feet. If he weren't so short he'd have brained himself on the trapdoor. He looked terrified.

"You can escort me up," I said. He would have plenty of

time to die on my behalf later on. No point chasing him down the stairs myself. "Rodrick, is it?" I had no idea what the coward's name was but "Rodrick" was popular in the Highlands.

"Yes, Your Majesty." A relieved grin spread over his face.

He unbolted the door and heaved it open. I let him walk out first. Nobody shot him, so I followed.

From the tower battlements I could see the Prince's army on the slopes, in even more disarray than my own troops. It would be an hour and more before his captains imposed order, the units reformed and merged, before the dead were heaped, the injured carted to the rear. A haze of smoke hung across the remains of the shantytown that had stood before the Haunt's walls. The brisk wind could do little to shift it.

Despite the fires in the courtyard below, it felt cold on the tower. The wind had teeth up there and carried the edged threat of winter. I crept to the east wall and looked out toward the ridge where the Prince had the bulk of his archers positioned. They seemed to be in some confusion. Trolls had emerged from several still-undiscovered exits and were busy parting the lightly-armoured bowmen from their heads again.

I ducked down. I'd had my head up for two heartbeats. It took an arrow three beats to fly from the ridge to the keep. And sure enough, several shafts hissed overhead. They all missed Rodrick, who hadn't had the wit to get behind cover. I knocked him flat. "Stay there."

I took the Builders' view-ring from inside my breastplate and held it to one eye. Making the image zoom in to one area still made me feel as if I were falling, plunging from unimaginable heights. I knew it must be a matter of moving lenses, as Lundist had shown me in my father's observatory, but it felt as if I rode the back of an angel falling from heaven.

"Jorg! Jorg!" Makin's voice from down below. He sounded worried.

"We're up here," I called.

A moment later Makin's head poked into view. At least I assumed it was him in the helmet.

"You didn't burn up then," I said.

"Damn near! I couldn't find Kent. I think he's gone."

"Watch this." I waved him over to my side. "It should be good. But don't stick your head up too high."

I took Makin's shield from him and held it over my head for extra cover. We peered over the battlements. The battlefield had fallen almost silent after the explosion, still with the screaming of course, but without the crash of weapons, the war-cries, the twangs and thuds of siege machinery. The drums were voiceless too—Uncle's six great battle-drums, brass and ebony, wider than barrels, ox-skinned, now burned-out and smouldering among the corpses in the yard. Beneath it all though I could hear a new drumming, a faint thunder. Makin cocked his head. He could hear it too. It sounded almost like another avalanche.

"That's cavalry! Arrow's brung up his cavalry, Jorg." Makin started to crawl for the wall overlooking the Haunt's ruined front.

I pulled him back. "There's only one place for miles a horse can charge, Sir Makin."

And they came, in a rushing stream of blue and violet cloaks, silver mail, thundering past Marten's hidden troops, the foremost with their lances lowered for the kill.

"What?" Makin almost stood up.

"I once told Sim about Hannibal taking elephants across the Aups. Well, my uncle has brought heavy horses across the Matteracks in the jaws of winter."

"How?"

I made quick circles with my hand, as if trying to spin the cogs of Makin's mind a little faster.

"The Blue Moon Pass!" Makin grinned, showing more teeth than a man should have.

"Even so," I said. "I emptied it out for him. And Lord Jost must have signalled that the marriage was sealed . . . and here they are."

The cavalry of the House Morrow sliced through the ranks of foot-soldiers sent up to hunt out Gorgoth's trolls. It helped that most of Arrow's troops had their backs to the Runyard, since they'd found rather more trolls than they had wanted to. In fact the trolls were making an impressive hole in Arrow's ranks all by themselves. They moved like wild dogs on the attack, hurling themselves into knots of men and leaving scattered limbs in their wake. Whoever bred them for war had surpassed themselves.

Riding onto the archers' ridge required that the cavalry slow, but they could traverse the whole length five and eight abreast at the canter, killing as they went. The archers were no match for armoured knights. Most broke and ran, tumbling back down the mountainside.

There were perhaps five hundred of my grandfather's cavalry. Gorgoth withdrew his trolls as agreed and left the men to fight each other. I couldn't tell what losses the trolls had suffered but they were not insignificant and I knew that Gorgoth would not permit them to rejoin the battle. He had wanted a homeland for his new-found subjects and they had paid the price I asked of them.

"Incredible!" Makin shouted. He kept shaking his head.

"It's not enough," I said.

The charge left bloody slaughter trampled into the grit, hundreds upon hundreds died before the momentum broke. And even without the cohesion of the charge, the knights wrought havoc, striking down with axe and sword at the heads of running bowmen. But you can't run five hundred men into four thousand and not expect to pay. The knights were wheeling now, finding their way down the back slope of the ridge and turning toward the Runyard again. Perhaps half of them survived.

"They were magnificent!" Makin surged to his feet. "Weren't you looking?"

"They were magnificent. And when they join us, we will have a little over seven hundred men in this broken castle. Depending on how many of the troops routed in that charge can be rallied and reformed, the Prince of Arrow will have somewhere between five and seven thousand men."

I went to look out over the Prince's main army. On the battlefield losses of the sort I'd inflicted would have set any army running long ago. But I'd been cutting away whole chunks of Arrow's force, one at a time, separating them, drawing them away, destroying them. I had whittled at his numbers, carved them to the bone, but I hadn't thinned his ranks in the way that erodes an army's morale. Not until Miana's explosion had the main bulk of Arrow's troops even felt the battle.

Now the explosion; that could have set them running, but it didn't, and that just told me the Prince's men were every bit as loyal and well trained as reported.

A glance toward the Runyard told me the Horse Coast knights were beginning to enter the sally port. A small number of men remained to lead the horses back up into the mountain passes. Marten and his troops would bring up the rear.

"Let's go meet them," I said. "By the way, this is Guardsman Rodrick. Guardsman Rodrick, Lord Makin of Ken."

"Lord now, is it?" Makin grinned. "And what would I be wanting with the Ken Marshes, not that they're yours to give?"

I led the way down. "Well, if we don't win, it won't matter that your elevation is a hollow gesture. And if we do win—well the Prince of Arrow has taken a lot of land recently so I'll have plenty to hand out."

"And I get the squishy bit?" Makin said behind me.

"Come meet my uncle," I said. "He's got lots of good recipes for frog."

I looked into my chamber as we passed. Miana sat on my bed, rubbing her head slowly with both hands as if she were afraid it might fall off.

"Lord Robert has arrived," I said. "Stay here. Guardsman Rodrick will protect you. He's one of my best." I turned to the guard. "Keep her here, Rodrick. Unless she comes up with a plan to destroy the remainder of the enemy. In which case you're to let her do it."

Makin and I carried on down. I caught hold of one of my knights, nursing a wounded shoulder and burned whiskers. "You! Hekom, is it? Go to the cellar beneath the armoury. The one with the fecking big barrels. You'll find our southern allies coming out of one of them. Send Lord Robert, and any captains he wants to bring, up to the throne-room."

Hekom—if it was Hekom—looked confused, but nodded and absented himself, so we headed for the throne-room. I caught hold of another man as we pushed past the wounded in the corridors. "Have my armour brought up to the throne-room. The good stuff. Quick about it."

Uncle Robert arrived with two of his captains as three page-boys set about strapping me into my armour. Several of my own captains preceded him, Watch-master Hobbs among them.

"There are rather more of the enemy than I was led to believe, Nephew!" Uncle Robert didn't wait on formality. In fact he only just waited to get through the doors.

"There are many thousands fewer than there were this morning," I said.

"And your castle appears to be broken," Uncle Robert said.

"You can blame your god-daughter for that. But it was a dowry well spent," I said.

"Good Lord!" Robert took off his helm. "The ruby did that?" He shook his head. "They told us to be careful with it. I didn't realize the danger though!"

"Rubies are hard to break," I said. "It's not the sort of thing that you're likely to do by accident."

He pursed his lips at that. "So, Nephew, I've come for you. Where do we stand?"

I still liked him. It had been four years since I saw him last but it felt like little more than a lull in the conversation. And he had come for me, just as a skinny boy had dreamed before he ran betrayed from the Tall Castle. Uncle Robert had come, with the cavalry behind him. That drained some poison from the wound.

"We stand about knee-deep, Uncle," I said.

"It looked more like chest-deep from where we entered those caves." He sagged slightly, the exertions of the fight catching up with him. Smears of blood crossed the brightness of his breastplate, a deep dent caught the light from odd angles, and the left side of his face had started to darken into a single impressive bruise.

I shrugged. "Either way we've got shitty boots and the situation stinks. He has thousands to our hundreds. He can besiege us in this keep from the ruins of my own walls. There is no question that he could wear us down within months, possibly weeks."

"If the situation is lost. If it were always lost. Why did I spend the lives of two hundred knights out there? Why did we even beat a path through the mountains in the first place?" His brows drew close, furrowing his forehead, a dangerous light in his eyes. I knew the look.

"Because he doesn't want to wait months, or even weeks," I said.

Makin stepped up from behind the throne. "The Prince has been attacking as if he intends to crush us in a day."

"He needs to now," I said. "He wanted a quick victory

before, but now he needs one. He didn't want to wait the winter out here. He had a huge army to feed, a timetable to keep to, other powers to consider, newly acquired lands to police. Being a prisoner of the Highland winter was never his plan. But now, he needs to win today, tomorrow at the latest. In a day or two his army will start to understand the scale of their losses, his captains will start to mutter, his troops will leak away, and the stories they tell elsewhere will lend Arrow's enemies courage. If he takes us today, then the stories will run a different course. The talk will be of how he crushed Jorg of Ancrath who levelled Gelleth, who humbled Count Renar. Yes, the losses were high—but he did it in a day! In a day!"

"And how does all this help us?" Uncle Robert asked.

"I don't think he can take us in a day. And neither does he," I said.

"Even so, we will still all die, no? It might ruin the Prince's plans, but that's cold comfort from where I'm standing." Uncle Robert glanced at his captains, tall men burned dark by the southern sun. They said nothing.

"It helps because it will make him accept my offer," I said.

"Offer? You told Coddin no terms!" Makin stepped off the dais to take a good look at me, as if I might not be Jorg at all.

"No terms!" The echo came from Miana, helped in by young Rodrick. She looked pale but otherwise unhurt.

"I'm not offering terms," I said. "I'm offering him a duel."

August 27th, Year 101 Interregnum
Arrow. Greenite Palace. Red Room.

Orrin is campaigning again. The bigger his domain grows, the less I see of him. He took Conaught in the spring with just three thousand men. Now he's marching an army toward Normardy with nine thousand. He even talks of taking the lands of Orlanth into his protection, though there are other realms to consider first.

He never speaks with desire, as if he wants those places for himself, to have them bow and scrape before his throne, or to fill his war-chests. He talks of what he can do for the peoples of those lands, of what they will gain, of how their freedoms will increase, their prosperity, their prospects. It would sound false from any other man. But Orrin believes it, and he can do it. In Conaught they already worship him as one of their old heroes reborn.

To me he speaks with desire. Since the day we were married he has made me feel treasured. Happy. And I know I make him happy too. Though there is always that touch of disappointment, expertly hidden. If I had not spent so very many days delving into the stuff of men's dreams I wouldn't see it. But I do see it and I'm cut by the knife I have forged and sharpened. Orrin wants a child. I do too. But it has been two years.

Sareth says in her letters that sometimes it can take two years, sometimes four. She herself has born no child in the years since Degran, but for little Merrith who sickened and died so quickly. I think grief made Sareth barren. Jilli and Keriam also say it can take two years, just as Sareth said. They say we're young—it will come soon. For the first year they believed it.

March 28th, Year 102 Interregnum
Arrow. Greenite Palace. West Gardens.

Egan is back in the palace. I say "back" but he has never been here before. Orrin had the palace built after the Duchy of Belpan surrendered to him, and Egan so rarely returns from campaigns that this is the first time he has laid eyes upon it.

He's been wounded again. In the side this time, falling off a horse onto something sharp he says. Egan always seems to mend quickly though, as if he just won't tolerate any kind of restraint, even if it's his own body that tries to impose it.

I've been reading Roland of Thurtan's On the Dreamlands and Below. *I like to read it on the balcony that overlooks the herb gardens. The formal gardens are . . . well, too formal, and too large. I like to look over the herb gardens with their little pools, the sundial and the moondial that I had put there, and to breathe in the scents. Also, it's not a book for reading indoors or in the dark. It only takes a paragraph or two of Roland of Thurtan before the walls seem to be closing in on you.*

Egan practises with his sword in the grand square every day, in front of the statue of his father. There's a sorcery in the way he moves. It reminds me of the dancers out of the Slav lands, those elfin creatures all grace and air, though he adds force to their grace. It's not until he brings in men to spar with that you understand how fast he is. He makes them look silly. Even the best among the palace guard.

Something in him scares me though. The passion with which he pursues each victory. Watch him fight and you wonder if there would be anything he might not do in order to have what he wants.

April 15th, Year 102 Interregnum
Arrow. Greenite Palace. Herb gardens.

Egan is still here. He recovered quickly, although they say it was a dire wound. He seemed eager to heal and be back doing what he loves—cutting a path through anyone who opposes Orrin. But now he idles around the palace. He even came into the library today—a place I've never seen him.

I both like and don't like the way he looks at me. Some animal part of me relishes it. Every reasonable part of me is offended. Although I can find nothing to like in Egan that does not start with what my eyes give me of him, there is still a mystery there. When he watches me it is with an instinctive understanding of women that is denied to the wise. Denied to Orrin.

Orrin and Egan are on campaign again this summer. The days are long and hot and lonely though there must be a thousand souls in this palace of ours, at least fifty of them ladies of quality brought in just to keep me company.

I have learned to travel in dreams, keeping every part of me focused and lucid though I walk through the realms of possibility and of impossibility. Or sometimes fly, or swim, or gallop. The path of the world is a line, a single thread through the vastness of dream, and if I follow that line I can scry what is real rather than wallow in the randomness of strangers' imaginations. I have sent messengers out to explore the places that I have visited in this manner, and confirmed the truth of my observations.

I dreamed of Jorg of Ancrath last night and in dreaming of him became tangled in the stuff of his own nightmares. The margins of his dreaming are set with briar so thick and sharp I woke expecting my nightclothes to be *shredded and soaked with blood. And a storm rages over it all, so fierce it shook the sleep from me. It seemed almost as if he'd set barriers to keep intruders out. Or perhaps it was all my own imagination. I can hardly send out messengers to check.*

This morning my head aches, the quill shakes in my hand, and I see the page through slitted eyes. They give fennel powder in Arrow rather than wormwood—it works no better. I would swap the pain behind my eyes for the cuts of that briar, but it seems to be the price I pay for pushing into the dreams of others.

May 22nd, Year 102 Interregnum
Arrow. Greenite Palace. Grand Library.

Orrin writes me that he has employed Sageous as an advisor of sorts! The heathen had settled in the court of Duke Normardy after fleeing Olidan's protection. Orrin writes that Sageous has proved useful in foreseeing the lie of the land ahead of their path and in interpreting certain troubled dreams he has suffered.

I have written back by fastest rider to beg Orrin to dismiss the heathen immediately. I would have written "hang" for "dismiss" but Orrin is too . . . even handed for that.

June 23rd, Year 102 Interregnum

I tried to visit Orrin's dreams as I have done every night since I discovered the capacity for it. Tonight I could find no trace of him, just a space in the dreamscape where I sought him, just blankness and the memory of the spice, the coriander seed that the heathen seems to breathe.

In desperation I sought out Egan in his sleep but found no trace of him either. The others in Orrin's retinue I haven't enough familiarity with to find among the hundreds of thousands who shape the dream-stuff.

I've a new physician, a dirty little man from the Slav steppes, but his infusions calm my head. He's older than old and what words he has of Empire Tongue are oddly shaped. Even so, Lord Malas makes good report of him and his medicines work.

June 26th, Year 102 Interregnum

I found Orrin dreaming! I couldn't walk in his dream, a golden thing of many layers, but it seemed to me that he has fought off whatever attempts Sageous has made to control him. Maybe he was right about being the one to hold the strings. It troubles me though that I am kept out. Perhaps it is a barrier fashioned by the heathen, or a defence of Orrin's own making, whether by conscious will or natural resistance to direction.

Where Jorg kept me out with thorns and lightning, Orrin used a calm and simple refusal. I hope he has sent Sageous scampering back to Olidan Ancrath in the Tall Castle.

July 12th, Year 102 Interregnum
Arrow. Greenite Palace. Ballroom.

This palace has stood for almost two years and no one has danced in the ballroom. Orrin would host a ball to please me, have his lords and ladies descend upon the palace in their carriages. Hundreds would come in satin and lace. He would dance with the precision and grace that amazed his tutors, be attentive to my needs, compliment the musicians. And all the time I would know that behind his eyes grander thoughts were circulating, plans, philosophies, letters being written, and that when the last revellers had been taken home dead drunk across their carriage seats, Orrin would be found in the library scribbling notes in the margins of some weighty tome.

Egan has written to me from the celebrations after the capture of Orlanth's last castle. I say it is Egan but I have never seen his hand before. It would surprise me if he has ever written a letter until now. Perhaps a scribe set it down for him, for the characters are formed with practised skill, but the voice is Egan's. He wrote:

Katherine,

We have Orlanth from the western plains to the borders of the Ken Marshes. Orrin concerns himself with plans for Baron Kennick. He will play politic, offer terms, massage the old man's ego. We should just roll through there without pause and leave it smoking in our wake.

Orrin has sent me to Castle Traliegh in Conaught, it stands in the middle of nowhere. After the excesses of East Haven he says he worries for me. He says I need rest.

I need rest like I need poison. What I require is to be tempered in the forge of war and to pitch exhausted into dreamless sleep each night.

Conaught is a haunted place. I dream such dreams here. I stare at the walls and fear the night. Even though I dream of you. They are not good dreams.

I don't know what to do. Orrin will hear no wrong of his brother. I have seen it before. Somehow he always finds an angle from which Egan's deeds can be viewed as excusable.

I've never done anything to encourage this passion, this obsession, in Egan. I favoured Orrin from the start. If I had wanted a savage I could have smiled on Jorg of Ancrath, and what a creature I would have been tied to then.

Orrin needs to send Egan away, to give him some castle on a disputed border, some war to occupy him. It can't be that he needs his brother always at his side. One blade can't turn a battle, surely, no matter how skilled.

July 18th, Year 102 Interregnum

I have searched for Egan in the dreamscape and he is still hidden from me. The messages I send go unreplied. I don't even know if the riders are reaching Orrin's army. Report has it that he is closing on the Renar Highlands. Part of me wonders if Sageous is Jorg Ancrath's tool. Has he unleashed his father's pet upon my husband?

October 28th, Year 102 Interregnum

I found Egan's dreams but they were dark and closed to me. I sensed the heathen's handiwork and worry at his plans. Has Orrin proved too difficult to steer? Egan would be easier, like a bull goaded this way and that by the fluttering of rags. It's maddening to be closeted in this palace with all that matters unfolding three hundred miles away.

October 29th, Year 102 Interregnum

Still no word from Orrin or from Egan, but reports come in of tens of thousands on the move, men under arms, all converging on the Highlands, and of Jorg Ancrath skulking in his single castle with less than a twentieth part of that force.

And still I worry. For Orrin with his cleverness and strength and patience and wisdom. Even for Egan with his fire and his skill. Because I remember Jorg of Ancrath and the look in his eye, and the scars he carries, and the echoes of his deeds that still vibrate through the dreamscape. I remember him, and I would worry if Orrin had ten times the number and Jorg stood alone.

November 1st, Year 102 Interregnum

I made a dream, a thing of light and shadows, and set it dancing in the head of Marcus Gohal, captain of the palace guard. It made it easier for him to agree with me when I demanded that he assemble a suitable force to guard me on my journey to my husband's side. It made him forget all thoughts of arguing. Instead he nodded, clicked his heels in the way the men of Arrow do, and gathered four hundred lancers to escort me south.

We set off early, before the dawn stole shadow from the sky, and we rode out at a gentle pace, the horses' breath puffing in clouds before them, the leaves golden and crimson on the trees as the first light found them.

And I felt watched, as if someone on high were paying close attention.

Brother Gog I miss. There is no sound more annoying than the chatter of a child, and none more sad than the silence they leave when they are gone.

48

Wedding day

"This is madness, Jorg. God made the Prince of Arrow to stand behind a sword. That's what everyone says about him. He's not like other men, not with a blade in hand. He's not human." Makin stood before the throne now, as if he were going to block my way.

"And it will turn out that he was born to die behind one too," I said.

"I've seen him fight." Makin shook his head. "I hope you've got something up your sleeve, Jorg."

"Of course," I said.

Makin's shoulders fell as he relaxed a touch. Uncle Robert smiled.

"The best damn sword arm in history is what I've got up my sleeve."

The protests started immediately, a chorus of them, as if my court had filled with disgruntled geese.

"Gentlemen!" I stood from my throne. "Your lack of faith dismays me. And you wouldn't like me when I'm dismayed. If the Prince of Arrow accepts my challenge I will meet him on the field and find victory there."

I pushed past Makin. "You!" I pointed to a random knight.

"Get my herald here." I felt reasonably sure I had a herald. I turned and looked Makin in the eye. "I did tell you that I fought Sword-master Shimon, didn't I?"

"A thousand times." He sighed and glanced at Lord Robert.

"Shimon said you were good, Jorg," Uncle Robert said. "One of the best he's seen in forty years."

"You see!" I cried. "You see?"

"But he met Orrin of Arrow two years later and judged him the better blade. And Orrin's brother Egan is said to be the more deadly of the two by a considerable margin."

"I was fourteen! I'm a man now. Full grown. I can beat Makin here with a chair leg. Trust me. I'll have the Prince of Arrow down and bleeding before he even sees my sword."

The levity was something made for show. I would fight the Prince. Win or lose, chance or no chance. The madness Sageous had set in me had been burned away and I would dare the odds against victory, however slim, but still—I had killed my brother. Flame could not consume that guilt. I would carry it with me to the battlefield and maybe they would bury it with me.

They found Red Kent trapped beneath the charred corpses of Lord Jost's men. I had him brought to the throne-room when I heard.

"You've looked better, Sir Kent," I said.

He nodded. Two of my guard had carried him in, bound to a chair so he wouldn't fall from it. "And felt better, Brother." His voice came as a hoarse whisper from lungs scorched by blistering air.

Even now, when neither of us knew if he would live or die, Kent kept his eyes lowered, humble amongst lords and knights, despite me elevating him to their rank. He would throw himself into the teeth of an army given but slight encouragement, but a throne-room full of men more used to silk than leather made him cower.

I stepped from my throne and crouched before him. "I would give you something for the pain, Brother Kent, but I want you to make a battle of it. Fight these burns. Win. I'm offering no terms for surrender." My own burn still screamed at me. Surely only an echo of Kent's pain and that of others from the courtyard, but still, it gnawed at me, throbbing in my cheekbone and the orbit of my eye.

Something on the edge of vision caught my attention and I turned away from Kent, back toward the throne. Two oil lamps stood to either side of the dais, enamelled urns in black and red, set on wrought iron stands. The flame dancing on each wick within its glass cowl looked odd, too bright, too orange, taking on too many flame-shapes at once. I held my hand above the glass and could feel no heat, only a pulsing vital force that raced along my arm making me want to shout out.

Never open the box.

"Highness, the herald has returned."

I snatched my hand back, almost guilty in the action. My herald stood at the doorway between two table-knights. He looked the part, handsome and tall in his livery, gold-spun and velvet.

"And what did the Prince of Arrow have to say to my offer?" I asked.

The herald paused, a gossip's trick to draw in more listeners, though we could be no more intent.

"The Prince will meet you on the field of combat to decide the outcome of this battle," he said.

I saw Makin shake his head.

"Well and good," I said. "And did he name his ground, or accept my invitation to battle on the Runyard ridge?"

"The Prince felt the ridge to be constructed more from troll than from stone and has identified an area of flattish ground close to Rigden Rock, midway between the castle and the current position of his front line. He will bring five observers to watch from a distance of twenty yards and expects that you will do the same."

"Tell him his choice is acceptable and I will join him there in an hour," I said.

The herald bowed and set off to deliver my words.

"Makin, I'll want you there. But first, get Olvin Green or if he's dead then somebody good with arrow wounds. I want him and six strong men to get up to Coddin. Have them treat his injury there if he's still alive and bring him down as soon as it is safe to move him."

Makin nodded and left the throne-room without a word, just setting a hand to Kent's shoulder as he passed.

"I'll want Lord Robert with me, also Rike, Captain Keppen, and Father Gomst."

Uncle Robert lowered his head in agreement, then stepping onto the dais and bending close, "Why a priest? Good swords are what's called for in case of treachery."

"The Prince of Arrow will bring five good swords. I'm bringing three, plus an archer in case the bastard runs for it, and a priest so that in times to come the truth may be told concerning what occurred."

I let them strap me into my armour, pieces of silvered steel, well crafted and without adornment. I carried no crest, no emblems on this mail. Decoration is for peacetime, for people playing games but not understanding that they do.

The Hundred War, you must know, is a game. And to win it you must play your pieces. The secret is to know that there is only one game and the only rules are your own. With the memory box gone I had all my plans in mind now. The trick was not to dwell on them—to give no edge of them for Sageous to take hold of. One slip and the game would be over.

Whilst the pageboys bolted and strapped and sweated, I held the Builders' ring to my eye. For a moment I saw Miana through it, across the room, and wondered if she might fit her hand through the ring and wear it as a bracelet on that tiny wrist of hers. And then the image formed. The whole world before me as a jewel of blue and white. A canvas on which even all of empire would not look large.

A small motion of my fingertip along the ridged edge of the ring and the point of my perception fell to earth, faster than an arrow. Faster than a bullet even. Oh yes—I know of those.

The imaged blurred with speed for a heartbeat, two, three, and then snapped into focus. However vast the telescope that must hang above us, it could offer no closer view than this, an image miles across in which the Haunt's outline could be seen but the details lay hidden. The mass of the Prince's army made a darker smear on the mountainside. I could see the shape of the larger siege engines, and the men around them like specks of dust. I moved my fingertip again and the image went black. By flickers I counted as it jumped through four voids where whatever eyes the Builders once had were now blind, and then, with my finger on the last of the ridges, a new scene. I could see the army and the smoking wreckage of my walls as if I stood on a nearby mountaintop. Stroking the metal side to side and moving my fingertip forward by hundredths of an inch I drove the view in closer, zeroing upon the ground by Rigden Rock.

In most places the Builders' ring can see no closer than the miles-high bird's-eye perspective I described, but in maybe one place in five there are other eyes it can use. By exploration and extrapolation I found the location of an eye that I now exploited. It sits on a high ridge in the Matteracks, entirely hidden from view when not in use. When I call upon it, a gleaming steel shaft rises from behind black doors set into the natural rock and lifts a black crystal dome into the air. I have stood below this dome and listened to the faint hum and whir as I change the ring's view. Some mechanical eye must sit within and answer my needs. I left it as I found it. These eyes, in the vaults of heaven and down amongst us, burrowed into the living rock, are a work of genius. Even so, I wonder at a people who felt the need to be watched in every moment and at every place. Perhaps it was what drove them mad. I would not be spied upon so. I would blind such eyes.

Fexler Brews went mad. Fourteen years after his echo was captured and held in that machine, he took a gun and shot himself. A Colt four-and-five they called that gun, though it looks no more like a horse than the Horse Coast does. I found Fexler, but it wasn't easy. I found him on my long and wandering return to the Renar Highlands and it cost me pain and lives. Lives I valued. A rare commodity. Fexler had put a bullet through his brain but even then the machines wouldn't let him go. They held him trapped between fractions of a second. I pushed away the thought, the image of the weapon in his time-frozen hand, rubies of blood motionless in the air about the exit wound. I forgot about the stasis chamber . . . before Sageous saw my remembering.

They say God watches us in every moment. But I think, in

some moments, when some deeds are done, he turns his face away.

"What do you see, Jorg?" Miana at my side now.

"That the killing ground is clear." I took the ring from my eye.

"Can you win, Jorg?" she asked. "Against this prince? They say he is very good."

I felt Sageous. I smelled him, picking at the edges of my thoughts, trying to filch my secrets.

"He is very good. And I . . . I am very bad. Let's see what comes of that, shall we?" I made a wall of my imagination and kept my mind from wandering forward to what would happen. My hands knew what to do—I did not need to think of it.

There is a strong-box built into the base of my throne at the Haunt. Before they set my helm in place, I knelt in front of the throne and set the heavy key into the lock-plate. I lowered the side and reached in with my right hand, slipping it into the straps of the small iron buckler within, then drawing it out. I closed my fingers around the curious grip of the object that the buckler hid, and smiled. Imagine Fexler Brews thinking I would take "no" as an answer. I left the box open and stood, stepping off the dais so that the pageboys could reach to strap my helmet on.

"Move my sword belt round, Keven," I said.

The boy frowned and blinked. He looked like a child. I supposed he was, no older than Miana. "Sire?"

I just nodded and still frowning he unbuckled the belt and refastened it with the hilt sitting on the steel above my left hip.

Some men name their swords. I've always found that a strange affectation. If I had to call it something I would call it "Sharp," but I'm no more inclined to christen it than I would my fork at dinner or the helm upon my head.

I walked from the throne-room, taking slow steps, with all eyes on me.

"Red Jorg," Kent said in a whisper as I passed.

"Red would be good, Kent. But I fear I am darker than that."

When I opened that box I got more back than memory.

The flames on the torches by the doorway flared as I passed, infecting me with strange passion. I felt watched by more than my court, by more than Sageous and the players who seek to move the Hundred across their board. Gog watched me. From the fire.

I looked back one time, to see Miana beside the throne.

Lord Robert fell in behind me. Captain Keppen and Rike joined us outside.

"Time to jump the falls, old man," I told Keppen as he stepped beside me. He grinned at that, as if he knew the hour was upon us and shared my hunger for it.

I led the way through my uncle's halls. Degran no longer haunted me from the shadows, the fact of my guilt no longer came bound in the promise of madness, but I knew my crime even so. Death waited for me on the slopes, one way or another. Death would be good enough. Death at the Prince's hands, death on the swords of his thousands, or the death Fexler had saved me from when he anchored into Luntar's little box those forces of necromancy and fire with their hooks sunk so deep into me and their pulls opposing.

And that reminded me. I took the empty box out one last time to toss it aside. Pandora's own casket had hope lurking within, the last among all the ills unleashed upon us by her misguided curiosity. She might have let hope fly, but not my way. Even so, I looked into the lidless box once more, hand raised to throw it to the floor. And there, on the polished copper interior, one small stain. One last memory? Reluctant to return? I set a finger to it and the darkness of it soaked through my skin, leaving only bright copper behind.

This memory didn't seize me, didn't lift me from the now, but settled in as recollection while I walked the Haunt's corridors. I remembered that last talk with Fexler, back in Grandfather's castle. Fexler had been considering the box as I held his view-ring to it.

"Sageous?" he had mused over the buzzing of the ring.

"Sageous? That filthy dream-thief did this to me? Put madness in me?"

"Sageous has done far worse than that, Jorg. He put you in the thorns." Fexler had paused as if remembering. "What kept you there is another matter."

Every thorn-scar had burned at his words. "Why?" I had asked. "Why would he do that?"

"The hidden hands that move the pieces of your empire have prophecies they like to share. They like to talk of the Prince of Arrow and his Gilden future. And then they have foretelling they are less eager to spread. The hidden hands believe that two Ancraths joined together will end all their power. Will end the game."

"Two?" I had laughed at that. "They're safe enough then!"

"When you survived against all odds it seems some value attached to you," Fexler had said.

And I had grown cold, knowing at the last how the players had tried to keep two Ancraths from joining on their board. They would have seen Olidan's sons die together. And when I escaped that end and became as useful to their games as Father dear himself, did they let me live because they knew I would never join my cause to his? Or had the possibility been considered long ago and had the wedge between father and son not been driven there entirely by our own hands?

"I will find the heathen and kill him," I had promised Fexler.

"Sageous is nothing but a savage, straining truth through superstition to dabble in dreams." Fexler shook his head.

"Still, he's hard to catch a hold of," I had said.

"Oh, how I wish he'd go away," Fexler had replied, his voice half song.

"What?"

"An old rhyme. An ancient rhyme I suppose. Sageous puts me in mind of it. *As I was going up the stair I met a man who wasn't there; he wasn't there again today; oh, how I wish he'd go away.* That's Sageous for you; the man who wasn't there. The thing to do of course is to change it around. *Oh, how I wish he'd always stay.*"

"What?" I wondered if ghosts could grow senile.

Fexler had come in close then and set his ghost-light hand to the box. "But none of this is any use to you until the puzzle of this box is done, this Gordian knot unravelled. I'll put it in the box."

"No!" I shouted it. I wouldn't let him take this memory from me.

"No what?" Fexler had asked.

"I . . . forget," I had said.

*   *   *

"No?" Makin asked at my side, back in the corridors of the
Haunt, the Prince of Arrow waiting outside with his sword and
thousands more behind.

I shook my head. My hand held the empty box, crushed now
in my grip, blood on it from old thorn-scars bleeding once
more. The box fell from me, and I kicked it to the wall.

"No," I said. "Just no."

Father Gomst waited for us in the courtyard. A path had been
cleared through the dead. They lay heaped to either side as if it
were the road into hell. And the smell of it, Brothers! It made
my stomach rumble. And worse, as I walked that path between
the corpses, stacked and charred, they twitched. Hands red in
ruin flexed at my passing, burned skin sloughing from fingers.
Heads lolled, dead eyes found me. The men with me, focused in
their purpose, didn't see it, but I saw, I felt them all, uneasy in
their new slumbers as the Dead King watched me through them.

Never open the box.

Death and fire had their hooks in me. Deeper than deep.
And each had started to pull.

"I should be tending the dying," Father Gomst said, almost
shouting to be heard over the screaming from the circle gallery
where they had been taken.

"Let the dying tend to themselves," I said. I knew that Father
Gomst would have been no comfort to me when I lay groaning
in the Heimrift. I saw Grumlow at the keep doors, hanging
back in the shadows. I waved him forward. "Show the dying a
little mercy, Grumlow," I said. He nodded and departed.

I knew I would have appreciated Grumlow's quick sharp
mercy back in the Heimrift rather than a slow exit accompanied
by Father Gomst's moralizing.

We walked along the pathway, cleared of the dead, but not
the grease of burned flesh, the pieces of skin, the charred out-
lines of men. No one spoke; even Rike looked grim. It was
appropriate though. My uncle, the Duke of Renar, had been a
burner. He had spread his own terror that way. And I had come
to take the place from him with Gog at my side, filling the

courtyard with cremations. The Prince of Arrow had it right when he called the Ancraths the darkest branch of the Steward tree. I had long wondered if I would stand against Orrin of Arrow when he came a-calling. He was perhaps the brightest fruit from the branches of the emperor's line. In the four years since I claimed the Highlands I had walked the empire, returning at last to suppress cousin Jarco's uprising in the west, then battled less tangible foes, sickness in my people and in the economy. In the same span the Prince of Arrow had built his strength and taken five thrones. It was perhaps only the repeated whispering of the wise, telling me I must cede him the empire throne, that made me think of opposing his march to the Gilden Gate. I do not like to be told.

Now though, with the copper box torn open and my memories and sins returned to me, I felt that more had been restored, as if I had been a shadow of myself, almost me, but with something vital stolen away, something so bonded to my crimes that Luntar had been forced to set it also into his box of memories. I might not live to see the sun set on this day of blood, but if I did, four years would not pass again and find me no closer to my goals.

We walked out through the ruins of the sprawl-town where burning chunks of the Haunt's outer walls had left only wreckage in their path. No trace of Jerring's stables where Makin had once rolled in dung to be ready for the road.

Even now I could end this. The Prince would accept a peace: his progress was too important to him not to. And who would say that he would make a worse emperor than I? I could match the very worst of his crimes with my own then trump them with darker deeds.

There had been times aplenty, in the clarity of high places among the peaks, when I had thought to leave Orrin of Arrow a clear path. But things change. A different Jorg approached the duelling ground, a different Prince of Arrow. This wedding day had seen Jorg Ancrath remade in an older mould. I had that old thirst on me once again. Blood would flow.

Music rose around me, faint at first. A piece my mother used to play on the piano. A rare instrument, a complex thing of wires and keys and hammers, ancient, but the notes she scattered from her right hand were clear and high, pure like stars against the black and rolling melody from her left. Sometimes just a single ice-pure note can catch the breath in your lungs, and a second, off tempo, thrown into the void, can command chills across your skin. A small run, a flutter of the hand over the blue notes, can take you any where, any time, make you feel new, or settle the press of years upon you, heavy enough to stop you drawing breath.

We walked through broken stone, charred timbers. The melody pulsed under the crackle of flame, her left hand running through the deepest notes. Rike towered above me on one side, my uncle walked on the other. I felt the high refrain. I saw my mother's hand finding the high notes, the black keys, the ones that made me ache inside my chest, like the cries of gulls above wild seas. After so many years of watching her hands play in silent memory, I heard her at last, I heard her music.

Down the mountainside, down toward the serried expanse of the Prince's army. Still the music, the deep slow melody, the high and broken counterpoint, as if the mountains themselves had become the score, as if the glories of hidden caves and secret peaks had been wrapped around the ageless majesty of the ocean and turned into the music of all men's lives, played out by a woman's fingers, without pause or mercy, reaching in, twisting, laying us bare.

To the level ground before the grey bulk of Rigden Rock. The music slowing now, the notes scattered, just the counterpoint played out in the highest octave, sad notes, faltering, faint. I glanced at Makin, remembering that first day when he handed me a wooden sword. All those earnest boys of his ready to learn his game. I'd shown them that it wasn't play, that it's always about winning, but I don't think they understood it even then, even with the best of them lying choking on the floor.

A great trebuchet lay burning by the rock. It must have ignited closer to the walls and been dragged this far before they realized it was a lost cause. I wondered if it were the one that threw the rock at my bedchamber. The flames watched me. They leaned toward me.

The Prince of Arrow stood waiting, the dragons still clutching his namesakes on the rainbow sheen of his Teuton armour. His five knights stood at the agreed distance and I left my seconds at the same remove. They made a funny line, Rike towering at the centre looking like six kinds of bad news. Makin and Robert to either side. Old Gomst on the right wearing every holy thing he owned in the hope that nobody would stick an arrow in him, and old Keppen on the left, a sour face on him as if he had no time for this foolishness.

I walked over to meet the Prince.

"Open your keep to me and we can end this." The Prince's voice muffled within his helm, dark eyes watching.

"You don't really want me to," I said. "Better this way." I turned my blade to catch the light. "Stop trying to be your brother. Him I would have opened the gates for. Maybe."

The Prince lifted his visor. He offered a fierce and joyless smile then pulled the helm clear, running a hand back across hair bristling, thick and short and black.

"Hello, Egan," I said.

"I liked you better as road-filth," he said. "It suited you."

Smoke from the burning siege engine drifted across us. I heard Rike cough.

"I like your armour. I may take it for myself when they pry it from your corpse," I said.

He frowned, black brows meeting. "You're right-handed. What game is this?"

I set my left hand to my sword hilt. "I often fight right-handed. I hope you haven't based your assessment of my skills on spies who saw that . . . I'm much better with my left."

Egan shifted his weight onto his back heel. "You fought Orrin with your right . . ."

"True," I said. "I was sorry to hear that you killed Orrin. He was a better man than both of us. Perhaps the best man of our generation."

"He was a fool," Egan said, fixing his helm in place again.

"Too easy with his trust maybe. I heard that you stabbed him in the back and watched him bleed to death?"

Egan shrugged. "He would never have fought me. He would have talked. And talked. And talked." He spoke as if it were nothing, but it haunted him. I could see it in his eyes.

"And how did Katherine take news of Orrin's death?" I asked.

I saw him pale. Just half a shade. "Prepare to defend yourself," Egan said. He drew his sword. I paid it no heed.

"I told Orrin that I would decide about him on the day he came to the Highlands again," I said. "I think that I would have followed him and called him emperor. I hope that I would have. You should have left it for two weeks—then you could have murdered him after moving through the Highlands. It would have worked out better for you."

Egan spat. "We are two fratricides met for battle. Are you ready?"

"You know why I've practised with the sword every day since we last met?" I asked.

"So it would take me a few moments longer to kill you?" Egan asked.

"Nope."

"Why then?"

"So you would believe that I'd stand against you in a fair fight," I said.

I raised my right hand, pointing the gun at him from beneath the plate-sized buckler.

"What's that?" asked Egan. He took a step back.

"It has the word COLT stamped into the metal if that helps. Think of it as a crossbow, but all squeezed down into one small tube. You can thank an echo called Fexler Brews for it," I said.

I shot Egan in the stomach. The bullet punched a small hole in his armour. I knew from testing on a watermelon that the hole on the other side would be larger.

"Bastard!" Egan staggered back.

I made to shoot him in the leg but the gun jammed. "Lucky that didn't happen first try, neh?" I drew my own blade, in my left hand.

He almost blocked the swing of my sword. I had to admit he was pretty good. The blade crunched into his knee and he went down.

The five knights Egan brought with him started to charge. I fiddled with the gun, banging it against the hilt of my sword. I raised it again and fired, once, twice, three, four, five times. They all went down with red holes in their faces. I would have missed with my left hand.

"Bastard!" Egan tried to crawl toward me.

"This is not your game!" I shouted. Loud enough for Arrow's thousands to hear if they hadn't been screaming for my blood as they surged forward. I shrugged. "I don't play by the rules you choose."

I knocked Egan's sword from his hand and waved my seconds forward. "Bring Gomst!"

The gun had no bullets left so I threw it and the buckler aside and crouched behind Egan to pull his helm clear. I had to use my knife on the straps. I may have cut him a little.

"You don't have to end like this, Egan." I took hold of his neck. "There's death in my fingers, you know? It hurt me when you named me fratricide, but it's true. I killed poor Degran without even thinking about it. Can you feel it yet? Can you imagine what I can do when I *am* thinking about it? When I actually want to hurt you?"

He screamed then, as loud as I've ever heard a man scream.

"See?" I said, when there was a gap. "I'm not proud of how I learned to do that—but there it is, the devil makes work for idle hands—I can kill parts of your spinal cord and leave you in that much pain for the years before you die. I can paralyse you and take away your speech so no one will know how you suffer and you will not be able to seek or beg for an end."

The Prince's soldiers came on at a run, but they had a lot of mountainside to cover.

"What do you want?" he asked.

I had already killed the link between his mind and his muscles so he knew I wasn't lying. I was only lying when I implied I might be able to restore it. "Let's be friends," I said. "I know I might not be able to trust you even if you called me brother . . . but do it anyway."

"What?" Egan said.

"Jorg! We need to run!" Uncle Robert put a hand on my shoulder.

I ignored him and let more pain flood through Egan. "Call me brother."

"Brother! BROTHER! You're my brother," he cried, then screamed, then gasped.

"Father Gomst, did you hear that?" I asked.

The old man nodded.

"Let's make it official," I said. "Adopt me into your family, Brother."

I hurt him again.

"Jorg!" Makin pointed at the thousands coming our way, as if I hadn't noticed.

"I . . . You're adopted. You're my brother," Egan gasped.

"Excellent." I let him fall. I stood and wiped his blood from my hands onto Makin's cloak.

"We need to run!" Makin took a few quick steps toward the Haunt to encourage me.

"Don't be silly," I said. "We'd never make it."

"What's your plan?" Makin asked.

"I'd hoped they would just give up. I mean it's not as if they like this pile of dung." I kicked Egan in the head, but not too hard: I might yet need that foot for running. "I've killed more than half of the bastards. Both their princes are gone. You'd think they'd just go home!" I shouted this last part at their ranks, close enough to see faces now.

"That's it?" Uncle Robert asked. "You just hoped?"

I grinned and faced him. "I've lived the last ten years on hunches, bets, hope, and luck."

The fire danced behind him as timbers fell from the trebuchet. The flames held that same strangeness as those in the castle, a flat brittle look. Crimson striations flushed through them, a stippled effect . . .

"I am going to watch you die." Sageous stood to my left, naked but for a loincloth despite the cold, every inch of him written upon.

He had surprised me but I tried not to let it show. I stepped toward him.

"I'm not here. Will you never learn, Jorg of Ancrath?" I could see he hated me. That in itself made a small victory, putting some emotion in those mild cow-eyes of his.

"Are you not?" I asked.

He looked at Egan, limp and bleeding in his rainbow armour. "I could have done great things with that one. Do you know how long it took to find a man so powerful and yet so malleable? I couldn't work with Orrin. He had less give in him than your father, and that's saying a lot."

"You set him to kill Orrin?" I asked.

"It wasn't hard. It needed the slightest push in the right direction. Sweet Katherine proved too tempting and poor Orrin was just in the way. Men like Egan have only one answer to things being in their way."

"So many little pushes, dream-witch," I said.

"You probably don't even remember the dream that made you beg to visit Norwood that day, do you, Jorg?"

"What?" Images bubbled at the back of my mind. The fair at Norwood. The bunting. I had wanted to go. I'd pestered my mother. I'd almost dragged them into that carriage. "It was you?"

"Yes." He showed me a tight vicious smile. "Your sins cried out for it." He mimicked me.

"I was a child . . ."

Sageous looked down at Egan. "They cry out for it now."

A cold fire rose through me. "I'll tell you what my sins cry out for, heathen. They cry out for more. They call for company." And I stepped toward him.

"I am not here, Jorg," he said.

"But I think you are."

I felt him try to weave my vision, try to walk away in dream. And then I saw her. A ghost of her. Katherine white with anger and the more beautiful with it. A ghost of her at his shoulder, waiting in the place he sought to run to, like a mirage on hot sand, her lips moving without sound, chanting something. I could see her sitting on horseback, with the same knights around her that she brought with her from Arrow's palace. Somewhere back in the mass of that army Katherine rode her horse blind, her eyes bound by visions as she cast spells of her own. And with each silent word from the tight line of her mouth Sageous grew more solid, more *there*.

I reached for him. "I met a man who wasn't there . . ." My hands almost found the heathen, the stuff of him slipping away as my fingers closed. What had Fexler said? It's all about will. Put aside the skulls, the smokes, the wording of spells, and at the bottom of it all is desire. "He wasn't there again today." Wanting makes it so. "Oh, how I wish he'd always stay." And my grasping hands found him. Whatever may be said about the aftertaste, in the moment revenge tastes sweeter than blood, my brothers.

I seized his head and tore it from his shoulders as though I were a troll and he only human, for he had walked too long in dream and his flesh was rotten with it, tearing like the scribbled parchment it resembled. He made his own silent screams then and tried to die. But I held him there. I let the necromancy bind him into his skull.

"There is not sufficient hurt in this world for you." And the fire that burned in my bones, that echoed in my blood, lit about my hands and he burned with it also, trapped, living, and consumed.

I threw his head toward the oncoming troops. It bounced flaming on the rocks, flesh bubbling, lips writhing.

Burning was too good for him.

I walked toward the flaming wreck of the trebuchet, the fire running up my arms now.

"Jorg?" Makin asked, his voice quiet as if at least half of him was hoping not to be noticed.

"Better run," I said.

"We can't outrun them," Rike growled.

"From me," I said.

The fire leapt as I approached it. It looked like glass, like a window. Behind me Makin and the others ran. I laughed. The joy of it, the roaring joy of destruction. That's why the flames dance. For joy.

"There's only one fire," I said, and I knew Gog watched me from it.

I reached into the blaze and found him, flame-made, his white-hot hand in mine, the fragments of his lost body still in my flesh, preserving me. In the core of me this new fire magic—call it magic, or understanding, or empathy—made war on the necromancy that still infected my blood.

The Prince's troops passed Rigden Rock, a spear flew by my head.

"Come to me," I said, "Brother Gog."

"Truly?" he asked. "There will be no end to this—like the sun beneath the mountain."

A million images tumbled through me. Faces, moments, places, brothers of every kind. The weariness of the world. And the fire consumed it. I knew then how Ferrakind felt.

"Let it all burn."

And Gog flowed into me. A river of fire, eating the death-magic and making something new, a darker fire that ran like poison, coiling about my limbs.

The first of Egan's army reached me and the fire lifted from my hands. The men shredded, their flesh lifting from them as sea foam before a wind, their bones igniting as they fell. The dark-fire ran, jumping from man to man as the soldiers tried to flee, tried to turn and run, only to find their comrades not yet understanding, surging forward.

I walked amongst them and death walked with me.

Death and fire. Ferrakind howled at me from the place where fire lives, a song of destruction, stripping away what makes me. Ferrakind and every other lost to flame, all one now, fused, screaming for me to join them. And in the dry place into which the dead fall, other voices, just as compelling, implacable. The Dead King reached for me, along the paths through which necromancy flowed into my core, flooding me. These two among the many, both of them fought to claim me, dogs over a bone. And while they fought death and flame blossomed about me in conflagration, and men died, in tens, in scores, in hundreds, in stinking, steaming, screaming heaps.

49

Wedding day

The warrior rides a black stallion. Smoke shrouds the castle ruins behind him and the wind gives only glimpses of the corpse-choked gap between high and broken walls. That same wind streams long dark hair across his shoulders, like a pennant, and flutters the remnants of his cloak. To his left and right more riders emerge from the fog of war, warriors all, their armour dented, torn, smeared with soot and blood. A huge soldier in battered plate-mail carries the standard, Ancrath's boar in black upon the red field of Renar. They come by ones and twos, slow in their motion as if the great distance from which they are seen has somehow robbed the urgency from their movement. Each hoof lands with the finality of tomb doors closing, no sound to accompany the action. Each bounce and jolt in the saddle takes an age.

Where the baked dirt flakes from the warrior's plate armour the metal shows the rainbowed hues of oiled steel. Beside him an older, dark-haired knight, half a smile on thick-lips, black curls plastered to his forehead, an eagle's head on his round shield, worked in red copper, fire-bronze, and silver, broad-sword at his hip, black iron flail secured to his saddle. A second man in plate-mail on a white charger rides to their left, at home in his saddle as any sea-dog on a rolling deck. His armour is worked with the gothic engravings of the Horse Coast, his cloak blue in memory of the sea, on his jousting shield the white ship and black sun of the House Morrow.

A priest follows them, perched uneasy on a fractious mule. The wind throws wisps of grey hair across his scowl.

The man at the centre, at the arrowpoint of this emerging army, stares straight ahead. A wolf skull hangs from the pommel of his saddle. A wolf or a large hound. The man's face is scarred, the left side rough and twisted, as if the sculptor had heard the work bell and left in mid-action, leaving his creation unfinished. Over one eye, fixed to the bossed rim and side of his helm by iron rivets, is a silver ring, big enough to rest against his eyebrow and cheekbone. If you knew the edge were ridged you might imagine you could see those ridges, but they are a prisoner of the distance between us, as is any message in that thousand-yard stare.

I got bored with watching myself and flipped the ring up so my view lay unobstructed.

They had found me naked, every item on me seemingly burned away, except for my sword on which flames still danced. That fire held to the blade for hours and even now from time to time I see reflections of flames in the steel. I've named my first sword. I call it Gog, though I think it holds only an echo of him, like that echo of Fexler Brews, a man who shot himself in a stasis chamber long ago with a Colt 45. The world turned, he said. And it left him behind.

I had opened my eyes as Makin wrapped me in his cloak. The wound on my chest was just pink edges and white seams—the fire burned every trace of the necromancer from me, and in the end, as it failed, that death quenched Gog. I felt the absence of both, like holes in the world. Gog is ended. I won't see him again.

The fire has left me for it was always his, never mine, and the necromancy too. I may have clothes and armour now, but I am naked against the world once more, with nothing but the sharp wit, tongue, and blade of the Ancraths to see me through.

I think if they had not fought each other over me, Ferrakind and the Dead King, if either had his sole attention on me as I opened myself to their realms and let those places burst through me in such reckless abandon, I would have been claimed. Such powers can't be mastered, not without cost, and that cost would seem to include losing all those reasons you wanted that strength for. And it is a sacrifice I would have paid in the moment, with the arms of thousands raised against me. In the end, my brothers, there is no price I will not pay to win this game of ours. No sacrifice too great that it will not be paid to stop another placing their will over mine.

We ride for Arrow. I feel they owe me a castle at the very least. A palace might be nice too. And all those dead soothsayers and seers of the future—we're friends now. I *am* the Prince of Arrow. Ask Father Gomst. He was there, looking whilst God turned away. Egan adopted me into his family. And he's dead now. Not at my hand, but trampled by his own men. So, I'm the Prince of Arrow, homeward bound, destined by right and vision to be the emperor and to sit upon that golden throne beyond the Gilden Gate.

We ride for Arrow, an avalanche that thunders from the Highlands. This world will bend to my dominion. The box is open, its memories free, old wickedness and sins loosed once more. I am not that boy, the wild boy on the edge of manhood who filled it. He stands in my past and soon the curvature of the earth will hide him as the years carry us apart. I am not that boy and his crimes don't stain my hands. I'm riding for Arrow. I will delve shoulder-deep in gore if the need arises, so deep no river could scour me clean though they cut through mountains. My dreams are my own now, dark and pure. If you would know them, Brother, stand in my way.

I told Sageous my sins cried out for more, and I intend to give them company. I will burn and I will harrow and Orrin's lands, Egan's bloodstained inheritance, will be delivered into my hands. I will stand King of Arrow, of Normardy, of Conaught, of Belpan, of the Ken Marshes, of Orlanth, and of the Renar Highlands. I will take these lands and make a weapon of their peoples. In fire and in blood I will bend them to my will, because this is a game with no rules, and I will be victorious if it beggars hell.

I write this as we camp after a hard day's riding. I make a crabbed hand across pages as white as gold can buy. Perhaps they were destined for more worthy thoughts, but I set mine here. Sageous wrote his words across his skin and it left him weak. My father keeps them to himself and it leaves him less than human. I write mine here, as if ink and paper can take the blame from me. The surgeons like to bleed a man, to let ill humours out, so that he may face the world anew. Perhaps they should just hand him a quill and let the poisons spill from him whilst he keeps his blood for its intended purpose.

Beside my pages are Katherine's, scavenged from the ruination below Rigden Rock. I saw her burn. I saw her among the flames, her horse screaming. Or was that a dream in the darkness that followed? In any event the wind scattered her words across the dead and I followed them to the corpse of a baggage mule. I said once, these feelings are too fierce to last. They can only burn. Make us ash and char. And we burned, both of us—but still I want her. Though if she stood here now, she would only hate me and pride would edge my tongue to cut her in return.

Pride has ever been my weakness and my strength, but there are three things only of which I'm proud. The first—I climbed God's Finger to stand alone in that high place and find a new perspective. Second—I went to the mountain for Gog, even though I couldn't save him from his fire, just as no one can save me from mine. Third—I fought the all-sword, Master Shimon with the sword-song all around, and we made a thing of beauty.

There will be pride to come, enough to drown in, but perhaps there will be no more things of which to be proud.

A time of terror comes. A dark time. The graves continue to open and the Dead King prepares to sail. But the world holds worse things than dead men. A dark time comes.

My time.

If it offends you.

Stop me.

Ready to find
your next great read?

Let us help.

Visit prh.com/nextread

Penguin
Random
House